To all those who have ever found comfort, even light, in the dark.

A SEA OF ETERNAL WOE

A LITTLE MERMAID RETELLING

Printed in the United States of America: First Printing, 2022

ISBN 978-1-7351315-8-0 (eBook)

ISBN 978-1-7351315-9-7 (paperback)

Published by Night Muse Press

Cover art by Maria Spada Design

Edited by Nastasia Bishop in collaboration with Stardust Book Services

Proofread by Fantasy Proofs

Illustrated by Nathan Hansen Illustration

NIGHT MUSE PRESS

EST. 2020

Acknowledgements

To Tessa, once again. Words fail this author any time I try to properly thank you, so my only hope is that I'm doing your Scarlett justice.

To Jena, Lisette, and Marie-Lyne, who not only put up with the screenshot snippets I'd send at 3am, but who encouraged me to send more.

To Jaxen and Raquel, who read this story in its infancy and didn't tell me to throw it in the trash.

To my readers, old and new. You're the reason I keep writing, and some days, you're all that keeps me putting one foot in front of the other.

And to Wendy and Cedric, even though you were nearly the death of me. I guess I was almost the death of you, too, so we're even… for now.

Also by R. L. Davennor:

The Curses of Never Series:

A Dance with the Devil

A Land of Never After

A Sea of Eternal Woe

A Forest of Blackened Trees – Coming Summer 2023

Others:

Dragon Lake: A Swan Lake Retelling

Lyres, Legends, and Lullabies: An Annotated Score Collection

Previously in the Curses of Never Series:

Wendy Maynard, an orphan longing for the sea, turned sixteen and aged out of the orphanage in which she was raised. At the docks, she met a mysterious boy named Peter Pan. Through a series of unfortunate events, Wendy became trapped in a cursed and dying Neverland, and was soon captured by Captain Hook and his band of pirates. Several revelations were made, including that Hook and Wendy are father and daughter, and a deal was struck. Once Peter was captured trying to rescue Wendy, they journeyed to Blackbeard's tomb, where Hook intended to kill Peter and break Neverland's curse. Wendy proved to be their savior in the end, but only by plunging a knife into her own gut. She was revived by one of Neverland's creatures giving its life in exchange for her own.

After the battle, Hook and his sister Elvira left Neverland and gave Wendy and Peter control of their ship. While *The Jolly Serpent* set off in search of a witch with the power to grant Peter eternal youth, Hook and Elvira sought to discover what happened to Wendy's mother, Scarlett, and soon happened upon a strange woman who claims to not only have the answers they seek... but that Scarlett Maynard is alive.

Before You Begin:

Please note several content warnings: this novel contains graphic depictions of violence and death, disturbing imagery, adult language, explicit sexual content, mentions and brief depictions of gender dysphoria, and transphobia, including misgendering. While *A Sea of Eternal Woe* may contain a handful of teenage characters, it was written and intended for a mature adult audience.

This book also features original music written and composed by the author! Head to the link below for a full playlist, and keep an eye out for the featured songs at the beginning of chapters to listen as you read.

https://soundcloud.com/rldavennor/sets/a-sea-of-eternal-woe

A desperate mother fled her curse
Not knowing what she sought was worse
Her daughter grew up all alone
For sins of the past, she must atone

A broken father freed at last
Determined to revive his past
A stranger tells him she's not dead
To free her soul, blood will be shed

Together now, they all must sail
They must survive, they cannot fail
For monsters lurk in depths below

In the Sea of Eternal Woe...

PROLOGUE — THE BARGAIN

Featured Song: A Lullaby of Eternal Woe

Kaara

A single, faint knock echoed through my chamber for the forty-seventh time today. I fought the urge to roll my eyes. Why must my visitors always knock so hesitantly, as if hoping I wouldn't hear? Anyone who found themselves on the other side of that door had run out of options, time, or both. They could either face me or die. Not a difficult choice for most, but there were consequences not even I had foreseen. Cowardice had become a rather large issue. Sniveling, groveling humans were not only hopelessly dull, they were the opposite of what I had come here to find.

I decided right then that I wouldn't entertain another, at least not today. Forty-Seven had precisely thirty seconds to impress me,

1

or I would turn them into a fountain to adorn the space to my left. I already had one on the right, but I wanted a matching set.

"Come in," I said through a smirk.

The door opened of its own accord, and in limped a woman. Her clothes were ragged and torn, her skin shone far too pale in the candlelight, and she smelled of Nightstalkers and death. She refused to meet my gaze. In one hand she clutched a mysterious parcel, while the other gripped the base of her bulging belly so tightly it was almost as if she were afraid its contents would come spilling out at any moment.

I rose from my chair, my interest instantly piqued. I hadn't seen this particular kind of desperation for quite a while. Was this mother-to-be's motivation for seeking me out selfish or selfless, I wondered? Could she actually be the one? After decades of scouring and procuring soul after unfortunate soul, searching for the only one capable of retrieving my trident, could she be the one? To not only be able to enter the Sea of Eternal Woe, but reemerge unharmed and whole? I sensed no taint on her; at least, nothing more than the curse lingering in her bones. Easily lifted if need be, but she'd need to prove her worth to me first. Either way, I'd already decided against the fountain idea, brilliant as it may have been. She had indeed managed to impress me, all without opening her mouth.

As she set the parcel onto the marble table currently dividing us, I gestured to her belly. Even if she had wanted to hide the pregnancy, she couldn't have, not as far along as she was. "Congratulations."

She shot me such a fierce glare that had I not been who I was, I might have flinched. The defiance impressed me almost as much as the fire in her voice when she spoke. "Cut the shit. I'm here for—"

"My dear." I spoke across her smoothly, gesturing for one of my nymphs lining the walls to fetch our visitor a chair. Already I admired her spirit. It would serve her well should she ever enter the Sea. "It's not shit. It's polite conversation. Around here, introductions come before demands."

The woman didn't falter. "You're Ursa?"

It wasn't my true name, but I nodded anyway. Posing as a human witch had proven more than necessary. If I revealed my identity as a goddess, I'd have both worshippers and the desperate alike showing up on my doorstep, and I didn't have the time nor the patience for that. "Indeed. And you are?"

She shoved away the chair my nymphs had offered her with surprising strength given her condition, choosing to remain on her feet. "My name is irrelevant."

"I'll be the judge of that." I kept my voice even but narrowed my gaze. Her defiance was admirable at first, but now it was hindering my game, my plans. And *no one* hindered my plans.

"No, you won't." Her fingers twitched at her sides, most likely missing the weapons she'd been forced to leave behind prior to entering my chamber. "I've been… away. And in that time, I've learned a lot about names and what they mean." She paused, gaze clouded over for a fraction of a second, but recovered quickly. "Because of mine, I've been hunted and kidnapped, beaten and abused, forced to run for gods know how long."

"I didn't ask where you've been." My fingers gripped the edge of the table so tightly my knuckles shone as white as the foamy tide. "I asked your name."

"No names," she said again, her tone a warning. She clearly sensed my irritation, for she added, "I suppose you're accustomed to being feared. But unlike most you bargain with, I've faced witches before, so if you want to scare me, you'll need to try harder than that."

Good thing I was far more than a witch.

Closing my eyes, I called upon a tiny fraction of the moonlight stored within me. Free from its cage at last, the raw, unfiltered magic surged through my veins, morphing and twisting my current form to nearly double in size. I'd have grown even taller if I had my way, but this chamber prevented it; still, it was more than enough to create an intimidating illusion. Dark hair swirled around my face as though underwater, and my eyes illuminated with amber fire. When I spoke, it was in the tongue of sirens.

"You will tell me your name, or there will be no deal, and if there is no deal… your child will emerge from your womb nothing more than a puddle of blackened, festering blood."

My display had the desired effect. She staggered back and would have fallen if my nymphs hadn't caught her. I exhaled slowly, bottling up the moonlight once again as I returned to my normal, unassuming self. Well, as normal as a goddess in human form could look. When my guest didn't move, I raised an eyebrow. "That wasn't a threat, just a warning. Now, will you please sit?"

She blinked, bewildered as the nymphs helped her into the chair.

As I sank into mine that far more resembled a throne, the woman wrapped both hands around her unborn child, remaining silent as a frightened deer. I frowned. My display hadn't been that intimidating. I could do without the defiance, but I liked her better with her fire. "Out with it, unless you'd rather I move on to the next poor soul."

"Scarlett," she blurted out, her voice significantly softer than it had been when we began. "My name is Scarlett."

My gaze snapped to hers. "Scarlett," I repeated. "Where in bloody hells does that come from? You're no redhead." Though limp and lackluster, her hair was a pretty shade of medium brown.

"It was my mother's favorite color."

"You carry her surname, then?"

"No. My father's."

"The one you say nearly got you killed?"

She swallowed. "Yes. Maynard."

It struck a chord of recognition, and as pieces began to fall into place, I smiled again. This was getting more interesting by the minute. "Ah, the infamous Lieutenant Robert Maynard. Betrayed his men and sold his soul, all to bring down a pirate that cursed him anyway—Blackbeard himself. And then Jamie Teach spread the scourge even further, infecting even you. And aren't you fucking one of his other sons—Cedric? Is he the father of your child?"

"What is it that you want?" Scarlett snapped, informing me her inner flame hadn't been fully extinguished after all. Good.

"What do *I* want? Scarlett, you came here of your own accord. Besides, we aren't done with introductions yet," I reminded her. "You have a final piece to your name. A middle name."

She frowned. "What does that have to do with anything?"

"Everything." My grin was nothing short of devilish now. "Names have power, dear. You know that. It's important that I know yours, or I won't be able to help you." All I needed was for her to hand it over willingly, to grant me full access into her thoughts and memories, but this was yet another secret I didn't intend to reveal.

Silence lingered as Scarlett hesitated. Her fingers clenched, crumbling what little was left of the stubborn façade she'd so carefully crafted. "It's not me I'm trying to help," she finally whispered, nearly imperceptibly soft, and that's when I knew.

She *was* the one.

Relief swirled within me strong as a tsunami, and it took effort to keep my facial expression unchanged. The Sea of Eternal Woe was exactly as it sounded: an endless abyss meant for lost things, both human and object alike, and the current home of a very powerful trident. It had once belonged to the God of the Sea himself until even Adais grew to fear its magic. To prevent the trident from falling into the wrong hands, Adais stashed it within the Sea. I could go after it if I wanted to, but that was precisely the problem. Anyone could enter the Sea, but only one of selfless heart and untainted soul could return to our world unscathed… and mine was the blackest in existence.

I'd been scouring the globe for centuries, conducting search after desperate search for someone capable of retrieving the trident in my place. I'd finally settled here in Afterport. It wasn't the plethora of pirates or the stench of the harbor that drew me in, it was the proximity to Neverland—or the Forest of Never as the locals preferred to call it. There, time stood still, and children would forever remain innocent and pure-hearted. I had assumed one such child would be my prize, until that little shit Peter Pan had begun corrupting them all. There were grown men wandering this harbor who weren't half as bloodthirsty as his Lost Boys. But perhaps I had never needed a child's innocence… not when a mother's selfless sacrifice could purify her soul of any previous misgivings. Whatever she had done and whoever she had been no longer mattered.

The Sea would wash her clean, or it would destroy her.

"Leave us," I ordered my nymphs, and in less than a minute, we were alone.

Scarlett glanced around worriedly, wrapping her arms even tighter around her middle. "What are you—"

"Relax." I cocked my head to the side, and at the movement, every candle in the room dimmed. Though it darkened the space to near blackness, it was a comforting kind of darkness, a cloak settling over my bare shoulders. Though I had no need to breathe, I inhaled deeply, concentrating on the rot clinging to Scarlett's very soul. She sighed, visibly relaxing as her pain eased up, so I seized the opportunity to ensure we wouldn't be disturbed. With a final snap of my fingers, the door latched behind us. At the sound, Scarlett shot up with surprising reflexes for someone nearly full-term pregnant.

"Witches," she muttered. "Gods, I knew better than to come here."

"Scarlett, sit down."

Her face flushed. "No. I don't want this. I've changed my mind."

7

"Over a locked door? We have discussed nothing even resembling a bargain."

"There's got to be another way." She snatched her parcel from the table and turned toward the now-barred exit.

"To what, break your curse? To save your lover?" I called after her.

"To save my child."

I let her yank on the massive handle before speaking in sirentongue for the second time.

"*There isn't, and you know it. You have already tried and failed.*"

Scarlett stilled. "I don't know what you're saying."

"*Don't lie.*" She'd come from Neverland, for fuck's sake, and it wasn't as if I didn't know about her legendary escape from Admiral Ruiz's mansion. "*I know you understand me.*"

With a heavy sigh, she backed away from the exit, but kept her parcel close to her chest. "To save my child, I'll do anything."

"I'm glad to hear it," I said, switching back to the common tongue and nodding toward her parcel. "That's your payment, I presume?"

"If you'll have it."

After returning to where I stood, she set it on the table, unwrapping the parcel as though its contents might lash out at any moment. I watched from a slight distance through narrowed lids, both curious and cautious. I had no idea what might lay inside, which meant that the wrappings had been enchanted with a cloaking spell, and a powerful one at that. Cast by whom, I wondered? And what could be worth going to such extremes to protect? Dozens of possibilities raced through my mind, but what Scarlett soon revealed hadn't been anywhere among them.

I gaped. "A music box?"

Without my magic, I wouldn't have otherwise known that's what the object before me was supposed to be. Ornate silver plating decorated the blackened wood, but the metal had already begun to tarnish, and part of me was doubtful it even worked properly; not with the key meant to wind it up bent like that, likely jamming the gears. The music box had clearly been well-loved by someone, possibly several someones, but its glory days were long gone. I shot Scarlett a glare. "Why in Adais's name would I have any use for this broken thing?"

"It's not what it looks like. It's enchanted," Scarlett said. "It will play any song you ask of it, even one that only you know."

My questions remained. Who would waste such a powerful enchantment, on a music box of all things, and why? I supposed there was no harm in trying it out. "Open it."

Once she did, I closed my eyes. If it truly worked as she said, I shouldn't need to ask with words. Thoughts, or even a single emotion, would be enough. Silence lingered for a brief while, but it wasn't long before a melancholy tune emerged, soft and gentle. I couldn't help but sing along.

"Lost, roaming forevermore,
Gods, monsters, friend and foe,
Never to go ashore,
Trapped in the depths below.

9

Hidden, deep in the waves,
Lie all those dead long ago,
Headed to their graves,
The Sea of Eternal Woe."

The song had hardly ended before Scarlett butted in, causing my eyes to flash open. "Well? Is it enough?"

I blinked, unsure I'd heard correctly. "*This* is the payment you brought for me to save your child from a curse?"

"It's all I have."

"It's not enough." I shook my head. "Not even close. It's unique, I'll give you that, but I've no use for an enchanted music box."

Scarlett closed her eyes, clenching her hands into fists. "Ariel."

"What?"

"You asked for my name, did you not?" Her fire once again burning bright, Scarlett spread her arms wide, giving her best attempt at a mock-bow as a pregnant person could. "I've given it, and I wish for my child to be free of this curse."

I couldn't help it. I laughed. She'd said it with such finality, with such *declaration* that it could only mean Scarlett had thought her full name worth far more than it actually was. "My dear," I managed between breathless chuckles. "My price will cost you far more than your precious dignity."

It was Scarlett's turn to laugh, which surprised me. There was a far darker undertone to hers, though. "I have no dignity left. Do you honestly think I'd be here if I did?" I opened my mouth, but she shook her head. "Don't answer that. Go ahead. Name your price. Anything but him or his freedom, it's yours."

"Him?" I echoed, raising an eyebrow. "If you're referring to the child, you're having a girl."

She snapped her mouth shut, gaze widening. "A... girl?"

"Or nothing at all if we don't strike our deal," I said. "Your choice."

Scarlett gritted her teeth. "I've already told you to name your price. Whatever it is that you want, I accept."

"Do you?" I pressed. "Because you're paying not once, but twice."

Her jaw dropped. "Twice? Perhaps you misunderstood. I don't give a shit what happens to me. It's her I need to save."

"This *is* about her, not you. Your child was conceived in Neverland. Its magic never lets anything it's created go willingly, and it has already staked its claim over her. It no longer matters where she's born. She's tied to that forest, so if she leaves, she dies. But take her back and she becomes a prisoner, forced to dodge Nightstalkers and nerisas for most of her too-short life."

Scarlett looked as though she'd been slapped.

"And because her mother is, the child is also cursed. She'll need to kill from the moment she's born, or she'll be killed." I met Scarlett's gaze. "But you alone could save her and pay double to secure her freedom. Her true freedom, both from the curse and from Neverland."

Scarlett stood silent and still but didn't look away. Deliberation didn't take long, not when the choice was obvious. She visibly shuddered before whispering, "What must I do?"

I grinned, clasping my hands together. "Anything and

11

everything I ask."

Scarlett's gaze snapped to mine. With our faces only inches apart, it made her glare that much more intense… and thrilling. "So I'm to serve you? For how long?"

I thought for a moment. "Does 'as long as your daughter lives' seem fair? If something were to happen to her, you walk free." I rested my opposite hand on Scarlett's belly, caressing gentle circles over the thin fabric of her tattered shirt. "This way, you know your sacrifice isn't for nothing, and that I'm a witch of my word."

She considered it before nodding. "Yes. But what about the second price? The one paid to secure her freedom?"

I laughed. "So eager. All in good time, dear. For now, go."

Scarlett blinked. "Go?"

"You're not free, but you're not mine… yet." I took a step back. "Have your child. Leave her somewhere safe, then return to me. You will then pay your debt in full, and we will begin." When she didn't move, I sighed. "This isn't mercy, Scarlett. Your labor will begin in three days."

Her hands shot to her belly, eyes wide with disbelief. "How is that possible? I've only been pregnant since I left Neverland a week ago. She's grown so rapidly. I knew it was unnatural, but surely it's not yet time."

"It's past time." I'd sensed as much upon touching her. "You conceived her over ten months ago, but time stood still while you were in Neverland. Now that you've left, the clock is catching up to you."

Scarlett bowed her head, hair shielding her pale face as she spoke. "I'll be back."

"I know."

She made quick work of packing up her music box. I unlocked the door, and without another word, Scarlett was gone. For a moment, I gazed at the space into which she'd disappeared before sinking back into my chair, a smirk playing on my lips.

"Well?"

My eyes shot open. Standing where Scarlett had only moments ago was Calypso, my favored nymph. Unlike the rest who wore simple pale blue robes, Calypso's were gold, contrasting gorgeously with her sepia skin. Gaze narrowed, she questioned me yet again, her dark curls bouncing over her shoulders as she spoke. "What was so special about that one? You were with her for an awfully long time."

I beckoned with my finger. "Come here."

Calypso glided toward me, settling into my lap without needing further encouragement. After draping her long legs over the side of the chair, she settled her head into the crook of my shoulder. I traced circles over her bare knee as I spoke. "She's the one."

"What?" Calypso shifted in my arms, pulling away just enough to look at my face. "That half-dead thing?"

I nodded. "She's giving up her freedom in exchange for her daughter's life."

"Ah. That is selfless, I suppose."

"Indeed. But her freedom only breaks Neverland's claim on her daughter—to also break her curse, there is a second price she must pay. I haven't settled on what yet, but it can wait until she gives birth

13

to be decided."

Calypso pondered for a moment. "What about her voice? I heard her singing to her music box on her way out. You could serenade Adais with it. It's quite lovely."

I snorted. "Even if I were to use another's voice, he'll know it's me."

"Couldn't hurt to try."

"Hmm."

We fell into a comfortable, comforting silence as only the two of us could, but it wasn't long before Calypso began trailing kisses up my neck. I wanted badly to let her reach my lips but pulled away before she could. Before we got lost in our passions, I needed to tell her something. "You have a part to play as well."

"Do I?" Calypso murmured, clearly distracted as she cupped my breast. "What's that?"

"Scarlett is more than likely going to leave her child at the orphanage, and that child will need someone to look after her. She might one day prove useful... even necessary."

At this, Calypso snapped her head up, nearly clipping me in the jaw. "You can't mean—"

"I do." Snatching her chin, I forced the nymph to look at me. "We will be apart, but it won't be forever."

I kissed her deeply then, claiming every inch of her lips and mouth with my tongue. Calypso went limp in my arms before reciprocating enthusiastically. She quickly grew breathless between kisses and caresses but forced the question I knew she'd ask between desperate pants. "You'll... You'll come back for me?"

"Always," I assured her. After all, Calypso might one day prove useful… even necessary.

And in the end, I would always claim what was mine.

I. THE STORM

Wendy

If there was one thing Neverland had taught me, it was that monsters were real. They walked among us, lived within us, and lurked in the most unexpected places. Sometimes, they were us. The damn things came in all shapes and sizes and weren't always as they first appeared, if they appeared at all. Monsters could be evaded for a time, but eventually, when at your most vulnerable, they would find you.

The one chasing us now fit that description exactly.

I gritted my teeth as I glared at its vague black shape. The mysterious creature had been trailing *The Jolly Serpent* for hours that felt like days, gliding like an ink stain beneath the surface of the waves. All anyone had gotten a glimpse of were its numerous

17

black tentacles that had occasionally poked above the water line, but that was more thanks to me. I wouldn't let us close enough to get a good look at it. We were already traveling at eight knots, an unsustainable pace as Mr. Smee had reminded me time and time again, but I wouldn't allow us to slow. To do so was to relent, and Captain Maynard never relented—at least, not the Captain Maynard I intended to be.

"Wendy?"

I flinched at both the intrusion into my focus and the name I was working to shed, at least in front of my crew. Without tearing my eyes from the monster or even turning to acknowledge my mentor, I spoke through pursed lips, ignoring the rain trailing down my face. "It's Captain, Mr. Smee."

"Not yet, it's not," he said.

I gripped the rail so hard my knuckles turned white, but I didn't respond.

"The men are getting restless and want to know your orders."

"So I am the one in charge?" Whirling around, I shot Smee a murderous glare. "Which is it, Samuel: I am, or I'm not?"

He sighed so deeply his red hat sagged. I swore it, too, had exhaled. Or perhaps its drooping was simply a result of this relentless rain. Mr. Smee was as drenched as I was, his clothes soaked, and his silvery beard plastered to his neck. Neither caught my attention as much as the vein throbbing dangerously at his temple. Though he practically shouted, it was a strain to make out his words over the thunder rolling in the distance.

"For fuck's sake. *You* give the orders, and I simply counsel you on whether or not they're decent. But you're no captain yet, not by a long shot."

"Slaughtering innocent children is the prerequisite for that, I suppose."

Gaze widening, Smee silenced abruptly. "Y-you—that was—"

"Maintain speed. We stay the course to Ursa. And if any man has objections?" I met his gaze, narrowing my own. "He can say them to my face, or not at all." Turning on my heel, I stalked away, but didn't get far before Smee's venomous jab twisted like the knife I'd once plunged into my own gut.

"If it's a choice between captains, I prefer Hook."

I froze for the briefest of moments but recovered quickly, refusing to allow any shred of emotion to rise to the surface. Keeping up my brisk pace, I didn't slow until I'd rounded a corner, and there, hidden by barrels containing cargo that wouldn't fit below deck, I sank to my knees. As my lower lip trembled and I fought to keep from sobbing, that gods-forsaken name repeated endlessly in my mind.

Captain Hook.

He went by many names. Cedric Teach. Son of Blackbeard. The Crow. I'd even heard a few of the men refer to him as Avery, and where that one had come from, I didn't even want to know. But none of his many titles affected me as much as what I'd finally dared to call him the last time we'd spoken: *Father.* I shuddered at the memory, horrified that I'd even acknowledged the truth to his face, but there could be no running from it. Not anymore. Hook may be many things and wear many faces, but above all, he was my blood, and the only thing I had left resembling family.

So why had I second-guessed keeping him alive nearly every second of every day since?

"You're going to let him get away with that?"

I cursed and scrambled back as a presence thudded onto the deck in front of me. Peter Pan raised his gaze to meet mine, eyes glittering both with their usual mischief and something I'd come to recognize as hunger, but not for sustenance. He drew the dagger at his hip, casually twirling it in his palm as he spoke. "It seems your mentor may have forgotten who he serves. I'd be happy to remind him."

"You'll do no such thing," I snapped, glancing up at the ropes from which Peter had descended. The winds were growing more violent by the second, and I didn't want to even consider how slippery and freezing it must be up there. "And will you stop swinging from the rigging like a goddamn monkey? You're going to mess up our sailing pattern."

"And here I thought it was my safety you were worried about."

"It is." Glowering, I only barely resisted the urge to rub my aching temples. "But like it or not, it's my responsibility to look after more than just you when we're on this ship."

Peter raised an eyebrow. "Grown men can't look after themselves?"

"I didn't mean literally. But if we go off course because of something you damage while you're up there, we die."

"Wendy."

My gaze flickered back to his. Though irritation washed over me when Smee had used my name, on Peter's lips it was something else entirely, especially when he adopted that too-serious tone that didn't quite match his boyish body. I faltered because of it, but still managed to keep some bite in my voice. "What?"

"You're acting the very definition of a bratty teenager. No wonder you're pushing Smee away."

My mouth dropped open, and heat immediately rushed to my cheeks. "I'm acting like a brat? *You're* acting like a child!"

"Correct," Peter fired back. "That's the entire reason we're on this ship to begin with, so that I might remain one forever. Or have you forgotten?"

"No." Of course I hadn't. Every minute we spent at sea and away from Neverland was another minute that Peter aged, and the only one who could ensure that stopped permanently was a witch known as Ursa. We'd been closely following the map to reach her, and though we'd been at sea for a week, we had several more to go, and that was only if dodging these storms and monsters didn't push us off course.

"At least I've got an excuse. What's yours?"

"I don't—that's n-not…" Sputtering, my voice trailed off, and I simply stared at Peter for a long moment. Having been on deck for the better part of the day, he too was soaked to the bone. His amber skin glistened with seawater and his mousy hair lay plastered to his forehead. The latter had grown since we'd left Neverland and now nearly covered his ears, but I hadn't yet gathered the courage to suggest a haircut. He hadn't tied up his shirt all the way, so the collar

21

plunged slightly, revealing a glimpse of the chest bindings I'd helped him secure just this morning. Paired with his breeches and boots, he looked a far better fit to be part of this crew than I did, and it wasn't helping my current train of thought. Peter said nothing while my gaze wandered, keeping his dagger drawn as he waited for me to confess what we both knew.

"I'm not him," I finally forced, though I couldn't bring myself to mention Hook by name. "I will never be him."

Peter raised an eyebrow. "You look every bit Hook's daughter from where I'm standing, and especially from the crew's perspective."

I threw up my hands hoping that the movement might distract Peter from my tear-filled gaze. "Then stop looking. Hook isn't here." He'd left me in command of *The Jolly Serpent* and its crew prior to setting off on his own mission: to find out what happened to my mother and his lost love, Scarlett. I'd given him the additional task of avenging her death if it proved to be murder, but if I was honest, it wasn't because I wanted or even cared about justice. It was because I never wanted to see Hook again.

"I didn't say it to upset you. It's just the truth," Peter said, continuing to push despite the death glare I shot in his direction. If it were anyone else speaking to me this way, I'd gut them where they stood, and Peter knew it. "Why do you care so much, especially about what they think?"

"Why do I care?" Tears streamed down my face freely now, but I prayed to the gods that the rain would conceal them. "Hook captained those men for decades, and that's who they're accustomed to. And I'm his blood, so they expect me to be him. But I'm not. Gods, I'm not, and I'll never come close. I'm not their captain. To them, I'm nothing but a scared little girl."

"You're the one who saved their lives."

"It doesn't matter. I'm Hook's daughter, yet I couldn't be further from what they expect of me. And if I don't belong here on this ship, then where else?"

"With your friends. With me," Peter insisted.

I smiled sadly. "I know. I mean a place." I couldn't voice the unblemished truth aloud: *I want to finally have a home.* Between the orphanage and then Neverland, it was something I'd never truly known. I'd hoped it could be this ship, but it seemed that the harder I clung to it, the more it was slipping from my grasp.

"Then stop trying so hard to *not* be your father that you're instead running in circles, and simply be yourself. Be Wendy." I flinched, but Peter pressed on. "You didn't kill her that day, you know. She's still in there."

My hand wandered to the still-healing wound on my stomach, to where I'd stabbed myself to break Neverland's death curse. It didn't hurt much anymore, especially thanks to the supernatural magic which was the reason I was alive at all, but the only parts of me Xephan's sacrifice had mended were physical. Mentally, I was barely keeping it together. Picking up the pieces of my father's crew combined with my inexperience commanding a ship had taken its toll over the past several weeks, and one ever-present fear consumed my thoughts more than Neverland's curse ever had. How was I to shine if I was constantly living in a Hook-shaped shadow? I thought I'd been hiding my insecurities well, but if there was anyone who could see through the metaphorical barriers I'd erected, it was Peter. He'd been doing it since before he knew me, and now that he did, it had become impossible to keep the boy out of my head. He may not look it, but Peter was far older and more powerful than I was, and I was still learning just how far those powers extended.

I spoke quietly, unsure if Peter could hear me over the rain. "How do you know?" I kept my real question buried: *How do you know me better than I know myself?* It was eerie, really. Was Peter a mind reader? It would hardly surprise me. "How can I still be Wendy if half of me is him?"

Peter opened his mouth to respond, but whatever he said was swallowed by a chorus of horrified shrieks.

"MONSTER!"

I wasn't certain how I'd gotten to my feet, only that I ran. Peter trailed so close behind that he nearly slammed into my back when I reached *The Jolly Serpent's* rail, mirroring the dozens of men who already peered over the side of the ship. Getting such a close view was hardly necessary, because the shadow that enveloped us wasn't the gathering storm.

It was a dragon.

A head so massive it dwarfed the entirety of our vessel towered at such a height that I had to crane my neck to make out the details of its face. Bright, intelligent eyes were set deep into the narrow, streamlined skull, and fins were arranged at regular intervals down its body. Scales blacker than the night sky glistened in the rapidly fading daylight, and trailing up the creature's neck were dozens of glowing blue lines. They pulsed in a rhythm not unlike a heartbeat, and if I concentrated, I could feel a gentle *hum* in the air. The dragon's energy grew stronger with each pulse, building to a swirling crescendo I wasn't certain I wanted us to be present for, but despite the crew's growing panic, I found myself unable to look away, or even to let go of my most pressing thought. The dragon was as terrifying as it was awe-inspiring, yet the bulk of its body remained hidden beneath the agitated surface of the waves, and there was no sign of the tentacles we'd seen earlier. Despite lacking them, the dragon could sink us with a single swipe of its tail, or even less effort if it really wanted to.

So why didn't it? I fixated on its gaze, fighting to ignore the chill creeping along my arms and spine as I pieced together what I knew. The dragon remained calm, immobile, and stoic, in complete contrast to the tentacled monster we'd been fleeing for hours. Both may be black in color but couldn't be more different in temperament and body type. My heart hammered against my ribcage as a terrifying possibility struck me. Were there two monsters? And was one trying to save us from the other?

The moment the thought took shape, the dragon rumbled. I almost mistook it for thunder, but there could be no mistaking the ripples which sourced from the creature's neck and belly. With a single bob of its massive head, the dragon rumbled once more before turning toward the heart of the storm, as slowly and methodically as it had appeared.

Almost as if it wanted us to *follow*.

"*Wendy!*"

I'd never heard Mr. Smee sound so desperate. Reluctantly tearing my gaze from the dragon, I turned to where he stood near the helm. One hand was all that kept his red cap from flying off his head while the other clung to the rigging, the latter the only thing keeping him upright when the ship rocked beneath us. His eyes blazed with an emotion I couldn't place as he shouted once more. "Get over here before we're fish food!"

I was already moving, but that didn't seem to matter. Intensity was etched so deep into Smee's face that nothing could have erased it prior to me reaching his side, but it wasn't until I did that I recognized it to be fear. The men surrounding me were in various states of it, but strangely, the only thing I felt was a numb, eerie calm. I couldn't explain how I knew, but whatever the dragon's intentions, hurting us wasn't one of them. "It's not a fish, it's a dra—"

"I don't give a rat's ass what it is. We need to get away from it and away from that storm. That's a ship killer, that is, and I'm not even certain I could get us through it." Smee locked his terrified gaze with mine. "But you, Wendy, have no chance, not with your inexperience. You need to give me control of the ship."

Despite everything, I nearly laughed. Between the storm, the dragon, and wherever that tentacle creature had slipped off to, only the Sea God Adais could help us now. "So what's your plan?"

He faltered. "Plan? We flee. What else is th—"

"Flee where? Off course? Back to Afterport? No." I straightened my spine, willing my voice to carry every ounce of the authority my father had gifted me. "We've lost sight of the tentacled creature, and if the dragon wanted to hurt us, it would have done so already. I... I believe it means for us to follow it. And doing so would keep us on course."

"Follow it? Into the storm?" Smee's eyes nearly bulged from his head. "Have you completely lost your mind?"

"You'll wish *you* had if you question me again."

"Did you not hear me say 'ship killer'? If the storm doesn't do it, that dragon surely will."

"And if we turn back, those tentacles will do it." I was shouting in full view of my crew now, but I didn't care. "If I'm to choose between monsters, I'll go with the one I can see. Now if you'll excuse me, Mr. Smee, I have a ship to command."

He shouted something else, but I was already out of earshot and ascending the stairs to the upper deck. The winds were picking up and the cold was so bitter it had each spray of seawater feeling like the stab of a knife, but despite the world coming apart around me, it was exhilaration rather than fear running through my veins. Now was the chance I'd been waiting for. If I could get us through this, no man could deny my ability to lead.

If I could get us through this, I'd earn the title of captain.

I knew I was in the correct position when my right hand rested on a part of the railing scuffed and damaged by something sharp and pointy. My father's hook. It was tangible proof that he'd stood in this very spot countless times before, and now it was my turn. Lifting my gaze, I scanned the goings-on below. A handful of men ascended the rope ladders leading to the sails, getting into position to hoist them the moment I gave the inevitable order. Already the sails were being battered more than they could reasonably take, and if we didn't get them furled soon, the strain would put the masts themselves in danger.

But the time wasn't yet. We needed to catch up to the dragon first; perhaps if we stayed close enough, we could not only ride the creature's trail, we could use its massive body as a shield from the worst of the storm. Perhaps that's what the beast had been trying to tell me. "Mr. Gibbs!" I shouted to the helmsman standing just below. "Stay your course. We follow that dragon, and I want you to get us as close as you can."

His already-terrified face went pale, but he nodded nonetheless. "Aye, milady."

Shrugging off the grossly formal honorific, I went back to searching the sea of faces below. *The Jolly Serpent's* crew was like a well-oiled machine; they had weathered many a storm under Captain Hook, and truth be told, needed little additional guidance from me. Despite the torrential downpour, the hatches had been battened, the men at the sails were nearly all in position, and those below had already secured any loose cargo to prevent it from rolling about with the ship. Even Smee had given up his attempts to change my mind, and other than shooting occasional disapproving glares in my direction, aided where he could. The only person missing was Peter.

I knew him far better than to hope he'd gone below. No—he was here among us, but where, I hadn't a clue. My gaze scoured the entire ship thrice over for any sign of his boyish figure or overgrown hair, but there was no sign of either by the time I couldn't ignore the sails any longer. The masts quivered dangerously, and the wooden beams groaned from the strain.

"Wendy!" Smee called. "You need to—"

"Furl the sails!" I all but screeched, cupping my hands around my mouth to help the command carry. "Get them up now!"

A chorus of *ayes* and *nows* echoed from above as the men scrambled to obey. My grip on the hook-marked rail was all that kept me upright as I craned my neck to better watch them work, to ensure each of the sails came up without a hitch. Little by little and heave by heave, the expanses of white disappeared as they were each rolled and secured to the masts, no longer subject to the relentless battering of the storm... all but one.

The men at the topsail were struggling. It was difficult to tell from where I stood, but something was either weighing it down or caught, but it hardly mattered; with the rest of the sails gathered and secure, the lone one remaining could damn us. The mast's groaning rivaled the thunder, and the winds continued to rock as much as the waves. I had no idea if they could hear me, but I screamed anyway. "Get that sail up now! Cut it loose, do something! It's going to—"

Lightning split the sky, and that's when I saw him.

There, far higher than I'd ever seen him climb, stood Peter Pan. Balanced precariously atop the mast to which the topsail was attached, he only had one hand gripping anything for support; one misstep and he would suffer a likely fatal fall. A mixture of fury and fear rose within me as I watched him attempt to locate the reason for the stuck sail. How many times had I told him to keep his feet on the fucking deck? Reminded him that Tink wasn't here, and that without her dust, he couldn't fly?

I yelled his name along with a curse. "Get down at once! You fall, you die!"

My final words were drowned in seawater as a rogue wave came crashing across the deck. I slammed against the wood as my feet were swept out from under me, and the only reason I didn't tumble into the ocean was my death grip on the rail. With an agonized cry, I pulled myself forward, loosening my grip only enough to wrap my arms around the wooden beams before tightening them once again. Salt burned my lungs, and tears of pain blurred my vision, but the storm didn't relent. If anything, it *laughed* as another swell gathered to our left.

I dared a glance up, and my heart caught in my throat. Peter had lost his grip and fallen, but not all the way; he now dangled from the mizzenmast, his weight held by a single fraying rope. It wasn't nearly as high as he'd been before, but it was still *too* damn high.

"Wendy!" Smee's desperate shout somehow carried over the storm. "We've lost the dragon, and this storm is a killer. You have to give me command if you want us to live!"

"Peter," I whispered hoarsely, no longer able to scream. His fingers were slipping, and that rope wouldn't hold for a moment longer. "Someone catch him!"

The moment the plea left my lips, he fell. Limbs flailing uselessly, Peter's body struck the deck with a sickening *crack*, and pain flooded through me as though I was the one who'd fallen. My lips moved in a silent scream, and I hardly paid attention to the voices speaking behind me.

"—gone mad, she 'as."

"Left us no choice."

True agony blossomed at my temple, and unable to fight its relentless pull, I slipped into blackness.

II. THE PAST

Cedric

Twice, I almost turned back.

There was nothing stopping me. I wasn't being forced or threatened to follow a complete stranger into a dingy tavern basement that reeked of magic among other, somehow worse, things. Darkness all but swallowed us whole, and I could barely make out Calypso's outline as she descended the creaking, moldy stairs. Cold seeped into my bones, and despite the numerous layers intended to conceal my scars, I shivered.

I have no idea how she sensed my discomfort with her back to me, but Calypso laughed all the same. "Don't tell me you're scared, Cedric Teach."

"I'm not." The truth, but what she had implied was right. I should be terrified out of my mind given both my surroundings and history—magic had never been kind to me—but the only thing making the hair on my arms stand on end was anticipation. The basement only got darker and creepier, but I continued to follow Calypso of my own free will, solidifying what I'd already accepted as fact. I'd give my life to find out who or what had killed Scarlett, my love and the mother of my child. But if Calypso spoke the truth and Scarlett was alive?

I'd light the world on fire and happily watch it burn if it meant that I could hold her once more.

Before I could linger on the bloody revelation, Calypso whirled around, nearly causing me to slam into her front. I caught myself at the last second, but before I could curse her name, she flashed me an unsettling grin and clapped her hands a single time.

The basement became illuminated by a combination of torch and candlelight. Though the light wasn't overpowering, it took my eyes a few moments to adjust to the sudden brightness. As I took in our surroundings, Calypso's dark gaze searched my face. Evidently my reaction wasn't what she had been expecting. "Unimpressed?"

"Where's the impressive part?" I raised an eyebrow. "Looks like a normal tavern basement to me." Supplies lined the walls, with many of the crates open and their contents half-used and rifled through. Rat droppings coated the floor. A random assortment of personal objects, likely things left behind by patrons over the years, were piled in one corner, and a dusty table with several rickety chairs sat in the opposite. I grimaced. If Calypso thought I'd trust one of them to hold my weight, she was even more wrong than her original guess regarding my sexuality.

"Not that. Me." Her eyes narrowed, still searching me intently. "I just used magic."

"And? You're not human, so I'm not shocked."

"You don't know much about nymphs, do you?"

"You're the very first I've had the pleasure of meeting."

Calypso smiled despite my tone dripping with sarcasm. The light down here was much better than that illuminating the main floor above, and I'd removed the hood obstructing most of my vision, so I got my first uninhibited look at her. She was tall and slender, standing nearly eye level to my frame. Her rich sepia skin practically glowed and was well-complemented by the low-cut dress barely clinging to her shoulders. Tight, dark curls tumbled partway down her back and bounced at the slightest turn of her head in a way that was almost distractingly gorgeous. There was no denying that the nymph was beautiful, almost unearthly so, but I hadn't been interested in any other woman since losing Scarlett, so if this was yet another attempt at seduction, Calypso had already failed. I opened my mouth to tell her so, but she beat me to it.

"Well, Cedric Teach, if you *were* familiar with nymphs, then you'd know that while we do have certain innate abilities, using magic outright isn't one of them. To wield it as I just did, we must be taught."

"Why do you keep saying my name?" I was only half-listening to what else she'd uttered, too fixated upon the way she kept addressing me, surname and all. It was the third time she'd done it. We'd hardly touched, yet this felt more intimate than if I'd let her strip me naked.

Calypso continued smiling. "Names have power," she said simply, "and I happen to like yours."

"Stop saying it." I set my jaw, doing my best to appear braver than I felt. Fear I could handle—I'd survived Neverland, after all—but vulnerability was a different beast entirely. I'd rather be surrounded by a dozen Nightstalkers than allow her to keep looking at me like that. "You said that you can tell me where to find Scarlett, so get on with it."

She frowned then. "You're shaking."

Was I? My body suddenly didn't feel like it belonged to me. Though Calypso had reached the basement floor, I lingered on the bottom stair, hand and hook gripping both sides of the railing to keep my knees from buckling. I didn't move, but the room began spinning, and my vision grew dark and spotty. "I… I don't…"

Strong arms encircled me, and it wasn't until I opened my eyes that it became clear that I'd fallen. I lay slumped in Calypso's lap, my head against her shoulder and her breasts pressed uncomfortably close to my chest. A low growl escaped my throat as I shifted to push her away, but the voice that responded wasn't the nymph's… and neither was the scent that had enveloped me.

"Are you sure you're all right?"

My breath caught in my throat as it constricted from the force of the shock. The words were warm and sincere, spoken by someone I'd known only in my dreams for the past sixteen years. But this wasn't a dream. I was too aware, too lucid. Never once had I considered my dreams to be so, not even nightmares in which I'd have done anything to escape. *Is it truly her?* Hope blossomed in my chest, but more overpowering was the icy doubt that prevented me from lifting my head, unwilling to feel such an enormous loss all over again. Scarlett and her memory might be an anchor holding me back, but I wouldn't drop it. I couldn't. Doing so would leave behind a gaping wound I wasn't sure I knew how to close, force me to feel agony I wasn't certain I could—

Fingers gripped my chin, gently pulling my gaze up, and there she was.

Scarlett.

She said something else, but I didn't hear it. My hand was everywhere, following the path my eyes traced as I drank her in. Dark locks framed bright eyes, freckled cheeks, a soft jaw, and full lips. I lingered there the longest, resting my thumb against Scarlett's mouth as my heart began beating out of my chest. Countless times I'd stared at her. Countless hours we'd spent together. I'd memorized her very existence from caresses alone, imprinted her soul on mine and vowed to never leave her should we be fortunate enough to meet again. And she *was* here. I didn't know how, but of that, I was certain.

"Y-yes," I forced, barely able to recall how to speak. "I'm fine. More than fine." Knotting my fingers into her hair, I pulled her lips toward mine, preparing to lose myself in the kiss I'd spent nearly two decades yearning for.

I wasn't prepared for the knife that buried itself into the wall behind us, missing Scarlett's face by mere inches.

My body sprang into action before my mind could catch up.

After ripping myself from Scarlett's grasp, I twisted to cover her form with mine, using both hook and hand to pin her in place. I handled her roughly, but she could take it. No doubt she'd protest my actions and remind me that she was no 'damsel' when all this was over, but it was an argument I'd gladly have if it meant she was safe. Shifting my focus, I turned toward the steps and our attacker, only to stare down my sister.

Elvira held a second blade in her hand, perfectly poised to let the dagger fly. She remained half-concealed in shadow, looking every bit a viper set to strike, but her eyes contained a startling mixture of fear and fury and her chest heaved as though she'd sprinted to reach us. "Move," was all she said. It was the only warning I'd get, because we both knew she wouldn't miss a second time.

"Absolutely fucking not." I tightened my grip on Scarlett. Beneath the anger, shock rippled through me. Scarlett may not be Elvira's favorite person, but never in a thousand years could I have envisioned standing between my sister and the woman I loved. "What in Adais's name are you doing?"

Almost before I'd finished speaking, a sob sounded from below. "Help," Scarlett whimpered. "Don't let her hurt me." A second realization struck, nearly with enough force to topple me over.

Scarlett wasn't fighting me.

My breath caught in my throat. The Scarlett *I* knew would be wrestling me tooth and nail for a chance to throw herself at anyone who so much as looked at her the wrong way, let alone *threw a knife* at her. I could imagine the vile obscenities she'd happily spew at Elvira in particular. My pirate queen wasn't immune to fear, of course, but I could count the number of times I'd seen her genuinely afraid with nothing but the fingers I had left, and Elvira was nowhere near that list. As ice cascaded down my spine, I dared a glance and pulled back in the same horrified motion, my worst fears confirmed as I stared at a beautiful, but very wrong face. It wasn't Scarlett I'd been holding. It wasn't Scarlett I'd almost kissed.

It was Calypso.

A second knife went flying once I was no longer in its way. With inhuman reflexes, the nymph plucked it from midair the moment before it would have buried itself into her chest. She flashed Elvira a grin, flipping the blade over in her hand. "How generous of you, Serpent."

Before I could say another word, they pounced on one another, hacking, whirling, and slashing with unnerving precision. Calypso was quicker than she had any right to be, and Elvira was downright lethal as she wielded all the skill our father, Blackbeard, had passed down to her. Her reflexes had slowed considerably while cursed and trapped in Neverland, but she had since regained her strength, and it showed. But old habits died hard, and judging from the intensity of her movements and the hatred painted across her features, Elvira was indeed going for the kill. Frustrated grunts and the clashing of steel filled the room, and I was nothing but a helpless bystander, unable to think of a way I could get between them without causing more harm than good… and that was if I didn't get stabbed in the process.

It took Calypso's hiss of pain to bring me to my senses. Elvira had grazed her upper thigh, and strange black liquid I could only assume was blood trailed from the wound and down Calypso's leg. She retreated to the corner with the table, perching on top of it to keep Elvira at a distance while she caught her breath. I barked Elvira's name, but she didn't tear her eyes from her prey, so I swore instead.

"Will you stop thinking with your knife and just *think*? She's far more useful to us alive than dead."

"'Us?'" Elvira whirled around. "I agreed to help you find Scarlett, not some nymph bitch for you to shove your cock into the second I turn my back. If that's what you want to do, be my guest, but in that case, there is no 'us.'"

Heat crept to my cheeks. "It's not like that."

"Then what is it like, Ced? Are you fucking her, or am I killing her?"

"I wonder whether you want to fuck *me*, Elvira," a male voice said.

Both our gazes snapped to the table, but Calypso was no longer there. Instead, from the shadows emerged a Black man, as muscular and handsome as I remembered him. Dreadlocks were tied into a loose bun at the back of his head, revealing a devilish smirk and eyes only for Elvira. He was shorter than me but taller than my sister, and thickly built around his upper body especially. It was why Jasper had found a place among my sister's crew more than two decades ago. First as a gunner, and later her quartermaster… and lover.

But even as Elvira drifted toward him, openmouthed, I reached for the pistol sheathed at my hip. Now that I observed from the outside, I saw what Elvira must have seen when Calypso had assumed Scarlett's shape. Jasper's outline flickered, and if I squinted, I could make out the nymph's true form underneath. An unsettling presence I recognized as magic flooded the room, informing me there was more to Calypso's power than just shapeshifting, but I'd need to interrogate her for specifics later.

"Get back! He's not real. He's not even alive, Elvira." The last time we'd seen Jasper, he'd ventured into Neverland's jungle and never came back. She knew as well as I did that only meant one thing. "You're falling for her trap just like I did."

Neither Elvira nor Calypso appeared to have heard me. With the knife held loosely at her side, Elvira reached with her free hand. "Is it really you?"

I gritted my teeth. Either my sister actually bought this ridiculous fucking fantasy or she was simply acting to get close enough to Calypso to kill her, and I couldn't allow either scenario to play out. Cocking the gun, I darted toward the woman I deemed the more dangerous of the two and pressed the barrel to her throat.

"Now do you see?" I hissed into Elvira's ear.

Before our eyes, Jasper's form and flesh alike melted away, revealing Calypso's golden-brown skin. The process I'd expected to be grotesque turned out to be shockingly beautiful, or perhaps that was just the nymph's magic seizing hold of my mind yet again as she transformed back into her stunning self—fully clothed, thank the gods. Her wound remained, as did the black blood staining the front of her dress. She shook her head, curls bouncing, and clicked her tongue disapprovingly. "*Tsk, tsk*, Cedric. That's no way to treat your sister."

"Shut up before I let her kill you."

Elvira batted away the gun, stilling only when I rested my hook against her collarbone and applied just enough pressure to let her know I wasn't bluffing. It didn't keep her quiet, though. "Oh no, please continue. I'd love to finish what I started."

"Enough." I shot each of the women a glare. "No one is killing anyone so long as you keep your word."

"So you did go striking deals with a nymph behind my back," Elvira hissed.

I ignored that and turned my attention to Calypso. Raising the gun, I pointed it square at her chest. "Talk, and spare no detail. I want to know everything you know about Scarlett Maynard."

Calypso raised an eyebrow. "I'd be happy to if you'd stop making threats you don't intend to follow through on. You're not going to hurt your precious sister and you're not going to hurt me, especially not with that. Fire it, and you'll attract half the town and surely sleep in a cell tonight."

I hated that she was right. With a curse, I placed the gun on the table but didn't loosen my hold on Elvira. I didn't trust Calypso, but I trusted my sister even less at the moment. "Get on with it."

The nymph slid back onto the wooden surface, making a show of pushing the pistol aside and crossing her legs so that her injured one was on top. "So impatient, Cedric Teach."

"Stop saying my fucking name."

"Are you seriously buying this little whore's act? She doesn't know anything." Elvira attempted to sidestep my hook, only freezing when I snatched her wrist; a warning. I wasn't above twisting it painfully behind her back if that's what it took to keep her away from the nymph. "If she did, she'd have talked by now."

Calypso eyed Elvira with disdain. "I warned you that she couldn't follow you here. There will be consequences if you allow your sister to hear what I have to say."

"Elvira stays," I said before Calypso had finished speaking. 'Consequences' seemed like a convenient excuse to get me alone once more, and there was no way I'd make that mistake a second time. "Any more reasons to keep stalling?"

"Just one." With a firm yank, the nymph tore a long strip of fabric from the bottom of her dress and began wrapping it around her wounded leg. I didn't miss the pain that flashed across her features, so it surprised me when she started speaking mid-wrap. "Scarlett is alive."

"So you've claimed," I said. "Where is your proof?"

Calypso shot me a glare. "She and I have the same mistress. Proof enough?"

"Who is your mistress?"

"Patience. We'll get there." She wound the fabric around her leg a final time before securing it with a tight knot. "First, we need to go much further back. You two might want to sit."

I spun Elvira to face me. "Will you behave?"

She glowered. "Only for you."

Neither of us trusted the half-broken chairs not to collapse beneath us, so we dragged a pair of empty wine barrels over to where Calypso sat. I made certain to position mine between the women, just in case, but the air of hostility between them had diminished, at least for now.

The moment we were settled, Calypso began her tale unprompted.

"At the beginning of time, there was the sea, and there was chaos—"

"The beginning of time?" Elvira's eyes widened. "My brother might have an entire night to waste on this nonsense, but I certainly don't. I have a perfectly good woman waiting for me upstairs."

Calypso held her gaze. "Interrupt me again, and I'll happily keep my 'nonsense' to myself."

"Please, continue," I said. "She'll keep her mouth shut." I shot Elvira a glare that hopefully communicated my unspoken threat: *Or I'll slice your tongue out myself.*

"As I was saying—the sea and chaos. Adais and Kaara, respectively. I trust you've heard of them?"

Elvira and I both nodded. I'd only heard Kaara mentioned in passing, but Adais's name, legend, and lore were staples aboard any ship. My father especially had been fond of the Sea God, and frequent offerings and prayers had been made in his name. I'd never been an outright nonbeliever in the gods, but after witnessing Blackbeard's downfall despite his devotion, it would take more than a little convincing to get me to follow in my father's footsteps.

"Their love birthed the world, and their children helped craft it. All was well for a long while. Adais commanded the seas while Kaara wielded her chaos. Her storms and devastation carved landmasses upon which life could thrive, and Adais, impressed with the way she handled such raw power, surrendered control of the tides to her in the ultimate gesture of love and trust. To this day, it is Kaara who rules over the moon and its tidal pull, day in and day out. They were such

44

a powerful team, each so intertwined with the other, that they vowed to love no one else for the remainder of eternity. But it could not last."

"Shocker," Elvira muttered. I kicked her in the shins, summoning a curse, but despite the interruption, Calypso kept going.

"Over time, Adais's loyalty waned. He began to take lovers of both man and beast and grew more brazen with his affairs the longer they were allowed to continue. It was a betrayal Kaara could no longer ignore. She rained chaos upon his domain, determined to flush him out no matter the cost, and even dry land began paying the price of her fury. All living things suffered a great deal. The earth nearly split in two as a result of the warring gods, and even then, neither could gain the upper hand. Knowing he could not hide forever, a desperate Adais began crafting a weapon in secret: one intended to end the feud once and for all." Calypso paused to meet my gaze. "A trident. Its name is in Godstongue and unpronounceable by mortals, but it most closely translates to Heartpiercer."

I'd heard bits and pieces of this lore over the years. The tales were often whispered around fires, in taverns, and as ghost stories meant to explain why our ships sometimes fell prey to unexpected storms. Real or not, the gods and their lives were legends, myths far too separated from my current reality for me to give an ounce of a shit who they were or who they fucked. Why Calypso was telling us now I didn't yet know, but something stirred within me at that name: *Heartpiercer*. That title could only be given to one type of weapon. "He intended to kill her."

The nymph nodded. "Only a god can kill another god, and Adais had every intention of spearing Kaara and being done with it. What he didn't anticipate was Heartpiercer's raw, unstable power… or that he would lose control of the trident." Calypso turned away, shrouding her face in shadow. "It was apocalyptic. Devastation unlike anything we'd ever known at the hands of Kaara. Cities crumbled, children perished, artifacts were lost to time—"

"'We?'" Elvira echoed. "You're speaking as though you were there."

"Nearly everything in Adais's realm was lost." Yet again, Calypso ignored Elvira's outburst—the nymph's tone was subdued and almost haunted. "His attempts to destroy the trident failed, so the only other thing he could do was hide Heartpiercer in a place that no one, mortal or god, would ever be able to retrieve it. The Sea of Eternal Woe."

At the mention of the Sea, I sat up a little straighter. "Hell, you mean?"

"To some." Calypso looked up, though the troubled look in her eyes remained. "It's a place where lost souls roam for all eternity. Anyone can enter it, living or dead, but only one of pure heart can emerge from the Sea whole and unscathed."

Panic constricted my chest. "Is that where Scarlett is?"

"No. But it's where my mistress intended for her to go."

"Your mistress…" My voice cracked as it trailed off. "Is *Kaara*?"

Calypso nodded, brow raised. "Surprised?"

A combination of things had my heart beating out of my chest, and surprise was only one of them. "H-how…"

"How did they meet? Sixteen years ago, a self-proclaimed witch set up residence in Afterport. She was in search of children who might be good candidates to enter the Sea but found Scarlett instead, the definition of selflessness. Desperate, pregnant, and willing to do anything to save her unborn child. She sold herself to Kaara in exchange for her daughter's freedom from Neverland and the curse." Calypso paused when I sucked in a sharp breath. "You're the father, I take it?"

I could no longer form words and barely noticed when Elvira's arm shot out to steady me. "Ced, are you all right?"

My fist clenched. How could I be any semblance of *all right* upon learning that the love of my life was indebted to a goddess? Already the revelation hurt far worse than when I'd simply believed she was dead; knowing Scarlett was alive yet out of my reach was an excruciatingly familiar kind of torture. My thoughts drifted back to what had happened at Admiral Ruiz's mansion all those years ago, to how helpless I'd felt when I thought she was slipping from my grasp. Back then, Scarlett was where she had chosen to be. She may have made a similar choice with Kaara, but it was only to keep Wendy safe. Would Scarlett keep making that choice if she knew our daughter was alive and well?

There was only one way to find out.

Lifting my head, I met Calypso's gaze. "Why are you telling me this?"

"I need a reason?"

"Don't play games with me, nymph." I shot up, causing her to flinch. "Kaara clearly sent you. What does she want from me? Am I to enter the Sea next?"

Calypso's demeanor turned icy, and she all but spat her reply. "I suppose specifying *former* mistress would have helped. I was there the day Scarlett and Kaara struck their bargain, and once Wendy was born, Kaara asked me to remain in Afterport to keep an eye on the child. I agreed, but only because she promised to come back for me. She… she never did." Her eyes closed, and she turned her head away.

Silence lingered until Elvira broke it. "Suppose a pretty thing like you hasn't known much rejection."

Calypso shook her head. "Not by her."

Rejection? I pieced together the clues—Calypso's change in demeanor, her tone of voice, her choice of words—and came to one plausible conclusion. "You love her."

"I did." Calypso snapped her gaze back to me. "But that ship has clearly sailed, which means I can't return to her empty handed if I hope to ever regain her favor."

I wasn't following what any of this had to do with me. "And you need us because…?"

"Because of that name you hate so much," Calypso said. "Teach. And not the Serpent. Just you."

"I share that name," Elvira piped up, but both of us ignored her, because I still wasn't following.

"What the fuck is your point?" I asked.

"The curse, Cedric." Calypso threw up her hands, exasperated. "Do you seriously think that chaotic, evil thing came from Adais? That he'd place such a burden on one of his most devoted subjects, on *Blackbeard*? No. The curse was Kaara's doing. What do you think she'd give to meet the one who survived such darkness?"

"But I didn't break the curse," I said slowly. "That was Wendy."

"Doesn't matter." Calypso stepped forward, closing the distance between us. Resting a single finger beneath my chin, she applied light pressure, tilting my face toward hers. "You bore that rot upon your soul longer than anyone else. Year in and year out, you could never go longer than a week without killing. And oh, you killed." Lips mere inches from mine twisted into a sultry grin. "What Kaara wouldn't give to meet the man who will never wash the blood from his hands… well, hand. If I delivered you, the elusive Crow? No doubt she'd have me back."

My breath hitched, mind spinning. Kaara, the goddess of chaos and discord, wanted *me*. It wasn't a question of whether I'd trade myself for Scarlett's freedom—I would in a heartbeat—it was whether it could truly be that easy. I leaned into Calypso's grasp, gaze narrowing as I drank her in. Gods, she truly was intoxicating; a drug I'd happily lose myself in had our circumstances been any different. "Why should I trust you?"

She grinned. "You shouldn't."

At least she's honest. Couldn't fault her for that. Tearing myself from Calypso's grasp, I uttered my response before Elvira could butt in yet again. "Fine."

A strangled cry of disbelief tore from my sister's throat. She stood up so quickly her barrel tumbled to the floor, but her shrill voice carried even over the racket. "There is nothing about this that is in any way fine. Do you even know what it is you're agreeing to?"

"Calypso will take me to Kaara. I get the opportunity to free Scarlett, and she gets back in her mistress's good graces." I shrugged.

"Did I miss anything?"

"Yes," Elvira snapped. "The part where you think this through. Weren't you the one telling me that just a bit ago?"

"There's nothing to think." Whirling around, I shot my sister a death glare. "Sixteen years, Elvira. Sixteen years of death, decay, and despair, of waking up every morning knowing I deserved every bit of it for chasing Scarlett away. I would have ended my miserable existence to join her had I not wanted to prolong my suffering for as long as possible. To end the curse which had plagued her. To exist in this world until I fully embraced the monster I'd already become." I shouted now, but I didn't care. "You weren't able to stop me when it was Ruiz who had her. What makes you think that you can stop me now?"

Something glistened in Elvira's eyes, but it had to be a trick of the light; never once had I witnessed my sister cry. "You know that I'd happily follow you to the ends of the earth, but if you're planning on giving yourself up without a fight, then this is where I leave you. Te amo, hermano. I cannot watch you place your own neck in a noose. Even if it is for the woman I know you love."

Fuck. The genuine hurt in my sister's voice was nearly enough to summon tears of my own. Before I knew what I was doing, I pulled Elvira close, draping both arms over her shoulders. She tensed at first but soon relaxed enough to squeeze my middle nearly to the point of suffocation. Calypso had long since retreated against the far wall, but unsure whether the nymph remained within earshot, I spoke in as breathy a whisper as I could muster, my words intended for Elvira alone. "I have no intention of handing myself over. I need you by my side." Only one of those statements was true.

Elvira didn't loosen her hold. "Promise?"

"Promise."

With a satisfied nod, she released me, but a dull, suffocating ache remained even as my sister smiled. "Then I'm coming with you."

I forced my own smile before glancing at Calypso. "What now?"

She made a show of stretching and yawning as she sauntered back toward us. "In case you'd forgotten, it's the middle of the night, and even nymphs need their rest. We leave in the morning, but only if this one promises not to throw any more knives at me between now and then."

Elvira snorted. "Don't count on it."

Too exhausted to scold either of them, I gestured toward the stairs. "After you."

My sister all but skipped away, taking the steps two at a time, no doubt to continue whatever it was she'd started with the woman she'd met on the dance floor. Rolling my eyes, I followed her, eager to retreat to the room I'd rented for the night.

But before I could, Calypso laughed darkly behind me. "You're a terrible liar, Cedric Teach."

I paused mid-step, swallowing hard. "Eavesdropping on me now?"

"Hardly. I just know you'll stop at nothing to save Scarlett. But before you walk yourself off a cliff, know this." Calypso leaned against my back, her breath tickling my earlobe as she whispered. "She *will* be the death of you, but it will be the most beautiful death you could ever know."

III. THE MUTINY

Wendy

Wendy, Wendy...

Gods, not that voice again. I gritted my teeth, attempting to cling to anything that wasn't that lyrical, almost mournful, soprano. Hadn't I escaped my mother's singing once I'd escaped Neverland? Was sending Hook after her murderer not enough for her spirit to leave me be? I tried to wave her away, but my hands wouldn't obey my command.

Wendy. You must listen.

"Not to you."

You don't understand.

Anger surged through me. "No, you don't understand!"

"Wendy!"

My eyes shot open at the sudden change in tone, at the voice that was most certainly not Scarlett's. More hazy darkness greeted me, and I became aware I stared at *The Jolly Serpent's* grimy hull. Everything ached, but worst was my pulsing skull, closely followed by my arms. Twisted at a brutal angle behind my back, I couldn't free them to ease the pain shooting from my shoulders to wrists. "W-what is—"

"Don't move," Peter said; at least, it sounded like his voice. "They hit you pretty hard. If you can sit up, do it slowly."

If I could? Confusion rippled through me until I attempted to do as he suggested. Only then did it become clear I'd been bound, arms and legs secured with tight, unforgiving knots at my wrists and ankles respectively. Red stained the wood upon which my head had rested moments before, informing me it was blood and not water trailing down my face. Combined with the incessant pounding at my temple, it was safe to conclude that I had indeed been struck.

Bits and pieces came flooding back. The storm. The dragon. My refusal to give up command. The crew's paralyzing fear. Peter's fall. At least he'd survived without significant injury, but had everyone else? "S-storm," I croaked through parched lips. "D-did w-we…?"

Peter nodded. Tied just as I was, he sat at a distance, huddled against a stack of musty crates. A light, almost golden bruise colored his cheek, and his shirt was ripped and torn, mostly near the shoulder upon which he'd fallen. "Smee took command and got us through it. As far as I can tell, everyone is alive. Shaken, but alive."

"Are you all right?"

He hesitated. "I'm alive."

"That's not what I asked." The horrific *crack* I'd heard upon him striking the deck replayed through my memory, and I tried to crane my gaze to his left side. "I saw you fall, and it looked bad. It sounded even worse."

"I...can't feel my arm, and my shoulder aches like a motherfucker," Peter admitted, grimacing as he shifted. "But I can move my fingers, so I don't think it's broken, just dislocated. I'm afraid to pop it back into place on my own."

Groaning, I tested my still-tight bonds. "I could help you if I were free. The boys at the orphanage used to dislocate their shoulders all the time when they wrestled, so I became rather good at mending them."

The corners of his mouth turned up. "Of course you did."

Unable to share in Peter's amusement, I guided us back to more pressing matters. "And the dragon?"

"Gone. No one's seen it since yesterday."

Yesterday? Had an entire day passed? Now that Peter had said as much, the midday light streaming through cracks in the boards above was telling, as were the faint voices and footsteps echoing from the same. "So why are we down here?"

Peter laughed darkly. "Do you really have to ask? They've mutinied, Wendy."

Vehement rage replaced any lingering bewilderment. *Mutiny?* Had I truly been tied up, beaten, and taken prisoner aboard my own ship? "Who did this?" I demanded, loathing the way I flopped about like a goddamn fish. "Was it Smee? I'll have his ass flogged so hard he won't be able to sit right for a month!"

"Does it matter?" In stark contrast to mine, Peter's tone was defeated and bitter. "You're no longer captain, and I'm no longer anything."

"Like fuck we're not," I spat. "Come on, you're up. See if you can help me."

"There's no point. It's over."

"What's over?"

"All of it, Wendy!" In an instant, Peter's fury surfaced. "Our mission. This voyage." He paused, lips barely moving as he whispered two words that nearly made my heart stop. "My life."

I shook my head. "Don't say that. We'll get through this."

"You might, but I won't." Peter met my gaze, but only after flicking his head to get the hair out of his face. Hair that was both too long and an unmistakable sign of the truth we both knew but couldn't bear to admit aloud: he was aging. "If we don't find Ursa, if I'm doomed to live in this body, then I don't want to live at all."

The more he kept insisting it, the more my fear threatened to strangle me. Here on this ship, Peter truly was the only thing I had resembling a friend or even an ally. I couldn't lose him. Not after we'd already come so far and were *so close* to attaining what he'd always wanted. I began tripping over my words in an effort to convince him otherwise. "What about Neverland? Tink? How could you do that to her?"

"Tink understands there's far more at stake than my immortality."

"You can't—what?" I did a double take as I struggled to recall what I'd just heard. "Did you just say immortality?"

"Quiet," Peter cut across me, suddenly leaning forward and tilting his head. "Do you hear that?"

"Nothing but you avoiding my question."

He gasped sharply, gaze widening. "It can't be."

I rolled my eyes. "You're going to have to try much harder than that if you think I'm going to forget the..." My voice trailed off as I did begin to hear something—a music I doubted I'd ever hear again—but before I could voice so aloud, its source darted in front of me and smiled.

"Hello, Wendy."

I gasped. "Tink?"

The fairy was exactly as I remembered her: brown skin, dark, textured hair, light eyes, gossamer wings, and clothes woven from flowers. Her glow wasn't nearly as bright as it had been in Neverland, but the tinkling bell noises which gave Tink her name were as strong and lyrical as ever. She offered me a simple wave before turning to Peter, who seemed to be rendered completely speechless.

"Y... y-you—"

"Hush," was all Tink said before fluttering to his ankle bindings. Whipping out a dagger small enough to fit in her palm, she began severing the ropes one by one.

"Where did you come from?" I asked while she worked, voicing the questions Peter seemed unable to. He simply watched us, openmouthed and frozen. "Have you been here this entire time?"

"Yes."

"And you didn't come out until now? You watched us weather that storm, watched me fall, and did nothing?" Seemingly recovered from his initial shock, Peter sounded equal parts incredulous and furious as Tink moved to free his wrists. "Tink, what in the gods' names are you doing here?"

"Saving your asses," the fairy snapped. "Or at least, trying to. Would you rather I leave you to rot?"

"No," I butted in. "We're very grateful, and I for one couldn't be happier to see you."

Peter shot me a murderous glare. "You shouldn't be."

I met his gaze, completely taken aback by his reaction. "Just because you're a thankless ass doesn't mean I have to be the same."

"You don't understand, Wendy," Peter said as Tink moved to the ropes around my arms. "It's not that Tink shouldn't be here, it's that she can't. At least, not for long."

With my hands now free, I rolled over and sat up to look at Tink while she worked on my ankles. "What is he talking about?"

Tink's light turned red. "A choice that wasn't his to make."

"We're bonded," Peter snarled as he rose to his feet, nursing his injured shoulder with his opposite arm. "How are the choices you make none of my concern?"

Bonded? I glanced between the two, bewildered yet unsurprised.

Much of their relationship made sense now, especially how deeply the pair seemed able to communicate without spoken words, but how had this not been relevant sooner? They had spent time both together and apart without issue many times before.

Tink's glow remained crimson as she rose to the level of Peter's head. "*I'm* affected by the bond, not you."

"That's not true and you know it!"

"Enough!" I hissed, coming to stand between them. I didn't think they'd hurt each other, but I needed to get their attention somehow. "Will one of you please tell me what's going on?"

"Tink is going to die," Peter blurted out between breaths, chest heaving from the force of his shouts. "She's already dying. Can't you see it in her light?"

I turned to the fairy, who now floated in midair with her arms crossed. I'd wondered if it was simply my memory playing tricks on me, but now that Peter had confirmed as much, the glow surrounding Tink was indeed far dimmer than usual. "Don't be dramatic," she said. "I've got time."

"How much?" I asked, dread twisting my gut into knots. The longer I studied her, the more I noticed the signs; Tink's skin appeared lackluster, and not even her wings fluttered as fast as I was accustomed to seeing them move. "And why? What happened to you?"

"She left Neverland." Peter's voice lacked fury, and now he simply sounded sad. "'Neverland never lets go.' It was true well before the curse took effect. Any creature born there can never leave, not unless they wish to die a slow, painful death. All the time that stood still while they were in Neverland catches up with them in the outside world, and here, no one can live forever. It's hard to say how much time she's got, but judging from how much she's already deteriorated, I wouldn't guess any longer than a month."

"Well then... I suppose we've no choice but to get you to Ursa before Tink's time runs out." I glanced at the fairy, determination surging through me as the path ahead became clear. "Will you recover if you return to Neverland?"

"I think so," Tink said. "I can feel it calling me back."

I nodded, turning to Peter. "And you're not dying?"

He shook his head but remained wary. "I wasn't born in Neverland, so I'm not bound to the island in the same way Tink is."

"Then we've got a plan." Clapping my hands, I began scanning the room for anything that might help us. "All we need to do is get out of here and get my ship back."

Peter grimaced, pulling his injured arm closer to his chest. "Wendy, it's not that simple. We don't even know what the crew is planning."

"I do," Tink piped up. "I overheard them talking before I freed you."

It couldn't be any worse than any of the bloody spectacles my mind wasted no time conjuring up. "Well, spit it out."

"There's good news and bad news," Tink said grimly.

Peter nodded. "Good news first."

"They're not going to kill you."

Relief flooded through me; this at least meant that the bad news wasn't life threatening. "Thank the gods."

"You're going to be fed to the monster… alive."

IV. THE TIDE

Cedric

"Remind me again how we're getting to the goddess?"

It was a question I'd never asked in the whirlwind that had been my morning. Calypso burst into my room well before sunrise, completely ignoring my demands that she get out or, at the very least, turn around while I dressed. Judging from the sour look on my sister's face, Elvira's wake-up call had been no different. After stashing Scarlett's portrait safely in my coat pocket, we settled our tab and departed the tavern, and the three of us weren't far from the docks now. The sun still hadn't fully risen, but the first rays of daylight were visible over the horizon.

"Patience, Cedric Teach," was all Calypso said. Despite limping due to her fight with Elvira the previous night, the nymph's pace was rather brisk, and Elvira and I trailed a fair distance behind despite our efforts to keep up. It wasn't a problem now, but once the crowds grew thicker, we'd be in danger of losing her entirely.

"Hey, Silvertongue, mind slowing down? Some of us aren't morning people," Elvira said, tightening her grip on my cloak. She hadn't let go of me since we'd left the tavern.

I gritted my teeth. "Will you stop calling her that?"

She shrugged. "Certainly, but my other ideas for nicknames aren't nearly as kind."

"She has an *actual* name, you know."

"So do I, but she hasn't once used it and insists on calling me Serpent," Elvira snapped. "Why should I show her more respect than she's shown me?"

We were so engrossed in our argument that we didn't notice Calypso had halted until we nearly ran into her. She raised an eyebrow, regarding us as though we were her misbehaving children. "As amusing as your bickering is, I'm afraid it will have to wait. Our transportation is only available to us for a very narrow window, so we must hurry."

At this, I perked up. "You secured us passage? On which ship?" There were a number of fine-looking vessels in the harbor, and though we'd only been away from *The Jolly Serpent* for a few weeks, I missed her more than I cared to admit. I took several deep inhales of the crisp, salty air, relishing the energy flooding through me despite the ungodly hour. I'd never been much of a morning person.

Calypso either didn't hear me or didn't want to answer. She began moving even faster, expertly weaving her way through the rapidly growing crowds as more people emerged from their homes to start the day. Keeping sight of her dark curls became far easier said than done. Up until now, it had annoyed me that Elvira insisted upon keeping hold of me, but unwilling to lose her in the chaos, I clasped my sister's hand within mine, yanking her along despite her continued cursing of Calypso's name. We battled the hordes for a few frenzied minutes until the nymph took a sharp turn down a mostly deserted road leading directly to the beach.

"Where is she taking us?" Elvira asked between breathless pants. There were no ships anywhere near here; the water was much too shallow for any vessel larger than a rowboat. There wasn't much of anything other than a handful of fishermen trying their luck with a combination of nets and wooden crab traps.

I shook my head. "I've no idea."

When we were a fair distance from the last of the fisherman, Calypso finally slowed, and so did we. She walked along the coast, her bare feet leaving delicate imprints in the sand, and she had even removed her shawl from her shoulders. I had no idea how she wasn't freezing half to death, especially when the tide began lazily engulfing her up to her ankles. Elvira and I remained huddled together, this time for warmth rather than the fear of losing one another. We traveled in silence for a good half mile. A deep, hazy fog obscured much of what lay ahead, but even through the mist, the outlines of several gnarled trees were visible. If I didn't know any better, I'd think Calypso was leading us back to—

"Neverland?" Elvira hissed through chattering teeth. "We spend half our lives fighting to escape that hellhole, and she expects us to go back?"

I was even less fond of the idea. Neverland hadn't done anything but take parts of me I was unwilling to give—my hand, my love, my daughter—and under no circumstances would I ever set foot in that forest again. I opened my mouth to tell Calypso as much just as a human silhouette emerged from the haze, though from the surf rather than the forest.

Freezing, I tightened my grip on Elvira's hand. The barefoot man strode toward us, his posture confident and relaxed. Only a single loose layer of brightly colored clothing clung to his frame, contrasting handsomely with his tawny brown skin and dark hair. He spared us a passing, dismissive glance before fixating on Calypso, his previously sharp features twisting into a wry grin. "Took you long enough."

"I was dragging along some dead weight."

"I can see that."

The stranger turned to meet my gaze, and only then did the resemblance dawn on me. There was an air of magic about him, inhuman and mysterious, and suddenly positive he was a nymph, I half-expected him to begin shapeshifting on the spot. "You're Calypso's brother."

"Observant too, it seems," he said to Calypso, voice heavy with sarcasm. "Are you certain he's the one?"

"Positive." Calypso gestured to her brother, then us. "Ceto, meet the infamous Captain Hook and his sister, Elvira Teach."

Elvira drew a mock gasp. "So you do know my name."

"Forgive me, but don't you keep saying we're short on time?" I glanced between Calypso and Ceto, brows raised. "How much farther do we have to go? If it involves Neverland in any way…"

"Rest assured that it doesn't. We have no use for that half-rotted forest. We simply needed to get away from prying human eyes." Calypso turned to Ceto. "Are they ready?"

"And eager," he said.

Before I could question who or what 'they' was, the tide surrounding the nymphs began to stir and bubble before receding, gathering into a single terrifying wave. Panic constricted my chest as the crest swirled over and above all our heads, continuing to rise until it had formed an impenetrable, easily ten-foot wall of water. I'd never seen anything like it. Shifting my weight, I prepared to sprint up the coast to put distance between us and the tsunami, but Elvira's arm shot out to stop me.

"Ced," she breathed. "Look."

I followed her gaze and gasped. There, still half-submerged within the tidal wave, were a pair of horse-like creatures. Reflective emerald-green scales covered every inch of their hides. Where manes and hooves should be were webbed fins, the latter of which pawed restlessly at the sand. Bright, intelligent eyes stared back at me, but there were no openings for nostrils along their snouts. Instead, gills ran vertically up both sides of their neck. They opened and closed rhythmically, almost frantically, and one of the creatures emitted a distressing cry.

Calypso winced. "Don't just stand there. Pick one and get on. They can't be out of the water for long."

"What… What are they?" I remained equal parts entranced and skeptical. One of the creatures was a fair bit bigger than the other and wouldn't quit staring me down.

"You've never seen a hippocampus before?" Ceto asked, incredulous. "What kind of pirates are you?"

Calypso shot her brother a look. "They're rather elusive. It took us a decade to find these, even with our gift."

"Your gift?" I echoed.

"There are only two," Elvira pointed out when Calypso didn't answer me. "As delightful as it sounds, I didn't imagine that you would be leaving us so soon."

"On the contrary, Serpent, it's *you* I hadn't intended to bring along." Calypso raised an eyebrow. "You're still very much welcome to turn back. It's not too late."

"We'll share," I butted in before this could turn into yet another argument. "I'm sure the big one can carry us both."

The largest hippocampus tossed its head back, and whether that was an invitation or a warning, I didn't know. Inhaling deeply, I approached, holding my breath until something slimy nuzzled my palm. The hippocampus stomped one of its hooves, but this time, it felt more like impatience than irritation.

Calypso was already sitting atop the other hippocampus. "Phorcys likes you."

"Phorcys," I repeated. The name sparked recognition, but from where, I couldn't recall.

"He'd like you even more if you'd get on."

As if on cue, Phorcys bowed his head, lowering his front half to the surf. It made mounting him easy, though I could have done without the wetness seeping into my rear. Elvira climbed on behind me, wrapping her arms tightly around my waist as Phorcys rose. I gripped his finned mane for stability as the hippocampus pranced about, and in my efforts to grip scales as slippery as a fish, I nearly missed Calypso's shout to Ceto, who remained on the beach.

"Get ready!"

Deeply focused, Ceto raised his arms, all the while chanting something I couldn't hear. The roaring of the ocean behind me drowned everything out but Calypso's voice, which somehow cut cleanly through the tidal wave seemingly taking its commands from her brother.

"Hold your breath and trust your mount."

Hold my breath? Panic seized my chest at the realization we were going under; Scarlett's portrait would be ruined. But before I could do more than take a shallow inhale, the wave came crashing over our heads. My body jolted forward, yanking Elvira's with me as we were plunged underwater. I slammed against Phorcys's neck with force identical to being sucker punched in the gut, and then we were rising. Something powerful and muscular writhed near the hippocampus's back. I threw my arms around our mount's neck as we picked up speed, moving through the water without the slightest bit of resistance.

We surfaced just in time, for my lungs had begun burning with a vengeance. Gasping, I blinked at my surroundings, reassured to feel Elvira at my back and see Calypso still atop her mount. We were drenched and breathless, but we at least had made it.

The same couldn't be said for Scarlett's portrait. Reaching into my pocket, I pulled out the drenched and ruined parchment. The ink that had once made up my love's likeness now gathered in incomprehensible swirls, running down the page and dripping into the ocean like blood from a brutal, gut-wrenching wound.

Calypso's gaze widened. "Oh, Cedric, I'm sorry. I'd forgotten all about that."

"This was the only portrait I had of her." The only possession which ensured I wouldn't forget Scarlett's face was as gone as she herself was. A sudden wave of grief threatened to drown me, and I might have gone under had Elvira's hand not closed around mine.

"It's all right, Ced," she murmured. "We'll get her back."

Nodding, I forced myself to raise my gaze. We were so far away from shore it was barely visible. Afterport was nothing but a faint gathering of sails, and Neverland a mass of dead trees. Impressive, but apart from Scarlett's, it wasn't the image that lingered in my mind's eye. "H-how—"

Calypso gave her hippocampus a fond pat. "There's a reason these creatures are so coveted. Hippocampi are the fastest and most graceful swimmers in all the realms."

"Not them. Ceto." I shifted to face her. "Did he just control the tides?"

"Children of Adais tend to have that gift, yes."

My mouth fell open. "The Sea God is your father?"

Calypso rolled her eyes. "I'd be far more concerned over your own fatherly role. Are you ready to face your daughter?"

"My *daughter*?" I did a double take, unsure that I'd heard correctly. "Aren't we headed for Kaara?"

"Yes," Calypso said, raising an eyebrow. "So is Wendy. It makes sense for us to join her, does it not?"

"No, because she and Peter are tracking Ursa."

Calypso laughed deep in her belly. "Oh gods, you truly don't know, do you?"

I swallowed. "Know what?"

"Cedric," she managed between breaths, "Ursa *is* Kaara. It's just one of her many aliases. A goddess couldn't parade around with her true identity on display—surely you of all people understand that."

Chills shot up my spine, and they had nothing to do with the fact that I was drenched. The last time we'd spoken, Wendy had made her loathing disgust for me more than clear. She could have killed me; I still wasn't sure why she hadn't. She could hardly stand to look at me as she'd handed me a task we had both thought impossible at the time, and though she hadn't said it aloud, the subtext behind her order was obvious: *I never want to see you again.* I laughed darkly. Up until now, we had been enemies, but the tides swirling between us had turned in an instant.

We had just become allies.

V. THE PLANK

Wendy

"The what?" My mouth dropped open. "I thought you said the dragon was gone!"

"It is, but the squid isn't," Tink said.

"The… squid? Is that what that tentacled thing was?" I didn't know whether to laugh or cry.

Peter nodded. "I'd believe it."

I stared between him and Tink, incredulous and rendered speechless. My skull began to pulse uncomfortably. Given my recent head trauma, it was pain I probably shouldn't ignore, but I pushed through it regardless because I had to think. It didn't matter that everything imaginable had gone wrong in a matter of hours, and it couldn't matter that I was no longer captain of my own ship. I had to form a plan, had to keep us safe, had to get us out of here—

Movement out of the corner of my eye, followed by Peter's gasp of pain, yanked me from my rapidly spiraling thoughts. He must have tried to use his injured arm to reach for me. "Are you all right?" he asked, though I didn't miss his barely suppressed grimace.

"Your shoulder." It looked even worse up close, and from the way he was holding it, definitely appeared dislocated. Though the light remained dim, more golden bruising colored the inflamed— and exposed, given the way his shirt hung in tatters—skin. I inhaled deeply. I might not be able to pluck a solution to our current predicament from thin air, but this, I could mend. "Kneel facing away from me."

He obeyed, albeit hesitantly. Once in the proper position, I gripped Peter's wrist, lifting his arm until it was parallel to the ground. With my opposite hand, I grasped the shoulder itself, squeezing both to brace the joint and make certain I could feel where the bones should reset. It had been a while since I'd done this for anyone, but once muscle memory kicked in, I was confident that I wasn't going to injure him further.

"This will hurt," I warned him. "Ready?"

"Yea—*fuck*!"

I didn't wait for his affirmation because anticipation always made it worse. All it took was a quick, firm tug, and the bone slid back into its socket with, to me, a satisfying *pop*, though far less so in Peter's case. He scrambled away the moment it was done, holding his arm close to his chest and continuing to curse under his breath.

Tink's light flashed crimson yet again, and she darted in front of me with the fury of a hornet. "You couldn't have given him a moment to prepare?"

"He'd have tensed up and I might have injured him further."

"I'm fine, Tink," Peter said stiffly. He flexed the joint as well as his fingers, probably shaking off the residual numbness. "At least one part of me is back where it belongs."

She flinched, but before either of them could say anything else, I butted in. "You've made your point, but what's done is done. Tink is here and neither of us can do anything about it. What we can do is make a plan, and first things first, we need to get the fuck out of here."

Both of them said something that sounded quite like a protest, but my mind didn't bother making sense of it. I spun on my heel, my gaze darting everywhere as I scanned for something, *anything* that could help us. We were in a supply closet similar to the one I'd been trapped in the very first night I'd spent on this ship, but the memory didn't bring a smile to my face. If anything, it fueled my desperation, because I couldn't fucking stand feeling trapped. The door was locked and held fast when I yanked on the handle, so I began rifling in the space between the forgotten crates and barrels. I could have worked with so much as a rusty nail, but most of the containers were empty, and those that weren't held nothing but various rotting rubbish. Dust began clouding the air, eliciting coughs from both me and my companions, but I refused to stop even as my eyes burned from the irritation. I refused to give up and refused to slow.

I refused to be a prisoner aboard my own goddamn ship.

It took Peter all but throwing himself in front of me to get my attention. He braced himself against the boxes I'd intended to search a third time, but it didn't keep me from attempting to reach around him. "Wendy, stop."

I shook my head. "It's dark over here. Maybe I missed something. Tink, can you help me? With your light, maybe I can—"

"You're not fucking listening. Will you look at me?"

The only reason I did was because of the way his voice cracked and rose. Tink hovered over Peter's shoulder, bathing his battered body in her dim light, and only then did it become clear what a mess he truly was. I may have eased the worst of his physical pain, but that wasn't the kind affecting him now. He hadn't kept his arm close to his chest solely because of his injury; it was to hold up his ruined shirt. And judging from the wrappings drooping around his sides, that wasn't the only thing that had come undone. My heart leapt to my throat. When did that happen, and how had I not noticed before?

"I can't go out there like this," Peter whispered, his eyes wide with terror. "I *won't*."

It felt invasive to stare and even more so to prod, but something wasn't adding up in my mind. For Peter's shirt to tear as a result of his fall made sense, but what had sliced his chest bindings into ribbons? I was the one who'd tied them and had weeks of practice doing so at this point. They were tight enough to get the job done, but not too tight, still allowing for proper breathing and movement. Not once had the bindings so much as loosened, let alone come undone without Peter or myself unwrapping them, and that was just it—they hadn't been unwound. They had been cut.

"Who did this to you?" My voice was hoarse.

"I… didn't see—"

"You blacked out, but Peter didn't." Tink's voice adopted a darker edge than I'd ever heard from her. "He fought them. Your crew didn't like that."

The emphasis Tink put on 'your' didn't go unnoticed, and she was right. I still considered them my responsibility, meaning their actions, however savage, were reflective of me. Red streaked across my vision, but for Peter's sake, I kept my tone even. "So they resorted to this?"

I was suddenly so angry I could hardly breathe. Of all the injuries the crew could have caused to make their point—bloodied his nose, kicked him once or twice, left a cut here or there—they had chosen to worsen an existing one. To poke and prod at the one thing he couldn't help nor control. My thoughts wandered back to a particular girl I'd known at the orphanage. I'd mentioned her to Peter on the day we met, but I hadn't disclosed the extent of the cruelty she'd endured before coming to confide in me. The teasing, the exclusion, and the assault perpetuated by both the other children and adults alike had been one of the worst injustices I'd ever witnessed, and that was counting Neverland's atrocities. She was just as much a girl as Peter was a boy, but the bodies they had been born into didn't reflect that to strangers without additional cosmetic precautions being taken. The girl was young enough to not need to resort to the more extreme measures, but Peter's body was changing, and his time was running out… literally. His breast growth meant that even with careful binding, he might begin to show, and it was only a matter of time before he got his first monthly. Given how much the former was already affecting him, imagining the potentially irreparable damage the latter could do to his already fragile psyche sent icy stabs of fear down my spine.

"It doesn't matter," Peter said, his mechanical tone yanking me from my thoughts. As though a switch had gone off, his expression suddenly hardened, all traces of emotion locked far away. "I just… need to be covered before I can go back out there. A blanket, a shirt, something—"

"Of course." Before he finished speaking, I had already shrugged out of my shirt. Gooseflesh immediately erupted along the newly exposed skin on my arms, but I suppressed the urge to shudder, putting on a brave face as I handed Peter the still-warm garment. I wasn't naked, though with nothing but a thin undershirt to protect my torso, I'd be in real danger of catching a chill, especially once we reached the upper deck. I shoved the fears aside. Like much concerning our current situation, it was a problem I'd need to worry about later.

But as the shirt passed between us, a bright flash of color caught my eye. My hands were coated in some sort of residue I hadn't noticed before, and still wet, the mysterious liquid had stained the previously unblemished linen.

"What the…?"

Without letting go, I brought both the shirt and my free hand to my face. Maybe it was a trick of Tink's dim light, but I swore the liquid was—

Peter yanked the garment from my grasp, almost tearing it. Before I could warn him to be more careful, he began weaving his arms through the sleeves, but his shoulders remained bare as my gaze flickered to them, particularly his injured one. The bruised and battered skin I'd touched only minutes before was flecked with...

Gold. The same color coating my hands.

My lips parted in a silent gasp, mind racing as I pieced together the damning evidence. Peter should be bleeding, and yet there wasn't a single drop of crimson in sight. Even his bruises were strange looking; a sickly yellow edged with light brown, completely lacking the shades of blue or deep purple I might expect anyone else to possess. A potential explanation began forming in my horrified mind, but before I dared to believe it, I brought my quivering palms to my face, inhaling deeply. The scent that flooded my nostrils was metallic—unmistakably iron.

If I didn't know any better, the golden liquid was Peter's blood.

Something unintelligible tumbled from my lips, but Tink ignored it as she shook her head, shooting me a warning glare. "Whatever it is you think you saw, you didn't."

"*T-think* I s-saw?" The nonsense I'd been speaking turned to barely incoherent stuttering. "It's r-right there—it's blood—"

"Blood is red, Wendy."

"It's s-sure as h-hell supposed to be!" My cries bordered on hysterics now, but my restraint had flown out the window. I pointed an accusatory finger at Peter, who had both donned the shirt and taken great care to ensure his wounds were now covered. "Even y-your bruises don't look right."

He raised an eyebrow. "Is there a 'right' way for a bruise to look?"

"Keep your voice down," Tink hissed, her too-dim light flashing a deep violet that I knew to be a warning. But I ignored her.

"I don't understand," I said, mind still racing. Vivid imagery of the day I helped Peter bandage his wounds following the nerisa attack back in Neverland popped into my mind's eye. "I've seen you hurt. I've seen you bleed. There was nothing special about your blood then, nothing at all like this…"

"You're absolutely right." Peter gave a curt nod. "There's nothing special about my blood. Wasn't then, and there isn't now."

At such a blatant untruth, I stilled. I knew what I'd seen, he knew what I'd seen, and here he stood trying to gaslight me. Me, the one whose resources he was currently utilizing for his own personal gain. Me, who'd defend him to hells and back. Me—his friend. Or so I'd thought. An explosive combination of fury and something else awakened within me, but I kept a careful lid on it, determined not to burst until the right moment. I had to go about this carefully if I wanted answers. Ever since we'd left Neverland, something had been off about Peter. Whatever was going on with his blood was far from the only secret he was carrying, and gods be damned, he was going to tell me what they were.

"You're lying." All traces of my stutter gone, I took a predatory step toward him. "And worse, you're lying to *me*. I'd choose your next words carefully."

His lip curled. "Is that a threat?"

Tink said something we both ignored as I laughed darkly. "If you need me to identify your threats for you, then I'd say you've lost your touch, Pan."

My words had the desired effect, and Peter flinched. I'd channeled every bit of Captain Hook that I could stomach into that sentence, and though I wanted to vomit, that look on Peter's face was worth it. As fucked up as it was, I wanted him to hurt as much as he'd hurt me, and at least right now, I didn't regret it. We stood in tense silence, breathing hard, as in my peripheral vision, violet flashed once more.

"Someone's com—"

Tink didn't finish her warning before the door burst open. I whirled around, bewildered, to find myself staring at a man I didn't immediately recognize. Broad and tall, his shape easily took up the entire frame, leaving no hope of Peter or me darting around him unnoticed. He was... Phil? Prescott? Phipps? He definitely had a 'P' name, but I stopped wracking my brain for the answer upon noticing where his leering gaze had dipped. My undershirt was not only thin but lower cut than I'd have ever wanted anyone on my crew to see, and my breasts would surely come spilling out should I bend over too far.

I crossed my arms over my front, equal parts embarrassed and disgusted to have been gaped at like some tavern wench on display. "How dare you."

"What?" He shrugged. "I was just admiring your foresight." Before I could ask what he meant, he hurled a bundle of white fabric at my chest. "Put this on."

I unrolled it to find, of all things, a dress. The cloth wasn't much thicker than my undershirt, and given its color, I was more than a little skeptical of its ability to conceal everything it would need to. "What the fuck is this?"

"Ah. Suppose a wild thing like yourself wouldn't know what proper young ladies wear. You slip it over your head like a shirt."

"I know what it is," I snapped. "What's it for?"

"Never you mind."

I glared. I hadn't worn a dress since my days at the orphanage and had no plans to start again now.

"That one's been rubbing off on you, I see." The man's gaze flicked to where Peter stood and back again. "But we could only find one of these. Otherwise you'd both be changing."

The meaning behind his words didn't sink in until I'd slipped my arms through the sleeves, prepared to pull the dress over my head. If they could have found one, they would have brought a second dress... for Peter to wear? I froze as fury ignited within me, then turned back toward the man. "You said that this is what young ladies wear. He isn't one."

Behind me came Peter's voice, unnervingly defeated and small. "Do as he says, Wendy. It's not worth the fight."

"Yes, it is," I snarled. *Especially after what you endured earlier.* After yanking the dress up and over my head, I took a step toward the crewman, voice seething with barely contained rage. "Whether you want to accept it or not, I am your *captain*, and you will treat him with respect or—"

Pain exploded across my cheek before I'd finished speaking. I hadn't been struck particularly hard, but given the existing and still-throbbing wound on my forehead, my knees buckled beneath me, and I staggered and fell. My vision flickered in and out, and the noise that filtered through my ears was muffled as though I'd gone underwater. I was only vaguely aware of something buzzing around my head, followed by a dull *thud* as something heavy struck the floor beside me. No matter how hard I blinked, my vision didn't get any clearer, but after about a minute, words at least became easier to make out.

"She's bleeding again."

"Can you help her? Do you have dust to spare?"

"Not in my current state."

"Then go check the hall. Distract anyone you find and buy us all the time you can."

Tinkling bell noises drifted away into nothing as a strong, reassuring arm snaked beneath my armpit, all but dragging my limp body to its feet. Fingertips brushed my hair out of my face, but gentle as they were, I flinched as they summoned a fresh wave of hurt.

"Wendy, can you hear me?"

I nodded, relieved to find that it was Peter, and not the crewman, touching me.

"I need you to walk, all right? And watch your step."

As long as I kept my eyes squinted slightly, I could make out the shapes in my immediate vicinity. I glanced downward, expecting to dodge a fallen crate or barrel... not a bloodied, crumpled body. An alarming amount of crimson had already begun pooling onto the wood, dripping through the cracks and into the depths below. Inhaling sharply, I had to bite my lip to keep from crying out in shock. "What... What happened?"

"Glass," was all Peter muttered, and he refused to elaborate until we had stepped into the hall. "I found a shard of glass."

"You stabbed him?"

"He hit you!" he snarled, shuffling along more urgently now. "What else would you have suggested that I do?"

"They wanted to throw us to a monster *before* you killed a man." As my wits returned, so did the use of my legs, and Peter became more of a guide than a crutch. Commotion had begun to sound overhead, but given that he seemed to have a plan, I followed where he led. "What do you suppose they might do to us now?"

Peter shot me a glare before motioning for us to duck behind more discarded cargo. His free hand still clutched the shard of glass, the only semblance of a weapon we had between us. "In case you haven't noticed, I'd rather not find out. And I didn't kill him. So long as I missed his vitals, he'll live."

I scoffed. "Yes, I'm sure he'll thank you for that—"

"Quiet."

I obeyed, albeit reluctantly. Noises indicating a struggle sounded just ahead. Peter was the only one with a clear view around the corner, and though I could stick my neck out to follow his gaze, I didn't dare. "What's happening?" I whispered.

Of all things, a smirk played on Peter's lips. "Tink is giving them a hell of a time. She just needs a moment and… *there*. Come on."

At his signal, I rose, rounded the corner, and found myself greeted by three more fallen bodies. Hovering above them was a triumphant Tink, her needle-like dagger flashing in the lamplight. I gaped. "How did you…?"

"Does it matter? Move!"

Peter's snarl didn't keep my mind from swimming with questions. We were nearly to the stairs, and though my companions approached them confidently, fear constricted my chest at the thought of what we might encounter on the main deck, where there would be far fewer places to hide. There were dozens of men aboard this ship, and it was only a matter of time before we provoked a fight we couldn't win. Even if we did manage to fight them off, where in hells would we go? What would we do? We were in the middle of monster-infested waters, more than a week's journey away from the nearest land mass, and had no supplies, no ship, and no other allies to speak of. Whether Peter chose to believe it or not…

"We're fucked."

Tink didn't slow, but Peter stopped in his tracks. "Excuse me?"

"We're fucked," I repeated, more stubbornly than I had the first time. "Unless I've magically been reinstated captain, there's no way out of this, Peter. You're a goddamn fool if you believe otherwise, and you're only making all of this worse."

He stared at me, chest heaving with ragged breaths as he spread his arms in mock exaggeration. Gold coated the palm that clutched the glass shard, and unlike before, he made no attempts to hide it. "Do you have any better ideas?"

"Not killing my crew would be a decent start."

"For gods' sake, they're not your crew!"

"They are if we want to live!" I wasn't anywhere near shouting, but I was no longer whispering, either. "They're our only way out. We have to face them. We need them, and unless you'd rather be thrown to the monsters, we need to show them that they need us."

Peter glowered. "They hate us."

"Have we given them reason not to?" Gods, what was I saying? This wasn't something I would have dared to utter even twenty-four hours ago, but here I was repeating Peter's own words back to him. "I've been nothing but a bratty teenager, and you're the spoiled child, remember? Think for one second about how this must feel for them."

"For *them*?"

I ignored the interruption. "They pledged their lives and loyalty to Hook, not me. I may be his daughter, but clearly I'm nowhere near deserving of the same respect he built up and earned over gods know how many years. And until a few weeks ago, you were their sworn enemy. You'd been picking them off one by one, torturing them when you got the chance."

Peter clenched his jaw. "Who told you that?"

"Doesn't matter. What does is what we do from here."

Before Peter could reply, Tink's light flashed a warning. "The sedative I gave those men is extremely temporary and will wear off any moment now," she said.

"Wait." I dared a glance back at the fallen bodies. "They're not dead?"

Peter laughed incredulously. "Of course they're not. Did you really think a fairy would be capable of bringing down multiple grown men on her own?"

"What's that supposed to mean?" Tink huffed.

"This is fantastic," I said, perking up at the news. "We can apologize, claim that the first one was an accident, tell them we didn't know Tink was here—"

"Apologize? Have you lost your damn mind?"

"—and grovel. After that, we do whatever it is they want us to, without question or complaint." I shot Peter a glare, raising my chin for good measure. "That's my plan, and it's the best chance we've got. We cannot do this on our own, Peter, and blindly hacking and slashing won't get us anywhere but to our graves even faster. Are you with me, or not?"

I'll never know if he was actually going to agree, because a gunshot split the air. It was closely followed by a cry from Peter, but instinct had me crouching to the floor before I could discern whether or not he'd been wounded. Without raising my body, I whipped my head in the direction of the noise, sucking in a gasp when I made out the familiar leering shape at the end of the hall. *Pierce.* His name finally came to me just as he limped into the light. One quivering hand gripped a revolver while the other was crossed over his bloodied middle, and he leaned heavily against the wall between steps. Though I was his closest target, Pierce stared right past me, through me even, his hardened face contorted in rage as he bellowed with all his might.

"Look alive, you fucks—the prisoners are loose! Nelson, Digby, Alder, DOWN 'ERE!"

Bodies came thundering down the stairs. I didn't catch a single glimpse of Peter through the chaos that ensued, through the tears of pain blurring my vision as I was yanked up by my hair. My arms were twisted brutally behind my back before being tightly secured by even more rope, both at my wrists and at my elbows; when they were done, my shoulders screamed in familiar agony. They all but dragged me to the upper deck, cruel laughter echoing in my aching skull every time I tripped over the dress I'd been forced to wear.

Though fear kept my body paralyzed, my mind raced with reckless abandon. Not only had I not seen Peter, I hadn't heard him since Pierce had fired his gun. Had Peter been shot? Was he wounded—was he dead? And where the fuck was Tink? If she'd evaded capture, could she do anything for us? Far more pressing than concern for my friends was the guilt eating me alive. Not five minutes ago, I'd suggested that we apologize to these men, that we do our best to try and talk our way out of this. Only now did I realize the idea hadn't just been hopelessly naïve, it was fucking asinine. Talking was for humans.

These men were monsters.

A groan slipped through my gritted teeth as my hair was yanked yet again, forcing me to stare straight ahead—or at least it would have if my eyes weren't closed. I was propped up between two bodies, my feet dangling uselessly against the deck. Though I could place them flat if I wanted to, I wouldn't, unsure if my aching, bloodied knees would even support my weight anymore.

"—fuck have you done? This was never part of the pl—"

"Unless you want to lose that tongue of yours, I suggest that you silence it."

The voice I recognized spoke again despite the threat, and my chest tightened. Would Smee truly risk himself to save me? I'd assumed he loathed me just as much as the others. "That's Hook's *daughter* you've beaten into a bloody pulp. What do you imagine he'd do to the man who so much as looked at her funny? Have you forgotten what he promised?"

"It's a damn good thing he isn't here then, isn't it?"

"And him," Smee continued. "Pan's hands are far from clean, but he's with her, and we can't—"

My eyes flashed open, but not because Smee had been punched in the face. Behind my mentor and the man leering over him was a scene straight from my nightmares.

Secured to the mast by his wrists and ankles was Peter. Given that he faced away from me, I couldn't get a good look at his face, but there was a shine to it. A wetness. He was crying, and I could hardly blame him; the shirt I had lent him had been ripped from collar to hem, exposing the entirety of his muscled back, tanned everywhere but where his bindings normally rested. Scars I'd long since memorized were now on display for all to see, but that wasn't what the men were laughing at.

"Shaking like a leaf."

"Not a leaf—a *girl*. Men don't fear a little flogging, not even when they're boys."

"But you're not one, isn't that right, Pan? Just a confused little girl playing dress up."

"Poking her nose where she shouldn't."

Peter jerked at that, yanking on his bonds as a snarl tore from his throat. "Whatever it is you deem me to be, this child killed more of you than anyone can count."

"You're no child. You're a fucking demon."

Pierce's boots clicked rhythmically against the deck as he closed the little remaining distance between himself and Peter. Just as Pierce had belowdecks, one hand clutched the wound Peter had given him while the other gripped a weapon; this time, a nasty-looking knotted whip. I screamed and thrashed but was paid no mind, a helpless spectator as Peter was to be tortured before my eyes, by the man least likely to show him any mercy, no less. *No.* Gods, no, this couldn't be happening—

The moment Pierce raised the whip, a ball of dim light streaked across his path, coming to a halt in front of Peter's back. A glimmer of hope ignited in my chest. *Tink.* I'd nearly forgotten about the fairy's existence in my panic, but here she was, come to rescue the boy with whom she shared a bond. I stood as straight as I was able, even putting weight on my aching knees. *Get him, Tink.*

Pierce's cheeks turned as crimson as Tink's light now flashed, and before he could react further, she darted toward his face. He shrieked, dropping the whip as she buzzed around his skull like a hornet, hopefully using her trusty dagger and more of that sedative. My lips twisted into a smile as I watched the glorious sight: a grown man brought to his knees by a single angry fairy. It captivated my attention until Peter screamed in agony.

I realized what had happened before I saw either of the telltale signs: the discarded whip now in Digby's hands, the golden blood trailing from the fresh gashes on Peter's back. His still-bound hands gripped the mast for dear life, and his trembling legs likely would have buckled if not for the ropes holding him upright. Save for Pierce snatching a freshly distracted Tink by her wings, everything stopped, and whispers started.

"What the fuck is that?"

"What the fuck is *she*?"

"That can't be blood."

"Cursed—has to be."

"And now he's brought it to us. They both have."

My heart hammered wildly against my ribcage. Everyone on deck now stared at either me or Peter. Some were disgusted, others fearful, and still others looked murderous. *Ravenous.* Talking wasn't an option, and never had been. There was only one way out, and it wouldn't change the simple truth.

We were fucked.

But I wouldn't allow Peter to be—at least, not more. I had to get him out of here, even if it meant facing a different monster. If he stayed here, he'd die a slow, torturous death, and I knew without asking which one he'd prefer. Swallowing hard, I spoke in a voice that hardly sounded like my own. "We'll go."

Pierce turned to me, brows raised. "What did you say?"

"You'd planned to throw us to the monsters, right? We'll go."

More low murmuring broke out among the men who didn't seem to have a discernible leader.

"No skin off our backs."

"If they're so eager to die, let them."

"Can make it look like an accident."

Once it died down, Pierce regarded me once again, this time with a demented smirk painted across his scratched-up features, no doubt from Tink's dagger. He still held the fairy between his fingers; Tink, to her credit, remained still and silent. "All right, then. Ladies first."

Before I could insist that they at least cut Peter down from the mast, the men holding me dragged me toward *The Jolly Serpent's* rails. There was a narrow space in which they parted—likely an unused gun port—where a board had been laid flat. As recognition dawned on me, I twisted in my captors' arms to face the jeering crowd of men.

"A plank?" My voice rose, incredulous. "You're going to make me walk the fucking plank? I thought that was just a myth!"

Pierce flashed me another twisted grin. "Myths are what monsters are meant to be. This, sweetheart, is real."

With my arms still bound, I was lifted onto the unassuming slab of wood where I was immediately greeted with an icy blast of wind. It bunched the skirt around my legs, but I was too focused on what lay below to care about the snickers behind me. There was no sign of any monsters, but the sea, black and cold, was a threat all on its own. We were far from the temperate waters of Afterport, farther than I'd ever been from home, and farther still from Peter's lifelong dream. It was his words and not the swords digging into my back which spurred me on.

If we don't find Ursa, if I'm doomed to live in this body, then I don't want to live at all.

I'd died once. I could do it again.

I strode leisurely to the end of the plank, closed my eyes, and jumped.

VI. THE CAPTAIN

Featured Song: Far Across the Seas

Wendy

Knives.

They pierced and stabbed at every angle, the blades as unrelenting as they were frigid. Despite the pain, the agony, I remained motionless, dazed from the force with which I'd struck the surface of the water. I was only vaguely aware that my skin remained intact, that there were no literal knives, and that the stabbing sensations were just my body's response to the intense, sudden cold that I couldn't escape. The specifics of my current hellish reality hardly mattered. I didn't care which claimed me—a monster, the sea, jagged teeth, or the simple act of drowning. Anything that stopped my lungs from burning, I'd welcome. Even Death themself.

Or herself. Or himself. Though my eyes remained closed, as my chest screamed for air, I began envisioning what Death might actually look like. I'd felt their icy touch the first time I died but hadn't lingered in their realm long enough to see their face. Would they be dark and brooding, like my father? Or bright and sunny, like Tink? Would they recognize me? Would they say anything before scooping me up, and would I even hear it? Right now, nothing roared in my ears but the gentle *hum* of the ocean. The distraction was a welcome one, and slowly but surely, the pain gave way to a tingling warmth as I continued to sink, unable to use my still-bound arms to swim for the surface even if I wanted to. My legs kicked uselessly, more out of instinct than anything I had consciously ordered my body to do, but they stopped after a while, going as limp as the rest of me as even my lungs ceased their plea.

I was alone in nothingness, slipping into unconsciousness when I heard it. My mother's voice, faint yet unmistakable as ever, singing a low, mournful lullaby.

> *"The tide is ever rising through the night,*
> *Silver waters bathed in restless light.*
> *Far across the seas,*
> *Together you and I will be."*

As beautiful as the melody was, I refused to acknowledge her. What was the point? If she was dead, I'd meet her soon, and if alive, she was far too late to save me. But despite my inner protests, she continued, her ethereal voice seeming to swell with the roll of the tide.

> *"The storms will come and go, the rains will fall,*
> *Listen now, and hear my silent call.*
> *Morning sings her song,*
> *And whispers 'my child, don't be long."*

Warmth surged through me… or maybe it was more cold. I could hardly tell the difference anymore. All I knew was that the abyss into which I was drifting seemed more appealing by the second, and that Mother's voice was urging me toward it. I was so exhausted, so tired of fighting, and so tired of *feeling*.

Don't give in, my darling. Not yet. You're close, so close, and so is he.

I very nearly asked which 'he' she meant before stopping myself. Peter made the most sense, but the moment she'd said it, images of Hook flooded my mind… but not the Hook I knew. This was a happy Hook, laughing and dancing, smirking and cracking jokes, possessing two good hands with which to cup Mother's face before he kissed her. He remained scarred, but less so, and wore clothing which suggested that he didn't care who saw the marks. A lump formed in my throat at such a blatant impossibility. If this was how she remembered him, the man that Hook had been prior to entering Neverland, what in hells had that forest done to him? What had Peter done to him?

Another sensation shuddered through me, this one unmistakably warmth. *Heat.* My eyes flashed open as the burning in my lungs subsided despite not having taken a breath—I suddenly didn't need to—and there, floating in the space before me, was a person.

No. A mermaid.

The glowing palm still lingering on my sternum may have been of more concern had I ever been this close to one of the creatures. I'd glimpsed mermaids in Neverland, but they were as scarce as they were skittish, and had always fled before I could get a good look at them. This one, though, grinned when they noticed me looking, and remained still as I trailed my gaze over their sharp features. What shocked me wasn't their inhuman characteristics... it was the parts of them that were. In every way, save for the fins protruding where ears should be, gill openings on either side of their neck, and the fish tail serving as their lower half, they were as human as I was. Silvery hair fluttered in an imaginary ocean breeze, and their bright blue eyes remained fixated on mine.

I spoke without thinking. "Who are you?"

The mermaid didn't offer a response, which made sense given that speech was nothing more than gibberish underwater. Still, I tried again.

"Are you the one making it so I don't have to breathe? Or is this a dream?"

They smiled, and the fingertips still resting on my chest pulsed with another warm glow. The light almost reminded me of Tink, but it was much stronger and more concentrated, seeping into my skin even through my clothes. My chest felt entirely weightless now, completely void of any lingering discomfort, and any desire to draw breath had abandoned my mind entirely.

"It is you."

The mermaid didn't confirm nor deny my words. Moving their hands to either side of my waist, they spun me around until my back was to them. My shoulders seared for a brief moment before the ropes binding my arms fell away, and I could move them again. Relieved, I spun back around to thank them.

But the mermaid was gone.

Panic constricted my chest—or possibly, the need to breathe again—but I pushed aside my mind's incessant plea to swim for the surface as I scanned the blackened waters for any trace of my companion. I screamed and begged but remained alone. The only response came in the form of Mother's voice yet again.

I love you, my darling Wendy, and I'll see you soon. Forgive your father. He's a better man when he's with you.

"Fuck my father," I forced, even as saltwater made its way down my throat. "Did you send the mermaid? Where are you?"

Silence.

Then a jolt rippled through me, a physical one, and it took a moment to realize that something had clamped one of my upper arms, something that definitely wasn't the mermaid. A monster, at last? Was it the squid, the dragon, or something else entirely? Before I could linger on the thought that no longer seemed terrifying, it dragged me, but not deeper. We were headed for the surface.

In a fraction of the time it had taken for me to sink, we rose. Whatever had snatched me was a powerful swimmer and shot through the water with inhuman speed and ease. We burst from the waves a moment later. Only once cold air struck my face did I recall how much I needed it, but when I opened my mouth to inhale, I choked instead. Arms—strong, human arms—pulled me from the water entirely before cradling me close to a chest. Someone said something my oxygen-deprived brain couldn't discern, so I instead latched on to the noise flooding my other ear, the one pressed against skin. *Thump-thump. Thump-thump. Thump-thump.* The heartbeat was quicker than normal, but still rhythmic and sure, serving as a guide that I could follow back into the world of the living. A harbor in which I could find refuge.

An anchor ensuring that this time, I'd remain.

"Breathe," came a hoarse whisper. "Please, Wendy, *breathe.*"

A violent cough shuddered through me, but once it passed, I attempted another inhale. The breaths came shallow and ragged, but they were breaths, and with each one the ache in my lungs subsided a little more. The fog shrouding my mind took longer to clear, but as it did, voices cut neatly through the haze.

"—thank me. I'm no healer. By rights, she should have drowned."

"Then clearly, your magic did something."

"Not the something you seem to think it did."

An animalistic snarl. "I'm going to fucking kill whoever did this."

"Only kill? Isn't that a bit tame for you?"

"Once her lips are no longer blue, then you can go on your murderous rampage. Just because she didn't drown doesn't mean that she won't freeze."

It was true; the shivers running through me were so violent I feared I might bite off my own tongue if I tried to speak. Though the body wrapped around me radiated heat, it wasn't nearly enough, not even when the arms tightened to all but cage me within their grasp. My eyes fluttered open, but immobilized as I was, I couldn't shift my head to get a decent look at who held me.

"Have them lower a rowboat. If they don't, Elvira, I need you to get aboard by whatever means necessary and *make* them lower a rowboat."

Elvira? A shudder that had nothing to do with the cold ran through me. If she was among my rescue party, that meant…

Then I saw it. Arms held me, yes, but one of those arms ended in a curved metal hook.

No.

No.

Reacting on instinct alone, I thrashed with all my might, kicking and bucking like a feral animal. The noises that erupted from my throat were within the same vein, unintelligible and hysterical as I fought to escape Hook's grasp in any way I could manage. His hold slipped at first, but not enough to release me, and once recovered from his initial shock, he pulled me even tighter against him, pinning my arms to my sides before draping one of his legs over mine to slam it against something slimy. A fish? A mermaid? Any other time I'd have cared, but right now I needed to be anywhere other than trapped within his embrace.

Hook's beard grazed my cheek as he snaked his neck over my

shoulder, careful to position himself where I couldn't slam my skull into his. "Shit, Wendy. Was almost dying a goddamn act?"

I still couldn't form coherent sentences, but whatever I screamed in response had the words 'fuck' and 'you' in there somewhere.

The next few minutes passed in a blur. Though I continued fighting Hook wherever and however I could, the burst of what I assumed was adrenaline wore off quickly, leaving me so exhausted I could barely hold my head up. I caught a fleeting glimpse of the fish-horse serving as our mount, or perhaps hallucinated it, before Hook transferred me to the rowboat he'd asked Elvira to procure, and then we were rising yet again. I squirmed and twisted, loathing the way I remained immobile in his lap, but the death grip he had on my wrists informed me there was no way out.

He exhaled against my cheek. "I'm beginning to wonder if you wanted to drown."

"I'm not a fucking damsel." I'd wanted to conjure something wittier, but that was what came out.

Hook froze. "What did you say?"

"Fuck you."

"I know, but after that."

"I'm not a damsel, and I don't need saving." I didn't voice the last bit: *especially not by you.*

Hook fell silent, and finally convinced that fighting him would do nothing but exhaust me further, I took the opportunity to scan my surroundings. Elvira sat to our left, her expression unreadable as she regarded us through narrowed lids. She was armed with at least a dozen knives strapped in various places along her lithe and muscular body, soaking wet, and twitching. Given the way both of her hands were hovering over daggers, I suspected the tremors were more anticipation for what was to come than they were a response to the biting cold. Gods, did she even get cold? The more time I spent around her, the less I was convinced she was entirely human.

To our right sat a third, a stranger I didn't immediately recognize. She was dressed in nothing more than a thin, nearly see-through dress with a plunging neckline and slits beginning at each hip, revealing long, slender legs. How in hells she hadn't frozen, I couldn't begin to guess. The longer I stared, the more familiar she became. It wasn't the rounded face, tightly wound curls, or high cheekbones that sparked intense emotion that I couldn't quite place… it was her dark, almost soulless eyes. I knew those eyes, and judging from the smirk that crept across her features, it would appear she knew mine. For some foreign reason, my thoughts kept drifting back to my days at the orphanage. Had I met her there? Had she visited me once? Had she been employed there—lived near there? There were endless possibilities, none of which I was able to settle upon even as she continued to hold my gaze.

Our staring match came to an abrupt end the moment the rowboat halted. I blinked; had we been hauled all the way back up the ship already? Evidently so, for Hook didn't hesitate to stand, lifting me as effortlessly as he lifted himself before stepping out of the rowboat and onto *The Jolly Serpent's* deck with me still cradled in his arms. Fury ignited once more. What would the crew think if they saw me like this, being carried like a child?

"Put me down!" Though my body ached all over and my strength was dwindling rapidly, I resumed my writhing, fully prepared to kick Hook in the face if that's what it would take to preserve any shred of dignity I had left. "I can fucking walk."

He glanced at me, raising an eyebrow. "If you insist."

With sudden gentleness that shocked me, he placed my feet on the deck, especially careful to keep his hook from snagging on my dress as he helped me stand. I'd have batted him away if it wasn't help I needed. My battered knees remained shaky and weak, and I'd have crumpled if I didn't have the railing to lean on. Our eyes met, and the blackness swirling within his left me completely unprepared when his good hand shot out to grip my chin with rough, calloused fingers.

Hook's already troubled expression turned downright feral as he studied me. I flinched when he raised his hook to my brow, but as gently as he put me down, he ran the sharpened tip over the wound on my head. I shied away a second time, unable to hide my grimace as the tender skin protested under his featherlight touch. When he spoke, his voice was low and animalistic; it almost sounded like one of the Nightstalkers back in Neverland. "Who did this to you?"

"Does it matter?" My voice didn't sound like me, either. It was too small, too defeated... too reminiscent of the terrified little girl I thought I'd killed back in Neverland.

"Answer me, Wendy."

Suddenly irritated he was so close, I shoved against Hook's

chest to put some distance between us. It wasn't enough—I moved more than he had, and my back was now pressed to the rail I still gripped—but it would have to do. "I just got thrown overboard. Pardon me if I'm not all that concerned over a flesh wound."

"Wounds," he corrected through gritted teeth. "You look like you were put through hell."

At the mention of hell, flashes of what had happened prior to my fall sprinted to the forefront of my mind, and so did a name: *Peter*. My blood turned to ice. To suggest what I'd endured had been hell when there was his ordeal to consider felt like a betrayal of the highest order. Had the crew kept their promise and cut him down, or was he still hanging from the mast, all the while subjected to psychological and physical torture? I said his name once, and when no response came, I sidestepped Hook. "Where is Peter?"

Hook whirled around at that, but not to answer my question. He posed his own. "Can anyone explain to me why I just plucked *my daughter* from the freezing sea?"

He hadn't threatened. He hadn't shouted. He didn't even sound angry, but the look on every single crewman's face suggested otherwise. Pale as ghosts, a few of them visibly trembled, and they had gone so still that the only sound was the roar of the waves.

When no one spoke, Elvira took a casual step forward. Similarly to her brother, nothing about her movements were predatory, and she wasn't even brandishing a weapon, but it didn't keep the men closest to her from scrambling back, tripping and stumbling over ropes and supplies in an effort to get away from her. "Cedric Teach asked you a question."

I gritted my teeth; I didn't have time for their theatrics and posturing. My gaze darted past the crowd, fixating on the mast—blessedly lacking a strung-up Peter. All that remained were a few scraps of rope. Shoulders slumping, I released a relieved exhale, but it didn't keep my heart from hammering against my ribcage. Where was he? Where was Tink? Had they been thrown overboard? Had the mermaid helped them, too? Or had the monsters found them first?

Questions, as well as horrific imagery, continued racing through my mind, but I managed to voice the only one that mattered as I addressed the still-silent crew. "Where is Peter? What have you done with him?"

More silence.

Balling my hands into fists, I half shrieked and half sobbed into the rapidly gathering night. "*Pet—*"

Something slammed into my side, nearly sending me tumbling over the ship's railing and back into the frigid ocean. Arms snaked around my waist so tightly I could barely breathe. A head nuzzled into the crook of my neck, coating my throat in fresh wetness, and the body it was all attached to released a shuddering sigh as to my right, something clattered to the deck. "Wendy…"

Peter. He was half-naked, bruised, and battered, but he was whole. After looping my arms beneath his armpits to rest on either shoulder, I pulled him tightly against me, careful not to touch any part of his still-exposed back. I allowed myself a moment's relief before shooting Hook a death glare. "He needs cover. A blanket, cloak, someth—"

He moved before I finished speaking, fixated on the nearest man wearing a jacket. Hook didn't need to say a word before the man had already shrugged out of it, and in another wordless exchange, Hook draped it over Peter's bare shoulders. I didn't miss the way Hook's eyes widened upon glimpsing Peter's back, but he didn't question either of us as we sank to our knees.

"Are you all right?" I whispered for Peter's ears alone, my voice hoarse. "Is Tink?"

He untangled himself from my waist as faint bell noises sounded from the space between our chests. A dim golden glow flashed within the somehow intact pocket of Peter's otherwise ruined shirt, but Tink didn't fly out or speak. My heart skipped a beat. "Is she…?"

"She's weak and hurting, but alive," Peter said quietly. "As am I."

I could only nod in acknowledgement rather than relief. There wasn't anything 'good' about this, but at least we were back together. And all the gods be damned, this time, I was determined for us to remain that way.

When I opened my mouth to tell Peter as much, a presence hovered over his shoulder. The strange yet oddly familiar woman from the boat knelt at his back, hand outstretched. I tensed, preparing to pull Peter out of her reach, but he reacted faster. With strength that I wouldn't have expected him to possess in his current state, he twisted both to shove me behind him and snatch the object he'd discarded earlier—a bloodied dagger.

"Touch either of us and you'll lose the hand." Peter waved the blade in a wild, reckless arc, forcing the woman to stagger back. Hook caught her before she lost her balance.

He glared and shook his head. "Put that down, Pan. She can heal you."

"I can try," the woman clarified. "I'm no healer, but I've got some magic and will do what I can to ease that pain of yours. I already did it for Wendy."

Peter made no move to lower his weapon. "Do you know her?" he whispered under his breath for my ears alone; though he couldn't see me, I shook my head.

"No. At least… I don't think I do. I've never seen her face before, but there's something oddly familiar about her nonetheless."

"Then you probably have met her before. She's a nymph—a shapeshifter," Peter said.

My lips parted in shock, but before I could voice it, the woman—no, the nymph—extended her hand once more. "I mean you no harm, Peter Pan. Are you certain you don't want my help?"

He nodded, tensing up yet again. "I'll manage on my own."

The nymph smiled as she withdrew her arm. "Suit yourself." She retreated to resume her previous position near Hook, but her gaze shifted to me as she moved, as invasive and unnerving as her stare had been on the boat. Searching. Waiting… for what, I didn't know, but once this was all over, I intended to find out, as well as how the hell I knew her.

Hook resumed his interrogation. "If none of you will come

forward freely," he said in that same bored tone, "then I shall be forced to assume that those of you sporting injuries sustained them as perpetrators of the violence these children suffered, rather than in defense of them."

"You think that any of us would defend *that*?"

My grip on Peter tightened at the sound of Pierce's voice. He stepped apart from the crowd, stopping out of arm's reach from Hook, but only just. I stifled a snarl. *Coward.* Raising his chin, Pierce shot an accusatory finger at Peter's back, every bit the image of a smug schoolboy telling on his classmate.

"That… that thing—"

"He is a child whom I left under your care and protection and was to be treated no differently than you'd treat my daughter." Hook raised an eyebrow. "Were my orders unclear?"

No differently than you'd treat my daughter might have floored me had there been a moment to linger on the thought, but Pierce fired right back. "That's precisely it. 'He' is a 'she.'"

Peter tensed in front of me, and for the first time since reuniting, Hook's demeanor visibly shifted. He stalked toward an unflinching Pierce, making a point to look down upon the shorter man even as Hook leaned on a nearby supply crate. Metal rattled as he laid his palm flat on the wooden surface—chains, perhaps. "It seems you may have taken my orders a bit too literally, Mr. Pierce. Peter was to be treated as my daughter's equal, not as a literal daughter. That would be foolish now, wouldn't it? He *is* a boy, after all."

Pierce's jaw clenched. "Not foolish. We all saw it, what's underneath—"

"You mean that in addition to beating and flogging him, you also assaulted him? A child, as it seems I must remind you." Hook clicked his tongue and narrowed his dark gaze even further. "Your crimes are certainly adding up, aren't they?"

"They're hardly crimes when perpetrated against a goddamn impostor! The so-called child you left us with isn't what we got, and we have every right not to feel deceived."

Hook's glare remained as cold as ice. "There was no deception, Mr. Pierce. I know precisely who and what Peter Pan is. I knew it when I gave the order, and I've hardly forgotten it now."

Pierce hesitated, face scrunching up as he pieced together the subtext. "You... You knew?"

"Yes. And?" Hook said, icy and detached as ever. Metal rattled a second time as my thoughts raced. How and when did Hook discover Peter's secret, and why had he actually kept it, let alone respected it? A month ago, they were sworn enemies hellbent on killing each other. Wouldn't it have better served him to do the opposite?

"Gods. You're just as sick as your daughter," Pierce spat. "How can either of you wrap your head around what he—she—hells, whatever the fuck it is?"

Hook cocked his head. "I'd be happy to show you."

A mirthless laugh. "What more is there to show that I haven't already seen? It's an abomination, unna—"

Pierce choked on whatever else he had been about to say when Hook lifted a heavy chain, the same one he'd been fidgeting with, and slammed it into the side of Pierce's skull. An agonized shriek tore from his throat as he staggered back, but he didn't get far. Hook delivered a savage kick to the man's ribcage, forcing Pierce to his knees. Only then did it become obvious that his skull had been split open. He remained conscious, but barely, twitching and breathing erratically as blood poured from the wounded side of his head.

Rather than put him out of his misery, Hook raised his gaze, his dark eyes flickering to mine before settling on Peter's. It took me a moment to realize what he was waiting for, but the unspoken question hit me right before Peter nodded: *Do you want to to finish him, or shall I?*

It was the affirmation Hook needed. With a sharp inhale, he brought the chain down a second time, connecting with Pierce's scratched-up face. He crumpled, landing flat on his back, but despite the fact his victim was no longer twitching, Hook didn't stop. Again and again he lifted the thick, weighted chain, sometimes even above his own head, landing blow after blow to the now-dead man's bloodied body. The dull squelching and slapping of flesh beneath metal became rhythmic and monotonous, not unlike the heartbeat I'd latched onto after being thrown overboard. The metal chain links clanging together were harsher and more irregular in comparison, as was the occasional *snap* and *crunch* of bone, but all of them were necessary when it came to composing the triumphant symphony that was Pierce's death.

I was no stranger to violence and had even found myself fascinated by it at times; Elvira's disembowelment of the crewman who disrespected her authority immediately sprang to mind. But something about witnessing my own father brutalize a man, even a man who deserved it, to the point where the body was no longer recognizable as a human being triggered something in me—something petrifying. The air in my lungs turned frigid, as did each breath I tried to draw after that. Horror unlike anything I'd ever felt crept into my bones, into my soul, slithering around the very essence of what made me human and chilling it to its core. I looked away from the worst of the savagery, ducking behind Peter's back, but there was no escaping the gruesome sounds that flooded the air, causing me to flinch with every blow Hook landed.

It went on for so long that I nearly vomited, but eventually, blessedly, Hook stopped. "I do believe," he said between haggard breaths, "that our friend Mr. Pierce has managed to 'wrap his head around' the concept."

The chain clattered to the deck, and a different type of silence fell as Hook began pacing across the blood-splattered wood. I lifted my head just enough to glimpse him. Carnage coated him from head to toe, ruining his shirt and jacket, but the monstrous look didn't bother me as much as I thought it would. At least now he matched the villain I saw in my head. As if he could tell what I was thinking, Hook met my gaze once more. His hardened expression softened, but before I could question why, one of the crewmen stepped forward.

Smee clutched his red hat in both palms, turning it over nervously as he spoke. "Forgive me, Capt—er, that's precisely it. Have you returned to resume your place as our captain?"

The contents of my mouth turned to ash.

Captain?

My mind continued to race, but my body no longer felt as though I was its host. Had Hook truly come all this way, plucked me from the ocean, and made such a show of murdering Pierce simply to take back everything he'd entrusted to me barely a month ago? To seize the ship he'd given me a taste of commanding? Had this entire voyage all been an elaborate test, a trial to see whether or not I was fit to rule in his stead? Had he wanted me to fail—expected it, even?

No. He wouldn't dare. Hook was many things, but surely not even he would stoop to these sorts of lows, especially not where his daughter was concerned.

Or would he? He hadn't even been aware of my existence until I'd set foot in Neverland, and we'd spent most of my time there as enemies. I'd broken the curse, yes, but my actions were also the direct cause behind why he'd chosen to leave Neverland immediately after; had I shamed him? Thrown a wrench in his plans? Made him look incompetent, or even weak?

Was this revenge?

I remained feeling as though I was simply a spectator to the goings-on rather than experiencing them within my own body as Hook's good hand clenched at his side. After closing his eyes for a brief moment, he turned to face Smee—though judging by the unmistakable authority with which he spoke, he addressed the crew as a whole.

"Yes. Captain Hook has returned."

The crew's roar of approval was drowned out by my own blood

roaring in my ears. They began chanting Hook's name, banging their weapons against the deck, and a few even raised their pistols into the air and fired them. It was several minutes before they settled down enough for Hook to continue, but even then, I still hadn't managed to rein in my spiraling thoughts, nor my trembling hands. There was an irritating wetness behind my eyes begging to be released as well, but I shoved it down; the last thing I needed was to fucking cry.

"You may have noticed my guest. This is Calypso," Hook said, gesturing to the nymph, "and she's to be treated with the utmost respect. Any man who lays a finger on her will lose it.

"As for tonight—dispose of Pierce's remains and bring any urgent matters to Elvira's attention, but otherwise, I'm not to be disturbed until morning."

"What about our course?" asked a voice near the back of the crowd: Mr. Gibbs, the helmsman. "Where are we headed, cap'n?"

Hook didn't miss a beat. "Stay the course you have." Confused murmuring broke out, but he was swift to silence it. "Our course is far from what I would consider an urgent matter. I will explain further come morning, but right now, I need my rest."

That was that. With Elvira and Calypso hot on his heels, Hook headed for belowdecks without so much as another glance in my or Peter's direction. The crew parted to allow him to pass, and several even began to wander leisurely back to their posts. It hit me then that Hook truly intended to leave me like this—without explanation, assurance, or apology—so I untangled myself from Peter and scrambled to my aching feet. Whether Hook remembered it or not, this was *my* ship, and I refused to give it up without a fight.

My mind and body rejoined one another the moment the words left my lips.

"You're not going anywhere."

VII. THE IMPASSE

Cedric

Wendy's words stopped me in my tracks.

I realized half a second too late that I should have just kept walking. She'd follow me, of that I had no doubt, but at least then we could talk privately, and not in full view of the men who had already tried at least once to kill her—and who would have succeeded if not for my timely arrival. The reminder of what they had done in my absence sparked yet another flash of rage, but I forced it down, reminding myself that enough blood coated my hands... for now. I had plenty of time to remind them what I was capable of.

The current problem I had to face was how not to make a goddamn scene. I'd stood still far too long, and the mutters echoing around me told me everyone was watching. *Fuck.* Wendy had cornered herself more than me with her outburst, but something told me she either didn't know or didn't care. Flexing my hand at my side, I spoke over my shoulder, but didn't turn around. "You're soaking wet and exhausted. You need to rest."

"No more than you do."

"Exactly." I didn't bother to hide my weariness. Smashing Pierce's head in had been a release I desperately needed, but after expending the energy it took to kill him, riding a hippocampus across choppy, freezing cold waters for damn near twelve hours, rescuing my daughter from drowning, and reclaiming my captaincy, I truly had no idea how I was still standing. The stump beneath my prosthetic throbbed painfully, a clear indication that I needed to remove the metal hook very soon, and though present company may not believe it, I was eager to wash the blood from my face and hair. "We'll talk later, Wendy. I swear it."

"Just like you swore this ship was mine?"

The crew drew a collective breath before falling silent as the grave. My heart skipped a beat not from fear, but from yet another burst of fury; did Wendy truly have a death wish? Either she'd drop dead from exerting herself past her limit—she couldn't even stand on her own, for Adais's sake—or my crew would expect her to face consequences for calling me out like this. Hells, part of me wanted to punish her, if only to teach her not to push her fucking luck.

It was that thought which fueled me to turn around. Wendy was already stalking toward me, so I met her halfway, ignoring the

118

warning in Elvira's tone as my sister said my name. Neither Wendy nor I stopped until we were a hair's breadth apart, and though she was swaying, she remained a formidable opponent.

Squaring my shoulders, I looked down at her through hardened features. I swear she'd grown taller these past few weeks. She'd certainly grown bolder, for despite looking as though she may burst into tears at any moment, she kept a lid on her most volatile emotions, more than I'd been known to do at times. Beneath the fresh scrapes and bruises, there was tanned skin, well-muscled arms, and an air of ruggedness about her—all marks of a young woman well-suited for this rough seafaring life.

All marks of Cedric Teach and Scarlett Maynard's daughter.

Wendy's resilience should make me proud, but given what I now knew of Scarlett, all the thought summoned was a lump in my throat. It wasn't as if Wendy got her best qualities from me, and she herself was well aware. She had even pointed out that part of the reason I'd wanted to be rid of her was because she reminded me so much of her mother, and Wendy certainly channeled every bit of Scarlett she had within her when she spoke again. "Well?" she pressed, clearly determined to get a rise out of me. "Shall we talk? I believe my quarters are free—the *captain's* quarters. If you've forgotten the way, I'd be happy to show you."

I inhaled sharply, equal parts impressed and fucking pissed. Now she'd done it; directly and undoubtedly challenged me. I wouldn't be able to let it slide even if I wanted to. Just because Wendy was my child didn't mean that she could do whatever she damn well

119

pleased, and it certainly didn't mean that I could go easy on her. If anything, I'd need to make her punishment more severe than a regular crewman's just to ensure there could be no accusations of favoritism. Or softness. The thought of such whispers alone made me see red. I'd spent decades crafting my fearsome reputation—had taken on the persona of *Captain Hook* for Adais's sake—and could lose it all in one instant thanks to Wendy's insolence.

But I couldn't say anything here, not without losing my temper, and if I lost my temper, I'd have to follow through on whatever threats came out of my mouth. I gave a stiff nod before turning on my heel, barreling past Elvira and Calypso before charging into the hallway I could have navigated with my eyes closed. Wendy's words had been intended as a jab, I knew, but it didn't keep me from needing to prove her wrong. I reached out with my good hand, allowing my fingers to graze the grooves in the bullet-filled walls I'd memorized more than a decade ago as I walked. Each crevice and imperfection summoned as much solace as the stench that flooded my nostrils: blood, piss, and shit. We'd aired her out the best we could upon the breaking of Neverland's curse, but though its crew was no longer rotting, *The Jolly Serpent* would forever reek of death. Crimson stained the floorboards we hadn't had a chance to replace, and I was certain that if we moved some of the supply crates around, we'd find scraps of decaying flesh that some cursed crewman had sloughed off long ago. Not even the rats would touch such filth. Every bit of it was abhorrent, disgusting, and vile, but I couldn't bring myself to care.

I was home.

The feeling only grew stronger once I'd thrown open the door to the captain's quarters. It was all here: my desk, my chests, and even the dresser that had once held Scarlett's shrine. I remained fixated on the now-empty surface even as far too many bodies crammed themselves into the room, my gut twisting into knots, but before I could break my self-imposed trance, movement flashed in my peripheral vision. A knife.

I only had time to bite out a single curse. My body reacted out of instinct alone, scrambling back until I reached the far corner, but I hardly noticed the pain that jolted up my spine upon slamming against the wall. The blade hovering directly over my heart was of far more concern, as was the fact that it was wielded by my daughter. She'd been stripped of all weapons prior to being tossed in the ocean, so she had to have swiped the dagger off someone. An irritated growl surfaced in my throat; who had been incompetent enough to let her disarm them, especially in her weakened state? "Where the hells did you get that?"

Wendy ignored me. "You fucking bastard," she snarled, face contorted with so much raw emotion she hardly looked like herself. She visibly trembled but seemed to be channeling her fear into rage. "You think you can just show up and save the day? Play the hero to the damsel in distress? That I'd welcome you back with open arms? That I'd want you back?"

"I—"

"You disgraced me. Embarrassed me. Made me look weak."

Elvira took a step toward us, but glancing over Wendy's shoulder at my sister, I shook my head. This fight was ours and ours alone. My phobia may have me reacting to the knife more strongly than I would have liked, but beyond that, it wasn't true fear holding me captive; Wendy may hurt me, but she wasn't going to kill me. Flicking my gaze back to hers, I summoned every bit of icy hostility I could muster. "You would have died. Was I supposed to just let you drown?"

"You were supposed to find out what happened to Scarlett and stay far away from me. Like you promised." Hurt. There was genuine hurt in her eyes, and I'd been the one to cause it. Her lower lip trembled, and her gaze now glistened in a way which suggested she might be about to cry. Perhaps a better father would have attempted to ease her conflicted anguish, but I'd certainly never claimed to be a decent one.

"I only promised one of those things, and it's precisely what I'm doing."

At this, Wendy dragged the knife up my body. "Lie to me again and I'll slice out your tongue."

"I'm not lying," I said through gritted teeth, squirming beneath the blade. "And I certainly didn't intend to embarrass you." I bit back what I badly wanted to add, knowing full well it would only add fuel to her inner fire: *You did that well enough on your own.*

"Intent doesn't change the truth, nor the consequences. And you're staring at yours."

That single word shattered the little restraint I had left. "You want to talk consequences?"

Something in my tone stilled her, and that was the only encouragement I needed. I slipped my hook just above Wendy's elbow before jerking it to the side. She didn't drop the knife, but with it no longer in my face, I was able to step away from the wall. Gripping her opposite shoulder with my good hand, I whirled her around, reversing our positions and leaving me the one in control. A whimper escaped her lips, but I knew I wasn't hurting her—at least, not physically. After pinning her where I had stood seconds before, I wrestled the dagger from her grip and leaned in, wanting her to hang onto my every word.

"What you did out there was idiotic beyond belief, and the crew will expect me to punish you."

"Then do it," Wendy shot back. She drew a series of rapid breaths which suggested her emotions were already stretched past their limit, and when she blinked, a few tears streamed down her bruised cheek. Her gaze flickered between my face and my hook, and suddenly, she seemed unable to look me in the eye. "I'm not afraid."

I raised an eyebrow, unsure if the façade she had erected was impressive or stupid. "Are you lying to me, or yourself?"

"Shut up," she hissed, but I didn't relent.

"Wendy, you're a mess, and you're going to hyperventilate if you don't calm down. This is precisely why I wanted you to rest before we talked, so you could clean up, dress your wounds—"

"Don't pretend like you care." She still wouldn't look at me.

More anger wasn't the correct emotion here, but it was what Wendy's words summoned all the same. My nostrils flared as I pulled her chin back up using my hook. "Don't care? For the last fucking time, I wouldn't have saved you if I *didn't care*. I wouldn't have killed Pierce if I *didn't care*. He was one of our best gunners, you know that, and his skill with a cannon will be damn near impossible to replace! He wasn't someone I ended to make a simple point, and I lost far more favor than I gained by that display. He was popular, had friends… friends who are surely my enemies right now. But I don't give a fuck what Pierce meant to this crew. I'd happily smash him to bits again. I'd do it a thousand more times if I had to." I lowered my voice then, speaking for Wendy's ears alone. "I didn't kill him because he hurt Pan. I killed him because he hurt *you*."

She held my gaze as I moved my hook again, this time to brush the stray hairs out of her face. Though I did my best to be careful, I must have grazed her bruise, because she grimaced when I passed over it. I dropped my arm then, seizing the opportunity to take inventory of her injuries. A wound at her temple. A bruise on her left cheek. Bloodied knees which suggested she'd been thrown to them multiple times… and those were only the injuries I could see, no doubt caused by more than just Pierce. He hadn't acted alone. I hoped the others responsible were shaking in their boots right now, because Pierce was only the beginning; I wouldn't stop until every person who had dared to lay a finger on her met the same fate.

I was so lost in my bloody thoughts that Wendy's voice made me start. "Now who's the liar?"

Too shocked to be furious, I blinked. "What? You think I'd lie about all that?"

"Just get on with whatever you came here to do. Are you going to punish me, like you said? Humiliate me? Turn me into one of those rats you call a crew?" She raised her chin, summoning that icy exterior despite the tears still streaming down her face.

I sighed before gesturing to my desk. "Sit down."

Wendy glowered. "No."

"Sit the fuck down before I do something I regret."

I wasn't sure which made her listen, the threat or my honesty, but she stomped over to the chair, making a show of crossing her arms and legs as she sat. Only once I was certain she wouldn't get up did I hand the confiscated knife to Elvira before allowing my gaze to sweep over the rest of the inhabitants in the room. My sister and Calypso had followed me, I knew, but I blinked in surprise upon noticing Pan lingering in the shadows. He remained disheveled and battered, still wearing the jacket I'd procured for him on deck as he regarded me through narrowed lids. It wasn't quite fear in his eyes, but he didn't look fully prepared to face me, either.

Something else stirred in my core. Sympathy, perhaps? I hadn't heard the full story, but Pan's appearance combined with Pierce's comments and the lashes I'd glimpsed on the boy's back were enough for me to get a general idea for what he might have endured. Peter Pan may be far from my favorite person—he'd cut off my hand, after all—and I may not fully understand why he went to the lengths he did to prove his boyhood, but no one deserved that type of ridicule over something they couldn't control. Clearing my throat awkwardly, I nodded toward one of my chests. "There's some shirts in there if you need one."

Something flashed in his dark gaze, but Pan didn't say anything as he wandered over to where I'd indicated and began rifling through the chest's contents. I watched him until Wendy spoke from behind me.

"You're stalling."

"I'm not," I lied.

"Will you just tell me why you're here? I don't understand why that's so hard."

I turned and opened my mouth to speak, but before I could, Calypso stepped in. "It's both hard and complicated, child. It involves certain truths not even your father has accepted yet."

Wendy bristled at *child*. "Don't call me that."

Calypso tilted her head. "It's what you are."

"The orphanage wouldn't have released me if I were still a chi— wait." Wendy sat up straight as all the color drained from her face. "I do know you."

"Took you long enough," Calypso said with a smirk.

I frowned, glancing between the nymph and my daughter. "You've met?" I asked, but before I'd finished the sentence, Calypso's earlier admission echoed in my head: *Kaara asked me to remain in Afterport to keep an eye on the child.* The question was, how?

Wendy threw up her hands. "You're working with Mrs. Hughes? Oh, this is just fucking perfect."

"Mrs. Hughes?" I glanced at Calypso for an explanation.

She shrugged. "I took the shape of one of Wendy's aides at the orphanage."

"Why is she here?" Wendy demanded, shooting up from her chair so fast it caused a bit of color to drain from her face. She wobbled a bit before gripping the back of it for support. "And why her, of all people?"

"Not a person. Nymph," Calypso corrected, but we both ignored her.

"She has information I need. That we both need," I said.

Wendy didn't buy it and was already shaking her head. "Bullshit. I never needed anything from that horrid woman."

"Perhaps you didn't before, but you do now. She knows how to get us to Kar—er, Ursa's realm."

"Don't we have a map for that?" Wendy pointed out.

"We certainly do," Pan said. He'd donned one of my shirts over the jacket, and the size meant that it hung nearly to his knees. "I risked my life multiple times in search of it—or have you all forgotten?" As he spoke, something came crawling out from beneath his collar. It took me a moment to realize it was Tink given how dim the fairy's light was. She settled atop Pan's shoulder without bothering to fly there. Gods, had they all been victims of the same awful violence?

"No one's forgotten," I said, still eyeing Tink, "but Calypso has information that cannot be found on a map."

Pan made a noise somewhere between disbelief and surprise. "You came all this way just to help me, then? I'm touched, Hook, truly."

"No—well, yes, but there's more to it than that. We're here to…"

My voice trailed off as I once again raised my gaze to the space Scarlett's shrine had previously inhabited. Given the loss of the portrait, other than the once-cursed medallion Elvira now wore around her neck, memories were all I had left of my Scarlett… and the memories were fading. Squeezing my eyes shut, I swallowed the emotion that had risen in my throat and made a conscious effort to ensure my hand wasn't visibly shaking. What was wrong with me? Why couldn't I just *say it*?

Something gentle squeezed my shoulder, and I almost jerked away until recognizing the touch. "Are you all right, Ced? Do you need me to tell them?" Elvira murmured, hopefully low enough for my ears alone.

"No. If Wendy is going to earnestly believe that I'm not the villain here, it needs to come from me." Turning, I waved Elvira away before sweeping my gaze over the room once more. Calypso gave me an encouraging nod, Pan and Tink looked skeptical and confused, and Wendy watched me the way a rat might regard the feral cat who had cornered it, but at least she'd sat back down. It was her eyes I met before speaking again.

"I've returned because Ursa has Scarlett. And I intend to get her back."

I told them everything: how Calypso and I met, her tale of the gods, and how Scarlett had found herself part of it all. Once that was done, I explained our journey—how we'd only gotten here so quickly thanks to Calypso, Ceto, and the hippocampi, and how, from afar, I'd witnessed Wendy's plunge into the sea, which is how I'd known to save her. I finished by explaining the deal I'd struck with Calypso and all that it entailed. The only details I spared were the ones no one else needed to know, such as how Calypso had fooled me by shapeshifting into Scarlett, and how Calypso and Elvira had nearly sliced one another to bits.

By the time I finished, my voice was hoarse, my throat raw, and the room silent save for the ship creaking around us. Pan had perched atop the chest to listen while Wendy, to my pleasant surprise, had remained in her chair for the entirety of my explanation. Though her head faced in my direction, her gaze was unfocused and far away, almost as if she was in some kind of trance. I said her name, but she didn't respond, so I turned to Pan.

"What's wrong with her? Can she hear me?"

"Oh, I heard you," Wendy answered faintly. She still hadn't quit staring off into space, though it almost looked as though she was focused on the desk—a certain drawer in particular.

I clenched my jaw as yet more irritation boiled beneath my skin. "Well, then? Do you have anything to say? Any questions?"

"Just one." She rose, thankfully more slowly than she had last time, and whipped her head in my direction. "What the fuck does this have to do with me and my captaincy?"

I blinked; I'd made certain to explain the goddess's ruse. "Ursa *is* Kaara, as I just said. Our goals are the same."

"No, they're not. I'm seeing Peter to Ur—Kaara, I suppose. Your little suicide mission was never part of the plan. My plan. Peter's plan."

"And I have done nothing to sabotage that plan—"

"Except sabotage *me*." I may have confiscated her dagger, but Wendy's tortured glare was sharper, and her words were

129

thick with hurt. "After what you just did, I will never be able to command this ship again."

I scoffed. "That's not true. My men are loyal and would happily obey you again should I give the order." *Especially after what I just did to Pierce.*

"Then do it." I didn't know at what point Wendy had gotten in my space, but we were once again standing nearly chest-to-chest. Her voice was no louder than a whisper, but the implied threat was more than clear. "Give the order, then get the fuck off my ship. You, your sister, and your whore."

Calypso hissed at that, but I managed to rein in my temper... for now. "No." Even if I wanted to give up my command, I couldn't risk Wendy doing something that might jeopardize Scarlett's rescue.

"So I'm right, then?" she continued, tone unchanged. "You did sabotage me?"

Despite my best efforts, my composure slipped, and my voice rose to a shout as I slammed my fist on the desk. "I did not fucking sabotage you, I saved you *and* Pan. I'm sorry if it came at the cost of your captaincy, truly I am, but had that actually been going well, you wouldn't have needed saving!"

"I never needed you, period!" Wendy's volume rose to match mine, but the trembling returned, as did the wetness glistening in her eyes. She'd flinched when I'd struck the desk, and her gaze kept flickering to that same drawer I'd seen her staring at earlier; despite being visibly distracted, every word she hurled at me landed harder than a physical blow. "And neither did Scarlett. Even if she is alive—

and I don't trust that nymph for one second—Scarlett abandoned both of us and never looked back. Don't you think if she wanted to be with you, she'd have come back by now?"

It was my turn to flinch. Not at Wendy's tone, but at her achingly familiar choice of words. It was as though she had plucked my deepest insecurities straight from my head before hurling them right where she knew it would hurt most, twisting the metaphorical knife for good measure. I'd been in this very place before, and it was somewhere I had vowed to never return. Forcing my reply through gritted teeth, I ignored the pain that had blossomed in my chest. "No. She's a captive, so she can't come back—"

"Scarlett is no captive. Didn't you just get done telling me she struck the deal with Kaara of her own free will? So she's precisely where she wants to be, or she's dead. My money is on the latter, but even if it's the former, she doesn't want to be with you." Wendy's face hardened. "And personally, I find it impossible to believe she ever could have loved a monster like you."

Something within me snapped.

I was aware of what happened next, and I wasn't; the blood roaring in my ears drowned out the voices demanding that I stop. There was screaming and slamming, the toppling of a chair, and then the entire desk had been flipped, only narrowly missing Wendy as she darted against the far wall to avoid the massive crash. Glass shattered, ink spilled, and one of the drawers separated from the desk entirely, spilling its contents across the floor. My legs moved of their own accord, expertly dodging the mess I'd created to meet my daughter where she cowered. Leaning down, I spoke in a scathing whisper I could hardly believe was mine.

"If it's a monster you want, it's a monster you'll fucking get."

At first, I thought Wendy was simply trembling again, but then she lowered her hands from her face, revealing freely cascading tears. The tremors were ugly, uncontrollable sobs. She'd been crying since the moment we'd entered this room, but my outburst, it seemed, had broken her. Upon glimpsing me standing so close, she scrambled back with a terrified whimper, looking at me as though she expected me to strike her.

"Get the fuck away from her!" I was barely aware of the hands shoving against my chest and remained frozen where I stood. It was several more moments before I registered the voice as Pan's, and only once he'd whipped out a shard of glass to press against my throat. "Back. Up."

Blinking, I staggered back into Elvira's waiting arms, suddenly aware of my surroundings once more. She clamped her hands over my shoulders, effectively holding me in place, but there was no need; I wouldn't have stopped Pan from darting to Wendy's side. They exchanged a few words I couldn't make out before Wendy lifted a quivering finger, pointing at the drawer whose contents had been scattered everywhere—the same one she'd been so fixated upon. Following her guidance, Pan soon extracted something from the rubble, holding it out for Wendy to see. Tarnished silver plating glimmered in the candlelight, and only then did I recognize the enchanted music box I'd forgotten my daughter still had in her possession. I hadn't seen it since leaving Neverland, and it hadn't occurred to me that Wendy would still feel an attachment to the old, broken thing.

But she cradled it to her chest the way a mother might comfort her child, continuing to sob uncontrollably. It was a while before Pan was able to help her to her feet, and she leaned heavily upon him as they began shuffling for the door. They stopped several feet from the door; though Wendy's back was to me, I had no trouble making out her surprisingly coherent words.

"*The Jolly Serpent* is all yours, Captain Hook."

VIII. THE TEMPTRESS

Cedric

I'd ruined my rug.

It was such a small, insignificant detail, but it was what my mind chose to focus on out of everything contained in the chaotic room. Though most everything else I'd banished to the floor could be swept or picked up easily, there was no erasing the ink stains. They blotted the once-innocent rug like droplets of blood, and where the vial had fallen, black liquid pooled the same way infection might settle in a festering wound. My lip curled at the cruel metaphor; I still didn't know whether I believed in gods, but if they were real, I had no doubt they were laughing at me tonight.

Prior to my loss of control, my quarters had looked as though I'd never left. Everything had been kept in its place: my charts, my stash of weapons and gunpowder, and even the chest of shirts and linens I'd allowed Peter to rifle through. Everything had been so neat and organized, well taken care of and looked after... until I'd ruined it in a moment of weakness. Shame prickled beneath my skin like the shards of glass beneath my boots, mirroring the mess coating the floor. *What a fucking disaster.*

Not wanting to stare at the carnage any longer, I flicked my gaze back to the parts of the room still intact, but this summoned a different kind of unease. What I'd prefer to believe was respect for my possessions could just as easily be read as disgust. I'd left all this behind fully intending for Wendy to make use of the supplies, but it appeared as though she hadn't touched any of it. All that had been used was the bed tucked into the far wall, and the sheets were so ruffled that I could imagine her leaping up the moment the sun rose each morning, fleeing the memory of me with as much disdain as she'd fled my quarters only moments ago. I released a haggard breath as I recalled the fear and revulsion in my daughter's eyes. I'd intended to return with answers, or not at all, and especially not like *this*, undermining the only shred of authority she'd ever known.

Gods, what have I done?

I needed to clean this shit up, I knew, but I needed to clean myself up even more. I remained covered in blood, and my prosthetic was aching so badly that the pain had spread to my shoulder. After righting the chair I overturned, I settled into it, desperate to feel something cool against my near-feverish skin. I shed my ruined coat before moving to untie the front of my shirt using my good hand. I remained sweltering but knew better than to attempt to remove such a thin piece of clothing with my hook. Laying my right arm flat on my lap, I rolled my sleeve up to my elbow and began the uncomfortable process of unscrewing the attachment from the iron sleeve which held it in place. It wasn't a pleasant thing to do on my own, but not even Elvira would be willing to help me now.

"That comes off?"

I whirled around with a curse. Leaning against the far wall stood Calypso, and having not realized she was still present, my heart fluttered wildly. Had she shapeshifted into the damn wall? But there was no disgust in the nymph's face, only curiosity as she took in me and my prosthetic. I nodded slowly.

"Do you need help?"

After I gave another nod, Calypso effortlessly dodged the mess before floating to my side. Wordlessly, she placed both of her palms on my bare arm, gripping tighter when I didn't protest her touch. With her helping hold me immobile, removing the hook was much easier—painless, even—and a minute later, I was free of all the metal which made my right hand a semi-functional limb.

"Thanks," I muttered, pulling the arm against my chest both to rub my aching stump and conceal the flesh beneath. Though calluses and scar tissue had long since formed over the amputation site, sores and bruises marked where the prosthetic rested heaviest. I didn't remove it nearly as often as I should. Part of it was laziness, but most of it was pride; it may have been damn near a decade since I'd lost my hand, but that didn't mean I could stomach being seen in public, or by my crew, as anything other than whole.

"Of course," was all Calypso said. She no longer touched me but remained in close proximity watching and waiting for gods only knew what.

The depth of her stare sent uncomfortable prickles down my spine. "What?"

"I just wondered if you wanted help removing anything else?"

I bristled and flashed her a warning glare. "Don't push me. Not now."

"Apologies, Captain." Calypso held up her hands in surrender before taking a single step back. "But it was an innocent question, given that you're drenched in blood."

Was it? I truly couldn't tell with her. One moment she'd say something wildly inappropriate and seductive, then the next echo exactly what I was thinking, proving that she understood me in a way no one else had for a very long time. Both halves of Calypso were dangerous on their own, but together? I dared a glance at her shape, at the plunging neckline of her dress which left little to the imagination where her breasts were concerned. A shuddering breath rippled through me, and heat shot to my groin. *Fuck.* She may be a daughter of the sea, but I had no doubt that was playing with fire. Unable to manage more in my irritating state of arousal, I simply said, "Oh," as I worked to calm my fluttering heart.

Calypso continued staring, her tone neutral and dismissive. "If you want me to go, just say the word. I'm sure I'll find a place to sleep some—"

"No." Before I knew what I was doing, my hand shot out to grip her wrist. She'd started to walk past me and out the door, but the thought of being alone, surrounded by nothing but the tangible reminder of what I'd just done, was unfathomable. I fumbled for an excuse. "You can't go out there, not dressed like that. Let's just say the crew may be willing to share their hammocks, but may not be, ah, gentlemen when it comes to… other things."

A grin slowly spread across Calypso's features. "Are you implying that *you* are a gentleman, Cedric Teach?"

"No." Despite my best efforts, heat crept to my cheeks. "What I mean is that I don't trust Elvira not to stab you in your sleep, and the only other female bunk is with Wendy. Starting tomorrow, you can share with her, but I think she needs to cool off tonight."

Calypso nodded, glancing at where I still held her. "That seems logical."

Abruptly, I released her, inhaling deeply as yet another flash of desire surged through me. She heard it—how could she not?—but said nothing, and this sparked a flash of annoyance. "Don't get too excited. We aren't sharing my bed."

"We aren't?"

"You take it. I'll sleep here, at my desk. Once I clean up, I mean." Resting here was nothing I hadn't done before, albeit unintentionally, on nights spent poring endlessly over Blackbeard's documents, searching for clues which might lead to breaking Neverland's curse. I'd wake with an aching neck and back, but I'd survive.

Calypso narrowed her gaze. "And why would you do that? It would be a tight squeeze, but we would both fit." When my eyebrows flew up in shock, she added, "In the bed, stupid."

"Don't be ridiculous. That thing is barely large enough to hold me." It was true… in its current state. I'd long ago modified where I slept to accommodate both me and Scarlett comfortably, but only by pulling out a hidden compartment, effectively doubling its width. I hadn't even shown Wendy how it worked. Perhaps that made me a bastard, but there were certain secrets I wanted to keep between me and Scarlett.

As if she read my mind, Calypso scoffed. "You're telling me you never made it work with Scarlett?"

I shook my head, my tone once again a warning. "I already told you not to push me."

"I'm not pushing. I'm being sensible. I won't be able to sleep knowing you're being a stubborn ass, and neither will you if you stay there. You'll wake so sore you won't be able to move, and that won't do. We need our captain to be functional tomorrow."

"Calypso—"

"What?" She crossed her arms, a challenge in her dark eyes. "I won't keep you from your own bed. Either we share, or I'm leaving."

I considered her words. The mere thought of being left alone was making my chest tighten, but there was also no way I trusted myself to be pressed up against her all damn night. I'd never touch her without her permission, of course, but that was precisely the problem; since the moment we'd met, Calypso had made it more than clear she was willing, and sharing the bed had been her idea.

But there was no reason we couldn't make things interesting, and if she was so determined to push, I'd shove. "All right. How about a little wager?"

Her mouth parted slightly. "I didn't take you for a betting man, Cedric Teach."

"But you did take me for a pirate." I tilted my head toward the exit. We currently stood an equal distance from it and had roughly the same amount of obstacles in our way. "We race to the door. If I win, you stay and help me clean this mess up… but we don't share the bed, and you don't ask."

Calypso raised an eyebrow. "And when *I* win?"

"I'll… share the damn bed."

"And you clean up on your own."

I nodded. "Fair enough. Do we have a deal?"

"We would, but you're forgetting something." She pulled her skirt up to her thigh, revealing the clumsily bandaged wound on her leg I'd indeed forgotten. "I'm not sure if I'm capable of running at the moment."

"Ah, right." I stepped over the toppled desk to reach her, bending over to get a better look at the injury my sister had caused. Blackened blood stained the rag she'd used to stop the bleeding, reminding me of the ink marring the rug. "Do you want to pick a different activity?"

Calypso smiled. "No need. We simply need to level the playing field."

I rose back to my full height, immediately wary. "What do you—"

Before I could finish my sentence, she stomped on my foot. *Hard.* A hiss of pain left my lips as a giggle left hers, and by the time I glanced up, she was already halfway to the damn door.

"You fucking cheater!"

She glanced over her shoulder but didn't stop. "Am I not racing a pirate?"

"That doesn't mean I would have resorted to dirty tricks!" Using whatever I could as a crutch, I began limping after her, though I more than suspected it was already too late.

But a step from the door, Calypso stopped. She turned to face me with a sultry smirk playing on her lips. "Dirty tricks, you say? I quite like the sound of that."

"Do you, now?" I halted an arm's length away, an idea forming in my head. She hadn't technically reached the door yet, and if I was quick...

"Very much."

I narrowed my gaze, dropping my tone to match hers. "Do you mean that? I prefer things rather rough."

"As do I," Calypso purred. She leaned in, closing the space between us. "Do your worst, Cedric Teach—"

I didn't hesitate and lunged before she finished speaking. Snatching her forearm, I yanked the nymph toward me. I caught her mid-stumble, using her own forward momentum to twist and shove her back against the nearest wall. My right arm acted as a brace, resting just beneath her ribcage, while my left hand barred her access to the door. I completed the entrapment by forcing one of my knees between her legs, effectively pinning her in place with my body.

A triumphant grin spread across my features as I inched my fingers toward our shared goal. "I win."

"Do you?"

Frowning, I glanced down, only to see her palm already resting against the door frame.

She grinned. "I suppose this means we're sleep—"

Another flash of red, and before I knew what I was doing, my hand flew to Calypso's throat. Her gaze met mine. There was no fear or even shock as I applied careful pressure to her neck—not enough to choke, but certainly enough to make breathing uncomfortable. She didn't fight or squirm. If anything, she sounded bored. "Interesting choice of foreplay."

"This is not foreplay."

"I didn't say I wasn't into it." She wiggled her hips as much as she was able, grinding against my groin, and gods damn it, my cock betrayed me. "Evidently, you are too."

My growing arousal fueled something dangerous within me, not unlike the beast Wendy had awakened. Leaning in with my upper body while pulling away my lower, I twisted my lips into a snarl. "For the last time, do not fucking push me."

"You're the one with your hand around my throat."

"And you're the one writhing against me like a goddamn cat."

Calypso continued grinning. "I can't help it, Cedric Teach. Call me twisted, but there's just something irresistible about a man covered in blood…" She moved her hand from the door to my hip, fingers drifting dangerously close to my ass.

At her touch, something between a snarl and a groan erupted from deep within my chest. Releasing her neck, I snatched both of Calypso's wrists with my good hand, shoving my right arm into her chest until air whistled from her lungs. She'd continued to push despite my multiple warnings, and the fact that my own body was betraying me made her attempts at seduction all the more infuriating. If nothing else was working, perhaps threats would. "I could kill you, here and now. Snap your pretty little neck and no one would bat an eye."

She clicked her tongue. "My, that salty of a loser, are we?"

"I'm not threatening you over a stupid game you cheated to win. I'm threatening you because you can't keep your fucking hands to yourself."

"You won't kill me."

"Perhaps I should."

Calypso's stare remained unflinching. "You won't, so quit lying to both of us."

Conflicting urges surged through me as pent-up energy demanded to be released. Throwing her over my toppled desk and fucking her senseless would be easy, and squeezing the life from her easier still, especially in our current position. But both were equally stupid, would damn my chances of ever reuniting with Scarlett, and I'd never willingly betray her. Calypso may be hopelessly attractive, but despite the fact that she acted like her more every day, she wasn't the woman I loved or even wanted. She was simply *here*, and I was the lonely bastard prolonging both of our tortures.

"See, that's precisely why you won't kill me, or even hurt me. You can't." Calypso's voice tore me from my increasingly violent stream of consciousness. "Because then you'd be alone, and you'd rather pry off your fingernails than be alone with your thoughts right now."

I hated that she was right with every fiber of my being. My voice was low, and I couldn't bring myself to look Calypso in the eye. "We aren't sharing the damn bed."

"If you say that one more time, I will knee you in the balls and walk out this door right now."

"And if you touch me without my permission again, I'll let Elvira stab you."

She glowered but nodded. "Fine."

I released her with a huff. Partly because my blood was boiling, but mostly because I didn't trust myself not to do something else I'd regret. Needing to distract my twitching hand, I turned toward the mess I'd created, bending over to begin picking up the scattered mess of papers. Just when I started to get lost in the rhythm of the repetitive movements, the door slammed shut behind me.

Calypso had gone.

I froze in place as an uncomfortable weight settled in my gut, more overpowering than my fear. More guilt, perhaps? It wasn't anger, because just like with Wendy, the only person I had to blame was myself. Calypso had been perfectly willing to stay, yet I'd pushed even her away, and now I was left to battle my demons in solitude.

Monsters I'd created, that I couldn't keep at bay on my own, that would overwhelm me if I—

My breath hitched as the knob turned, and a moment later, Calypso reappeared carrying a bucket and rag. Her eyes widened upon glimpsing the look on my face, and she shook her head. "Oh gods, did you think that I'd gone for good?"

"No," I lied before hastily returning to gathering up the papers; thankfully, she didn't press.

Despite bargaining for the contrary, Calypso helped me clean up. We worked in silence, keeping out of one another's way as we restored my quarters to their former neatness, though neither of us was able to fully scrub the ink stains from the ruined carpet. Righting the desk came last. Though Calypso barely broke a sweat as we lifted the structure in tandem, with only one hand to use given that I'd removed my hook, the task left me breathless. It had taken a fraction of the effort to overturn it than it did to make it right.

Exhaustion I could no longer fight threatened to drown me. I was too tired to care that a woman who wasn't Scarlett was going to share my bed, and I wouldn't have hesitated to crawl into the sheets a bloody mess had Calypso not slammed the bucket and rag on the desk's newly organized surface, splashing a bit of water onto it. "For your face."

I mumbled my thanks, but she didn't acknowledge it, turning to stalk across the room. I brought the wet cloth to my cheek before I could tell where she'd gone off to or why. Like ice to a flame, the coolness of the fabric melted a bit of tension from my shoulders, and the more blood I washed away, the more I felt like myself. Though my heartbeat never settled, my breathing evened out by the time Calypso reappeared. She clutched a rolled-up piece of parchment in her hand but tossed it on the bed before I could question what it was.

She shook her head disapprovingly, curls bouncing over her shoulders. "You missed a spot. Several spots, actually."

"I've got a mirror somewhere," I mumbled, beginning to rummage around in the desk.

"Cedric," Calypso said, and my head snapped up, but not because she was suddenly an arm's length away... but because it was the first time she hadn't addressed me by my full name. "You'll strain eyes you can barely keep open. Nymphs see much better in darkness. Let me help."

It was an order more than a request, and the candles were still burning plenty bright, but I nodded anyway.

Calypso didn't move. "You're sure?"

"Yes."

The desk that creaked when someone so much as looked at it didn't make a sound as she settled on top of it. She shifted so she had easy access to both the bucket and me, her bare legs dangling to my left. While holding my gaze, she wrung out the bloody cloth, only bringing it to my forehead when I didn't squirm or protest. Evidently I'd neglected my hairline, for she lingered there the longest, her dark eyes flicking back to mine every few seconds. I didn't miss the tension in her arms that wasn't there before.

147

She jumped when I finally spoke. "I'm not going to bite, you know."

"Bite? Now that's an interesting idea." Calypso chuckled, visibly relaxing. "But it's not that—it's your threat. I know you gave me permission to do this, but I'd very much prefer not to feel Elvira's blade a second time. I think she coats her weapons in poison."

"*Shit.*" I'd completely fucking forgotten about that. "She does. Do you need an antidote? Is your wound—"

"It's fine, and should be healed by morning, thanks to all the time we spent in the sea." Her eyes glittered. "But it's nice to see that you care so much."

Is that why my heart hadn't stopped racing? Did I... *care* for Calypso, even though we'd known each other for less than two days? Or was it what she represented that I was so terrified of losing? If anything happened to the nymph, I'd lose all hope of finding Scarlett, and with it, quite possibly my will to live. Without Calypso, I'd have no purpose, no future, and if things kept up the way they were with Wendy, no daughter. I'd have... nothing. I'd *be* nothing.

Not wanting to dwell on the horrifying realization, I changed the subject. "Why are you doing this?"

Calypso snorted as she worked the rag into a particularly stubborn patch in my beard. "Because I offered, and you said yes."

"Not that. This." I gestured vaguely all around us. "Why are you here? What's in it for you?" It was a question I'd asked her once before, and she'd given a sensible answer. But with the way she was looking at me, the way she spoke to me, and especially the way she touched me, it was one I was beginning to doubt.

Her voice remained nonchalant, but her mask slipped for a fraction of a second, and I didn't miss it. "I already told you. I need to get back into Kaara's good graces."

"By handing over me?"

Calypso ceased her scrubbing to shoot me a glare. "It's not as if I'm dragging you to her kicking and screaming, or that I lied about what awaits you. You readily agreed to our deal back at the tavern. Have you changed your mind?"

"Not at all." *Not as long as Scarlett is alive.* "I'm just trying to understand, because you like me. You've liked me from the start."

"Like you, or like tormenting you?" Calypso's lips twisted into a wry grin.

"Both, for reasons lost on me."

"And?" Though I couldn't possibly still have blood on me, she continued to idly scrub at my cheeks. "I can like you but still use you. They're not mutually exclusive."

"They're not," I agreed, "but aren't you making it a bit complicated for yourself?"

She went still then. Though her right hand still held the rag to my face, her left clenched into a fist. All the amusement had left her in an instant, her energy shifted, and it was an uncomfortably long time before she spoke again. "Do you know how old I am, Cedric Teach?"

I'd have shaken my head if she wasn't touching it. "No."

"I've been around for a millennium, give or take a century. I stopped counting after the first few." Whether Calypso meant years, decades, or centuries, I didn't dare ask. "I've been in Kaara's service for most of that time. And I've been her favorite since long before you, your father, grandfather, or great-grandfather even possessed a family name. Out of all the beings who serve her, Kaara, a goddess, chose me."

I genuinely couldn't tell if I had offended Calypso or simply poked at what was clearly an old wound, so rather than speak, I waited for her to continue.

But she didn't; in an instant, the rag was gone from my face, and she crossed to the bed and back again, retrieving the piece of parchment she'd previously discarded. She fingered the frayed edges, her gaze icy as she spoke. "I do like you, Cedric, but make no mistake—there is nothing 'complicated' about the arrangement you and I have. I will always choose Kaara, just as I know you will always choose Scarlett."

The way Calypso said Scarlett's name had already made my breath hitch, but I stopped breathing entirely the moment I was handed the parchment. I turned it over, and there it was: Scarlett's portrait, unblemished and restored, looking almost better than it had on the day it was illustrated.

My voice shook more than my trembling hands. "H... H-how did you get this?" I asked Calypso, unable to tear my gaze from Scarlett's fiery expression. It was all there, every miniscule detail I'd come to memorize and cherish. Her freckles, the strands of hair she could never quite tame, and even the tiny scar on the bridge of her nose from where Compton's blade had once nicked her. My jaw clenched at the memory, but Scarlett held my gaze, unafraid and unwavering, as if to say, *We both carry scars that can never be erased, but they're in the past. What matters are the choices you make from here.*

Calypso chuckled softly. "It clearly meant a lot to you, and I felt bad that you had to lose it. I warned you that my magic was limited, but it turns out restoring sodden portraits is within my skill set."

I was moving before she finished speaking. With the portrait still clutched in my good hand, I wrapped my opposite arm around Calypso's waist, pulling her tightly against me. "Thank you," I whispered into her ear, hoping she'd mistake the wetness on my face as residue from the rag and not the tears they were.

Then my mind caught up to what I'd just done, and I staggered back, keeping my gaze trained to the floor. "Sorry, I didn't mean—"

Calypso smirked. "Now who's touching who without permission?"

"It was a mistake. Won't happen again."

Dropping her tone to an exaggerated growl, she spoke in what I could only assume to be a terrible mockery of me. "It better not, or I'll have to make another horribly violent threat I have no intention of following through on." She tipped back her head and cackled before returning to her normal voice. "You're a strange man, Cedric Teach."

I raised an eyebrow but relaxed my shoulders, relieved that she wasn't mad. "I'm the strange one?"

She nodded. "That's twice now I've told you not to trust me, and of all things, you thank me."

"You're honest." I shrugged. "That's far more than I can say for the vast majority of the other bastards I've encountered in my life."

Calypso's lips parted in mock offense. "Bastard? I'm far too pretty for such a vulgar term. I prefer temptress."

"Well, temptress, it's getting late," I said, fighting a smile of my own. "We should sleep if we've any hope of functioning tomorrow."

"Agreed."

After setting Scarlett's portrait near the shrine I intended to rebuild at the first opportunity, I crossed back over to where Calypso was waiting by the bed. She watched me through narrowed lids, searching my face carefully, and asked, "We're sharing, then? You've given up arguing about it?"

I didn't answer right away, instead busying myself with pulling out the compartment that would give us twice the room. "You called a truce, didn't you? You're choosing Kaara, and I'm choosing Scarlett. No reason for me to complain about sharing when there's nothing for either of us to worry about."

Calypso scoffed. "There was never anything to worry about. I may have fucked with you to get a rise out of you, but I'd never have actually fucked you. You're certainly attractive as far as men go, but I bedded enough of them in Afterport to satiate me for quite a while."

"You prefer women, then?"

"I find all sorts of people attractive, and my preference isn't dictated by what's between their legs." She paused, tone softening. "But these days, yes, I do find myself craving a certain goddess in particular."

Me, too, I found myself thinking as I finished making up the bed. Scarlett may not be a literal goddess, but to me, she may as well be; I'd been praying to her memory since the moment I'd lost her, considered my soul intertwined with hers, and had even set up a shrine with which to worship her. As Calypso dimmed the candles using her magic and we settled into the sheets, I ensured I faced the shrine, turning my back to the nymph. She fell asleep quickly—at least judging by her breathing—but I laid awake for hours, my lips moving in a silent promise to Scarlett alone.

I love you.

And I'm coming.

IX. THE DARK

Featured Song: A Young Girl Fair

Wendy

The walk back to Peter's room was a blur.

My knees ached, my head throbbed, and my chest grew tighter with each frantic inhale as we moved through the now pitch-dark halls. Even if I'd been thinking clearly, the hour would have been impossible to discern; all I knew was that it was late, much later than I'd stayed up in recent memory, and given the lack of voices to drown them out, the creaks and groans of *The Jolly Serpent's* hull were almost deafening. More than once, Peter and I nearly lost our footing, catching ourselves just before we would have slammed into the unforgiving walls as the ship rocked beneath our feet. *Choppy waters, then*, I thought. *Maybe a storm is coming.* I began making a mental list of the men I'd need to check in with come morning to ensure we were still on course... until reality came crashing back with a vengeance.

I was no longer captain. And such worries were no longer my responsibility.

Clutching my music box tighter to my chest and banishing the crushing thought, I waited for Peter to open the door before shuffling into his quarters. Funnily enough, he'd converted the closet in which I'd once been held prisoner into his home. The space was modest and cramped but suited him perfectly; there was a hammock piled high with blankets, a small chest for his belongings, and even an empty crate he'd repurposed as a side table, currently sporting a dimly lit candle. Best of all, he had a window. The moon, bright and nearly full tonight, cast additional illumination into the space, giving me a reasonably clear view of Peter's expression as he turned to face me. His lips didn't move, but his eyes posed the obvious question as Tink crawled back out from beneath his collar to perch on his shoulder: *Are you all right?*

Of course I wasn't. The last person I'd ever have wanted to see had just shown up out of nowhere, humiliated and taken everything from me before completely losing his shit, proving he was just as capable of hurting me as he was anyone and everyone else. I'd survived the horrors of Neverland, yet the most terrified I had ever been in my life was back in that room—the room that, until ten minutes ago, had been *mine*. I'd stopped sobbing, but was still crying, and I ached all over, especially at my temples. The short list of the things I needed included a bath, a warm meal, and sleep, but most of all, I needed an apology.

No. I balled my hands into fists. *Fuck an apology. I need my goddamn ship back.*

"I agree," Peter said slowly, informing me I must have spoken aloud, "but right now, you need to get yourself cleaned up. We all do."

I could only nod as he pointed to the crate-table, eyes still blurry with tears.

"You can put your music box there. It will be safe, I promise."

I clutched it as though my life depended on it and didn't move at Peter's assurance. It didn't matter that it had been weeks since I'd last listened to its song, or that I'd done my best to cut my emotional ties to the damn thing by stashing it out of sight. It was my security blanket in the same way some children clung to stuffed animals. The moment Hook exploded, the music box had been all I'd wanted. In an instant, I'd reverted back to the scared, lonely girl I'd been at the orphanage: Wayward Wendy, the girl with no friends.

And in that same instant, Captain Hook had again become my enemy.

I'd be angry at him later, I knew, but true weariness had begun to take hold, and right now all I felt was drained. Drained, broken, and numb. With quivering hands, I placed the music box where Peter had indicated.

His voice was apologetic behind me. "We should have grabbed your clothes while we—"

"It's fine," I cut across him, not wanting to discuss or even think about anything to do with Hook. "I can borrow yours until we're able to retrieve mine, if you don't mind, that is?"

Peter shook his head, but before he could reply, someone else did. "Would that scrawny kid's shirts even fit you?"

I took a sharp inhale upon recognizing the voice, and my suspicions were confirmed when I glanced over Peter's shoulder. Casually leaning against the doorframe stood Elvira. Though her tone dripped with its usual sarcasm, she regarded us with something that looked a lot like pity, but I was too focused on the wave of fury that had ignited within me to care. Balling my hands into fists, I spoke through gritted teeth. "Get the fuck out."

She dipped her head apologetically. "I realize I'm guilty by association and one of the last people you want to see right now. But I had a hunch you might need more than you left that room with." Lifting her arms, Elvira revealed an array of things we did indeed desperately need: a bucket and rag for washing, clean clothes, including a few of my own garments, blankets, and even fresh linen bandages. She met Peter's gaze. "Throw me out if you want, but if you'll have me, I'd like to help."

He turned to me. "What do you think?"

I snorted. "I think she's trying to erase her brother's mistakes."

"I'm not," Elvira said flatly. Setting the bucket on the floor, she tossed the rest of her offerings on the hammock. "I love Ced, flaws and all, but he's a grown ass man who can clean up his own messes. What he did back there was wrong, and I'm not here to apologize for it. He'll do that when he's ready. I'm here because you two— well, three," she conceded, glancing at Tink, "have been treated like absolute fucking shit, and I want to make sure you're all right. It's the decent thing to do, and the least I can do."

Stunned, I simply stared at her. Not only because of what she'd said, but because Elvira seemed so far from the empathetic type that it was nearly impossible to imagine her taking care of us, despite the fact that she was in front of us offering that very thing.

As if she read my thoughts, she sighed deeply. "I can do more than kill, you know."

"What do you want?" Peter blurted out, and the valid question broke my stunned disbelief.

"Yes—what is it you want?" This definitely seemed too good to be true, and if there was anything I'd learned aboard this ship, it was that favors didn't come without a price, likely one that I couldn't or wouldn't be willing to pay.

Elvira didn't answer right away. Instead, she strode toward the crate-table, regarding my music box. I tensed, preparing to dart in her path, but she didn't touch it. "Ced didn't seek my counsel."

"What?"

"When he gave you command of this ship," Elvira said, glancing up and locking her gaze with mine, "Ced didn't seek my counsel. He just did it. Had he asked my opinion or discussed it with me, I'd have told him it was a fucking horrible idea, and I may have even taken steps to undermine him. I'm sure he knew as much, which is precisely why he didn't tell me about his plans."

The unexpected revelation shocked me so much that more tears sprang to my eyes, spilling uninhibited down my cheeks. Not even Elvira had believed in me?

"Wendy, it's not what you think." Elvira's voice softened, and her expression carried more emotion than I'd ever seen her show. "I'd have advised Ced against it not because I didn't think you deserved it, or even that you wouldn't grow into the role someday, but that's precisely it—someday. Not at sixteen. Not after you'd only set foot on the deck a handful of times. And certainly not immediately after fucking dying. Are you even fully healed?" She shook her head, and I didn't answer since the question was obviously rhetorical. "As Ced displayed so beautifully back there, he can be impulsive when he's pushed. Learning he had a daughter *and* that he could leave Neverland, all in a matter of weeks? It was a lot for him to take in. It's no excuse, but he doesn't think this shit through. He may have believed handing over the ship was the right thing to do, but the way he went about it was all wrong, and it set you up for this spectacular failure. Had he given it a shred of thought, acted with his head instead of his heart, he would have seen as much. He should have stayed, should have taught you himself. He should have apprenticed you. He should have been a father. Not gone chasing after the ghosts of his past while ignoring what's in his present, because that's precisely what she is… a ghost."

Head spinning, I took a few steps back, leaning on the hammock for support as I allowed Elvira's confessions to sink in. She and I hadn't had many one-on-one interactions, especially ones where Hook wasn't around, so to learn she would have had my back perhaps more than anyone else—save for Peter and Tink, of course—was nothing short of astonishing. I didn't know what, if anything, I should do with the information.

Peter spoke before I'd fully allowed it all to sink in. "Is Scarlett the ghost? I thought Hook said she was alive?"

"That's what that nymph bitch claims," Elvira spat. "But personally, I think she's a fucking liar, and that she's manipulating Ced for her own gain. I have no idea what her goal is, but I intend to find out. He's obviously far too obsessed with the idea of Scarlett actually being alive to see that he's being played, but even if he does, I doubt he cares. He'd do anything to get her back... and that's what terrifies me. He'd sacrifice this ship in a heartbeat. And without question, most, if not all of the men. He's made it more than clear that he'd sacrifice even me if it were to save Scarlett. He'd see the world go up in flames, allow everyone and everything to burn to ash, all for her." Elvira's voice trailed off, and when she spoke again, it was so low I almost didn't hear it. "Knowing that, it almost makes me wonder if he'd sacrifice *you*."

I swallowed as images of what she described flashed through my mind's eye. "Why are you telling me this?"

"Isn't it obvious?" Peter huffed, crossing his arms. "She's saying whatever it is she thinks you want to hear to get us on her side."

"Watch it, boy," Elvira growled, her tone adopting that familiar unhinged edge in an instant. "And do not misunderstand me: I'll be loyal to Cedric until my dying breath. There are no sides where he and I are concerned."

I frowned. "But you just got done saying you'd have undermined him for me—"

"Yes. For you." Something else flashed in Elvira's gaze, but it was gone in a flicker of candlelight before I had a chance to read it. "You may choose not to acknowledge it, Wendy, but I do: you're my niece.

And in Scarlett's absence, you may as well be my daughter."

The words I'd been about to say caught in my throat.

"I am not here to undermine or betray my brother. Adais knows I'll go along with whatever foolhardy plan he devises from here, however reckless it may be, without question or complaint. It's not as if he'd listen to me, anyway. But I also have a responsibility to protect you, even if it's from him, and that will be damn near impossible unless you know exactly what game you're playing... and what your opponents are capable of."

When Elvira reached for me, I didn't shy away. Her touch was icy as she encased my hand within both of hers, but the coolness actually helped when it came to gathering my swirling thoughts. Though Peter had a point, everything Elvira had said was in line with how she'd always behaved where I was concerned. On the day we'd met, she'd drugged and taken me hostage, yes, but she'd also whispered guidance and encouragement into my ear prior to leaving me alone with Hook, even arming me with one of her own daggers. She'd been by my side when we'd entered Blackbeard's tomb, there to keep me warm even in the unnatural cold. She'd stitched me up after what transpired there. I believed her when she said she was loyal to her brother, but given all that, it wouldn't be unreasonable to believe she might also feel a certain loyalty to me. Forming words took more effort than it should, but I forced the burning question from my lips. "But why?" Our shared blood was a convenient excuse, but my gut told me there was something she wasn't telling me. "And why tell me this now?"

Elvira gave a crooked smile. "Us blondies have to stick together, don't we?"

"The truth, please."

When she next spoke, it was excruciatingly slowly, almost as if each word caused her physical pain. "If I tell you, you can never tell another soul... especially not Ced."

I nodded, but Elvira's gaze flicked over to Peter and Tink, who leaned against the now-closed door. They had been so silent that I'd honestly forgotten they were present. Tink had curled into a fetal position against Peter's neck and looked to be asleep, but I doubted that would matter to Elvira, and it wasn't as if the fairy wouldn't be privy to the information given her bond with Peter. "I trust them," I assured Elvira. "They'll keep your secret—won't you, Peter?"

"Course," he answered automatically, but Elvira shook her head, unconvinced.

"I'd prefer this be for Wendy's ears only. If you could just step out for a mom—"

"And leave you alone with her?" Peter took a step forward, suddenly on high alert. "Not a chance."

"Oh for fuck's sake, if I wanted to hurt her, I could poison her before you could take another breath, let alone make any pathetic attempts to stop me," Elvira snapped. "And this is rather serious. If Ced found out... well, not even I know what he might do. To all of us."

Peter and I shared a wordless glance, but before anything could be decided, Elvira spoke again.

"And what I have to say is about Scarlett. If nothing else, Wendy deserves to hear it first. Alone."

At that, I nodded in Peter's direction. "It's all right. I'll be fine."

He clenched his jaw. "I don't like this."

"Go. Please. Give us two minutes."

I expected him to argue further, but he only hesitated for a fraction of a second before finally slipping from the room. Elvira's grip on my hands didn't relax until the door clicked shut, but she didn't speak right away, either. Head bowed, she stared at the floor, blonde hair shielding her face as she drew a series of harrowing breaths, looking more haunted than I'd ever seen.

Ordinarily I'd have asked her if she was all right, but I knew Peter wouldn't give us even a second longer than he'd promised. "We don't have much t—"

"Scarlett told me she was leaving Neverland. And I was the one who helped her escape." Elvira drew another deep breath, the words tumbling faster now that she'd made her initial confession. "She'd discovered she was pregnant and refused to raise her child in such a monstrous place. But she also knew getting out wouldn't be easy, and that Ced could never know. He had to think she was dead, because if she didn't come back—and there was a strong possibility of that—she didn't want him coming after her. If she couldn't be there for you, she wanted you to at least be able to find your way back to him someday."

A wave of understanding washed over me, followed by bile rising up in my throat. "So she's… she's really…"

"Dead. Yes." Elvira reached up then, tucking a strand of hair behind my ear before I had a chance to pull away. "It's why she made me swear to watch over you."

"But…" I raised my gaze, eyes narrowing as details began

following into place. "If you knew how to leave Neverland this whole time, why didn't you? Why did you let me grow up alone, or at least not come visit me? And how the hell was leaving even possible? The curse wouldn't let you, so that doesn't make any—"

The door flung back open, interrupting my tirade; evidently, our two minutes were up. Brows raised, Peter glanced between us, crossing his arms before leaning back against the doorframe.

Elvira pursed her lips. "Questions for another time."

"No, questions for now," I hissed through gritted teeth, yanking myself from her grip. "Tell me or I'll—"

"You'll what, Wendy? Tell Cedric and get both of us killed?"

I scoffed. "He won't kill me. I've done nothing wrong."

"All right—just me. But then who's going to answer your questions?" Elvira's eyes burned. "I'd have carried that secret to my grave. You're the first and only soul I'll ever tell. If you think you can learn what you seek any other way, think again."

Peter bristled, stepping away from the wall and back into the space. "Is that a threat?"

"Not at all. It's a promise."

"You didn't even like Scarlett," I cut across Elvira, seething now. "Hook said you hated her. Why should I believe you'd keep her secret, especially one as big as this?"

Elvira cocked her head. "You'd believe him over me?"

"I don't know who to believe. You're all fucking liars."

"Believe what you want," Elvira spat. "Scarlett and I have a complicated history spanning many, many years. Cedric was the only one closer to her than me, but there were still things she told *only* me. It's not as if I could disclose it all in one sitting even if I wanted to."

I glared daggers at my aunt. "You know, for someone who claims to be loyal to Hook, you sure keep a lot of secrets from him."

An icy silence washed over us as we stood in stalemate. It took some time for the awful taste in my mouth to become tolerable again, and it took an equal amount of time for Elvira to quit looking like a cornered feral cat. Peter stood between us, his expression as defiant as it was unsure, but he was the first to make a decision.

"Thank you for the supplies, but I think we can manage from here."

Five minutes ago I'd have argued that she stay, but Elvira's outburst had erected my mental barriers once again, and now I wasn't sure what to believe. I nodded my agreement, not missing the flash of disappointment that crossed Elvira's face.

But she recovered quickly, shrugging it off as her icy nonchalance returned. "Suit yourself. But before I go, I have one more favor to ask."

Peter groaned, but for some reason, I found myself asking, "What is it?"

"May I listen to your music box play a tune?" Elvira glanced at where it sat. "All this talk of the past has got me feeling nostalgic, and hearing that old thing play has always calmed me."

The question shocked me so much that I gave a single nod, and it was all the encouragement Elvira needed. She wandered over to the crate-table, winding the key with great care. Closing my eyes, I prepared to hum the music box's song, but that's *not* the melody which floated through the space. My eyes flashed open in alarm, but

Elvira wasn't fazed; if anything, she was entranced by the unfamiliar tune, and soon began to sing along.

> *"Once there lived a young girl fair,*
> *Hidden in the wood.*
> *Had she not a single care,*
> *Her heart was pure and good.*
>
> *Then one day a stranger came*
> *To her lonely wood.*
> *He said 'Oh! What an awful shame,*
> *That here, you spend your childhood!'*
>
> *She laughed and said, 'Good sir, don't fret,*
> *This wood I do adore!'*
> *He said, 'But surely you'll regret,*
> *Never seeing more.'"*

I didn't know whether I ought to be disturbed or fascinated. Shuffling closer to Peter, I whispered into his ear between verses. "This is *not* the song it's supposed to play."

"I know," he said, out of the corner of his mouth, face white as a sheet.

"What the hell is she singing?" The lyrics sounded vaguely familiar, but I couldn't put my finger on why.

"It's a nursery rhyme," Peter answered automatically, and when I gave him a quizzical look, he added, "Some of the Lost Boys used to sing it."

Elvira, seemingly oblivious to our confusion, continued on.

> *"She shook her head and backed away,*
> *And wouldn't take his hand.*
> *He cursed and said she'd rue the day,*
> *That she had made her stand.*
>
> *She fled, and ran back through the trees*
> *Of her beloved wood.*
> *Soon she fell down to her knees,*
> *Move, she knew she should!*
>
> *Frozen now, she lay in place,*
> *Her limbs all stiff and cold.*
> *As one by one, they were encased*
> *In string made out of gold.*
>
> *Once there lived a young girl fair,*
> *Who met a man no good.*
> *A puppet caught in devil's snare,*
> *A girl turned into wood."*

At last, the music box ran out of steam, and so did Elvira. She leaned heavily against the table, still except for the rise and fall of her chest, face once again concealed by her hair. The sight was almost as disturbing as her song, but before Peter or I said anything, she leaped back up, causing us both to flinch. She grinned before bowing her head. "Thank you. Needed to get that out of my system."

"What... What the fuck was that?" I forced, lips parted in disbelief. "What did you do? That isn't the song the music box plays. If you messed with it, if this is a fucking trick—"

Elvira laughed. "You mean you don't know?"

"Know what?" My hands balled into fists at my sides as blood roared in my ears; I didn't have much patience left to spare.

"The music box is enchanted, Wendy. It will play any song anyone asks of it, even in a thought or dream." Elvira spared it another glance. "I should know—I was the one who stole it on Scarlett's behalf."

My body moved before my mind caught up, and I snatched the music box from the table before wrapping it in my embrace once more. An uncomfortable mixture of confusion and disbelief rippled through me, but for the first time in my life, holding the music box wasn't easing the pain. My safety blanket had been snatched from beneath me, leaving me to free fall into the unknown. I couldn't even hear my mother's voice anymore.

The only sound was Elvira's unhinged cackling.

"—you hear me? Wendy, look at me."

Firm hands gripped my upper arms, shaking me just enough to bring me back to reality. I slumped forward before I could catch myself, landing against a chest—Peter's. His scent enveloped me, woodsy and wild, just like Neverland's forests, and his hold tightened enough to hold me upright. Blinking rapidly, I managed to open my eyes just as he spoke to Elvira, his tone so stiff and cold that it could have been Hook's.

"Get out of here. Now."

At the sight of us, Elvira's gaze softened. "As you wish." She turned and got halfway to the door before halting, sparing a final glance over her shoulder. "Wendy?"

Despite my better judgment, I replied. "What?"

"This wasn't how I intended for tonight to go."

She disappeared then, slipping into the darkness as if she were a shadow instead of a serpent. The door clicked shut, seemingly of its own accord, and I didn't protest when Peter took my music box and set it back on the side table before guiding me to the hammock. There was a soft *thud* as a pile of fabric struck the floor, an arm snaked behind my knees, and the floor slipped out from under me. When I next opened my eyes, the ceiling greeted me, followed by Peter's furrowed brow.

"I'm worried about you. You got hit in the head twice that I know of, have been fainting all day, your forehead is bruised to hell—"

"Speak slower," I cut across him. I made a feeble attempt to sit up until Peter's hand shot out to stop me.

"Don't think I won't tie you to his hammock if I have to. You need to rest."

"So do you." I settled for turning on my side to face him, watching as he dragged a small crate over to the edge of the hammock. "How have you not collapsed?"

He didn't answer right away, instead busying himself with dipping a rag into the bucket of water Elvira had brought us. "Don't worry about me. I'm fine."

"And Tink?"

He glanced at her sleeping form. "She needs to rest, but she'll be all right."

I opened my mouth to argue but shut it again when the rag met the wound on my temple. Though Peter was careful, it still hurt like hell, and a shuddering groan rippled through me. It wasn't just pain that surfaced at his touch—it was everything. The past twenty-four hours replayed clear as day in my mind, forcing me to experience every ounce of fear, shame, shock, revulsion, and finally agony all over again. Unintelligible muttering tumbled from my lips, and a few tortured sobs erupted from my throat. Peter either wasn't prepared or wasn't able to keep me from bolting upright, and he cursed before staggering to his feet, nearly kicking over the bucket in the process.

"For Adais's sake, Wendy," he started, but silenced abruptly upon noticing my quivering hands.

"H-hold me." It was all I could manage between shuddering breaths, and all I could think of that might get the panic to stop. "P-please."

Peter didn't hesitate. Moving gently but urgently, he climbed into the hammock behind me, wrapping both arms around my middle and pulling my back against his chest. He snaked his neck over my left shoulder, pressing his cheek to mine, all the while whispering, "It's all right. It's all right."

My heart continued to beat out of my chest and the tears continued to fall, but I forced myself to focus on Peter's words. His touch. Tink's rhythmic breaths from where she still lay sleeping against his neck. His heartbeat, once my sobs had ceased long enough for me to feel it. Little by little, the panic dissipated, and it

171

became just him and me. I had no idea how long we sat like that, but when I opened my eyes, near-darkness greeted me; only a single candle was left burning, and it was hanging on by a literal thread.

Peter must have felt me shift. "We should sleep," he murmured, but I shook my head, unwilling to close my eyes if it meant facing more nightmares.

"How are you this okay?" I whispered into the blackness. I intertwined my arms with his, hoping it would encourage him to hold me even tighter. "And why am I such a wreck?"

"Wendy," he all but sighed. His fingers searched until they found mine, and he squeezed so hard I almost gasped. "Do you remember the day we met?"

"Clear as day," I said, and smiled at the memory.

"What you probably don't know is that I followed you to the docks all the way from the orphanage." He chuckled softly. "And that wasn't something I'd ever done before. I'd been keeping a close eye on all the children there after losing the Lost Boys, you see, on the lookout for any suitable new recruits. I wasn't after girls, especially not one as old as you, but from the first time I saw you, I knew you were special. You nearly punched a boy in the face when he purposely walked through a picture you were drawing in the sand."

I scowled. "That was Tom. He was a dick."

"So when you aged out," Peter continued, "I simply had to see what you would do, where you would go. I followed you, only to watch you do the very same to a grown man. It was that very moment I knew we would be fast friends, even though you were a girl."

I'd let the comment go the first time, but I couldn't let it slide the second. "What's that supposed to mean? Haven't you ever heard that old saying: 'One girl is more use than twenty boys?'"

He nodded. "Of course I have, and it isn't wrong. But before you, I had an… aversion to being friends with girls. It wasn't because of who they were, though. It's because of who I am, who I want to be, that I felt the need to surround myself with boys." He paused, shaking his head slightly. "I'm not proud of it. Perhaps we could have met one another sooner. Either way, I'm proud to know *you*. You're many things, Wendy Maynard, but a 'wreck' is not among them."

I was grateful Peter couldn't see the heat which sprang to my cheeks.

"As for how I'm okay," he murmured, softer now, "I'm not. I just have a different way of dealing with my pain than you do."

My chest tightened. "But you are dealing with it, right? It's not good to keep all that bottled inside. If you'd like to talk about anything—"

"No," Peter said, a little too quickly for me to believe him.

"I have ears," I reminded him softly. "I heard what they said about you. We both know it isn't true, but that doesn't make hearing it any easier."

"Please, Wendy. I said I don't want to talk about it."

"I have eyes, too." Pushing him probably wasn't a good idea, but the words tumbled out before I could stop them. "How's your back?"

Peter tensed behind me, loosening his grip in a way that suggested he might leap from the hammock at any moment. "If you're asking about my blood—"

"Damn it, Peter, I'm asking about *you*," I hissed. Admittedly, I did still want answers regarding his strange golden blood, but now very much wasn't the time. "You spent the last hour comforting me. Why won't you let me do the same for you?"

He hesitated before responding. "What did Elvira say?"

I blinked at the sudden change in subject. "What?"

"When she made me leave. What did she say to you?"

"That I shouldn't keep letting you avoid my questions, especially the serious ones," I grumbled.

Peter sighed deeply. "Wendy, this is important."

"As important as the fact that you're allowed to keep secrets from me, but I have to tell you everything?"

"I never said that."

"No. But you sure implied it."

He fell silent then, but thankfully didn't leave. As still as statues, we breathed almost in unison until blackness surrounded us. The candle had either burned out or I could no longer keep my eyes open, and it was impossible to tell how much time had passed. I whispered Peter's name, unsure if he'd answer, but a soft grunt informed me he was still awake.

"Will you stay with me tonight?" I asked, the words so soft they were nearly imperceptible. Given our last exchange, I half expected him to tell me to fuck off, so the gentleness in his tone surprised me.

"Of course. I can sleep on the floor."

"No. I want you here," I admitted, pressing my cheek closer to his. There was no chance my dreams would be free of nightmares, and I couldn't bear the thought of waking up with him out of reach. "Just like this."

He nodded. "Then right here it is."

We shifted until all three of us were comfortable. I laid on my side facing the wall, Peter curled around me, and Tink slept just above his head, partially tangled in his hair. Peter traced lazy circles on my upper arm until he fell asleep, snoring softly against the back of my head. Though sleep took much longer to claim me, my panic never resurfaced, kept at bay by my friends' presence. There may still be secrets between us, ones so heavy they threatened suffocation, but I trusted Peter and Tink more than I'd ever trusted anyone else in this world—perhaps more than I'd trust anyone else ever again.

And whatever there was still to face, at least we'd face it together.

X. THE MORNING

Featured Song: A Lullaby of Eternal Woe
Cedric

A hand clamped over my mouth, and I jolted awake.

My eyes flashed open, taking longer than I'd have liked to adjust to the sudden illumination. It wasn't morning, but it wasn't dark, either; the candles Calypso had extinguished with her magic were back to their full brightness, aided by the light of the almost-full moon. The ship tossed and turned as it navigated its way through choppy and turbulent waters, and I vaguely remembered rolling into the person sleeping next to me… *Calypso*. Fuck, had I been snoring? Touched her by accident? I made an attempt to face the nymph, only to be met with a softly clicking tongue coming from the opposite side of the bed. The hand came from there, too—I simply hadn't noticed in my still-groggy state.

"*Tsk, tsk,* I wouldn't do that, Cedric. You might wake her."

My chest twisted into knots at the achingly familiar voice, quickly followed by a surge of fury. Ripping the hand from my face and holding it by the wrist, I spoke in a low growl, my tone an icy warning. "That trick won't work a second time, Calypso."

Scarlett—or rather, Scarlett's shapeshifted face—raised an eyebrow. "What the fuck are you talking about?" she hissed, struggling against my grip. "Calypso is right there."

"Don't play games with me—"

"Cedric, *look.*"

Whipping my head to the side, I did a double take upon realizing Scarlett was right. Curled on her side facing me, Calypso drew steady, even breaths as she slept, her tangled dark curls draped messily over her pillow. Had I not been able to feel body heat radiating from her in gentle waves, I may have thought this was yet another illusion, or even a dream; it sure didn't feel like one, but this didn't make any sense. Scarlett couldn't *actually* be here. But then again… it hardly made any sense that I had ridden on a hippocampus across monster-infested waters, somehow able to locate my ship despite it being in the middle of nowhere. Had she done the same? I turned back to her, sputtering now. "H-How…"

"Shhh." Scarlett gripped my chin, holding me in place as she silently moved from the floor to the bed, climbing atop it to straddle me. A shuddering groan escaped my lips as she settled her hips against my groin, creating delicious friction, but quick as a serpent, she leaned forward to cover my mouth once more. "I said, be quiet. I didn't come here to put on a show… not for her, anyway."

Scarlett was so close I could kiss her. Though her tone was serious, her warm brown eyes carried a hint of mischief, and the smirk at the corner of her mouth informed me her words were as much a command as they were a dare. And gods, I wanted to meet that challenge. I wanted nothing more than to tear her skirts aside and begin driving into her right then and there; my cock was already straining against my breeches, begging to be put to good use. But one nagging thought held me back, the voice of reason I wished more than anything would shut up and let me enjoy this. Swallowing, I forced the words from my lips, not wanting to wait until we were in the middle of it to spoil the moment. "But… is this real? Are you really here?"

Scarlett moved her hand to grip the back of my head. Tangling her fingers in my hair, she tugged, forcing my chin up and bringing my mouth to meet hers. "Tell me—does this feel real?"

When we came together, I nearly unraveled on the spot. She met my parted lips eagerly, slipping her tongue into my mouth and claiming what had always been hers, and hers alone. Moving to the silent rhythm of our own melody, we kissed as though we were drowning and only had one another's air to breathe, like we'd die happy if we never surfaced. I surrendered to Scarlett's every whim and command, melting beneath her touch and following where she led, precisely how she led. To everyone else, I may be a pirate captain, but for her, I'd be anything. I'd do anything, any way she wanted it. Get on my knees. Worship her. Bow to her. Slow, fast, urgent, sweet, rough… I didn't care, I just thanked every god in existence that she was here, truly here, and that I could *touch* her, at long last.

I reached out to do just that, starting with her breasts, but she batted my hand away and broke the kiss. "No, Cedric. Not yet." She splayed her palms over my chest and, before I could say another word, slipped her fingers beneath the collar of my shirt and tore it damn near in half. My initial shock quickly dissipated when she began roving her hands over my now-bare chest, gently raking her nails down my ribs in the way she knew I liked... perhaps too much.

"*Fuck*," I groaned, unable to suppress my shudder despite the fact that Calypso lay sleeping mere inches from us. The last thing I wanted to do was wake her, but I couldn't deny that her mere presence heightened the eroticism of the moment. At any moment, she could wake and see us, and however fucked up it was, the thought of getting caught in the act was intoxicating.

Scarlett laughed softly again, seemingly reading my thoughts. "I'm beginning to wonder if part of you wants to wake her. But here, this should help you to keep still..."

She tore my shirt again, this time fashioning two long strips from the already ruined fabric. Positioning both wrists above my head, she waited until I nodded in agreement before securing them to the wall with the strips, tying my arms down to my elbows to keep even my stump firmly in place. Sitting back, she took a moment to admire her handiwork, but I hardly minded; it gave me an opportunity to get a good, long look at her in this candlelight.

My pirate queen was dressed a white, nearly see-through chemise paired with a leather corset she must have donned with me in mind—it was one of my favorites given how beautifully it showed off her cleavage. Both her hair and skirts spilled wildly over her shoulders and legs, but what I fixated on were her lips. Now that I'd gotten a taste, I'd do anything to taste them again. Round and full, they begged to be kissed as much as her breasts begged to be ravished, but propping myself up in my now-compromised state to do just that would be next to impossible. It didn't keep me from trying. I arched my back and yanked on my bonds, but neither got me anywhere.

Scarlett grinned at my struggle. "I'll never get tired of watching a powerful man allow himself to be rendered so helpless. Do you remember our safeword?"

Desire surged through me; if we needed the safeword, this was about to get all kinds of interesting. "Fathom."

"Good. Close your eyes."

I did, and more chills shot down my spine in anticipation. When thirty or so seconds passed where nothing happened, I said Scarlett's name; that's when something light and soft began tracing up my unprotected sides. My first instinct was to squirm—whatever touched me was borderline ticklish—but I forced myself to relax and enjoy the sensation, barely stifling another moan as yet more arousal flooded through me. Scarlett remained straddling me, a fact of which I was hyper aware, and it was a struggle not to grind against her following each and every miniscule movement. Judging from the way she kept chuckling, not all of her squirming was involuntary. Little tease.

"Keep that up, and I might not be able to—*ah*!"

My whisper turned to a hiss as tiny flecks of heat splattered across my chest, but the pain from each was quick to subside, giving way to an odd sort of pleasure I'd never quite experienced. In stark contrast with the featherlight touch from before, the dull ache left behind was intoxicating. Opening my eyes, I realized it was hot wax that had been dripped on my chest; each tiny droplet was already beginning to harden where it met my skin. Scarlett paused when I raised my gaze to hers, tilting the candle she held back upright. "Too much?" she questioned, but I shook my head.

"No. Do it again."

She raised the candle nearly above her head, moving it in slow circles as she slowly dripped crimson wax across my chest. The sensation was as intense as it was arousing, especially with the way Scarlett began reacting to my increasingly desperate actions. I strained against my bonds, gritting my teeth as I struggled to reach her, but though she leaned slightly forward, it was never enough to meet me in the kiss I urgently craved. Her lips parted in a silent moan, her gaze heady as she drank me in; soon, I could no longer keep my hips still. Impatient and frustrated, I gave a few quick thrusts, but it did the opposite of what I wanted—with another disapproving click of her tongue, Scarlett picked up her skirts and slid off the bed.

A whimper escaped me as my cock twitched in protest. "Where are you going?"

"Nowhere. Yet."

Creeping silently as a ghost, Scarlett placed the candle back in its holder before crossing to the other side of the room. She lifted the desk chair and brought it to the edge of the bed, remaining just out of reach as she sank into it, never once breaking eye contact with me.

"How's the view?" she asked.

"Fine, but…"

My voice trailed off as she lifted both her legs to prop them on the edge of the chair, spread them, and parted her skirts, giving me an uninhibited view of what lay beneath. No undergarments, just her, visibly wet and glistening even from where I lay bound. "How about now?" she asked again, her voice heavy with lust.

"E-even… Even b-better," I managed, unable to tear my eyes away from the glorious sight. Scarlett began palming her own breasts, nearly causing them to spill from the chemise as she threw her head back in yet another silent moan. I jerked against my bonds once more, the movements involuntary at this point—I just needed to feel her, to taste her, to fuck her, *something*. I whispered her name between desperate pants. "Please, let me touch you."

"No," she said firmly, her gaze never wandering from mine. "I want you to see what you do to me. How wet you make me. How I was forced to pleasure myself while we were apart. You are welcome to join, though, on one condition… that you find a way to free yourself. I tied you in a way that shouldn't be impossible to escape, especially if you want me as badly as you claim."

I wasn't entirely certain that I believed her; for being strips torn from my shirt, these fuckers were tight. I tested them once more, even straining until my wrists ached, but of course they didn't give. My frustration and arousal had built to a point to where it was almost painful, but Scarlett seemed to be fueled by it. Ignoring the string of curses I whispered under my breath, she brought a pair of fingers to her mouth, wetting them thoroughly before reaching between her spread thighs. She paused there, flashing me a final seductive grin. "Prove that you want me, and claim what's yours. Otherwise, enjoy the show."

It didn't take long at all for her to get herself going, despite starting off slow. Scarlett only spent a minute or so tracing lazy circles before speeding up, her breaths quickening to match the pace with which she pleasured herself. Heat crept to her cheeks, her eyelids drooped, and she very nearly closed them, but at the sound of my voice, she refocused on me.

"Don't you dare look away—not when I know exactly what you're thinking about." Though my tone was even, so as not to wake Calypso, my heart thrashed wildly against my ribcage. I'd stopped struggling so violently against my bonds, trying out a new tactic instead: small, calculated movements, feeling for the slightest give in the makeshift rope.

Scarlett answered between breathless pants, never once slowing her fingers. "Oh? And what's that?"

"Those may be your hands, but you're imagining they're mine." These goddamn restraints still hadn't loosened, but I refused to let the frustration show on my face. Impatience had gotten me nowhere, and I needed to be methodical about this. "You wish it were my fingers touching you, slipping inside you one at a time… yes, just like that, Scarlett."

Her lips parted in a silent gasp as she did precisely what I was describing. One digit disappeared within her, then another, and she rocked her wrist back and forth, fucking herself agonizingly slowly.

"There you go, slow and steady, just like you like. Just like *I* know you like." I barely stifled a gasp of my own as finally, my bonds gave a fraction of an inch. "I know you feel good. But I could do it better. You know I could."

An audible moan slipped from her lips, and *fuck*, that sound was everything. I'd do absolutely fucking anything to hear it again. Arching my back, I yanked sharply, growling in triumph when the ropes finally loosened, making it a simple matter of untangling myself from them. All sense of self-restraint gone, I moved frantically, all but snarling under my breath as I worked my way to freedom.

"You'd better not come until I get over there. I want it to be *my* fingers you come apart on."

Or my mouth, I thought eagerly, shooting upright as I tossed the ropes aside. Eyes on my prize, I darted forward, completely missing the fact that though my arms were free, my feet remained tangled in the sheets.

And I fell.

I hit the floor hard, nearly smacking my head on one of the chair legs. Though I managed to protect my skull, my knees weren't nearly as lucky; agony shot up my thighs as I crumpled, taking the bedsheets with me. Cursing both from the pain and embarrassment, I threw the blanket aside only to be immediately assaulted by bright sunlight filtering uninhibited through the windows.

It was… morning?

Glancing around wildly, I took in my surroundings. No candles, no moonlight, and certainly no Scarlett. No Calypso, either—her side of the bed was empty and abandoned, meaning I was totally alone. My hand flew to my shirt, finding it unblemished and whole, and there certainly wasn't any candle wax coating my goddamn chest. That's when reality slapped me in the face, making my blood run cold.

It had been a dream after all. A glorious dream, but a dream nonetheless. Bringing my hand to my forehead, I dragged it down my features slowly, lingering upon each and every scar. The dull, ever-present ache in my chest returned with a vengeance, weighing on my already heavy heart like an anchor. How could I have been so stupid? I should have fucking known it wasn't real; getting to see, much less hold Scarlett again was seeming like more and more of an impossible reality with each day that passed without her.

The weight of my grief made standing difficult, as did the bulge in my pants. One thing that was very much real was the raging erection my dream had left me. It was so sensitive that even despite the looseness of my breeches, the handful of steps it took to reach my desk were borderline painful. I'd absolutely need to take care of it prior to leaving this room; the last thing I needed was for the men to see me in such a state. In search of a towel, I yanked open a handful of drawers, locating what I sought a moment before noticing the scrap of parchment on the desk's surface. A note was scrawled in barely legible cursive:

It seemed you were having a rather pleasant dream, so I didn't want to wake you. You'll (hopefully) be pleased to know that Elvira hasn't stabbed me yet, so I didn't want to push my luck by oversleeping. Gone to explore the ship—let me know if you need me. You need only whisper.

- C

P.S. Judging from the intensity of your moans, I definitely want to hear about this dream at the earliest opportunity. I expect details.

I winced. Calypso had heard me *moaning*? The day hadn't started, and it already couldn't get any fucking worse. The dream alone had been torturous enough… an agonizing reminder of what I may never have again.

Straightening, my gaze fell upon Scarlett's portrait. A static expression stared back at me, voiceless and unmoving, so unlike what I'd just experienced in the dream. Felt in the dream. Tasted, touched…

A groan escaped my lips as I palmed my cock through my breeches, and the little remaining self-control I possessed snapped. Fully awake and alert now, I leaned over the desk, yanked myself fully out, and began to stroke, never once looking away from her. Let Scarlett see what she did to me, how mad she still drove me despite the distance, the sixteen years that had passed since I'd seen her. The curses, the chains, the secrets, the lies… I laid it all bare as I worked myself to a climax. Higher and higher I climbed, the pleasure and heartbreak coming in equal waves as I finally approached the edge.

I cursed her name as I came, coming into the towel and nearly collapsing on the spot. My vision blacked out before I'd even closed my eyes, my muscles twitched with involuntary spasms, and my breathing was as erratic as my heartbeat. If I didn't have the table to lean on, no doubt I'd have fallen a second time; I couldn't remember the last time I'd orgasmed that hard.

I was still recovering when the door swung open so violently it nearly broke off its hinges… and in barged my sister.

Elvira had a split second to take in everything, from my still-twitching cock to the heat that no doubt colored my cheeks.

Swearing, I threw the used towel on the desk and whirled around, hastily tucking myself back into my breeches and fumbling over my words. "What the fuck? Haven't you ever heard of knocking?"

"For fuck's sake, Ced, once wasn't enough for you?" Elvira slammed the door shut before stalking toward me, looking not embarrassed, but furious. "No wonder that snide little bitch was looking so pleased this morning."

"What are you—"

"I'm not stupid, Cedric!" Elvira practically roared. "I know she slept in here last night, and this room reeks of sex. Don't you dare lie to my face."

Upon registering her accusation, my humiliation turned to fury in an instant. I raised my voice to match Elvira's, my shouts booming off the walls. "You think I slept with Calypso? That I'd even touch her?"

"Your eyes undress her every time you so much as glance at her!"

Fuck, she'd noticed? "That's not true."

"You know what, forget it." Elvira threw up her hands and turned, speaking as she headed back for the door. "If Silvertongue has you lying for her now—lying to *me*— then there's no hope for either of you."

Darting forward with speed that shocked even me, I threw myself against the wall, effectively blocking my sister from escaping. Holding her gaze, I forced myself to level my tone; shouting, while tempting, wasn't going to get us anywhere. "Elvira, look at me. I'm not lying."

She looked ready to stab me but thankfully didn't.

"I had… a dream," I admitted, loathing the blush that returned with a vengeance. "About Scarlett. One so good it left me, ah, wanting. And I couldn't exactly go out there with a massive fucking erection, so I was taking care of it."

Elvira raised an eyebrow. "The nymph did sleep in here, though."

"She did, because I don't trust you not to hurt her. But sleep was all we did—we didn't fuck. And even if we did," I added, cutting across my sister before she could interrupt, "it remains lost on me why you care so much."

"Because it's fucking distracting," Elvira snapped. "While you were in here dreaming, your daughter nearly died. Again."

I went completely still. "What?"

"Pan came and found me before dawn. Said Wendy keeps slipping in and out of consciousness and talking nonsense, that she may have been hit in the head too many times. She was up most of the night tossing and turning with nightmares Peter couldn't help ease. And of course, it's likely that the stress *you* put her through isn't helping."

"You couldn't have opened with that?" I was already fumbling with my hook and its attachments, attempting to don the prosthetic as quickly as possible. Though panic was what had originally set me into motion, I felt eerily calm as I moved to throw on the rest of my clothes—or perhaps it was just adrenaline.

Elvira's tone was icy. "Given last night and what I just walked in on, I wasn't entirely certain that you'd care."

I forced myself to ignore the jab. "Is she all right?"

"For now, yes. Calypso was able to get her to sleep and is sitting with her."

A relieved exhale escaped me as I yanked on my boots. "Then thank Adais for that 'nymph bitch,'" I growled, shooting Elvira a glare as I stood. "Where is Wendy?"

"That old supply closet. Pan turned it into a hovel of sorts."

After making sure I had both a pistol and a dagger on my person, I turned to go, but not before addressing Elvira one last time. "I don't care how you do it, and I don't care if all he's guilty of is looking at her wrong, but I want every man responsible for harming my daughter to be strung up in the brig. You have thirty minutes."

Her gaze darkened as she gave a single nod. "Consider it done."

I stormed off then, weaving my way through the halls as quickly as I could without tripping over or banging my hip on anything. The handful of men I passed gave me a wide berth, and rightfully so; I honestly wasn't sure what I'd do if I got my hook or hand on any member of this godsforsaken crew, innocent or not.

I reached the closet quickly. Instinct would have had me barging in unannounced, but at the sound of a faint melody drifting through the open doorway, I froze in place. A voice intertwined with the song, singing lyrics as eerie as they were soothing.

"Lost, roaming forevermore,
Gods, monsters, friend and foe,
Never to go ashore,
Trapped in the depths below.

Hidden, deep in the waves,
Lie all those dead long ago,
Headed to their graves,

The Sea of Eternal Woe."

I'm not sure why Calypso's singing surprised me, but it did. Haunting and otherworldly, her voice almost sounded like a cross between a siren and a human. It was a while before I dared to creep closer, and only because of Wendy. Had I been here for any other reason, I may have succumbed to whatever spell Calypso was obviously weaving. The notes she sang lingered in the air like a comforting blanket, settling atop my shoulders and soothing my racing heart. It was a fight to keep my eyes open, but good thing I did; the moment I peered into the room, a crimson ball of light came shooting at my face like a hornet.

With a curse, I stumbled back, throwing up my hand to cover my face. The light wasn't deterred and kept darting in and out of my personal space, all the while rattling with furious-sounding bell noises. It took me a moment to recognize the language as Fairies-tongue, and by then I'd also caught a glimpse of Tink's doll-like shape. "Piss off," I growled, lifting my hook, but before I'd raised it over my shoulder, my entire right arm was slammed back against the opposite wall. Something sharp rested against my groin, forcing the rest of my body flush against the wood, and blinking, I found myself staring into Pan's boyish face.

Except he didn't look quite so boyish anymore. He wasn't yet a man, but he certainly wasn't a child as I'd claimed only yesterday. His hair had grown so long it nearly touched his shoulders, his features were hardened and serious, and the strength with which he gripped my shoulder wasn't anything to scoff at. Something was different about his aura, too, but there wasn't time to linger on what as he pressed the dagger even closer to the inside of my thigh, dangerously close to my manhood. "If you weren't Wendy's blood, I'd kill you here and now."

I deserved every bit of this, I knew, but it wasn't enough to keep my fury at bay. Pan could threaten me all he wanted, but later; right now, I needed to see Wendy. "Careful, boy," I snarled under my breath, not wanting Wendy to hear us. "Remember our deal." We'd sworn it under eerily similar circumstances, over what we feared might be Wendy's deathbed: if she lived, I agreed I wouldn't harm Pan so long as he didn't harm me.

He spoke through gritted teeth. "Fuck the deal. It was off the moment you did *this*."

I bristled. I'd never pretended to be a fucking saint and certainly had many things for which I could take responsibility—but why did everyone seem incapable of separating me from things I had nothing to do with? "I shouldn't have lost my temper, and I'm sorry for what you both went through at the hands of my crew. But the former I can do nothing about, and the latter is being taken care of as we speak."

"Why should I believe a single thing that comes out of your mouth?" Pan tightened his grip on my shoulder, while beside him, Tink's light flashed red. "I gave trusting you a shot, and so did Wendy. Look where that's gotten us. Look where it's gotten her."

He didn't release me but sidestepped just enough to allow me to see into the room. Beneath a pile of blankets nearly as large as her body, a pale-faced Wendy lay sleeping. Her face had swollen, the bruises had spread, and the wound on her head didn't look anything but worse. One of her arms dangled from the hammock, her fingers twitching from what I could only hope was a pleasant dream. Calypso sat with her back to us, humming softly to the music box's melody as she slowly waved her hands up and down Wendy's trembling body.

Rage ignited like gunpowder at the sight, swiftly followed by a metaphorical knife burying itself into my gut. Pan was right—whether I liked it or not, if anyone was to blame for what had happened to Wendy, it was me. Perhaps that meant that I wasn't privy to details regarding her condition, that I shouldn't even be here, but it didn't stop me from voicing my questions regardless. Speaking loud enough for Calypso to hear, I ignored Pan's muttered curses. "What happened to her? How did she get like this?"

Calypso turned her head slightly. "Are you serious? She was struck in the head multiple times, nearly froze and drowned, has a panic disorder, and you scared the shit out of her yesterday."

I set my jaw. "Is that all?"

"Unfortunately not. It would appear your daughter is rather sensitive to magic of any kind."

What the fuck does that have to do with anything? "And that's a problem because…?"

"Because we're practically drowning in it, and it's only going to get worse the closer we get to Kaara." Calypso shifted until she fully faced me and Pan, not looking the slightest bit surprised at our current position. "Such sensitivity can be as much of an asset as it is

193

a handicap; I suspect it was why she was so in tune with Neverland's curse and creatures. But the curse was only a taste of Kaara's power. This is the real thing, and Wendy is suffocating."

I swallowed. "Is there anything that can be done?"

Calypso shook her head. "She'll adjust in time, but for now, this is Wendy's fight. I've eased her into it as best I can, and she's in no physical pain. But she's still having nightmares."

My chest throbbed with another stab of pain as I dared a final glance at Wendy. I badly wanted to go to her, to brush the hair from her forehead and tell her how sorry I was for yesterday... for everything. But not only did I suspect that Pan would let me nowhere near her, it wasn't as if words would do much good. Without action to back them up, any promises I made would be empty and meaningless.

If I wanted my daughter to truly believe that I cared, I'd need to prove it.

My voice was hoarse as I addressed Pan. "Take care of her, and come and find me the second anything changes."

He frowned and stepped back but didn't sheath his knife. Tink continued flitting about his head, still chattering away in Fairies-tongue I couldn't comprehend. "Where are you going?" Pan asked.

"To make this right."

If I had stormed off angrily before, it was nothing compared to how I moved now. Face hardened and jaw set, I kept my hand on my pistol, finger hovering over the trigger as I made my way to the brig. Elvira's thirty minutes weren't quite up, but I suspected that wouldn't matter; my sister was nothing if not efficient and had never failed me before. Lower and lower I descended into the ship's hull, taking the stairs two at a time, all the while imagining what I might do to the filthy rats guilty of abusing my daughter. No—not rats. They were fucking insects, and I'd crush them as easily as I'd crushed Pierce.

But not without making them suffer long and hard first.

My eyes had yet to adjust to the darkness, so I heard them before I saw them. A handful of muffled whimpers broke the monotony of the ship's hull groaning and creaking as we navigated through still-choppy waters, the noises as terrified as they were desperate. A smile played at the corner of my mouth as I envisioned what they must be thinking; if I'd do what I did to Pierce so publicly, what horrors awaited them here, far away from prying eyes?

I turned a corner, and illumination greeted me. Lit by lamps on either side, our brig's crisscrossed metal bars stretched from floor to ceiling. We didn't have a large one—I didn't take prisoners often, given that they were just extra mouths to feed—so the three men currently occupying it were crammed tightly together. Just as I had requested, they were strung up by their wrists, and Elvira had chained them by their ankles as well. Six frightened eyes watched my every move, but they'd silenced their pleading, likely knowing it wouldn't do them any good. They'd sealed their own fates when they'd hurt Wendy, and I was simply carrying out the sentence.

As I stepped closer, movement flashed out of the corner of my eye. Elvira slipped from the shadows before gesturing proudly to her handiwork. "These are the three who laid hands on her. Smee alone tried to stop them, and the rest were bystanders. Given that we

195

can't operate the ship without a crew, however, I unfortunately must advise that we look the other way for now."

I nodded as I took in the terrified faces before me: Nelson, Digby, and Alder, all men known to have been close with Pierce. I wasn't particularly fond of any of them, Alder especially, and given that he was in closest proximity to me now, he was who I chose to fixate on. Pulling open the door, I slipped inside the brig, smirking when the men did their best to shuffle away from me, even with chained ankles.

"Scared? Good. That means you know precisely why you're here."

With unrestrained ferocity, I lashed out at Alder's chest with my hook. The intention was simply to rip open his shirt, but in my carelessness, I struck flesh instead. No matter. I dragged my arm down, tearing both skin and cloth. Alder screamed through his gag, thrashing uselessly, but I didn't stop until I reached his naval. Crimson splattered across the floor as I yanked my hook out, leaving Alder's chest a dripping, bloody mess.

His eyes started to roll back in his head, but with a snarl, I gripped his chin with my good hand, forcing him to look at me. "Oh, no you don't. I'm just getting started."

But the moment I pulled my dagger from my belt, the ship rocked violently beneath us. Had I not gripped the bars of the brig just in time, I'd have fallen into Alder's bloodied chest, and it was several harrowing moments before *The Jolly Serpent* righted herself. Even Elvira was caught off guard; having not been standing near anything to hold, she slid into the far wall. Faint shouts came from above, and though it was nothing that sounded overly concerning, I still wanted to know what the hell had just happened.

I locked eyes with my sister. "Go investigate."

She dashed off, leaving me alone with my rage, and the next several minutes passed in a blur. I hacked, slashed, kicked, and punched, all the while picturing Wendy's broken form. The bruises she'd suffered, the wounds. I inflicted the same upon Alder and more, barely surfacing to draw breath into my own lungs. I wanted him to scream, I wanted him to *bleed*, I wanted him to—

The ship rocked a second time, taking me completely by surprise. It rolled in the opposite direction, slamming me against the door of the brig and sending pain shooting up the shoulder I landed upon. With a groan, I righted myself but remained dazed even as the ship returned to its normal position. More shouts echoed this time, sounding far more urgent than before; unfortunately for me, too urgent to be ignored.

Alder was slipping in and out of consciousness, so I addressed Nelson and Digby. "It appears your punishment will have to wait, but don't worry. I'll be back."

After slamming and locking the door to the brig, I ascended the stairs two at a time, reluctantly fleeing into the light.

XI. THE UNSEEN
Cedric

The main deck was absolute chaos, but not at all for the reasons I'd been expecting.

Incoherent shouting assaulted my ears as men sprinted to and fro. Screams of terror intermingled with the handful of crewmen attempting to take control without a clear leader. Nothing significant was getting accomplished, and I still couldn't tell what the fuck had even happened. Unsure whether the ship would tilt again, I made certain I had a firm grip on the nearest railing before assessing the weather. It was lightly drizzling but not full-on storming. Clouds completely obstructed the sun, and thunder rolled softly in the distance, but judging by the still-calm winds, we had a while before the storm would reach us, if at all. The ocean was agitated, but it shouldn't be anything *The Jolly Serpent* couldn't handle with relative ease; she was a man-o'-war, after all. So what the hells had tilted us so severely not once, but twice?

There was one person I had yet to spot among the disaster happening in slow motion before me. "Elvira!" I cupped my hand over my mouth in an attempt to help my shout carry, but my voice was quickly swallowed among the rapidly spreading panic. In the short time I'd been on deck, even more of the men appeared to have seen a ghost, and I was beginning to wonder if they were aware of something I simply wasn't.

I shouted my sister's name a few more times, and not only was it useless, but I still hadn't glimpsed a single flash of that telltale blonde hair. It seemed I'd only get answers by questioning a member of the crew. I reached for the nearest man, snatching him by the shoulder with my hook. Without releasing my grip on the railing, I yanked him toward me, ignoring his yelp of pain as metal pierced the skin near his collarbone.

"What the fuck is going on?"

It was several moments before Hudson's gaze fixated on me, and when it did, all the remaining color left his face. He raised a quivering finger, pointing at my face and chest. "A-are ye a-all r-right, Captain?"

I'd forgotten I was covered in blood. "Fine. Answer the damn question."

"W-we don't kn-know," Hudson stammered, not looking the

least bit reassured by my own answer. "Some mmen swear it's the squid, others claim it was the d-dragon."

"The squid… or the *dragon*?"

"But n-no one's s-seen either," he added, as if that cleared everything up. "So we don't know for sure."

I cursed so vehemently that Hudson flinched. "Where is my sister?"

"E-Elvira? Haven't noticed 'er."

Useless. Fucking useless, all of them. Calypso had warned me of the monsters that lurked in these waters, of course, but if one of them was the cause of our current predicament, surely the crew would be able to decide which one; it wasn't as if the beasts were subtle. I shoved Hudson away with a growl, ripping my hook from his flesh without gentleness or mercy before continuing my way across the deck, not daring to let go of the railing for even a single stride. Keeping my knees bent, I ensured my center of gravity remained low, prepared for the ship to slip out from beneath me at any moment.

I'd given up on spotting Elvira and instead began searching for the second best thing: Mr. Smee's bright red hat. It took another moment for me to spot it, but when I did, the crimson fabric was difficult to fixate upon given the unnerving way it flopped about like a dying fish. Another five seconds and I realized Smee was waving his hat around in what looked to be a signal, but what in hells he was trying to communicate—and to whom—was anyone's guess.

"Mr. Smee!" We were closer now than we were before, but there was too much chaos between us for him to clearly hear me. He glanced up, but not in my direction, and I gritted my teeth before trying again.

"*Sam—*"

The ship rocked a third time, jarring and sudden, and despite my best efforts, my legs slipped out from under me. My side of the vessel lifted while the other half tilted down, and the angle was so severe that for a moment, I wondered if we might capsize. Tightening my grip on the rail, I somehow managed to keep hold of the slippery wooden surface even as the shoulder forced to bear my weight felt as though it might rip from its socket. Blood pooled in my mouth from where I'd bitten my tongue, but I used the discomfort as an anchor, refusing to allow my battered body to slide across the deck as so many were around me. Screams assaulted my ears, swiftly followed by sickening *cracks* and *slaps* as flesh and limbs alike struck various obstacles; the masts, the cannons and crates which had yet to come undone, the hull itself. I wasn't in a position to see them, but I swore there was also the sound of bodies tumbling into the ocean, and with the way this ship was rocking, the poor souls the sea had claimed were likely never to be seen again.

"Adais have mercy," I whispered as *The Jolly Serpent* righted herself, crashing against the waves with a force that rattled me to my core. A paralyzing fear seized my chest, and for a moment I stood frozen, unable to so much as breathe as I came to terms with my current reality. I'd spent my entire life aboard ships of every size and type, had presumed I'd experienced everything there was to encounter while at sea, but never once had I gone through anything resembling this. How could we save ourselves from something we couldn't even see? I now understood and empathized with the panic and chaos unfolding around me, and even felt a strong urge to partake in it, but more than any of them, I couldn't afford to lose my head. Not if I wanted us to live.

But what could be done; what could I do? We were either battling the oddest storm I'd ever encountered, or Hudson had spoken true, and a monster was responsible for our plight. I supposed it made sense that one could be thrashing about in the waters below, tilting the ship and agitating the waves in a way that had nothing to do with the storm, but how in hells that could be remedied remained lost on me.

I was still deep in thought when another chorus of screams rose up, but as far as I could tell, the ship wasn't rocking—at least no more than it had to be in order to balance us atop increasingly agitated waters. Whipping my head in the voices' direction, it immediately became apparent why the men were newly distressed: not only had a cannon come loose from its restraints, it had rolled halfway across the deck to land on some poor soul's lower half. I couldn't see his face, but his howls of agony were more than enough to inform me some part of him had been crushed… as was the blood pooling in alarming amounts beneath his body.

Crossing the distance in a few hurried strides, without hesitation, I knelt at the cannon's side. There was no way I'd be able to lift it from the crewman completely, especially with only one functional hand, but I braced both arms beneath the base and heaved nonetheless. My shoulders screamed in protest, and I gritted my teeth from the strain of it, but I wasn't on my own for long. Within seconds, a man appeared on either side of me, joined by at least two more on the opposite side of the cannon.

Our combined strength was just enough to lift the half that had our crewmate trapped, and only then did I realize his leg had been shattered and partially pierced by one of the wheels. Blood actively spurted from the gruesome wound, splattering all over our worried faces. If it was the femoral artery that had been severed, this was a far more urgent scenario than I'd originally thought.

But the man couldn't be freed—not yet. Two more men were trying and failing to yank him to safety while a third searched frantically for where and however else he could still be caught. What none of them seemed to realize was they'd be freeing a corpse if we didn't stop the man from bleeding out in front of us.

"Someone get that leg a tourniquet!" I had no idea to whom I was speaking; I couldn't move my head from its current position pressed against the cannon's side. "Tie it off above where he's bleeding."

I had to repeat myself before someone obeyed, but once they did, the blood flow slowed significantly. He remained trapped, though, and the longer we sat there like fools, the more worried I became that the ship would tilt yet again. If the cannon's weight were to shift even slightly, it could not only kill the man we were working so hard to save, it could take any number of us along with it.

"It's his foot!" someone finally exclaimed—Smee. I hadn't the slightest idea when or how he'd gotten here, but I'd never been more grateful for his uncanny ability to remain calm even in the most stressful of scenarios. "You there, lift a bit higher, yes, there!"

The men in question scrambled to obey, and gods, it fucking worked. I half laughed, half sobbed when the victim was pulled several precious inches to freedom. Just a little farther, and—

Yet another shuddering jolt took us all by surprise. It wasn't a full-on tilt, but the cannon slipped from my arms regardless, beginning to inch backward and toward the gunport from which it came. The men in its path caught and stopped it, but only barely, and it was clear from their cries they wouldn't be able to hold it for long. Heart pounding, I scrambled to my feet and darted around to assess the situation, but it seemed to be good news. Not only had the trapped man been completely freed, no one besides those who held it remained in the cannon's chosen path. If it kept heading in that direction, there was a good chance it might fall overboard, but losing a cannon was far better than losing human beings.

Positioning myself among them, I braced my back against the cannon's side before nodding to my companions. "Go—get out of here! I'll slow it down."

The man to my right threw me a look of surprise. "But Captain—"

"Just go!"

Hesitantly, they abandoned me one by one, leaving me the sole obstacle between the cannon and the sea. Though I wasn't bearing anywhere near the cannon's full weight—*The Jolly Serpent* had more or less leveled out, for now—there was no way I could remain where I was for long. I'd need to be strategic regarding when and how I darted, light and quick on my feet, like... Well, like Elvira.

Gods, where the hells was she? The thought had been a fleeting one, but part of me had wondered if whoever Smee had been signaling with his hat could have possibly been my sister, but he was nowhere near close enough for me to ask him now. I was alone, and I may well be dead if I didn't move soon. Tensing my legs, I shifted my weight forward and was preparing to leap to the side when I heard it.

"Ced?" The smallest of whispers cut cleanly through my racing thoughts, spoken by a voice that made my heart stop.

Elvira.

I looked straight ahead. Drenched, quivering, dangling from the side of the ship and clinging to the empty gunport for dear life was my sister. Her wide, terrified gaze communicated everything already plain for me to see. I couldn't let go of the cannon, not even for the time it would take to pull her to safety. If I tried, I could just as easily get us both crushed if the cannon were to fall. But her white-knuckled grip was slipping, she was weak, and having no idea how long she'd already been hanging there, I didn't know how much longer she could hold on.

My blood ran cold as I stared at her, and a single fear became all-consuming. Was I about to watch my sister die?

"Hold on. Just hold on." Words tumbled from my lips, but as useless and empty as they were, I couldn't stop. They were a plea far more than an order, because of all the people I had to lose, I didn't want Elvira to be one of them. She couldn't be one of them. She'd been part of my life longer than anyone else, by my side even longer than Scarlett; losing my sister would mean losing part of myself, a part I'd never have any hope of getting back.

As if she read my thoughts, Elvira nodded, and the simple gesture was enough for logic to seize control of my panicked mind. Help. We needed help, and fast, but who would hear either of us if we screamed? We were too far removed from the rest of the crew, and they'd paid me no mind even when I'd been standing among them, shouting at the top of my lungs.

But maybe that was it... I didn't need to shout. Some faraway part of my mind recalled what Calypso's note had said: *Let me know if you need me. You need only whisper.*

With my next breath, I did just that. "Calypso—can you hear me? Please, help us. Help Elvira." So much was still happening around us that hearing my own whispered words was impossible, but I didn't care how ridiculous it looked or sounded. To save Elvira, I'd do anything.

It was another handful of breaths before anything happened, but suddenly, there she was. I caught only a glimpse of Calypso's billowing dress before she knelt at the gunport. Seizing each of Elvira's wrists, in an impressive feat of strength, she heaved, pulling my sister back aboard in a single yank. If anything, it was a bit too overzealous; the women went careening backward, landing in a tangled heap of limbs and skirts.

Elvira got back on her feet almost immediately, hissing something I couldn't understand—not because I was distracted, but because Calypso's voice was *in my fucking head.*

Move away from that cannon, Cedric Teach, and get your sister out of here.

My body obeyed before my mind could decide whether or not I'd imagined the nymph's unspoken command. Abandoning the cannon, I darted to my left, purposefully crashing into Elvira on my mission to get us both as far from that damned gunport as possible, then dragged her along until we were a good few meters away from what could have been my sister's demise. Slipping one arm around her waist and hooking my prosthetic firmly to the hull, I braced us for yet another tilt before turning back toward Calypso. I opened my mouth in a silent cry, for the sight before me wasn't at all what I had been expecting.

The nymph stood perched atop the rail, perfectly balanced despite the waves thrashing beneath us. Both her hair and dress whipped violently around her lithe form, but the chaos of it suited her, somehow; had the circumstances been any different, I may have once again found myself entranced by Calypso's ethereal beauty. But I couldn't shake the thought that she may be about to jump—was that why she'd ordered me to get away? So I couldn't stop her?

Finding my voice, I screamed her name, but Calypso's only response was to raise her chin and smile at the sea. She brought both her arms to shoulder level before her lips began moving in what appeared to be some sort of chant, though I was too far away to make out her words. On and on she went, gradually lifting her arms higher and higher, until her head tilted so far back I wondered if she might bend over backwards. But her stance remained as sure as her footing, and after about a minute, there was a visible shift in the waters surrounding us. The waves went from turbulent and unpredictable to smooth and relatively still, nearly immobile by the time Calypso's form slumped and she actually did go careening backwards, crumpling into a limp heap on the still-bloody deck.

It was difficult to tell if the world had at last gone truly silent or if it was simply a result of my own blood roaring in my ears. I vaguely registered Elvira saying my name as I made my way over to Calypso, both hurried and slow all at once given that I was terrified over what I might discover. What had just happened… and what had been the price?

I knelt beside the nymph before taking her in my arms. She stirred then, dark eyes fluttering open for a fraction of a second before closing once again. A chuckle escaped her. "Cedric Teach, did I have you worried?"

Of course she did, but I wouldn't dare admit that aloud. "What just happened?" I kept my voice low while it was only the two of us. "What did you do?"

Calypso waved her hand lazily. "Child of Adais, remember? Ceto isn't the only one who can manipulate the sea."

Shock rippled through me. "And you waited until now to—"

"Because this is what it does to me," Calypso finished, opening her eyes to glare up at me. She gestured to her battered body, quivering and still mostly limp. "And just because I *can* do it doesn't mean I'd like to make a habit of it. You know, just as your sister ought to make more of an effort not to fucking drown."

"Me?" Elvira's indignant screech was so high-pitched it caused me to wince. She stomped toward us, coming to stop at my back. "Are you saying this is my fault?"

"I'm saying you're far too experienced of a quartermaster and a sailor to let the crew's panic get so out of hand. That man is dead because of your carelessness."

The three of us glanced to where the rest of the crew had gathered, around the man we'd worked so hard to free from the wayward cannon. I still couldn't make out his face, but the copious amounts of blood pooling around his broken body were telling enough. "Who is it?" I asked.

Elvira ignored me. "In case you haven't noticed, Silvertongue, not all of us have sea magic. What would you have had me do?"

"I wouldn't have you here at all!" Shoving my arms away, Calypso forced herself upright, meeting my gaze before turning back to Elvira. "I warned both of you that she shouldn't be here, and that there would be a price for thinking you know better than the gods. If you think this pays it, think again—this is only the beginning of your suffering."

"Says who?" Elvira sneered. "You? The little nymph wh—"

"Elvira," I said, my voice a low growl. "She just saved your life. Be very careful what you say next."

My sister drew a series of audible huffs but stalked away rather than argue further. Calypso rose a moment later, waving away my attempts to help her steady herself. "Don't you have a crew to worry about?" she asked, her tone clearly dismissive.

"Yes, but are you all right? Is Wendy?"

Calypso nodded. "She's probably awake now, but that hammock should have kept her from tumbling anywhere."

"That doesn't answer my other question."

She sighed. "Just go, Cedric Teach. We have plenty to discuss later."

I'd have probably pressed her further if I wasn't worried she'd start asking me about my dream, so I forced myself to turn away, fixating instead upon the men still gathered around our fallen comrade. Pushing my way through the crowd, I trailed my gaze up the corpse's body, over his shattered leg and sunken-in chest, coming to rest on his pale face… his young pale face, framed by wild mousy curls.

For a harrowing moment, I mistook him for Pan, but it wasn't Wendy's friend: it was Wylan. One of our youngest, yet most promising hands, made to die a gruesome death I wouldn't wish upon anyone other than the fucking bastards still chained in my brig. Calypso may have declared Elvira the one at fault, but I knew the truth—Wylan's death was on my selfish hands, only the first of many more men I'd lead to slaughter before all this was over, all in the name of finding Scarlett.

At the thought of her, that ever-present ache in my chest swelled. Gods, I needed to hit something, and I needed to hit something now, but thankfully I had the perfect outlet strung up and waiting for me.

The trek back to the brig was a blur, and I was breathless by the time I yanked open its metal door. Two terrified faces greeted me; the third was too quiet, too still, and I frowned. Alder had bled out. A shame that I hadn't been there to watch the light leave his eyes, but I still had Nelson and Digby. I raised my hook and gave each of them a beaming, twisted smile.

"Now, where were we?"

XII. THE DANCE

Featured Song: Storm Dance

Wendy

The urge to stab my father grew more overwhelming every day. To my meager credit, no one noticed the violence and irritation festering within me; no one *noticed me*, period, especially given how much of the past week I'd spent unconscious. It was business as usual as far as the crew were concerned, and I'd never seen *The Jolly Serpent* run smoother or more efficiently. Cleanup and repairs following the strange disturbance I'm told claimed Wylan's life had taken less than a day. We hadn't encountered any more monsters or obstacles to speak of and were making such good time that the boatswain, Hector, kept proudly declaring that we were ahead of schedule to anyone willing to listen. Even the goddamn weather appeared to be on Captain Hook's side. Other than the night of his return, it hadn't stormed once. There had been nothing but clear skies and strong winds, more often than not in our favor, making navigation an absolute breeze. I should be happy—thrilled, even.

But I'd never been more pissed off in my short life, especially at *him*. Hook had tried to approach me a handful of times, probably to make some half-assed apology, but I hadn't let him anywhere near me. How anyone could stand the man was far beyond my comprehension, and indeed, many of the crew couldn't. Hook clearly relied on fear and intimidation as his main leadership tactics, and that alone didn't make him popular. But there was far more buried beneath the surface, traits no one could ignore. Hook was confident, efficient, and knew how to run a ship. He didn't hesitate, didn't waver, and he certainly didn't cry or have nightmares so vivid they plagued his waking hours. He didn't snap or crack under pressure, and he wasn't so sensitive to magic it felt like he was slowly drowning and suffocating all at once. He didn't act like *me*.

Despite how much I loathed him, not even I was immune to Hook's undeniable charm. Those who weren't afraid—Elvira and Calypso, mainly, but also a handful of veteran crewmen—lit up when they saw him, and Hook was different around them, too. He spoke calmly, sought their counsel, and generally acted like a respectful, even likable human being. There was a mutual trust within his inner circle that had obviously been built over many years, possibly even decades, and witnessing it was nothing short of fascinating given that I'd tried and failed to do that very thing in my short time as captain. The more I observed such interactions, the harder it became to hate him.

But you do still hate him, I reminded myself, deepening the glare directed toward my father for good measure. He and Calypso stood on the upper deck, muttering words I couldn't make out in between watching what everyone else was watching: Elvira and Peter sparring on the lower deck, a display that had become a common occurrence over the past week. Not only had Peter become restless after several days spent by my side, but after what Hook had done to Pierce, none of the rest of the crew had dared to so much as touch Peter, even if only to spar. Elvira proved the perfect solution, for not only was she just as restless, she was his match and more… at least, she usually was. Peter had been fighting abysmally today, having already fallen prey to multiple blows he normally would have dodged or parried with ease.

No sooner had the thought crossed my mind did he grunt as Elvira elbowed him roughly in the stomach. Doubling over, he brought one arm to his chest while the other shot out to grip a nearby crate. Tink, who had been sitting on my shoulder, buzzed her wings in irritation. "That was a cheap shot," she muttered, but I just shrugged.

"Kaara isn't going to play fair, so neither should Elvira."

"See? Wendy gets it." Only when Elvira spread her arms in mock triumph did I realize she'd been standing within earshot of me and Tink. "Are we finished for the day, boy? Or are you in

215

need of yet another nap?"

Brushing his too-long hair from his face, Peter lifted his head just enough to shoot her a murderous glare. "No. Again," he insisted, but his tone betrayed his exhaustion, prompting me to sit up a bit straighter on the barrel I occupied. For the past two days, something had been off with him. He hadn't been sleeping well, he'd complained of headaches, had been far more irritable than usual, and he'd even gotten seasick this morning. I'd tried to talk to him about it, or at least attempt to convince him that maybe he shouldn't train today, but he'd stormed off before me or Tink could so much as ask him if he was all right.

Elvira, though, wasn't buying Peter's obvious lie. She clicked her tongue before waving her hand dismissively. "You look ready to keel over, and that's hardly the challenge I need to keep my skills sharp."

Tink breathed an audible sigh of relief, but before I could call Peter over to join us, Elvira's voice boomed so loudly it made me flinch. She tossed her head, grinned wickedly, and pranced across the deck, all the while twirling a knife between her fingers. "It seems I'm in need of a new sparring partner. Any takers?"

She may as well have asked for the captain's head on a spike. Any man still watching averted his gaze, and a few even hastily returned to their work.

Elvira spat on the deck before seething, "Cowards. You know, it's days like these I'm embarrassed to call the lot of you crewmates."

"I hope that doesn't include me, Elvira."

Hook hadn't raised his voice in the slightest, but the deck had fallen silent nonetheless. He ambled down the stairs, shedding his jacket as he walked, and faced his sister with nothing more than a thin linen shirt covering his well-muscled torso. He rolled up his sleeves, exposing at least a dozen scars I'd never glimpsed before, and cocked his head in a silent challenge.

Elvira narrowed her gaze, looking unimpressed as ever. "That remains to be seen."

"I've touched a nerve. Good."

"You've gotten on my nerves since the moment Father fucked you into existence."

Hook half-laughed, half-scoffed. "Keep talking like that and I'll kick your ass more than I was already planning to."

"Keep stalling and I'll skin yours."

Even Hook stilled at that, and the smirk vanished from his features. Recovering quickly, he asked, "It's to be blades, then?" He gestured to the knife at her side. "Fists might be, ah, cleaner."

"What, are you scared?" If I hadn't been sitting so close, I may not have been able to make out Elvira's icy whisper. Something feral flashed in her eyes, but it was gone when she blinked. "It's not like it matters. Whichever one we choose, you're at an advantage with your hook."

"I won't use it, then," Hook said before she'd finished speaking, and my eyes widened; was he about to offer to take it off? Did that damned hook even come off? But before I could picture what he might look like without it, he snatched a coil of rope from a nearby stack of crates and offered it to his sister. "Tie it behind my back."

Elvira raised an eyebrow. "You're sure?"

"Positive."

A few minutes later, brother and sister stood inches apart. Hook's right arm had been secured exactly as he had offered, and from the way he'd gritted his teeth as Elvira yanked the knots, the rope didn't have the slightest bit of give. Each sibling had been armed with a supposedly blunted sword, but I had no doubts it would keep either of them from drawing blood—especially Elvira. The memory of her sinking those sharpened teeth into a man's hand the day we'd met flashed briefly in my mind's eye.

Mr. Smee must have had similar images filtering through his brain, for he approached the pair cautiously. Ample space had been cleared for what was obviously going to be more than a simple spar, and word regarding Hook's challenge had quickly spread; any man who wasn't absolutely required at his post had gathered around to watch. Peter had squeezed onto the barrel beside me, and if we were pressed any closer together, I'd be forced to climb into his lap. It made for an easy bridge for Tink, though, and she crawled from my shoulder and onto Peter's with ease.

"My money's on Hook," Peter said, practically vibrating with excitement. "Elvira is damned good, but she's been training with me all afternoon, and he's fresh."

"I don't know." I spoke without turning my head, unable to take my eyes off the formidable pair. At a casual glance, Hook and Elvira didn't look related, let alone like siblings. His short hair was dark and coarse where hers was blonde and wispy, cropped to a length that barely reached her shoulders. But when sized up to one another, there could be no doubt they were both children of Blackbeard; though Hook had a good six inches on his sister, they had identical profiles, identical unhinged gleams in their eyes. They even settled into similar stances despite needing to hold their weights differently. But there was something about Elvira's focus in particular that was making my skin crawl. Where Hook's movements were calculated, hers were predatory in a way that suggested she had no plans to lose this fight. "You heard the way she threatened him. I think she meant it."

Peter scoffed dismissively. "She always means it."

I opened my mouth to argue but shut it when Smee began rattling off the rules. "The first to disarm his or her opponent win—"

"No." Elvira didn't take her eyes off her brother. "Disarmed or not, the first to surrender loses."

Hook narrowed his gaze, hesitating briefly before nodding. "Fine."

"There is to be no intentional drawing of blood, nor unnecessary roughness—" Smee continued, but Elvira cut him off a second time.

"I'd think the captain of a vessel as fine as this should be able to handle a punch or two. Wouldn't you agree, Ced?"

For a moment, I thought Hook might fall into the trap Elvira had clearly laid for him. He set his jaw before opening his mouth, but shut it just as quickly, conceding with yet another dip of his head.

Elvira's devilish smirk confirmed my suspicions. The goal hadn't been to get her brother to snap back, rather to worm beneath his skin, angering or unsettling him enough to throw off his focus. Judging from the look on Hook's face, she'd succeeded at both. "Well then, that should cover it, don't you think?" She glanced innocently at Smee. "Whoever surrenders first loses, and roughness is permitted."

"Y-yes," he stammered, red hat bobbing as he nodded. "S-so if b-both parties are read—*ah*!"

It was impossible to tell which of the siblings moved first. They met in a violent clash of steel, only narrowly missing poor Smee as they twisted around, effectively reversing where they'd stood only a moment before. Staggering back before their blades could lock, they each took a moment to catch their breath. With only one arm to steady himself, Hook wobbled for a fraction of a second, and Elvira cackled.

"At least Pan had no trouble staying on his feet!"

"It's true," Peter sniggered, but I barely heard him over the ringing of swords as they met once again. Though he may have gotten off to a sloppy start, Hook found his rhythm quickly, and just in time; Elvira had never lost hers. She immediately went on the offensive, and her blows were as relentless as they were precise. In quick succession, she went for his gut, heart, and even his throat, but Hook blocked each with practiced ease. Despite myself, I sat up a bit straighter so I might get a better view. I hadn't watched my father fight since he'd dueled Peter at the tomb, and though I'd never admit it aloud, his skill impressed me as much now as it had then. It got me wondering…

"Was he always left handed?" I asked Peter before I could rein in my curiosity. "You know, before you—"

"Before I cut it off?" Peter flashed me a grin. "No. He had to learn to fight all over again. Honestly, though? He's just as good as he was before, ever since he got the hang of it. And it's not as if he's afraid to use that damn hook."

He was right about that much; even through all the parrying and whirling, each time Hook's back was to me, I noted his right arm straining against its bonds. But Elvira's knots held firm, rendering the limb useless and seemingly putting Hook at a clear disadvantage. He'd spent the entirety of the match simply blocking or dodging Elvira's attacks and had yet to attempt one of his own.

I wasn't the only one who noticed. Elvira laughed between blows, driving Hook farther and farther into a corner, presumably where she planned to pummel him until he surrendered. "It seems I was mistaken in hoping our dear captain would pose more of a challenge. You're rust—"

Her taunt turned to a grunt as Hook finally caught her in a trap of his own. Taking advantage of one of Elvira's particularly overconfident thrusts, he locked their blades together before yanking, effectively pulling her off balance. In the time it took her to stabilize herself, he'd slipped past her, very nearly clipping her shoulder in the process.

"Rusty?" Hook feinted at Elvira's left side before jabbing at her right, landing a blow to her upper arm and smirking when she hissed. "Or did you simply underestimate me?"

She glowered. "I of all people know far better."

If I thought they moved quickly before, it was nothing compared to how they moved after that. Brother and sister became a whirlwind, slashing and hacking without mercy. They used the entirety of the space allotted to them, never remaining in one spot for too long, and always hypervigilant of their surroundings. There were no more close calls; the pair were true equals, despite having different strengths, and knew precisely how to use them to their advantage all while concealing their weaknesses. Elvira was light on her feet and quick as a viper, while Hook never let his guard down, not even for a moment. Narrowing his eyes into dark, almost black, slits, he never missed an opportunity for an opening, and only failed to block a small handful of Elvira's blows.

Before long, they settled into what looked quite like a dance. It was difficult to tell with how quickly they were twisting and whirling, but I swore I saw smirks decorating both their faces; they were *enjoying* this, and they weren't the only ones. The men began roaring their encouragement, chanting the name of their ideal victor, and it seemed to be an even split down the middle. Even I began to doubt which of the siblings might win. The way this was going, we were likely to be here all night.

I turned to Peter to point out as much, and that's the precise moment a high-pitched shriek pierced the air. Whipping my head back around, my gaze landed on Elvira as she staggered back a few steps, flicking her free wrist and scrunching up her face in a grimace. "Fuck, Ced, be careful! Nearly broke my damn fingers!"

His focus immediately shattered. Blinking, he lowered his blade. "Shit, I'm sorry. Are you—"

Elvira lashed out so fast I almost didn't see her move. Ducking into a crouch, she spun and kicked, knocking her brother's legs out from beneath him. Hook fell on his ass with a dull *thud*, and I felt the residual vibrations even from where I sat. Before he'd recovered from the shock of it, Elvira stood, straightened, and dug the point of her dulled sword into her brother's throat.

"So I was right." She spoke so softly I almost couldn't make out her words. "All it takes to get your attention is a pretty woman crying wolf."

Hook clenched his jaw. "'Pretty?' Not the word I'd use."

She cackled at that. "Don't pretend for one second you wouldn't fuck me if I weren't your sister. Shall I flash my tits next?"

"*Elvira.*"

"What?" She glared, clearly unfazed by the warning in his tone. "If you want me to shut up, make me."

With a snarl, Hook brought his blade up to meet hers, but given both his position and the fact that he only had use of one arm, Elvira parried the blow with ease. She jabbed and twisted, and in a handful of practiced movements, had disarmed her brother. When his sword clattered to the deck, she flashed him a devilish smile but didn't remove her weapon from his neck.

"Give up?"

"No," Hook hissed. Forgetting the blades were dulled for a split second, I gasped when he closed his fist around Elvira's sword. With a savage yank, he ripped it from her grasp before tossing it aside; it seemed Elvira wasn't willing to fall prey to the balance trick a second time. He staggered to his feet then, and the now-weaponless siblings began circling one another, each silent footstep deliberate and calculated. "Not until you've told me what your problem is."

"My problem?" Elvira's nostrils flared. "No, you hijo de perra, *you* have the problem, and it's between your fucking legs."

"Oh shit," Peter said under his breath. "She only slips into Spanish when she's pissed."

I didn't have time to ask him how he knew that. Elvira rattled off something else, but before she could finish, Hook took a swing at her. She ducked before landing a punch of her own; though Hook grunted, the pain only seemed to fuel him. They exchanged a handful of blows before full out tackling one another, slamming onto the deck in a chaotic flurry of kicks, punches, and even bites. The sheer savagery of it made their sword fight look like child's play. It lasted for a few tense minutes in which no one seemed to know what to do. The crew's chanting had long since died down, having now turned to stunned silence, but no one dared interrupt their captain and quartermaster. Though Hook fought like hell, his one arm proved no match for Elvira's two, and it wasn't long before she had him pinned. Perched on his back, she held his free arm in a death grip, twisting the limb at such a brutal angle that he cried out in pain.

"Eres tan cabeza dura que no necesitas a nadie," Elvira spat. "¡Puedes solo con el mundo!"

"English, dammit," Hook said through a grimace, but she ignored him to rattle off something else in Spanish, a phrase delivered with such venom that I could only assume it was far worse than whatever she'd uttered previously.

"Elvira!" It took a moment to recognize Calypso's voice. In a single soundless leap, the nymph jumped from the upper deck onto the lower one, taking a few cautious steps toward the pair. "You're going to break his arm. Let him go."

Elvira glanced at the nymph, curled her lip, and turned her focus back to Hook. "Ríndete," she said before repeating herself in English. "Surrender."

His expression remained contorted in agony, but he didn't utter a word.

"Give up, brother. Last chance."

Silence.

"Fine," Elvira whispered, almost imperceptibly soft.

I didn't quite believe my own eyes when she released his arm only to wrap both hands around Hook's throat, and I was far from the only one. Shock crossed my father's face as she began to squeeze. He made a few feeble attempts to claw at her grip, but it was far too late; Elvira's hold was too strong, too fueled by pent-up frustration and rage.

It suddenly felt as though I was the one being suffocated. I'd spent every bit of my free time over the past week imagining all the ways in which I might stick a knife between Hook's ribs, but watching the life leave him right before my eyes was a different thing entirely. There wasn't time to dwell on what I actually wanted or why; I didn't recall giving my legs the order to move, but I was on my feet regardless, and halfway to Hook when a dark, blurry shape came hurtling toward Elvira. It hit her so hard that she went flying back several feet before crumpling against the rail, slumped over with her blonde hair shielding her face.

I stopped in my tracks to take in the scene before me. Hook was a sputtering, gasping mess, Elvira lifted her head to reveal a bloodied lip, and Calypso stood between my father and aunt. I swore the sea swelled when the nymph spoke, with each of her icy words directed at Elvira.

"That's enough."

I'd seen Elvira angry, and I'd even seen her unhinged, but I'd never seen her quite like this. I couldn't tell whether she was about to laugh, cry, or throw herself at Calypso. But Elvira did none of those things; chest heaving, she held the nymph's gaze as she licked the blood from her lower lip. "You seriously think I'd have killed him?"

"What was I supposed to think?" Calypso fired back.

"That I was adhering to the terms he agreed to!"

"The ones you baited him into? They were brutal and unnecessary, and you know it."

"I know perfectly well what he can take. He's *my* brother."

"That didn't stop you from murdering your other brothers. Why is Cedric any different?"

Elvira visibly tensed. "Careful, Silvertongue. I wouldn't speak on things you know nothing about."

"I know plenty. I've seen plenty."

"You've seen nothing." Using the rail for support, Elvira managed to pull herself to her feet. "But I'd certainly be happy to show you."

Hook snapped Elvira's name, his authoritative tone causing both women to flinch. He untied the rope around his waist, freeing his hook, but remained seated on the deck in the same spot where Elvira had tackled him. His hand lingered at his throat, and his voice was slightly hoarse when he spoke again. "Stand down."

"No," Elvira said, eliciting shocked murmurs from the crew. "You and I weren't finished. If Silvertongue here is willing to continue in your place, it may just preserve the only sliver of dignity you have left." Whipping a dagger from her belt, she took a few predatory steps toward an unwavering Calypso.

Hook shot up quicker than I would have thought possible, and though he wobbled a bit, he found his balance quickly. Snatching Calypso's wrist, he pulled her behind him, effectively placing himself back in the path of his murderous sister. "Stand *down*. I won't say it again."

Elvira stilled, tightening her grip on her blade. "That's it, then? You choose her?"

"I don't know what the fuck you're—"

Spinning on her heel, Elvira threw up her hands and muttered what I could only assume were curses in Spanish before switching back to English. "A lifetime I've been at your side. A lifetime I've defended you. Risked everything for you—my pride, my birthright, and even my life. All for the 'last born, least wanted,' the filthy Crow, the—"

"Don't you dare," Hook whispered, but Elvira looked him directly in the eyes and did just that.

227

"Malparido."

I had no idea what the word meant, but judging from Hook's reaction, Elvira's utterance of it wouldn't be easily—if ever—forgiven. He drew an audible inhale before stumbling back into Calypso's waiting arms, the expression on his face more wounded than I'd ever seen him, and he wasn't the only one. Elvira snapped her mouth shut, bringing a quivering hand to her mouth as a shadow crossed her face.

But before I could decide if it was regret or simply more anger, she fled below deck, and no one heard or saw any trace of the Serpent for the rest of the afternoon.

It finally stormed later that night. Rain pelted the deck with such force that I had originally been convinced it was hail, and *The Jolly Serpent* was back to tossing and turning as she battled turbulent and choppy waters. That was the worst of it, though; there was thunder and a bit of lightning, but it remained on the horizon, and the winds weren't strong enough to warrant furling the sails. Further sheltering us was Calypso's magic. For two hours now, she'd stood at the prow, using whatever abilities she possessed to keep the waves subdued— or so she'd claimed. I suspected her use of magic was less to do with actual necessity and far more to do with putting as much distance between herself and Elvira as possible.

They weren't the only ones avoiding each other. Hook had locked himself in his cabin shortly after his sister's outburst and had yet to reemerge. I hadn't seen Peter or Tink since then, either, and could only hope that wherever they were, he was at least confiding in the fairy given that he clearly didn't want to talk to me.

The crew, at least, seemed oblivious to all the tension. Only a handful of men were needed above deck, so the rest gathered below, more than content to drink and dance the night away. Having strung up the hammocks, their quarters had been converted into a space that rather resembled a tavern. A small group of musicians played against the far wall, led by Smee on the fiddle, while an intense game of cards took place on the opposite side of the room. Those who weren't dancing or watching the match were either engrossed in personal conversations or listening to Mr. Gibbs recite what sounded like a ghost story. I'd walked in partway through so had missed the beginning.

"...always searching for the perfect voice, one capable of seducing the Sea God as she once did. 'Tis why there's so few female bards. They're afraid that if they sing too prettily or loudly, Kaara will hear and take their voice for herself."

"But how?" Hector piped up. "A voice can't be stolen. It can't be touched or snatched."

Mr. Gibbs nodded. "Aye, not by humans. But Kaara can pluck a voice straight from a lady's throat, swallow it, and use it for herself. It leaves them with a terrible itch, I'm told, but they don't suffer—not if they're near the ocean. Kaara sics her flesh-eating sirens on them before they can so much as open their mouths in a silent scream."

229

Grimacing at such a brutal mental image, I turned my attention elsewhere, this time to the musicians. They had just wrapped up their previous piece and were beginning another. Raising his fiddle, Smee began by bowing a regular rhythm, and the rest of the group were quick to join him. The guitar strummed a joyful melody, the hand drum picked up the pace, and finally, the whistler began playing the main tune. Their piece was quick and lively, and it wasn't long before another handful of men began clapping and dancing along. The sight was enough to bring a faint smile to my lips, and I'd only just begun to tap my feet in time when faint light flashed out of the corner of my eye.

I turned my head just in time to see Tink take a tumble mid-flight. Darting forward, I cupped my hands and caught her, but not without banging my still-sore knees against the harsh wooden floor. Muttering a curse, I shot her a glare. "Didn't Peter warn you not to waste your energy on fly..." My voice trailed off at the pained expression on Tink's small face. "What's wrong?"

"Peter," she sniffed, and only then did I realize she was crying. "Something's wrong, very wrong. But he won't let me near him. He sealed off our bond and locked himself in his room and won't come out! I'm so scared. He's never shut me out like this, not once in all the decades we've been together."

I forced myself to remain calm, at least outwardly. "Is he still feeling sick? Has he gotten any worse since this afternoon?"

"He was complaining of stomach pains, but it didn't sound like anything serious, and he seemed to think sleeping it off would help. He laid down and I joined him, but the next thing I knew, he was shouting and cursing at me to get out." Tink shuddered. "He's never shouted at me, Wendy."

My heart threatened to beat out of my chest, but while I still had my wits, I focused on what I knew for certain where Peter's symptoms were concerned. Headaches. Trouble sleeping. Irritability. And just today, nausea and abdominal pains. My free hand wandered to my own chest out of instinct, settling on my lower belly, tracing the scars left from where I'd stabbed myself and taken my own life. The memory summoned Peter's earlier declaration, loud and clear as ever: *If I'm doomed to live in this body, then I don't want to live at all.*

Ice flooded through my veins, because suddenly, I understood *everything*.

With Tink cupped safely in my hands, I picked myself off the floor, fled the party, and sprinted for my friend.

XIII. THE BASTARD

Cedric

Malparido.

I wasn't sure which hurt more—the insult itself or that, of all people, my sister had been the one to say it. The two wounds combined had already festered, and nothing had been able to ease the ache in my chest. Not rum, not pacing around my quarters like a caged animal, and certainly not Scarlett's staring. The logical part of me knew her portrait remained as static as ever, but the emotional part was convinced her bright eyes had narrowed in disapproval. It was no great surprise. She never liked it when I drank.

"What?" I spread my arms in a mock challenge. I'd removed my hook—had thrown it across the room, more accurately—so only had one functional limb with which to grip the nearly-empty bottle. "Shit hurts. I haven't been called that since… Since…"

Since Blackbeard was still alive. The man who was my father by blood but had never once acted like one. Not to me. He'd sat there and laughed, *laughed*, the first time I'd heard that damned word. A mere five years old, I had no idea what it meant at the time, but I learned quickly; it became more commonplace than my own fucking name. There wasn't a direct English translation, but the most widely agreed-upon meaning was the one that hurt the most.

Ill birthed. Or 'miscarried,' which was what Blackbeard had hoped would happen to me. His 'last born, least wanted,' his bastard, his son who couldn't—

I nearly leaped from my skin when the door swung open. No knock, no greeting, and I'd definitely locked myself in here… and there was only one person aboard this ship who had a habit of picking locks, especially mine. Barely restrained rage coursed through me, and I tightened my grip on the bottle, speaking without turning my head.

"Elvira, get the fuck out."

"It's me, Cedric Teach."

Not my sister, but still not someone I had any desire to see. I spoke over my shoulder this time, careful not to show too much of my overly emotional face. "The door was locked."

Calypso sighed. "I may look human, but for the thousandth time, I'm not. Magic, remember?"

"Whether or not it stopped you, it was intended to keep you, and everyone else, out," I snapped, not bothering to rein in my

234

temper. "I'm busy."

"Really." It was a statement rather than a question.

"Yes."

"Are you drunk?"

Probably. "No."

Calypso shook her head before taking a few steps toward me. I only knew because of the noise her wet clothes made when she moved; her footsteps were as silent as ever. "You're slurring your words, and you have a bottle in your hand. And gods, you fucking stink. Can't any of you damn pirates be bothered to take a bath every now and—"

"What do you want?" I whirled around then and was immediately irritated at how close she stood. Drenched from head to toe, her curls were plastered to her face and neck, and the way her sopping-wet dress clung to her shapely frame didn't leave anything to the imagination. Both nipples were hardened and erect, and I hated myself for how much effort it took not to reach out and squeeze them. "You didn't come here to chastise me." *And you're certainly not bathing me.*

She narrowed her dark gaze. "I came to check on you after your sister nearly killed you."

"Since when are you the ship's healer?"

"Cedric."

"I'm fine." True if she was asking only about the physical. Light bruising colored my neck, and the area was tender, but it was nothing that wouldn't heal in a matter of days. The rest of my body ached all over, but I was honestly grateful for the tangible distraction.

"That bottle says you're not."

"I'm fine, and I'd very much like to be left—"

"Sit." She gestured to my chair. "And stop lying."

I didn't have much choice but to obey. After wrestling the bottle from my hand, Calypso placed her palm on my chest, slowly guiding me to where she'd directed. My exhausted muscles protested the movement, and a groan escaped my lips the moment my sore ass touched the hard seat. She raised an eyebrow. "'Fine,' huh?"

"This is nothing." She could claim I was lying all she wanted, but this was yet another true statement. "I've been through far worse. *Survived* far worse. Aren't my scars proof enough of that?"

"And how many of them were left by her?"

She didn't need to specify for me to know that 'her' meant Elvira. "Less than you'd think." I grimaced as the pain in my chest, the gaping wound ripped open by a single word, flared once more. "But no more talk of my sister. Please."

I wasn't sure if Calypso would listen, but she fell silent for a few blessed minutes as she gave me a thorough once-over. Making note of every bruise and scrape, she used her magic to dull the worst of my pain. She lingered at my neck the longest, using her fingernails to trace the marks my sister's had left. One by one, the stinging sensations began to subside, and despite myself, I relaxed into the nymph's touch. She wasn't actually healing anything, and the marks would remain, but thanks to her I wouldn't feel any discomfort while my body mended itself.

"Well," she said once finished, seemingly unable to draw out my inspection any longer, "it seems you were right. You've been beaten to a pulp but should feel good as new in a few days."

"Shocker," I muttered, rising to my feet before she could stop me. "If that's all, then, I'd like to return to—"

"Drinking yourself silly?" Calypso's gaze narrowed. "Wallowing in self-pity? Talking to a piece of parchment?"

I drew a sharp inhale, irritated but unsurprised by what she knew. "No."

"Then what, Cedric Teach? Because unless you can give me an actual answer, I'm not leaving this room."

"Don't you have a sea to calm?" She wasn't dripping anymore but remained soaking wet, and given what had happened the last time she'd used her sea magic, I didn't have the slightest idea how she wasn't shaking like a leaf. She'd been out there for what, the past two hours? More?

Calypso eyed me up and down. "It would appear I have a *you* to calm."

I half groaned, half snarled, and, before she could dart in my path, snatched my drink from where it had been set on the side table. There wasn't much left, so I downed the remainder in a single swig, throwing out my free arm to thwart the nymph's attempts to confiscate the bottle a second time. The rum burned my throat as it went down, providing a momentary distraction to that damned hole in my chest... but the ache returned the moment I lowered the drink from my lips, the one that had nothing to do with my physical wounds.

"*Fuck.*" I itched to throw the bottle but didn't want to be picking glass out of my already ruined rug for the rest of the night. After somehow managing to place it back on the table in one piece, I resumed my pacing, desperate for something, anything, else to occupy my head. But as it had for hours now, that singular word kept repeating over and over, each time uttered by a different one of my past tormentors.

Malparido. Malparido. Malparido.

Calypso knew better than to approach or say anything. She simply watched me pace, the expression on her face unreadable. After a while, she sank into the chair I'd occupied a few minutes prior, pulling my jacket off the back of it to drape across her own shoulders, but she never once took her eyes off me.

At first, her presence didn't bother me—what difference did it make?—but before long, it began to drive me mad. What sick enjoyment was she eliciting from watching me suffer? I didn't slow or even look at her as I spoke, each word laced with venom. "Enjoying the show?"

"No more than I enjoyed your little show earlier." Calypso pulled the jacket tighter before crossing her arms; perhaps she'd finally gotten cold. "But it's obvious the two are connected."

"Is it?"

She rolled her eyes, undeterred by my sarcasm. "You're clearly hurting in ways my magic can't ease. So will you please talk to me before you explode?"

"About what, exactly?" I stopped in my tracks, balling my hand into a fist as I turned to face her. "You heard what Elvira said."

Calypso nodded. "So did everyone, including your daughter."

"Don't fucking remind me."

"But even knowing that, your reaction seems a little extreme."

"Extreme?" A bitter laugh tumbled from my lips. "No. What's extreme is disowning your own son at birth. Allowing him to be treated worse than the rats that roamed the ship, called a *malparido* far more often than his actual name, forcing him to earn his place, earn his father's approval, all while his brothers and sister were treated like fucking royalty the moment they tumbled from their mothers' cunts."

I'd never seen Calypso's eyes so wide, but now that I'd opened the floodgates, truths I'd buried poured uninhibited from my lips.

"I am undoubtedly Blackbeard's son, but I was treated like a bastard. My crime wasn't being born to the wrong woman, though— it was being born at all. By the time I arrived, Blackbeard already had two perfect sons and a glowing prodigy of a daughter. Even if I could have compared to their skill and prowess, I simply wasn't needed, let alone wanted. Jamie was Blackbeard's eldest and heir, Lucas was there to take Jamie's place should anything ever happen to him, and not only was Elvira the spitting image of her mother, she was everything that Blackbeard could have ever wanted in his daughter. I was nothing but a disappointment and a mistake."

Calypso only spoke when I allowed the silence to linger too long. "You keep mentioning your siblings' mothers. Were you all born to different women?"

"Yes and no." I shouldn't be telling her any of this. Not only because I kept it locked away for a reason, but because none of it mattered; my father and brothers were dead, and the past couldn't be rewritten. But the words kept coming regardless, willing and more than eager for the chance to slip past my crumbling defenses. "Jamie and Lucas were full blood brothers, but the rest of us are only half siblings. Blackbeard was fondest of Elvira's mother. Even though she died before I was born, she was all he ever talked about." Another bitter laugh. "But I suppose I owe her, in some twisted way. If it weren't for her death, I wouldn't exist at all. Blackbeard was still grieving her when he fell into the arms of my mother."

I closed my eyes, piecing together the bits I'd been fed over the course of my existence. "She wasn't a wench or a whore. Her father owned the tavern Blackbeard stumbled into that night. Adais knows why she took pity on him, but she did, and they spent a few days in one another's arms before parting ways for what was meant to be forever. But the winds weren't on Blackbeard's side, and after a relentless battering by some of the fiercest hurricanes that coast had ever experienced, *Queen Anne's Revenge* was forced to dock in that otherwise sleepy portside town to resupply. It had been eight months to the day since Blackbeard left…"

"And your mother was very pregnant," Calypso finished, the look in her eyes once again unreadable.

Swallowing, I nodded. "But very weak. Not only had carrying me been hard on her, her father was beyond furious that of all men, a pirate had been the one to steal her virtue. He warned Blackbeard that unless he took me in, I'd be given to the sea before I could draw my first breath. Word had spread of my lineage, and none of the orphanages or nunneries would dare touch a pirate's spawn—especially not Blackbeard's."

Calypso clenched her jaw. "And they say the gods are cruel."

"I've no idea why Blackbeard remained in port for that entire month, but he did," I continued; if I stopped, I'd bury the tale forever. "Perhaps he tried to convince my mother to flee while she still could, to run away somewhere where she and I could both be safe. But even if she wanted to, I suspect she was far too sickly. She didn't survive my birth."

"And so Blackbeard became saddled with a motherless child he didn't want."

"It was that or drown me, and I suppose even his soul wasn't black enough to stomach that," I spat through gritted teeth. "But aye, he showed mercy, if you could call it that, and I spent the next twenty years repaying him for it. In every way possible, he made my life a living hell. He didn't even give me his name, not at first. Until I was sixteen, I was known as Cedric Fletcher—my mother's surname—rather than Cedric Teach. Though as I've already mentioned, most were fonder of *malparido* or Crow, the latter of which came about because the animals were commonly seen picking through our rubbish."

Calypso's gaze softened. "Cedric Teach, you are not rub—"

"Don't." Having finally recognized that look in her eyes, I took a step back to ensure I stood out of her reach. "I am what I am, and I don't need your fucking pity."

"That's not what I was offering." She stood then, still wearing my jacket draped over her shoulders. "It was reassurance, not pity. Your past is as much a part of you as your scars, and you needn't be ashamed of either."

"I'm not ashamed," I said, turning away so she could no longer see my face. "Some parts of me are just easier to deal with than others."

Silence lingered for about a minute before Calypso finally dared to state the obvious. "And Elvira wounded a particularly sensitive part by calling you that awful word."

"Can you blame me?" I whirled back around, voice rising as my hurt spilled from me in waves I could no longer hold back. "Jamie and Lucas were delighted to share in Blackbeard's mistreatment of me, and they teased and tormented me relentlessly. *Sadistically*. But it was different with Elvira, and it was from the start. With everyone else, she was a little brat, just as violent and awful as Blackbeard had raised her to be, but for whatever reason she had a soft spot for her youngest brother. It was complicated, of course—she had to be careful not to be too obvious, or she'd lose favor with Blackbeard. And she still teased me, but her version of it was more like the way schoolchildren tease their crushes. She did it because she was fond of me. Still does."

Calypso raised an eyebrow. "Did she nearly kill you because she was 'fond of' you, too?"

"Elvira would never kill me, not even if I begged her to." That much I knew for certain, because that much had actually happened. "She's just incredibly angry with me right now, and that led her to go a bit too far... even for her standards."

"So that makes it okay?"

"Of course it doesn't." Calypso and I stood chest-to-chest now, glaring daggers at one another. "I'd like to strangle *her* right now, to be honest. But I can hardly blame her for how she feels. You warned me that Scarlett would be the death of me, and here I am dragging an entire crew into this mess"—Wylan's lifeless, bloodied face flashed in my mind's eye—"my *daughter* into this mess. Elvira doesn't understand why I'd take such a risk."

"And she hates me because I do?"

"She hates you because she thinks we're fucking." I averted my gaze for the next bit. "And you're not special for it. She's never liked anyone I was intimate with, not even Scarlett."

"But we aren't fucking."

"We're sharing a room, you're breathtakingly gorgeous, and anyone with eyes can see that I'm attracted to you," I admitted, daring another glance at her. "So it's not as if she"—*or anyone*—"would have any reason to believe me. But... that's not all."

Calypso drew a deep breath, as if she wanted to interrupt again, so before she could, I cut across her. "Elvira is most angry with me for not being a better father to Wendy."

My sister had told me as much the night we'd disposed of Digby, Nelson, and Alder's bodies. Once they'd been sewn up with rocks and pushed overboard, she'd punched me in the face, threatening to break my jaw the next time I made Wendy cry. I'd happily let her do far worse should I be foolish enough to make that mistake a second time.

"Are... Are you serious?" Calypso's lips parted. "How the fuck are you meant to know how to be a proper father when yours was a piece of shit?"

"That's hardly an excuse, nor Wendy's fault."

"No. But it's not yours, either."

"And that's not for *you* to decide." I turned away again, taking a few steps back. "My point was that Elvira is right. About everything."

"Cedric, you're allowed to be upset, but—"

"Then let me be upset." I spoke over my shoulder, my words icy and detached. "And get out." Confiding in the nymph had clearly been a mistake; no outsider had ever understood my fucked-up family. The only person I wanted now was Elvira, but whether it was to finish what we'd started earlier or apologize, I wasn't certain. Until I was, she and I needed to stay the fuck away from each other.

A heavy silence weighed on my shoulders, and it was a few moments before Calypso replied. "Do you mean permanently, or only for—"

"Just get the fuck out. I need to think."

I could feel Calypso's glare burning a hole into my back, but it wasn't until she quoted Elvira, even going as far as mimicking my sister's tone, that I spun around. "That's it, then? You choose her?"

"She's my sister."

"*Half* sister."

"Sister," I growled, placing emphasis on each syllable, "nonetheless."

For a moment, I thought Calypso was about to throw herself at me, argue, or both, but before I could so much as tense, she whirled around, shed my jacket, and marched for the door. She made an impressively theatrical exit, her still-wet skirts sweeping behind her as she disappeared down the hall, leaving the door wide open. Though she hadn't spoken them aloud, her parting words were crystal clear: *Fuck you.*

I muttered my own string of curses under my breath as I crossed the room to shut myself inside, and had I not been breathing so deeply in an effort to restrain my temper, I doubt I'd have picked up the faintest of odors lingering in the doorway. The damp, woodsy scent immediately took me back to the forests of Neverland, but there was a bitter floral aftertaste to it, one I'd recognize anywhere: naxal root and wolfsbane. The main ingredients Elvira used in her poisons.

I stiffened and froze. Though I couldn't see her, my sister had undoubtedly been listening at the door; knowing her, she was likely still here, just lingering in the shadows. How much had she heard, and was she about to hurl a knife at me for spilling our family's darkest secrets to a stranger? Worse—was she about to go after Calypso? I may have sent the nymph away in anger, but I certainly didn't want her harmed on my behalf.

"Elvira?" I whispered into the blackness. My eyes were still accustomed to my room brightly lit with candles, and for all I could see, I may well be stepping into the abyss if I dared take another step.

Only silence answered me. But I stood in place for a full five minutes and, toward the end, swore I could make out the faintest silhouette lurking at the very end of the hall. And unless I hallucinated that too, the silhouette gave what looked to be a forgiving nod.

When I next blinked, the shadow was gone.

XIV. THE DEAL

Wendy

It took my eyes far longer than I'd have liked to adjust to the dark halls leading to Peter's room. Even the silence took some getting used to; though blood had been roaring in my ears since the moment I'd suspected what had Peter so upset. Noises from the party—Smee's music, in particular—were still rattling around in my cluttered mind, making this already difficult task no easier.

Tink remained silent and still as I walked. The hurt in her voice and that genuine expression of pain on her small face weighed heavily on my shoulders and didn't at all bode well for what I was about to attempt. The fact that not even Peter's oldest friend had been able to console him was nothing short of horrifying—and left me his only hope. But the closer I got, the more I couldn't shake my deepest fear. What did I have to offer that a fairy didn't, and what in hells would we do if I failed?

I stopped a few feet from his closed, and presumably locked, door. "Peter?" I called into the blackness, not bothering to knock. I knew already I wouldn't get an answer but wanted to at least announce that I was here. And a voice, even if it was my own, helped to counter some of the anxiety surging through my veins. "Are you in there?"

Nothing but the creak of the ship.

Sighing, I leaned my forehead against the door, raising my free hand to scratch at the uneven grooves. Hopefully it was just as irritating of a sound on the inside as it was on the outside. "Tink told me what happened. She's worried about you. We both are." Still nothing, so I kept talking. "I know something's up with you. You haven't been yourself for days. If you want to be alone, that's fine, but you have to at least have the decency to tell us to our faces. Otherwise, we'll be sitting out here all night, stiff, lonely, and freezing. You don't want that, do you?"

Something shuffled just behind the door. My heart fluttered expectantly, but it was back to eerie silence a heartbeat later. Turning, I sank to my knees before addressing Tink. "You're bonded to him, right? Can't you sense anything?" I had my suspicions, of course, but given that Peter wouldn't talk to me, maybe the fairy would.

She shook her small head as her light flashed a pale blue. "He's shut me out. I can't feel a thing."

"What about before today? Before what happened?" I pressed. "Surely you know or felt something."

"Nothing. This is what he's like, Wendy, always keeping his deepest emotions under lock and key. He doesn't behave any differently around you than he has with me for the past fifty years."

There was an irritation to Tink's tone, and her light had turned an orange that bordered on crimson, but I ignored both to fixate on the most shocking revelation. "Fifty years? So Peter is…"

"Much older than he looks, yes. But you already knew that."

I supposed I did. "And you bonded with him when he first arrived in Neverland? How does that work, exactly? And why haven't I ever met any other fairies? Can they bond with people, too?"

Tink opened her mouth, but before she could speak, something shattered against the back of the door, causing me to flinch so violently I nearly threw poor Tink across the hall. A slightly muffled shout followed, the voice unmistakably Peter's.

"Quit spilling all my secrets, Tinker Bell!"

I scrambled to my feet, but not without gaping at the fairy cupped in my hands. "*Tinker Bell?*"

Her light flashed blood red. "Do not call me that. Ever." Raising her voice to a high-pitched squeak, she shouted right back at the still-closed door, her wings buzzing like a dragonfly. "If you want me to shut up, come out and make me!"

"Yeah!" Whirling around, I gritted my teeth. It had just occurred to me that Peter had thrown and broken something, and that my music box was still in that room. Fury ignited within me; if he so much as *touched* it, I was prepared to raise absolute hell. "If you break my music box, Peter Pan, I swear to all the gods I'll—"

The door flung open then, cutting me off and revealing Peter's slumped-over form. He'd crossed one arm over his abdomen while the other gripped the frame for support. Broken glass littered the area surrounding his feet, and though I couldn't tell what he'd smashed, it was immediately clear my music box was safe. I couldn't see Peter's face given that he stared at the floor, but his pain was undeniable. The only question was whether it was physical, mental, or both. "You'll what, Wendy?"

Peter's snappish tone would have further stoked my temper had his appearance not been so pathetic. My mind had gone blank, and I'd completely forgotten what I'd been about to say. "I... I'll—"

"I haven't touched a single one of your possessions. You and Tink take the room, and I'll sleep somewhere else tonight. I want to be alone."

He took a shaky step, but his knees immediately buckled. I reacted instinctively, dropping Tink and darting forward in the same motion. I caught Peter around the waist, and he sagged nearly limp against my chest. It wasn't his near-fall that concerned me most, though; it was the heat radiating from him in waves. "You're burning up."

He only grunted in response. Behind us, Tink's wings fluttered, and I could only hope she'd broken her own fall, because Peter was my primary concern now. It took some awkward maneuvering and special care to dodge the glass, but I was eventually able to help him into the hammock we'd shared every night since Hook had returned to *The Jolly Serpent*. Only once Peter had curled into a fetal position atop our mountain of blankets did I notice his quivering. A sheen of sweat coated his brow, and he still wouldn't look at me. The clothes he wore were baggy and loose, even more so than usual, and I'd already discerned that he wasn't wearing his bindings when our chests had pressed together. His hair nearly reached his shoulders now, the mousy strands as wild and untamed as Neverland itself, but that was far from a comforting thought. Knowing I needed to be strong, at least on the outside, I fought hard not to cry as I drank him in. I'd accept Peter no matter how he chose to look or present, but his current appearance was nothing short of haunting.

"Peter," I said softly, voice cracking as I choked up. There were so many questions on the tip of my tongue—*what's happening to you? Are you all right? Why did you frighten Tink?*—but none of them mattered as much as the one I finally settled on asking. "What can I do to help?"

He said nothing for a long while. The violent shivering continued, but I could no longer tell whether it was from the cold or whatever emotions he was currently feeling. Perhaps both, and that would explain the intensity of the tremors. "Get out."

I flinched, but not because of the words or their meaning. Peter didn't sound anything like himself. "Didn't you say a moment ago that Tink and I could have the room?"

"Yes, well, it would appear that I can't leave. So *you* leave."

"And where would you have us go?"

"I don't care."

My temper flared once again, so I made a conscious effort to remind myself that it was his illness talking. "Please, if there's anything—"

"Was I unclear?" Peter sat up so suddenly it was unnerving, his too-pale face shining in the candlelight. "Get the fuck out."

If he was trying to scare me, it was working. That look in his eyes was identical to Hook's the moment before I'd pushed him too far and caused him to snap. Was Peter about to do the same—yell, lash out, smash and break things? My heart hammered in my chest, and I very nearly took a step back, nearly gave in to demands that were clearly the result of him feeling cornered with nowhere left to flee. Desperate. Trapped. Out of options.

But he wasn't, not as long as he had me. And he certainly wasn't my unpredictable father. This was Peter, my friend, and I'd be damned if I let him face whatever this was all on his own.

I swallowed and cleared my throat before speaking. "No."

His gaze narrowed. "No?"

"You heard me." Balling my hands into fists, I dug my fingernails into my palms, utilizing the pain to steel myself against whatever bullshit excuse Peter might try to throw at me next. "I'm not leaving. I'm not buying your lies. And I'm certainly not going to keep letting you avoid me like this. I don't care if you've been like this for half a fucking century, and I don't even care if you actually talk to me. That, I won't force. But no, I am not leaving you, and I'd really appreciate it if you'd stop asking." Chest heaving, I shot him a final glare. "Was *I* unclear?"

Peter seemed to have been rendered speechless. Blanching, his lips parted slightly, but no sound came out. He slipped one of his hands beneath the blankets; I almost thought he was searching for something, but the limb didn't reemerge. He just sat there, completely still, and the bewildered silence lasted so long I began to worry that I'd actually hurt his feelings.

My stupid stutter returned with my nervousness. "I-I don't mean t-to violate your p-p-privacy, I just—"

The tiniest of sobs uttered from Peter's throat, and when he closed his eyes, what looked to be long-repressed tears streamed down his cheeks. Immediately I stiffened and froze as my worst fear became a reality. Just as Hook had done to me, I'd made Peter *cry.*

Oh, fuck. Fuck, fuck, *fuck.*

I should have never been so harsh with him, should have never spoken to him that way. Not when he was this fragile and prone to a breakdown. Not when he said things like *If I'm doomed to live in this body, then I don't want to live at all.* I couldn't nudge him any closer to that ledge, not when he approached it himself on a daily basis. Instinct demanded that I reach for him, comfort him and make this right, but until he gave the word, I didn't dare come any closer. "Peter, I-I'm—"

"It's happening." A harrowing whisper, one that terrified me more than any Nightstalker's ever had. "It's happening, and I can't stop it."

I knew what he meant without him having to name it. It came as no surprise; he'd been so obviously aging for weeks now, but no one had the heart to say it to his face, least of all me or Tink. "I know," I said softly. "And so did you." I kept the rest of what I wanted to say to myself:

I tried to talk to you about it even then, but you refused to listen to me.

"Knowing and experiencing are two very different things," Peter snapped, yanking me from my thoughts. "And I certainly didn't expect it to hit me this damn hard."

"You knew it was a possibility," Tink's small voice piped up from the floor. "The longer someone stays in Neverland, the more their aging catches up with them once they leave."

"I know how it fucking works!" Peter's tone rose to a shout, one that flooded the entirety of our small and cramped space. His visible hand balled into a fist while the other shifted slightly beneath the blankets. "It's just... I prepared for this. I took precautions, thought that it might affect me differently, given my..."

His voice trailed off, and I suppressed a curse. Had he been about to mention his strange golden blood? I still hadn't pressed him over that, but considering his illness, perhaps now was the time. "Given your what, Peter?"

Another sob wracked his body, and all I could do was stand there like a helpless fool. Seeing anyone cry was difficult for me, let alone someone I cared about so deeply. Tears of my own pooled in my eyes, and when I blinked, a handful of them escaped. Peter, having turned his attention to whatever was under the blankets, thankfully seemed oblivious to my emotion. Once he'd caught his breath a bit, he pulled back the sheets with his free hand.

A concentrated grouping of blotchy golden stains marred the fabric upon which we'd slept, as shiny and reflective as the blood that had seeped onto Peter's clothing the day of the mutiny. My suspicions now confirmed, I recognized them immediately for what they were, and paired with his physical symptoms, everything made perfect sense. He wasn't sick. He was menstruating. I tried to say as much aloud, but my throat went dry the moment I opened my mouth, and all I contributed was stunned silence.

"This wasn't supposed to happen. Not to me." Peter spoke in a numb, faraway voice. "Or at least, not yet. I'm only twelve, not nearly—"

"But you've been leaving Neverland for years, haven't you?" My mouth remained dry as ash, but I couldn't stand to hear him sound as defeated as he did. "You'd go in and out, and every single time you left, you were aging. They may have been short trips, but they've added up, it seems. You barely looked twelve when I met you, and now that you've been gone for weeks, you look…"

Peter glanced up unnervingly fast. "I look *what*, Wendy? How old would you presume me to be?"

I hesitated for a fraction of a section before giving in to the intensity of his glare. "Sixteen," I admitted softly. "You and I look the same age now."

He flinched.

"And unfortunately, sixteen year olds can usually be expected to have gotten their monthl—"

"Girls. Sixteen-year-old *girls*," Peter snapped, cutting me off. "Not boys."

He was pushing now, trying to say anything he could think of to get me to back down or leave. But that tactic hadn't worked a few minutes ago, and it certainly wasn't going to work now. "Who's to say it can't happen to boys, too?" I shot back. "Or to other people? Anyone with the body parts you and I have typically experience this in some form or another. It's absolutely nothing to feel ashamed or embarrassed of."

"Tell that to all the men out there."

I snorted. "If those so-called 'men' bled from their dicks every month, you can bet your ass they'd be useless and bedridden for an entire week. But you? You put on a brave face and sparred with *Elvira* of all people, something none of them dared to do even when pressed."

His jaw ticked. "You're just making shit up to make me feel better."

"No, *you're* just making shit up to try to push me away." I took a step toward him. "It's not going to work, Peter. Not with me. Now are you going to let me help you, or do promises mean nothing to you?"

"Promises?"

"Yes. Back in Neverland, on the same day we met, you made a promise to come to me if this ever happened to you. I got mine when I was thirteen, so I've learned a thing or two about how to deal with things like… that." I gestured toward the ruined blankets. "I can get you cleaned up. And I may not possess Calypso's ability to take your pain, but I probably still have some suggestions on how to relieve those cramps of yours. You'll feel better once it's done, I swear."

I thought he might argue further, but after a brief hesitation, Peter gave a small nod.

Thank the gods.

We worked tirelessly for the next half hour. After we stripped the hammock of its soiled bedding and replaced it with fresh, I turned my attention toward Peter, showing him how I wrapped and layered rags in my undergarments to keep myself clean and dry during my cycles. Though he communicated solely through head shakes and nods, the focus in his gaze told me he was listening. I left the room while he situated himself and did my best not to eavesdrop as he and Tink exchanged a few words. Hopefully, Peter was apologizing for how he'd treated her.

When I returned, the fairy sat perched on his shoulder, though she didn't look at all pleased about it. She buzzed her wings in irritation, trying and failing to shove Peter's unruly hair out of the way. "Are you ever going to cut this, or is it just my new reality?"

Peter was still clutching the scissors we'd used to cut rags into strips. Meeting my gaze, he held them out to me, asking, "Can you?"

"What—cut your hair?" I took the scissors cautiously. "Are you sure?"

"Yes." He ran a hand through the tangled strands. "I should have had you do it weeks ago, but truth be told, I've been in denial. I need to stop running from the things I don't want to face."

I exhaled in relief before smiling. "Words I thought I'd never hear you say. But yes, of course."

Peter sat on a small crate, remaining perfectly still while I worked. Tink moved from his shoulder to settle in his cupped hands, equally quiet and stiff, and I nearly finished the haircut before realizing the intense, eerie looks they were giving one another. Swallowing, I resisted the urge to wave my free hand in front of Peter's face. "Uh, hello? Can you hear me?"

He didn't move anything but his mouth. "Of course I can hear you, and so can Tink. We're just communing."

"Communing?" I echoed.

"I shut her out for most of the past few days, so we have a lot to catch up on."

"How does that work, exactly?" I tilted Peter's head to one side so I could have better access to a part I still needed to trim. "Your bond?"

He thought for a moment. "It's... difficult to explain. Unless either of us closes off our mind, it's as if she's always in my head, and I'm in hers."

"So you can read each other's minds?"

"Not in the way you're likely imagining it. Thoughts aren't anything like spoken words. They're fleeting, messy, and confusing, and having someone else's entangled with yours can easily become overwhelming. Emotions are even worse—sometimes it's impossible to tell whose are whose. We spent at least a decade striking a balance."

I grimaced; this honestly sounded horrifying. "And what's the purpose of the bond? What does either of you gain?"

It was Tink who replied. "Answering that requires a bit of a history lesson I'm not sure I'm ready to divulge just yet. But the bond was my choice. I asked Peter, not the other way around."

They both fell silent then, wordlessly informing me that this was all I was going to get out of either of them for a while. Refocusing on the haircut, I made a few more calculated snips and ensured the result was relatively symmetrical before calling it done.

"All finished," I informed Peter. "I'm sorry we don't have a mirror, but I think Hook does in his desk somewhere."

"I'll swipe it tomorrow and have a look." He ran his hands through his freshly cropped hair and grinned. "Thank you, Wendy."

"Any time," I answered honestly before drinking him in. Not only did he finally resemble the Peter I'd come to know and love, he looked genuinely content. Lighter, as if at any moment he might rise into the air and begin zooming about the room. But his cheeks still lacked their usual color, and though he wasn't likely to admit it, surely he was still uncomfortable. "How are you feeling?"

"A little better."

I raised an eyebrow, unconvinced. Before he could stop me, I brought the back of my hand to his forehead. "You're still a bit feverish."

Peter ducked out of my reach and made a face. "I'm fine."

"Clearly you're not, but there's nothing shameful about that. It's just uncommon to experience symptoms this severe. Nausea, fever, cramps—"

"Wendy—"

"Irritability." I crossed my arms. "Even more than usual. You got the whole package. It could be because it's your first."

"No." Tink had finished climbing back onto Peter's shoulder. "It's because of his bl—*hey!*"

Peter had shrugged so violently it nearly sent the fairy tumbling back to the floor. He shot her a glare as she righted herself, hissing under his breath, "None of that. Not now."

She'd been about to say *blood*. I glanced between them, eyes narrowed, but the moment I opened my mouth, Peter snapped at me, too. "Don't ask. Please."

I sighed deeply but decided against pressing the issue... for now. "Fine. Are you certain you don't want me to fetch Calypso?"

"More than certain." He rolled his eyes. "She can't actually heal or relieve pain, you know. She's a nymph. Everything she does with that magic of hers is simply an illusion."

"Everything?"

"Everything."

I wasn't sure why the revelation sent chills up my spine until Calypso's borderline obsessive attachment to Hook sprang to the forefront of my mind. I'd heard Elvira call her Silvertongue on more than one occasion. If Calypso could spin pretty lies with her magic, what lies was she spinning with her tongue... and had my father already been caught in the nymph's web? How long had she been working him, sinking her claws deep into the crevices of his clearly troubled mind? Had Elvira been right all along? Were we sailing straight into a trap that we should have seen coming long before today, straight into a den of monsters both beast and human?

There was so much I didn't know. So much *none* of us knew. No one could seem to agree whether or not my mother was actually alive, Peter wouldn't tell me about his blood or past, Hook was losing his mind more every day, he and Elvira were literally at each other's throats, and no one seemed overly concerned that it wasn't a witch we were after—it was a goddess. Weather dependent, we were only a few days away from Kaara's domain, and as far as I was aware, we didn't have a concrete plan regarding what to do when we got there... at least, not one I'd been told.

I gritted my teeth. What else was being concealed from me?

"...all right?"

I shook my head, clearing it of thoughts I couldn't afford to get lost in. "Hmm?"

Peter frowned. "You were staring off into space."

"Sorry. I suppose I'm tired."

"I am, too. Shall we?"

A few minutes later, the three of us had piled into the hammock. The only light was from a single candle that burned so low it could extinguish at any moment, and the only sound came from my music box. It sang a melody I'd never heard before, though Peter had been humming along until it reached the third verse. He laid in his usual position directly behind me, his body curled around my own, while Tink had burrowed herself in the narrow space between Peter's chest and my back. As comfortable as I was physically, my mind was anything but and continued its endless stream of questions. I wanted desperately to voice them aloud, to have someone talk me through my anxieties, but the gentle exhales against my neck had grown so steady and rhythmic I began to wonder if I was the only one left awake.

"Peter?" I whispered into the stillness.

A faint grunt was the only response, and I bit my lip. He wasn't asleep yet but was well on his way. Still, I couldn't allow him to drift off without at least mentioning the unknown that he alone could resolve.

"Will you make me another promise?"

Another incoherent mumble, but I took it as a yes.

"I don't mean to push you, truly I don't. But someday soon, and I mean *soon*, I'd really like for you to tell me about your blood and what it means."

Peter stiffened, and the arm wrapped around me twitched. "Why? Why does it matter?"

It didn't, not really. But I was tired of being kept in the dark, tired of being treated like a child, and most importantly, I wanted him to be safe. "How can I protect you if I don't know what you are?"

"I'm human, Wendy. And I don't need protection."

"Maybe not, but I'd like to help anyway."

He remained tense but answered after a few beats of silence. "All right. But only if you tell me Elvira's secret."

I closed my eyes. *Fuck.* Evidently I was as guilty of withholding truths as the rest of them, but I wasn't about to admit it aloud. "It's about my mother."

"So? Mine is about what I am."

"Didn't you just say you were human?" I very nearly sat up as anger flared deep in my chest. "Was that another lie?"

"He is human, Wendy, but it's complicated—"Tink started, but I cut across her.

"So is what Elvira told me."

Peter huffed. "Well, then it appears to be an equal trade."

Unable to find fault in his logic, I forced myself to relax before grumbling, "I suppose it does."

"Do we have a deal, then? Mine for yours?"

He'd asked innocently, as if he didn't know full well that neither of us planned on divulging our well-kept secrets for anything less than life or death. Still, it wasn't as if I had another choice; Peter now knew precisely how badly I wanted to know what he was. He would be on high alert now, never lowering his defenses for even a moment, never letting down his guard. Perhaps with time I could discover a way to trick him, to twist the words of our bargain until they revealed some hidden meaning, an undiscovered shortcut or cheat... but that required time and energy, neither of which I possessed at the moment. It left only one option.

I exhaled deeply before nodding. "Deal."

XV. THE REVELATION
Wendy

I wasn't certain if it was due to my racing thoughts or because I'd spent so much of the past week asleep, but I found myself unable to shut my eyes for any longer than five minutes. An hour before dawn, I finally gave up trying. Extracting myself from Peter's arms was as easy as it was difficult. He slept like a damn rock, so there was no danger of waking him, but his limbs were as heavy as a corpse's. After a brief struggle, and plenty of wiggling, I finally broke free. Dressing quickly, I threw on a jacket and matching breeches before tying back my hair, slipping on my boots, and strapping a pair of daggers to my side. I'd have to track down a pistol later. Sparing Peter and Tink a final glance, I exited the room, closing the door behind me before scurrying down the hall.

My body thrummed with nervous, pent-up energy demanding to be released. I felt as though I could sprint the perimeter of the ship and not even break a sweat, as if I might actually be able to spar Elvira and win. But experience told me this was nothing more than adrenaline-induced panic, and that once my heart quit beating out of my chest, I'd drop dead from exhaustion.

It wasn't just my racing thoughts that had gotten me so worked up. All night, strange prickles had run up and down my spine, and even now, every hair on my arms stood at attention in response to something I could just... feel. There was a mysterious charge in the air, one that had nothing to do with a storm or lightning. The sensation was sickeningly familiar, though I'd experienced it only once before, on *that* night. The night before everything had changed, before my father had returned to the ship, before the crew had mutinied. Before my spectacular failure.

Before the dragon.

Next to my mother and her voice, the massive beast was what I dreamed of the most. I'd long since memorized the pattern of the glowing blue lines that decorated its body, the shape of its intelligent eyes, the knowing look it had given me, and me alone. What I hadn't yet figured out was what the dragon wanted from me and why, but perhaps I was about to... because it was close. Its presence enveloped me like a soft blanket, beckoning me, inviting me, calling me—

I had been about to break into a full-blown sprint when I heard the voices coming from a cabin: Hook's cabin. Stilling, I remained in the shadows, not daring to so much as breathe as I scanned the area. His door was cracked just slightly, but whether he didn't realize or didn't care, I couldn't be certain. Though the dragon's pull grew stronger with every passing moment, urging me onto the main deck, curiosity kept me rooted in place, as did Elvira's combative tone filtering into the hall.

"...to our deaths? I know you don't believe me, but you have to start trying. She's dead, Cedric. You believed it in Neverland. You had accepted it in Neverland. For fuck's sake, what changed? And don't say *her*. The nymph is pretty, I'll give you that, but not pretty enough for you to abandon all reason simply because her lies are equally as attractive."

Something slammed onto a hard surface, followed by a snarl of frustration. "We're nearly there, and now is when you decide to push me?"

"I've tried both diplomacy and my own fists, but you won't listen to either. So now I'm fucking screaming." Elvira had already been speaking loudly, but true to her promise, her next utterance was a booming shout. "You're going to kill us all, Cedric, and for what? A memory? A hope?"

"Scarlett is alive. I can feel it."

"You couldn't 'feel it' in Neverland!"

"It's hard to feel much of anything when you're fucking rotting, don't you think?" Hook's shout was laced with so much venom I swore it seeped into the hull of the ship. "I could only think clearly once the curse was broken."

"Seems to me you've only been thinking with your dick."

Another snarl. "You truly want me to strangle you, don't you?"

"With only one hand? You can fucking try."

I couldn't see who had thrown themselves at who, but sounds that followed were only those of a struggle. Brother and sister seemed hellbent on finishing what they'd started, only this time they didn't have any witnesses to their savagery. Wood scraped against the floor, objects of varying weights fell and were tossed around, and incoherent grunts sounded from both of them. Gods, if what they had done on deck was how they fought in public, what the hells would they do to one another in private? I almost, *almost* approached the door, but ultimately decided against it; involving myself would either do nothing or make the fight even worse. Rolling my eyes, I only took a handful of steps forward before everything suddenly, unnervingly stopped, and they began speaking once again.

"I'd die for her more than gladly. Is that what you want me to say?" Hook's voice, as desperate as it was breathless. His scarred face flashed in my mind's eye, and his haunted expression made my breath catch in my throat. I'd heard and seen him sad, but this was beyond grief… this was a confession plucked straight from the depths of his soul.

"Anyone with eyes can see that. I'm more interested in whether you'd sacrifice *her*." A heavy, poignant pause. "The daughter you claim to want to save. The daughter that Scarlett gave up everything—her freedom, her very life—to save. What about Wendy?"

My blood turned to ice.

What about Wendy?

Yes, what about me? What about what *I* wanted, what my mother had willingly given up so I might one day have? What about what Hook had put me through? His torments, his threats, his lies, his truths, namely the ones I'd be far better off not knowing. What about what he'd done, the lives he'd taken to survive in Neverland all those years, the sins for which he might never atone? What about this very ship that he'd given and taken from me all in a matter of weeks?

What about my agency as a fucking human being?

My hands balled into fists. He had chosen this life. All of it, from Scarlett, to seeking out Neverland, to his obsession with the curse, to me. I may have walked into that damn forest of my own free will, but the rest had been decided for me, all because Hook was the father I'd never asked for.

Without hesitation, I marched to the door and wrenched it fully open, immediately fixating on Hook. His lips parted in shock, but I held up a hand before he could utter a damn word; it was my turn. I was done being silent. Done sneaking around in the shadows, hoping and praying I'd overhear the answers no one would hand over willingly. And I was definitely done cowering before him, because in the weeks since that night in his cabin, I'd learned a very important lesson.

Sometimes it wasn't about standing up. It was about refusing to sit back down.

Which was why I said, cold as ice, "Yes. What about me?"

Hook simply stared at me, blank faced, while Elvira glanced between us, seemingly unsure who to defend. She didn't have to worry about me, though. I didn't need her protection, not where

Hook was concerned. "Go on," I urged him in that same cold tone. "I want to know the answer."

He swallowed. "How much have you heard?"

No *I'm sorry*, no explanation, but I'd expected nothing less. "Enough."

"Wendy—"

"Don't 'Wendy' me." It was him who flinched when I took a step forward, not back. "I want the truth, and I want it now."

"The truth?" A joyless laugh tumbled from his lips. "You're my daughter. I'd do anything for you."

"Bullshit. You've never done a single thing I've asked."

"In the name of keeping you safe—"

"You call this safe?" I gestured around wildly. "If that were true, you'd have turned this ship around and dumped my ass back in Afterport."

Hook set his jaw. "Would you have stayed put if I tried?"

"Of course not, but that's not the fucking point."

"Then what is?" His eyes glistened as he ran his hand through his ruffled hair, and his voice cracked when he spoke again. "I love you, Wendy. I love your spirit, your strength, and your good heart that was somehow spared from the blackness shrouding mine. As irritating as it is, I love that you push and challenge me to grow. It's almost impossible for me to believe that Scarlett didn't raise you, because you're so much like her it's unnerving. You even quote her sometimes, and when I look at you, it's often her I see staring back at me.

"But I love her, too. I've never stopped. Scarlett is my other half, the light to my dark, my everything, and she gave me you. She protected you, saved and spared you when no one else would or could. She's the reason we met at all, and we both owe her our lives. So how can you stand there and ask me to choose?" Hook glanced at Elvira and back again. "How can either of you stand there and ask me to choose?"

I couldn't move. Couldn't breathe. Couldn't think. There were a lot of things I'd expected Hook to say, but '*I love you*' had been nowhere among them.

How was I supposed to respond to that? What did he expect me to say when I was quite literally incapable of believing it? How could the man who had tormented me so, who had haunted my waking hours as much as my nightmares, claim to *love me*?

I opened my mouth, but no sound came out. All I could hear was static, my own blood roaring in my ears as I fought to make sense of it all. It was as if the floor was crumbling beneath me, as if I was drowning and would never again surface for air, as if language would never make sense again. My breathing quickened, my pulse spiked, and the room began to spin, not at all helped by the intensity of the dragon's pull. The urge to turn around and flee became overwhelming, and I didn't have any idea whether it was because of Hook's confession or the beast sinking its claws into my psyche.

I was only vaguely aware of Smee entering the room; somehow, his stutter cleanly sliced through whatever Elvira and Hook had been trying to communicate to me. His face was pale, he was visibly shaking, and he wrung his hands as he approached. "C-Cap'n?"

"Get out," Hook snapped. "We're fucking busy."

"A s-ship's been spotted."

Elvira did a double take. "What?"

"A-and it's u-under a-attack."

"By whom?" Hook was already reaching for his jacket. "I haven't heard any cannons."

"N-not by a-another s-ship, Cap'n." Smee swallowed. "By the d-dragon."

I hadn't moved but could picture it clear as day. The dragon that had once spared me now wrapped its serpent-like body around a warship much larger and grander than our own, intending to crush it into smithereens before letting all its occupants drown. They couldn't be permitted to go any farther, couldn't reach *her*, and they certainly couldn't be allowed to live. Let them drown, let them freeze, let them suffer and die the way they allowed so many dragonkind to suffer... so many of *my* kind...

"Wendy!"

I blinked at the person shaking me—Hook. But before he could utter a word, I slipped from his grasp and darted away, trying to disregard the fact that somehow, some way, I'd just been inside the mind of a *dragon*. Ignoring my father's cries, I took the stairs two at a time, nearly tripping over my own feet on multiple occasions. The energy thrumming within my chest swirled and thrashed around, begging and pleading to be released; but how I would do it, I couldn't begin to guess. All I knew was that I needed to reach the main deck, and I needed to reach it now.

At the top of the stairs, an icy gust of wind all but slapped me in the face. Gritting my teeth, I planted my feet and pushed through the pain, at last giving in to the full force of the dragon's relentless pull. It guided me toward the rail, urged me to shove my way through the horde of crewmen, and at last, I saw it with my own eyes: the dragon and its prey.

The sight before me was precisely as I'd envisioned mere minutes ago. The beast had wrapped the entire length of its body around the most decorated warship I'd ever seen, and it held the vessel captive from bow to stern. Those mysterious blue lines pulsed erratically, not unlike a frantic heartbeat, and contrasted sharply against its onyx scales. The distance between our two ships made it impossible to discern individual voices or faces, but it would have hardly made any difference given the complete and utter panic, and rightfully so. One of the masts had already been brought down, and another was soon to follow. The dragon opened its massive maw, revealing no less than three rows of glittering teeth before aiming for the mainsail.

I reacted without conscious thought. One moment, my feet were planted firmly on the deck, the next, I stood on the rail. Panicked voices screamed for me to get down, and hands grabbed at my ankles, but I paid them no mind. Closing my eyes, I forced them all to the edge of my psyche, focusing on the dragon alone.

"Leave them be." I spoke no louder than a whisper but forced every ounce of authority I possessed into my words. "Release them, and do not come back."

The moment I opened my eyes, our gazes locked. Irises as stormy as the sea dilated until the color was no longer visible. The dragon growled so deeply it rattled *The Jolly Serpent's* hull, and unless I was hallucinating, I could understand it.

You know not what you ask.

"Leave," I repeated, though with far less conviction than before. "Now."

Are you certain, Wendy Maynard?

"Yes."

For a harrowing moment, I thought the beast was about to lunge for me. But just as I considered leaping back to safety, the dragon slowly but surely began to untangle itself from its prey. Inch by precious inch, it lowered its massive body back into the sea, even going as far as to ensure it wasn't overly disturbing the waves that rippled against the sides of *The Jolly Serpent*. Though it was several minutes before they realized what was happening, the crew of our neighboring ship eventually fell completely silent, seemingly speechless as they watched the dragon release them at nothing more than a young woman's command.

At last, only its head remained visible. The dragon and I stared one another down, unblinking and immobile, but with a final unimpressed snort, it disappeared beneath the waves.

I suddenly became very aware of my own breathing. The crew kept up their attempts to pull me back onto the ship, but I remained where I was as I fought to regain control of my senses. Smell was first, followed by touch, then hearing, and only then did noise come floating in on the breeze, its source the other ship—and of all things, it was a laugh.

"Who is that magnificent girl? I insist, nay, *demand* to meet her at once!"

They spoke in English, but not only was it the strangest accent I'd ever heard, the sheer entitlement was making my skin crawl. Blinking, I forced myself to take my first real look at the vessel before me. It had drifted much closer since being freed and would be upon us soon. Not only was the entire ship painted *white* of all colors, ornate gold plating decorated every visible port, mast, and railing. Paired with the elaborate uniforms most of the crew appeared to be wearing, the realization struck me like lightning; if these people weren't royalty, I'd go give my father a hug.

What the fuck had I gotten myself into?

XVI. THE PRINCE

Cedric

I couldn't decide which was more shocking: the fact that we weren't the only ones suicidal enough to be traversing these waters, or whatever the hells Wendy had just done. By the time I emerged from belowdecks, she was already balanced precariously on the rail, and there was no way I could think to reach her without increasing the likelihood that she'd take another tumble into the sea. I wondered whether I should begin removing my boots and jacket in preparation to dive in after her, and then it happened.

Not only did she speak to the beast in a voice that sounded barely her own... it listened.

Calypso's words echoed in some faraway corner of my mind.

"Your daughter is rather sensitive to magic of any kind. I suspect it was why she was so in tune with Neverland and its creatures." Did Wendy possess… magic? Did her power extend to other beasts as well? Was that how she had managed such a feat? Had she always possessed such an affinity toward monsters, or had her power only manifested after she'd broken the curse? And why hadn't she ever told me?

Questions buzzed in my head like a nest of hornets, doing absolutely nothing for the pounding headache that was the unfortunate result of how much I drank last night. As much as I wanted to go to Wendy, now that the adrenaline had worn off, I could barely see straight. Thankfully a short-haired Pan emerged from belowdecks a moment later, weaving his slender body through the crowd to help her down. The men surrounding me broke into puzzled speculation, but I remained at my hangover's mercy until long after the dragon disappeared. At some point, Elvira appeared by my side, and it took her shaking my shoulder for me to snap out of my pain-induced trance. "Ced—look. They mean to board us."

That certainly got my attention; *The Jolly Serpent* hadn't been boarded by another crew, friendly or otherwise, in decades, and I'd be damned if it was going to happen now. *"What?* Who the fuck are they, and what do they want?"

"Wendy, by the sounds of it," Elvira said under her breath, fixated not on me but the odd white warship. "As for who they are, I've no—"

"I do." Calypso all but materialized beside us. Raising her arm, she pointed to the flag hoisted high on their mainsail. It was difficult to make out the design given how it fluttered in the morning breeze, but the fabric was dyed a deep gold, the hue matching the metal wastefully adorning the ship's ports. "Those are the Engelbert's colors. Their lineage has ruled Adra for centuries, and they're faithful servants of all the gods." When neither me nor Elvira responded, Calypso rolled her eyes and sighed dramatically. "I'm assuming your blank stares mean you've never heard of them."

"I feel like I fucked one once," Elvira offered unhelpfully.

"You'd best hope it wasn't any of the royal family, because it appears at least one of them is coming aboard."

"Royalty? And they want my daughter? Fuck no." High society was all the same to me—lords, ladies, admirals, officers, even kings and queens—and I didn't trust anyone with any such title as far as I could throw them. It appeared I was alone in my distrust, however, for it soon became apparent that my men were making all the necessary arrangements for the strangers to come aboard. Rage ignited within me. "I didn't order this. Stop this, don't let them—"

"Be quiet, Ced." Elvira dug her nails into my wrist before shooting me a fierce glare. "What would you have us do instead, open fire? It's a little late for that, and they'd blast us to bits when they decided to return the favor."

"And I don't know about you, but I'd rather we not piss off royalty," Calypso added.

"You two agree on something?" I glanced between them warily before running a hand through my hair. Perhaps I had a worse hangover than I thought. "Hells. Are you sure I'm not hallucinating?"

The nymph shook her head. "Unless your mind could have

conjured up a ship called *The Glistening Pearl*, then no, you're not."

Elvira doubled over in a fit of laughter, and I wasn't certain whether I should join her or gag. "*The Glistening* what?"

"You heard me." Calypso pointed to where the name was inscribed upon the ship's hull and smirked.

"Brilliant," Elvira managed between cackles. "Absolutely fucking brilliant. Like ships, pearls are rather wet and slippery... well, they ought to be if you've done it right."

I fought the urge to roll my eyes. "Grow up."

"No, Ced, lighten up. I'd ask whether you even know where to find such a pearl, but I think that might be a better question for this so-called prince."

"Once again I must agree with the Serpent," Calypso said, still grinning. "Whoever came up with that was either a genius or incredibly stupid. And judging by everything else I'm seeing..."

"My money's on the latter," I finished, narrowing my gaze as I took my first proper look at the vessel before me. Everything about it, from its sails to its decks, seemed to have been designed for looks rather than practicality. *The Glistening Pearl* was twice the size of *The Jolly Serpent*, but she only carried half as many guns, her masts were only half as tall, and she'd been painted *white*, for Adais's sake. Though she looked to be in relatively good shape, especially considering the damage the dragon had inflicted, the color meant that every blemish and barnacle marring the hull stuck out like a sore thumb. None of that was even touching on the gold, and I suspected the added weight of such adornments were the main cause behind

The Glistening Pearl's limited functionality. I hardly expected *The Jolly Serpent* to be able to outrun a bloodthirsty beast, but she'd have a hell of an easier time than the monstrosity before me. "Whoever built that ship should never be allowed near one again."

Elvira *shushed* me again, all traces of amusement gone as she trained her gaze forward. "They're coming."

Indeed someone was. Both our ships had been anchored, and a bridge had been erected between them. Unintelligible voices speaking a language I didn't immediately recognize drifted from *The Glistening Pearl*, and half a dozen bodies prepared to come aboard *The Jolly Serpent*. My heart skipped a beat upon realizing my daughter was nowhere within my reach. "Get Wendy, and keep her behind me," I hissed out of the corner of my mouth, uncaring who obeyed.

A minute later, our two parties faced one another. Calypso and Elvira stood at my left and right respectively, with Mr. Smee at Elvira's other side. Wendy and Pan had been placed at my back, and when I spread my arms in welcome, I did all I could to shield them both from prying eyes. "Welcome aboard *The Jolly Serpent*," I said through an empty smile, but I didn't bow. I refused to bow. "To whom do we owe the pleasure?"

There were six of them: two guards, three advisors, and a man I could only assume was a king or prince given how he was dressed. His elaborate jacket shone as white as his ship and had even been decorated with threaded golden trim, presumably to match. He was reasonably handsome, sporting pale skin that clearly hadn't seen much of the sun, wavy black hair, and striking blue eyes, and couldn't be any older than thirty. But he didn't return my smile. His crew drew a collective breath, and two even took a step back, including one of the guards. The prince's mouth fell open, and he gasped dramatically. "Your *hand*—"

"Ah, yes. My apologies for waving it around so brazenly." I lowered my prosthetic. "Though I suppose there's no need to explain why I'm called Captain Hook."

A grin spread across the man's features, and he threw his head back and laughed. It startled me, but not the laugh itself; it was his tone as well as his accent I found unsettling, for I hadn't yet been able to place either. "Fascinating," he said when he came up for air. "What did I tell you, Amira? I knew meeting pirates wouldn't disappoint."

He addressed the light skinned and silver-haired woman at his side, who didn't acknowledge her charge other than to raise an eyebrow. She and Elvira appeared to be far too busy staring one another down.

"But for Adais's sake, where are my manners?" The man clicked his tongue, interrupting my thoughts before I could worry about whether or not he planned to do anything about the fact that we were pirates. "I am Prince Herbert Elmer Clyde Engelbert the Seventh of Adra, and I believe thanks are in order. We owe that girl hiding behind you our lives."

Elvira snorted, and I might have joined her in laughing at that utterly ridiculous name had I not been fighting tooth and claw to keep the hostility from my tone. Herbert wouldn't so much as look at Wendy if I had anything to say about it. "She accepts your thanks," I said coolly, silently praying that Wendy would see sense and keep her mouth shut. "All we seek in return is to continue our voyage in peace."

"Peace?" Amira echoed in an identical accent to her prince's, still looking confrontational as ever. I didn't miss the way her fists clenched at her sides, her palms clearly itching for the impressive array of weapons holstered and sheathed at her side. "Kaara nor her realm do not know the word, as your nymph should damn well know."

Herbert's gaze snapped to Calypso who, of all things, flinched. Though she was more than capable of defending and speaking for herself, I acted upon the surge of protectiveness that flooded through me, sidestepping slightly to place her behind me. Holding Amira's glare, I said, "Thank you for the insight, but my request still stands."

"You misunderstand, Captain Hook." Herbert held up a hand to silence his companions. "We have no intention of jeopardizing or delaying your mission. In fact, I believe our goals may be more aligned than we think."

"Do you." A statement rather than a question. I didn't give a shit where these fools were headed or why, so long as it didn't interfere with me getting to Scarlett any more than it already had.

Herbert nodded, oblivious to my irritation, and flashed Calypso a toothy grin. "I'm engaged, you see, but not to any woman. In fact, she's not human at all. I was on my way to collect her from Kaara's court, a mission I may now complete thanks to that charming girl of yours. But—and forgive me, as I know it's bad luck to glimpse

283

her prior to our union—does my bride-to-be happen to be standing before me at this very moment?"

Calypso shoved me aside so fiercely I nearly took a tumble. She got as close to the prince as his guards would allow, quite literally bristling. Her skirts and hair whipped around in a breeze that wasn't there, her hands balled into fists, and her tone was laced with so much venom I hardly recognized it as hers. "My goddess would never barter me like a piece of property."

Herbert waved away his guards, and I tensed as he got within arm's reach of the murderous-looking nymph. "No one has been bartered, Miss…"

"Calypso," she bit out.

He smiled and took her hand within both of his. "Then as honored as I am to meet you, lovely Calypso, you are not my bride. I'm told she asked for my hand personally, so if this is the first you are hearing of the arrangement, it must be one of your sisters I am to wed."

I held my breath as Herbert brought Calypso's hand to his lips, wondering if she was about to stab him. *Is he truly that idiotic?* But she yanked herself from his grasp before his mouth made contact, stepping back to resume her place at my side. "Lucky her," she replied icily.

"Of course, I do hope you'll join us for the wedding. It will be held here, on *The Glistening Pearl's* very deck." Herbert made a grand sweeping motion toward his ship, as though he expected us to be impressed by the ridiculous-looking vessel. "That is, assuming you are also on your way to Kaara's realm?"

Elvira and I exchanged a look, but before any of us could reply, a massive white shape bounded between Herbert's feet. Knocked off balance, the prince fell on his ass, but the shape wasn't deterred. Forcing its way between me and Elvira, it halted in front of Wendy, its wagging tail slapping me in the thigh until it sat on its haunches. It took me a second to piece together the dragging leash and fur, but by then, Herbert had been helped to his feet.

"Bad dog. *Bad* Arktos!"

He picked up the leash and gave it a savage tug, but the fluffy white dog didn't move. Arktos remained fixated on Wendy, continuing to wag his tail as his tongue lolled out of his mouth.

Herbert uttered a disgusted sigh before throwing the leash back onto the deck. "My apologies. An engagement gift from my parents, though as you see, he's not very obedient. Odd, though. He's not usually this friendly to strangers."

Everyone remained silent and still as Wendy knelt before the massive dog. They regarded one another for a moment before she held out her hand, and without hesitation, Arktos placed his paw within it.

Elvira scoffed. "Not obedient, huh? Or just not obedient to you?"

"Perhaps he senses that we owe this girl our thanks." Herbert fixated on Wendy in a way that made my stomach twist into knots. "What is your name?"

"Don't answer that," I snapped before I could help myself. Though Wendy shot me a glare, she remained blessedly silent.

Herbert clicked his tongue. "Protective, I see. You care for her."

"I care for everyone aboard my ship, which is why I must insist that you allow us to pass—"

"Have you ever wanted to speak to a god, my dear girl?"

That shut me up, but not because I took it in any way seriously. Wendy, however, was a different story. "What?"

Amira took a hasty step forward. "My prince, I must caution that you do not—" she began, but Herbert ignored her.

"You're looking at one who is god-touched." He spread his arms, and maybe it was a trick of the light, but I swore his blue eyes illuminated for a split second before resuming their normal hue. "And my gift is that I am a mouthpiece for the gods. They speak through me, and I can even summon them on occasion. Would such a demonstration be sufficient thanks for sparing our lives, girl-whose-name-I-do-not-know?"

While he spoke, Calypso snaked an arm behind my back before tugging insistently on my jacket. I lightly nudged her foot in response and fought hard to keep from stomping on it. She clearly had something to tell me, but how would I decipher her message here in front of all these people? And what in hells did she expect me to do with the information once I had it?

Her behavior kept me distracted to the point where I missed warning Wendy not to humor whatever the prince was playing at. "Any god?" she asked in a tone that surprised me. Did she believe in gods, even after everything she'd seen and done in her short life?

Herbert beamed. "Which were you thinking?"

"Adais."

Calypso cursed, Amira shook her head, and Herbert's eyes widened. "The Sea God himself?"

"I know of no other Adais," Wendy said coldly.

"Well, you see, it's usually much simpler to summon, well, a *lesser* god—"

"I am not interested in speaking to a lesser god. I am interested in speaking to Adais." Wendy crossed her arms. "Unless you wish to leave your savior dissatisfied?"

Herbert stammered a reply, but I didn't hear it. Leaning down, I grabbed her upper arm and squeezed until she grimaced. "What are you playing at?" I hissed for her ears alone.

She tried and failed to shake me off. "That dragon was a sea monster, was it not? I want to know why it obeyed me."

"You mean you don't know?"

"Of course I don't," Wendy snapped, louder now that she was clearly irritated I hadn't released her. "It's not as if I've gone around conversing with dragons my whole life."

"But he's lying," I whispered through gritted teeth. "There is no way that moron can speak for the gods. What kind of outlandish, bold-faced claim is that?"

She elbowed me in the ribs so sharply I had no choice but to let her go. "I'll decide for myself, thanks." To Herbert, Wendy said, "You must excuse my father. He's a bit of a skeptic."

Heat flamed my cheeks, but not for being called a skeptic. My brat of a daughter had just disclosed our relationship to complete strangers who could now do whatever they liked with that information. And judging from that satisfied smirk on her face, she'd done it solely to piss me off.

"Father and daughter, eh?" Herbert's gaze narrowed as he scrutinized us. "You don't look that much alike."

And you don't look half as stupid as you sound, I nearly snapped. "She takes after her mother more than me." *Clearly.*

The prince smiled at Elvira, whose lips curled in disgust. "I can see that. Your wife is as beautiful as a daylily in bloom, and as radiant as a nautical sunrise."

I barely stifled a gag while my sister took a calculated step forward. "This 'radiant' flower would rather gouge her eyes out with thistles than stand in your presence for another mo—"

"She's my sis—I mean, not her mother, nor my wife," I said quickly, speaking over Elvira. *Fuck.* Wendy's little confession would have me spilling my entire family tree, and not only did I not trust myself to linger on the topic, I wasn't positive Herbert would survive a second attempt to flatter any of the women in my company. "In any case, let's get this over with. You're right—we're seeing Calypso safely back to Kaara's realm, and we don't want to keep the goddess waiting."

"But I want what he offered me," Wendy butted in, her murderous expression rivaling Elvira's and Calypso's. "Surely it won't take long."

Herbert nodded, gesturing back toward *The Glistening Pearl*. "It will be quick, I assure you. Captain Hook, you and your daughter may come with me."

"What?" I'd have reached for Wendy again if she wasn't being so careful to avoid me. "Why can't you do it here and now?"

The prince raised an eyebrow. "If I'm going to summon a god out of thin air, especially one as powerful as *Adais*, I require certain tools. Bring whomever you'd like aboard my ship if it will make you feel safer, but as I need to focus, only you and your daughter may bear witness to my power. I'd prefer her alone, but always enjoy impressing the skeptics."

As if I'd let a strange man be alone with my sixteen-year-old daughter. I nodded stiffly. "Fine." I rattled off a list of names that included Elvira and Smee but left out Calypso and Pan. They could decide for themselves whether or not they wanted to accompany us. Keeping Wendy in my sights while simultaneously doing my best to dodge the glares of Herbert's guards, I made my way across the bridge, stopping only when a hand clamped down on my shoulder. Calypso's scent enveloped me as she leaned against my back, curls brushing my earlobe. "This is a mistake, Cedric Teach."

I shrugged off her grip but kept walking, speaking with my head turned in the nymph's direction. "Try convincing Wendy of that, because in case you didn't hear me, I wholeheartedly agree."

"My father is not to be trusted." Calypso fell into step beside me. "And that's if he does agree to speak with you. He hasn't spoken to me in damn near half a century."

"Then we have nothing to worry about."

"I'm serious—"

"Is there a problem?" Amira all but materialized at my other side, raising an eyebrow as her gaze darted between us. Only now that I was so close did I notice her eyes were an odd stormy gray, in a way matching her silvery-white hair.

"Not at all," I lied smoothly. "Calypso was simply telling me what I ought to expect from your prince's... ah... demonstration."

"Was she, now?" Amira's expression didn't soften. "Then I suppose you hardly need me to enlighten you regarding what will happen should you dare harm a single hair on his head."

"I've no intention of harming your prince, nor any of your crewmates."

"Good. See to it that doesn't change no matter what the gods force him to say." Shifting her focus to Calypso, Amira said, "Remember: when he speaks for the gods, Prince Herbert is only a vessel. Nothing more."

With that, she stalked away, leaving me more puzzled than ever. Amira clearly didn't miss much, and if she was half as competent with her weapons as she was her words, she was a force to be reckoned with. "Why do you think someone like her serves the likes of him?" I asked Calypso.

"She's a Starchild. What do you expect?" she muttered under her breath, but before I could ask what in the hell that meant, she, too, darted away, leaving me no choice but to find and join Wendy and Herbert.

The Glistening Pearl was as ridiculous up close as it was from afar. If it weren't for the rigging and masts hanging above all our heads, I may have even doubted I was on a ship, for our surroundings resembled anything but. Herbert was bragging about precisely that when I finally caught up to him and Wendy, who had several shadows. Arktos remained at her heels, and Pan seemed reluctant to leave her side, even despite the prince's rambling.

Upon glimpsing me, Herbert beamed. "Ah, there you are, Captain Hook! I was just telling your daughter all about these lovely rail fixtures."

"Fascinating," I muttered.

"But now that we're all here, we may as well get started. Say goodbye to your friends. Arktos, *stay*, st—" He sighed in relief when Amira stepped in to take the dog's leash. After thanking her, the prince turned back to us. "You two, come."

Wendy said a quick goodbye to Pan before falling in step behind the prince, remaining silent after that. Given Herbert's insistence upon privacy, I expected him to lead us into his or someone else's quarters, so I was surprised when we headed for the stairs leading to the upper deck. I was even more surprised to find that we were the only ones up here.

"Are you certain this is…?"

"Of course." Herbert scoffed. "You didn't expect me to summon the *Sea God* holed up in one of the cabins, did you?"

There was a lot I hadn't expected about this prince, but I kept that to myself as we made our way to what was apparently the final destination: *The Glistening Pearl's* stern. It was quiet, still, and unassuming—save for the strange patterns etched in what looked to be chalk on the deck below our feet. While I tried to make sense of them, Herbert busied himself rummaging through a crate tucked in the corner, emerging a moment later with both a large conch shell and a piece of chalk. After drawing the shape of a wave

291

at the center of one of the patterns, he discarded the chalk before gesturing to the deck.

"Sit."

We obeyed, albeit hesitantly. While Herbert worked, the sea began to toss and turn below us, and it wasn't the only element we'd evidently disturbed. I didn't like how the wind had begun to pick up, nor the way clouds gathered over our heads and our heads alone. And neither did Wendy, judging from how pale she'd gone. I wanted to warn her that she may come away from this encounter disappointed, either by a lack of answers or the answers themselves, but I didn't dare given our proximity to an unfazed Herbert. Assuming a cross-legged position directly in front of us, he placed the conch shell within the wave-like shape he'd drawn before balancing his arms, palms up, on his knees.

The same moment his limbs fell into place, his eyes flashed open—this time, unmistakably glowing. I flinched, and Wendy's arm shot out to grip my knee, but I was too focused on the prince sitting before me to register that my daughter had sought me out for comfort. Unease prickled at the back of my neck, but not because I didn't believe this was real… because I was beginning to believe that it was. Had Herbert truly been touched by a god and gifted this power, and were we truly about to witness it?

When the prince spoke, it was in a voice that sounded nothing like his own. At least a dozen individual tones could be plucked from the sound, with variants of all ages and sexes, and I'd never heard anything so unsettling. Before I realized that I'd done it, I took

Wendy's hand, and we listened with guarded apprehension as the prince spoke in singsong chant.

"*Greatest god of depths and sea, hear me now: I summon thee.*"

The winds picked up, and waves crashed audibly against the hull of the ship. Every hair on my arms had stood at attention, and all my instincts were screaming for me to bolt.

"*Freely I give my body and soul. Take my voice, take control.*"

The conch shell began quivering violently. Herbert tensed, but nothing else happened, at least not that I could see, until he threw back his head and began yelling at the sky.

"*Adais! Adais! ADAIS!*"

His final call morphed into a scream as the multitude of voices in which he spoke faded away… except for one. Doubling over, Herbert's face disappeared from view, and the only thing that told me he was still conscious were the deep, haggard breaths he drew every few seconds.

"Your Highness?" I said slowly, unsure if that was even his proper title. "Are you—"

"*Listen to me exceptionally carefully, Cedric Teach and Wendy Maynard. I have mere moments before Kaara will sense my presence here, even in spirit.*"

Herbert lifted his head, and I flinched. Though his eyes weren't glowing as bright as they were before, there was something else in his stare that made me want to crawl out of my skin. The singular voice in which he now spoke was ancient and deep, so low-pitched it rattled me to my core, and unequivocally belonged to Adais. "*You intend to strike a deal with Kaara. Instead, strike a deal with me.*"

Wendy dug her nails into my palm hard enough to draw blood, but too fixated on the fact that we were conversing with a *god*, I hardly noticed. A question tumbled from my lips before I could rein in my tongue. "What could you possibly want from us?"

"*The same thing Kaara wants—Heartpiercer, my trident. She intends to use its power to kill me and, should she obtain it, will succeed. But Heartpiercer cannot remain in the Sea of Eternal Woe, for as long as it is anywhere other than back in my hands, Kaara will never cease her efforts to get a hold of it. So retrieve it, but retrieve it for me.*

"*And before you interrupt, Cedric Teach, yes. I am fully aware that Kaara holds Scarlett Maynard captive, and that you intended to barter Heartpiercer for her freedom. Wendy seeks the Golden Child's immortality as well as answers regarding her power. Do as I ask, and I will ensure you both have all you wish and more, but do as Kaara asks, and you will have nothing to show for your efforts but betrayal, disappointment, and loss far greater than your deepest fears.*"

I opened my mouth to reply, but unable to choose from the endless stream of questions now filtering through my mind, no sound came out. This entire voyage, I'd done everything within my power to keep a singular goal within my sights: Scarlett. But long before we'd found ourselves sitting before a man speaking on behalf of a god, things had begun to change. Elvira's resentment, Calypso's secrets, Wendy's distrust, and whatever it was that Pan had up his sleeve, were gaining far too much momentum, each adding height and fury to the tsunami set to sweep my feet out from under me at any moment… but it wasn't going under that terrified me. It was that there were fates far worse than drowning.

"*Oh, and one other thing,*" Adais added, tearing me from my spiraling thoughts. "*Use extreme caution when dealing with my daughter.*"

The Sea God abandoned Herbert's body in a similar fashion to the way he'd inhabited it, only in reverse. Opening his mouth, the prince threw back his head, and unless I'd imagined it, the faintest plume of smoke drifted from his parted lips. He slumped forward then, body swaying until his unconscious form landed in a crumpled heap, splayed limbs contrasting against the carefully drawn chalk shapes.

It was only when the sea and winds calmed slightly that I became aware of how heavily I was breathing. Wendy's exhales were just as ragged, and it was several moments before either of us realized we still held hands. She snatched her arm away, as if I'd burned her, before managing, "What in hells was that?"

"Either an incredibly elaborate magic trick, or…" My voice shook slightly. "We just spoke to the Sea God himself." I'd never admit so aloud, but I firmly believed in the latter. Never in my life had I sensed such raw strength and power from a voice alone, and I knew beyond a shadow of a doubt that it was only a taste of what we were due to face in mere days… perhaps hours.

If that's what the Sea God was capable of making me feel… What would the Goddess of Chaos herself have in store?

"No, you spoke to him," Wendy said, either oblivious to or uncaring about my fear. "Bastard wouldn't let me get a word in edgewise."

"And what would you have said?" I demanded, shooting her a pointed glare. Yes, this was the distraction I needed; if Wendy got me angry enough, I might forget about my sheer and utter terror. "Adais already knew precisely what you wanted."

She turned away, grumbling under her breath in a way that was difficult to understand. "No one knows what I want, not even him."

"Then what do you want?"

"I want to know why the gods gave me a father like you!" She shot up, hands balled into fists and tears gathered at the corners of her eyes. "You're fucking insufferable, you know that? The man—no, the *monster* I left in Neverland held a gun to my head, threatened to cut off my hand, and threatened to kill me and my friends on more than one occasion. And those are just the things I *know* about. I was so glad to be rid of you, glad that I hadn't dirtied my hands with your blood. You don't deserve mercy, especially not from me, and you don't deserve a moment's peace. But you're seeking it anyway, and judging from what Adais just said, you're going to get it. You're going to find Scarlett, rescue her, and get to ride off into the sunset and live out your happily ever after as if none of this ever happened. As if *I* never happened."

Perhaps I had been wrong in wanting to argue, because now I was so pissed that red gathered at the corners of my vision. None of this was anything I hadn't heard before, and to be honest, having my previous crimes thrown in my face over and over and *over* again was getting pretty fucking old. "You think I don't know that?" I didn't recall standing, but somehow I was on my feet, giving me the opportunity to lean into Wendy's face and snarl. "That I don't torture myself over what I've done every second of every day?"

"Good. That's a fucking start." Her eyes burned as she stood her ground, and she looked so much like Scarlett it was unnerving. "But still not nearly enough for me to even think about forgiving you."

I couldn't stifle the mirthless laugh that tumbled from my lips. "Forgiveness? Wendy, in case you haven't noticed, I still haven't forgiven myself, and I wouldn't expect it even if I took a damn bullet for you. And as for you and Scarlett," I continued, holding up my hook to silence her, at least for the moment, "I already told you once that I'm fully aware I don't deserve either of you, and that neither of you ever needed saving."

"Oh, but that didn't keep you from trying. You showed up unannounced at the worst possible time, all to rescue me from what—you?" It was Wendy's turn to utter a joyless laugh. "You put on a ridiculous act, lying through your teeth and doing whatever you could to make me think you cared. Killing Pierce, defending Peter, and playacting the perfect captain while I'm forced to sit around and do nothing. *Know* nothing. Do you think I've forgotten the past? That I've forgotten who you are?"

Wendy didn't have to say it for me to know precisely who she saw staring back at her: the villainous Captain Hook. Not Cedric Teach, not Blackbeard's son, not lover to Scarlett Maynard... and certainly not her father.

Her hurt made sense. Her rage had been fueled by me and me alone. Even still, that look she gave me now hurt far worse than any physical injury I'd ever sustained, and I was half-tempted to cut off my remaining hand if only to make her stop.

"You're stubborn," I finally said, unable to think of anything else, "and cling even harder to your hatred and loathing of me any time I do something that suggests I might actually be capable of something other than villainy. I shouldn't be surprised. Scarlett did the same thing when I first met her."

"Shut up about Mother," Wendy snapped.

"You're the one who brought her up."

"And you're the one who made her run away and forced me to grow up an orphan."

I hadn't thought she could hurt me any more, but those words proved me so, so wrong. Inhaling sharply, I reached for the rail, no longer able to hold myself upright on my shaking knees. Closing my eyes, a single question formed in my psyche, one whose answer would tell me whether or not Wendy and I would ever be able to salvage any semblance of a relationship.

"Do you hate me?" I asked quietly, turning my head toward her.

Wendy blinked. "What?"

"It's a simple yes or no question." I fought with everything I had to keep both my face and expression as neutral as possible. "Do you hate me?"

She opened her mouth and closed it again, silently telling me both everything and nothing. We stared at one another for what felt like an hour, chests heaving and fingers twitching, until finally she conjured up a response. "I—"

It happened quicker than lightning. One moment I was staring into Wendy's conflicted face, and the next, something slimy twisted itself around my ankle. There wasn't time for me to scream before I was yanked over the side of the ship, my lower half left to dangle as my hook shot out to grip the edge of the rail. All the while, whatever held my ankle continued to tug savagely, and unless I gave in and *soon*, I feared it might rip my damn leg off.

A flash of blonde, followed by Wendy's strained shout. "Take my hand!"

I obeyed, she pulled with all her might, but both were useless. There was no doubt I was going down, but I'd be damned if I took my daughter with me.

Meeting her gaze, I whispered, "I'm sorry."

Then I let go.

XVII. THE MERMAID

Cedric

I f it was possible to be both unbearably hot and impossibly cold all at once, that's precisely what my body was currently putting me through. The sun beat mercilessly on my unprotected face, but when I tried to lift an arm to shield it, agony shot from shoulder to wrist. My entire being ached, from my neck all the way down to my toes, and the parts of me still clothed were sweltering. Where skin touched water, though, I was so cold that I almost couldn't feel anything through the numbness.

I forced my eyelids open a sliver. A mistake. Sunlight assaulted my vision, adding my eyes to the list of things that hurt, and an involuntary curse tumbled from my parched lips. I ran my tongue

301

over them, wincing at the cracks and dried blood. A flash of anger ignited within me. Gods, was there any part of me that hadn't been damaged? Was I alone? Where the fuck was I, and how long had I been here?

Fighting through the pain, I brought my left arm to the ground beside me. Curling my fingers slightly, it dawned on me that they were sifting through sand. And sand plus water equaled...

A beach. Had to be. Waves rolled audibly in the background, matching the rhythm of the tide as it rolled on and off my half-submerged body. Blurry and jumbled memories returned a little at a time: the dragon, that arrogant prick of a prince, the voice of Adais himself, Wendy's outburst, my fall... A shiver shot down my spine that had nothing to do with the cold. This was bad. I'd been tossed overboard, miraculously not drowned, and washed up on a beach somewhere. The question was, *what* beach, and would my crew know where and how to find me? Would Wendy know how to find me? Would she care enough to?

This wasn't just bad, this was horrible. Beyond horrible, and wounded or not, exhausted or not, I couldn't stay here, out in the elements where anyone or anything was liable to find me. I had to scout my surroundings, assess my injuries, get something to eat—somehow—possibly build a signal fire... *No.* I halted my racing thoughts as I rolled onto my side, blinking in the still-too-bright sunlight. Overwhelming myself before I'd even stood up wasn't going to do me or my chances of survival any good. I had to keep my wits about me if I had any chance of being found. I had to be logical, had to be methodical—

Logic leaped out the window when I opened my eyes and saw a mermaid.

Shoving my pain aside, I scooted back, unable to force myself into an upright position fast enough. My hand flew to my side out of instinct, but there was nothing but an empty holster and sheath, meaning my weapons must have been lost to the sea. No matter. I always had my hook. It was the reason I'd chosen it over any other useless chunk of metal after Pan had chopped it off. Raising my arm, I waved it around threateningly as I finally sat up, only to realize the limb was much too light.

My hook was also gone.

I pulled my stump back into my chest, suddenly feeling more vulnerable than if I were stark naked. I was weaponless, defenseless, and weak, and my only hope now was that the mermaid wasn't out for blood. Luckily, I hadn't known the creatures to be violent. Even in Neverland, they preferred to flee rather than stand their ground. But this one wasn't fleeing. She remained in place, her crimson-red tail twitching slightly as the tide washed over it. Where ears would be if she were human, gill flaps opened and closed, doing their best to keep her alive and breathing while out on land. Her dark brown hair covered her face in a way that meant I couldn't get a decent look at it, though I wasn't fully certain that I wanted to. Given my past experiences with sirens and nerisas, it wouldn't surprise me all that much if this mermaid had fangs.

I had no idea if she would understand English, but there was little to no chance of her comprehending my broken and garbled Spanish even if she did speak the language. "Stay back. Don't come any closer, or I'll…" My voice trailed off. What would I do? "I'll kick you."

The mermaid's eyes widened, her lips parted, and she raised a hand to pull the hair away from her face. A face that looked far too much like…

"Scarlett?" I hadn't meant to whisper her name aloud, but as I was learning more every day, I had little self-control when it came to her. Or rather… things that reminded me of her, because Scarlett wasn't a mermaid, and there was no way this was real. I had to either be hallucinating or there was magic at play, and neither were options I was willing to entertain. With a growl, I shook my head, demeanor switching in an instant. "You're not real."

She froze, and it gave me a chance to study her features in more detail. One of the mermaid's eyes was a piercing blue while the other was a warm, familiar brown. Her hair was nearly an identical shade, falling a few inches past her shoulders—longer than I remembered it. Shells the same color red as her tail covered her breasts, held in place by a string so thin I was surprised it hadn't snapped. Beyond the obviously inhuman features, though, it was uncanny how much the mermaid bore a resemblance to Scarlett; they shared everything from round lips, to the faintest freckles, to the scar on the bridge of their noses…

I inhaled sharply. That scar was *identical* to Scarlett's. The placement, the shape, the way her freckles were arranged around it… That simply couldn't be a coincidence. Could it?

But before I could open my mouth to give a voice to the insane thought, the mermaid lowered her arm and began drawing in the sand with her finger. No… writing. She was writing words, English words by the looks of it. There was still a fair distance between us, so I dared to drag myself slightly closer to make out her message, written sideways so neither of us would have to read or write upside down.

No need for hostility. I saved you.

"I wasn't hostile," I lied automatically.

She erased her message before writing a second one. *You threatened me.*

Heat crept to my cheeks. "Yes, well, you startled me."

Thought you might, so took your hook.

"You took it?" Anger flared within my chest; that hook had been custom made for me, and wouldn't be easily, if ever, replaceable. "Give it back."

The mermaid didn't bother to tell me no. *Shouldn't you thank me?*

"Thank you for what?"

She looked as if I'd slapped her. *Saved your life. Scydra would have drowned you.*

"Scydra?" I echoed.

The squid, she scribbled impatiently. *She owes me, but was that a mistake?*

"Why, though?" I narrowed my gaze as distrust stirred within me. "I'm grateful for your intervention, yes, but what was in it for you?"

She stared at me long and hard before taking her time scrawling a new message. *Are you Cedric Teach?*

It was my turn to feel as though I'd been slapped across the face. "Who's asking?"

Don't lie. You know me.

"No." I shook my head. Whatever magic was affecting me, I wouldn't fall for it a third time. I couldn't afford to, and neither could my fragile heart. "You simply look quite a lot like someone I… I used to know."

Same. She gestured to my arm before writing again. *Except you had two hands.*

"And the Scarlett Maynard I knew was human," I snapped before I could help myself, pulling my damaged arm closer against my chest as shame flooded through me. This was precisely why I never went in front of strangers without my hook.

She wasn't fazed by my embarrassment. *I never said my name, but you know two. Do you know the third?*

Of course I knew. It was on the tip of my tongue, and I nearly blurted it out, but I shook my head again, scooting back. "I don't know who you are—*what* you are—but you're not my Scarlett."

Ignoring the wave of nausea the sudden movement summoned, I staggered to my aching feet. Knowing the mermaid wouldn't be able to follow, my intention was to run farther up the shore, but I'd barely taken two steps before losing my balance. My forehead seared with agony as I went careening backwards, and unable to throw out an arm to break my fall, I tensed, preparing to tumble back into the unforgiving surf.

But before I struck the water, arms snaked around my back and legs, effectively trapping me in a tight embrace. The breath *whooshed* from my lungs as I was pulled against a sturdy chest, and fingers shot out to grip my bearded chin. The mermaid pulled my face toward hers, leaving me no choice but to gaze into those odd, mismatched eyes. A wave crashed against the mermaid's back, but she paid it no mind. She was too busy staring at me as though she'd seen a ghost.

Instinct told me to protest. To push her away, to squirm. But she held me captive in more ways than one, and the longer she stared, the calmer I felt. I couldn't explain why. I didn't trust her. I trusted my desperate, lonely heart even less, but the spark of recognition remained. And if I didn't know any better... it was growing into a flame.

Finally, words returned to me. "I-I should g—" I started, but before I could finish, the mermaid released my chin. She reached instead for one of my scars, gently tracing the mark from its origin near my forehead to its end on my outer cheek. I remembered precisely how I'd gotten it. And judging from the look on the mermaid's face, she did, too.

My lips parted in shock. I had at least half a dozen scars marring my face, yet that was the one she'd chosen to acknowledge. The one left by Scarlett herself at my request, back when I was a relatively scar-free fugitive tired of having such a recognizable face. Scarlett had been so reluctant to do it, but efficient when the time came, digging the blade just deep enough to leave a permanent mark, but not so deep that it caused me unnecessary pain. I'd never regretted my choice for an instant, especially not after I lost her. As long as I lived, I'd possess the scar. The reminder of her, her memory, and what she meant to me.

And as long as I'd lived, I'd never told another soul she'd done it.

I released the breath I'd been holding, whispering her name along with it—her middle name. It was a question as much as it was a plea, one I hoped she'd be able to see in my eyes. I couldn't bring myself to voice it aloud, but it was there, repeating in my mind like a mantra: *Please don't break my heart. Please don't break my heart.* This had to be real, she had to be real. Another fractured reality wouldn't simply shatter me. It would kill me. And by the gods, I hadn't come this far just to die; not without seeing her, without *holding* her, the real her, at least once more. "Is this real? Are you real?"

Still holding my gaze, she gave a nod so slight it was nearly imperceptible.

Tears immediately welled behind my eyes, but not for the reasons I'd been expecting. I'd imagined this moment countless times, in every possible way—dreams, nightmares, visions, elaborate fantasies—but not a single one of them had gone quite like this. With her as a mermaid, and with me... whatever I was. Broken and damaged, scarred and monstrous. Partly to blame was Neverland, but mostly to blame was me. The things I'd done, the torture I'd often intentionally put myself through, all of it was to become my own self-fulfilling prophecy. Because I'd lost her, I felt the need to turn myself into someone who didn't deserve her.

I didn't realize I'd looked away until Scarlett pulled my face back up. Her fingers lingered below my jaw, gently twisting the unruly strands of my beard, but though her caresses were soft, her expression was anything but. She glanced at my missing hand and back again, slightly tightening her grip on my chin. Though she still hadn't said a word, I knew that look in her eyes well enough to know what she was asking. *Who did this to you?*

"No one you know," I managed, voice hoarse. "It was a misunderstanding, and it's done now."

Something flashed in her eyes, but as quickly as she'd broken my fall, she released me. She remained in close proximity though, writing in the sand with far more urgency than she had the first few times. *I thought you were dead.*

I half laughed, half sobbed. A few of the tears I'd summoned streamed down my cheeks at the movement. "I thought *you* were dead."

Where have you been? Neverland? Why come here now?

"Can you speak, please?" I blurted out. The writing didn't necessarily bother me, but if this was real, if this was her, I wanted every bit of her I could get. "I'd like to hear your voice."

Scarlett's head snapped up, and she swallowed before slowly shaking her head. Bringing a few fingers to her throat, she clawed at it as if hoping she could reach inside and yank something out. When she dropped her hand, the marks remained, shining brightly against older scratches which suggested she did this often.

"Oh." I racked my brain trying to recall whether I'd ever heard a mermaid speak out of water. "Are you not capable... as you are?"

Another head shake, followed by writing in the sand so quick it was nearly illegible. *Worse. Kaara has my voice.*

"I see." Gods, why did this feel so awkward, so formal? "Is she also the one who did... *this* to you? Can you change back to human form?"

I asked first. What are you doing here?

I opened my mouth to speak but shut it again. How was I supposed to answer that? The truth was what Scarlett deserved, but somehow I didn't think she'd take kindly to *I thought you were dead until a nymph showed up and told me that you weren't, so without a shred of actual proof, I embarked on a suicide mission across monster-infested waters for the million-to-one chance of seeing you again. Oh, and I dragged our daughter into it, too.*

Our daughter. *Wendy.* If nothing else, I had to be completely honest about her, about how resilient and brave and strong she was, all thanks to Scarlett. If Calypso had been telling the truth and Scarlett had given up everything for our daughter, it was the least I could do. "I'm here for you. We both are—me and Wendy." When Scarlett didn't react, I added, "Our child."

She drew an audible intake of breath—the first I'd seen that wasn't through her gills—and threw a hand over her mouth as her eyes began to glisten. It was a few moments before she was able to write again, and it was a noticeable struggle for Scarlett to regain control of her quivering limbs. *She's alive?*

I nodded. "Intelligent, capable, and beautiful. Every bit

your daughter."

Scarlett wrote more before I'd finished speaking. *What did you call her? I named her Gwendolyn.*

"Gwendolyn?" I repeated, the unusual name feeling odd on my tongue. "Where did that come from?"

It means fair and blessed. She was born with such light-colored hair.

"Ah." The meaning made sense, at least. "She must have shortened it at some point. I've only known her as Wendy."

What does she look like? What is she like?

At this, I hesitated, because as far as I knew, Wendy hated me and everything I'd ever stood for to my core. Laughing nervously, I said, "You'll meet her soon enou—"

Scarlett moved so fast it was unnerving. Twisting her body and balancing on her tail, she did the mermaid equivalent of straddling me, settling on my lap and caging my helpless body between her outstretched arms. The pose was anything but arousing. A dangerous, yet all-too-familiar, fire ignited behind her eyes, and when she mouthed her question, I'd have given anything to disappear into the foamy tide behind us.

She's here?

I'd fucked up. Severely. But it was too late to backtrack, and even attempting as much was liable to get me in far deeper trouble than I already was. "W-Wendy?" I stammered. "She's not *here*, per say."

Scarlett's tail slapped against the waves with such ferocity that I flinched. *You brought her here?* she mouthed again, her movements exaggerated given that I wasn't experienced reading lips. *To this place? To Kaara?*

"She was already on her way here for a different purpose," I said quickly, regaining a bit of my composure despite the fact that Scarlett hadn't quit looking at me like she wanted to kill me. "We simply joined forces."

No. Her eyes burned. *You fucked up is what you did.*

Had I, though? Instinct screamed for me to do what would have been easiest: to nod, to grovel and beg her forgiveness, to say whatever she wanted to hear to calm her. To fix this. But there was an old wound festering within me, one Scarlett's words had prodded, and it summoned fury and rage I hadn't realized I'd bottled up for so long. I was far from innocent in all this, but neither was she.

Sitting up a bit straighter, I met her challenging glare. "That may be true, and I won't bother denying it. But so did you. None of us—not me, not you, and certainly not Wendy—would be anywhere near here if you hadn't left me. Lied to me. Led me to believe that you were fucking *dead.*"

She had gone completely still, but didn't interrupt, so I continued before she could.

"Do you know what that did to me? Can you even begin to imagine it?" Tears streamed uninhibited down my face, but they were the least of my worries. "If it weren't for Elvira watching me like a hawk, for her shoving knives into my hands and forcing me to kill rats so the curse wouldn't take me, I would have ended it myself. Would have happily strode into that forest and let some monster devour me. I drank myself silly until they started hiding the rum.

Searched in vain for the bullets they kept under lock and key. Tried to leave the prison Neverland had become, sometimes wandering those everchanging trees for days at a time. When none of that worked, I forced myself to sleep, hoping desperately I wouldn't wake up. But that was the worst idea of them all… because in dreams and nightmares alike, there you were."

I squeezed my eyes shut, reliving the pain all over again. "You left my side, yet you refused to leave my fucking mind. I began to see you everywhere. It was glimpses at first—a flash of your hair, a hint of your smile. But over time, and especially these past few weeks, it became far more. It was as if you were standing over my shoulder everywhere I went, whispering in my ear, but every time I'd turn around, you were gone. Until you weren't." I paused, swallowing. "I knew I'd lost my damn mind, but by that point, I was too lonely to care. I wanted you any way I could have you, even if it wasn't real. *Especially* if it wasn't real. Easier to believe a lovely dream than to accept a tragic reality."

Glancing up to look her in the eyes, I drew a deep, shuddering breath before speaking again. "So yes, I came after you, yes, our daughter is here too, and no, I won't apologize. For what? Missing you so badly it ached? Wanting you every second of every day? Loving you with my entire soul?" I shook my head, lowering my voice to a growl as my sorrow turned to pent-up frustration. "I'm not sorry. I *refuse* to be sorry. Don't you get it? I'd rather die in this hell than live in the one your absence created."

Too distracted by my haggard breaths and fluttering heart, it was several moments before I realized how close we had gotten. Scarlett remained on my lap, but at some point had leaned into where our chests touched. Locking her tear-filled eyes with mine, she mouthed two simple words.

I'm sorry.

The depth of her unflinching gaze told me how much she meant it. The fact that she kept opening her mouth but closing it again told me how much more she desperately wished she could say. And the closeness of our bodies reassured me that maybe, just maybe, we could survive this hell, just as we'd survived every other hell that had come before. *Together.*

I nodded, voice hoarse. "I know."

She shifted her weight; with her arms no longer bearing the brunt of it, she splayed her palms on my lower back. I shuddered at the contact, but not from the clamminess of her touch. Scarlett froze, cocking her head in a silent question, but I was already shaking my head. "Don't stop." *Never stop.*

Her hands began their journey upward, both too fast and agonizingly slow. One traced my spine while the other lingered below it, outlining shapes I didn't bother trying to picture. I was both cursing and glad for the shirt that still clung to my frame, for as much as I longed to feel her skin-to-skin, I worried I may come apart by her featherlight touch alone. Expertly she worked me, her deft fingers playing me as if I were the instrument who would sing only for her, and by the time she settled both palms against the nape of my neck, I was breathless all over again.

Then, with a single kiss, Scarlett Maynard reclaimed me in mind, body, and soul.

Any lingering doubt I still possessed over whether or not she was real receded with the tide. She tasted like the sea, her tears and *mine*, and when my arms shot out to grip her waist, I knew I'd never again let her go. The faintest of whimpers emitted from her throat when I touched her; fueled by it, I tangled my hand in her hair. Pulling her head back, I deepened the kiss, and she opened for me eagerly. We became lost in one another, drunk on what we'd been deprived of for so long. Not even a wave crashing over our heads was enough to break us apart. With Scarlett's tail acting as our anchor, we remained exactly as we were, and had we both been human, it would be impossible to tell where one of us ended and the other began.

It felt as though we were just getting started when a faint shout cut through our too-perfect reality, shattering it in an instant. I almost ignored it—almost. But I knew that voice, and the voice knew me.

"*CEDRIC*! Cedric Teach, are you here? Are you alive?"

Calypso. My heart skipped a beat at the realization. If she was here, had found me, there was a good chance Wendy had, too. My family could be whole again, here and now. Pulling away from Scarlett, I inhaled deeply in preparation to shout right back.

But before I could so much as squeak, her hand clamped over my mouth. Utilizing those inhuman reflexes a second time, Scarlett twisted and shoved until I was pinned to the ground beneath her, once again glaring daggers at me. *Her?* she mouthed, once again looking absolutely furious.

She still had her hand over my mouth, so I couldn't do more than shake my head in confusion. With a frustrated huff, Scarlett released me, allowing me to sit up as she scribbled a barely legible message in the sand.

You brought Calypso here?

I blinked. "You know her?"

She's Kaara's.

"I know that. How else do you think I found you—blind faith? I was determined, but not that determined. I had a little help."

Scarlett's lips parted in shock, but before she could write anything else, Calypso called for me again. There was still no sign of the nymph, but her voice was much closer than it had been before, so close that it wouldn't surprise me if she came waltzing down the shore at any moment.

I turned to Scarlett to warn her as much, but she was no longer there; in the space she'd previously occupied, there sat my hook, prosthetic attachment and all. Gaze darting around wildly, I caught a glimpse of her just as she was disappearing beneath the waves. My heart sank faster than an anchor, and the hole in my chest widened so much I feared it might tear me in two. *No.* I'd just gotten her back—had just touched her, just kissed her—and I'd be damned if I'd lose her again. Ignoring the rising, turbulent tide, I followed her into the surf, uncaring that I chanced drowning for the second time today. I all but screeched Scarlett's name, and only then did she turn to look at me, remaining up to her neck in water.

"Where are you going? Why? Was it something I said? Will I ever see you again?" Desperate questions poured uninhibited from my lips, the words themselves borderline incoherent. The water was to my elbows now, and the bottom was only getting steeper. Soon I'd be forced to tread water. "Don't go. Please, Scarlett, stay with me!"

She hesitated for a fraction of a second, and if I didn't know any better, something flashed in her one blue eye. But a moment later, she was gone, having slipped so soundlessly beneath the waves that it left me wondering if she'd ever truly been here at all.

XVIII. THE STRAY

Wendy

I love you, Wendy.
Do you hate me?
I'm sorry.

Damn him. Damn Captain fucking Hook to hells and back, to the depths of the Sea of Eternal Woe, to Davy Jones's locker, to wherever his torment would be the most punishing. His words, especially the '*I love you,*' hadn't quit haunting me since he'd uttered them, and each time they replayed in my mind, my fury ignited anew. This was the same man who'd gambled with my life on more than one occasion. Who'd slaughtered innocent children in cold blood. Who was covered in scars from head to toe, a good number of which had likely been earned committing other atrocities I could only begin to imagine.

He wasn't supposed to love me. He was supposed to loathe me as much as I loathed him, meant to keep making my life a living hell if he insisted upon being in it, to keep playing the villain to my... whatever I was. And it had felt damn good to tell him as much, even if I didn't really mean half of what had spilled from my lips.

But he wasn't supposed to die.

That much became clear the moment my father's hand slipped from my grasp. I'd lost sight of him shortly after, but it hadn't kept me from screaming his name until my throat was raw and hoarse. It hadn't kept me from nearly punching Calypso in the face when she claimed there was nothing her magic could do to get him back. And it certainly hadn't kept me from using whatever powers I possessed to summon any creature that may be able to rescue him.

The only beast that answered my call was Herbert's dog, but not in the way I had intended. It didn't matter how many times I tried to shoo him away—Arktos had designated himself my second shadow, refusing to leave my side despite multiple attempts to wrangle him into a cage, belowdecks, or at least secure his leash to one of the masts. The closest anyone got was when a pair of guards succeeded in dragging him away, but following an agonized shriek, Arktos trotted back over to me looking rather satisfied as blood dripped from his muzzle.

They left us alone after that, and it gave me plenty of time to wallow in my guilt. This was my fault, and my *selfish* fault at that. I'd been so busy screaming at my father that I hadn't paid any attention to the prickles creeping up my arm, nor noticed the arrival of the squid until it had wrapped an inky black tentacle around his leg. I should have warned him, should have pushed him out of the way, should have done *something*, but I hadn't. And now the guilt was eating me alive... ironic considering that was more than likely the fate that had befallen Cedric.

Elvira was the sole reason I hadn't leapt into the sea myself. After Arktos deemed her presence acceptable, she had held me for hours, acting as both a punching bag for my rage as well as a shoulder to cry on. Her patience never waned, even when curses spewed from my lips and violent tantrums erupted from me on more than one occasion. "The lookouts say we'll reach the mainland in a few hours," she reminded me countless times, "and Ced is a strong swimmer. He's probably washed up somewhere, and we'll form a search party the moment we go ashore."

It was bullshit and we both knew it. If we found anything at all, it would be a corpse, and for Elvira to insinuate that I didn't know otherwise was an insult to my intelligence. But part of me suspected it was far worse than that. I didn't believe for one second that my aunt would be this calm if she truly believed her brother was dead, and I didn't miss the venomous glares she and Calypso were shooting at one another when they thought I wasn't looking. Once darkness fell, I even caught them speaking in hushed tones near the wedding arch Prince Herbert had erected. Unfortunately, I didn't pick up on a single thing they were saying, and they were much more careful to stay out of sight after that.

I didn't know about what or why, but I did know I was being lied to. Again.

But as angry and bitter as I was, the emotions became secondary to my exhaustion, because for the second night in a row, I didn't sleep a wink. Unwilling to return to *The Jolly Serpent* where reminders of my father would be inescapable, I remained onboard *The Glistening Pearl*, huddled at the prow and scanning the moonlit waters for a head, a body, a piece of driftwood… literally anything resembling Cedric or something he may have clung to. I barely noticed Peter draping a thick blanket over my shoulders, nor when Arktos settled his massive head in my lap. They fell asleep huddled against me, their slumbering bodies holding me together even when I wanted to do nothing more than fall apart.

The lookouts finally declared *"land ho!"* an hour before dawn, and we anchored a hundred yards from shore without incident. I'd have been the first one into the rowboats had Elvira not barred me from disembarking until I swallowed the pieces of half-stale bread she shoved into my hands. Tears blurred my vision as I forced the food down—I hadn't taken the time to properly chew—but the moment she was satisfied I wasn't running on no sleep and an empty stomach, Elvira allowed me to join the others. The prince handpicked a dozen or so of his crewmates to come ashore while Peter, Tink, Elvira, Calypso, Mr. Smee, and Arktos crammed themselves into the rowboat I'd selected.

Had our circumstances been any different, I may have enjoyed the journey to shore. The sea was calm, the morning bright, and the beach was as ordinary as it was unassuming, leading into a healthy-looking jungle. In stark contrast to Neverland, everything was alive and green. Colorful birds circled overhead, their cries echoing faintly on the breeze, and I could sense a wide array of other creatures dwelling within. But something other than worry about Cedric had my gut twisting into knots, and I turned to Peter when the weight of the unease became overwhelming.

"Somehow I didn't imagine Kaara's realm looking like... this."

"Neither did I." He spoke without looking at me, fixated upon our destination. "No sign of Hook, either."

"We'll find him," I replied without missing a beat. "He's out there somewhere. Has to be."

"How her realm appears to mortals changes at her leisure," Calypso piped up, looking more energized than I'd ever seen her. Warmth colored her cheeks, a faint smile played on her lips, and she sat balanced on her ankles, as if she were eager to leap out of the boat at the earliest opportunity. "Kaara must be in a good mood today."

"Can't imagine why," Elvira muttered, so softly I almost didn't hear her.

"What does it look like when she's in a bad mood?" I dared to ask.

Calypso met my gaze. "Like Neverland does in your nightmares."

With that terrifying image seared into everyone's brains, we remained silent until reaching the shore. Once the rowboats had been tied and secured, we split into groups, with Peter, Tink, and Arktos making up mine. The dog immediately set off sniffing along the shore, but I purposefully allowed all the others to go ahead as I dragged my feet, much to Peter's confusion.

"What are you doing?" he asked. "Aren't you dying to find Hook?"

I brought a finger to my lips and replied in a voice barely louder than a whisper. "I'm dying to throttle him for worrying me so badly. But I also need to figure out what Calypso and Elvira are hiding, and suspect that once I do, Hook won't be far behind. Don't you think it's odd that Elvira didn't seem to give a fuck about his disappearance?"

Peter shrugged, nearly displacing Tink from her perch on his shoulder. "Maybe, but it's not like they haven't been arguing lately. Perhaps she's finally gotten tired of his bullshit."

"She's his sister. I doubt the bonds of blood would be broken that easily."

"No offense, Wendy, but if you think your family holds blood in high regard, you haven't been paying much attention."

I forced myself to ignore that and whistled as softly as I could muster. Though he had wandered a good thirty yards ahead, Arktos immediately stilled before snapping his head up and trotting back to my side. "Is Cedric here?" I asked once he was closer. "My father?"

Arktos whined as Peter's mouth dropped open. "So do you just... have a dog now? One that understands you?"

"He's certainly not mine," I said, cringing a bit at the thought of what Herbert might do if I tried to keep Arktos permanently, "but let's find out if he understands." Clearing my throat, I turned back to the dog and summoned the most authoritative tone I could muster. "Arktos, take us to Captain Hook."

Another whine, and this one came accompanied with him dipping his head and placing a paw over his snout. I tried not to think too hard about what that response meant. "In that case, take us to Elvira and Calypso."

The moment the command left my lips, he bounded off without hesitation, leaving Peter and me struggling to keep up. We sprinted along the glittering coast, keeping close to the tide as it ebbed and flowed at a rhythmic pace. Gulls took off back into the sky, squawking indignantly as Arktos ran straight through their gatherings, but the moment I began to wonder if this was all just a game for an oversized puppy, I heard them: Elvira and Calypso's raised voices, both shouting Cedric's name.

I snatched Peter's arm and skidded to a halt, digging my nails into his flesh to silence him when he opened his mouth to protest. With another low whistle, I summoned Arktos before leading us up the shore and into some foliage, where I motioned for everyone to duck out of sight. Tink's wings buzzed, and Arktos whined again, but I *shushed* them both before peering through a gap in the leaves.

The two women were far enough away not to have noticed us, yet close enough to hear so long as they shouted. Between calling for their captain, they appeared to be continuing whatever argument I'd stumbled upon last night. It was difficult to make sense of anything that was being said while my heart rate was still elevated, but before long, intelligible words began to float on the breeze.

"...have killed you in that tavern."

"Didn't you try just that and fail?"

"This is the last time I ever listen to my lovesick brother and not my instincts. Gods, had I just stuck a knife between your ribs, none of this would..."

They kept going back and forth, but I stopped listening because Elvira's words all but confirmed my instincts. Cedric was alive and she knew it—the question was where.

"Wendy," Peter said slowly. "What are you—"

"Come on." I rose to my full height, uncaring that twigs and dead leaves were now tangled in my hair. "I've heard more than enough."

Peter said something else, but I ignored it as I marched across the sand toward Elvira. It was a while before she noticed me, and only at the last second did she dodge my swing toward her face. She recovered almost instantaneously, green eyes narrowed into slits as she drank me in. "I may have put up with that shit for hours last night, but try it again and I'll break your fucking nose."

"Break my leg if it will help you sleep at night. I imagine that's rather difficult for a liar like you," I snapped. "Is that why you're such a bitch all the time? The lack of sleep?"

Beside us, Calypso threw back her head and laughed. "Wendy, I think you just became my new favorite person."

"Shut up. You're even worse than she is." It took all my effort not to whip out my dagger and hurl it in the nymph's direction. "It's not a fucking contest when you're both to blame. One of you needs to come clean *right now*, or I swear to Adais I'll sic this dog on you." Arktos appeared at my side and, without further prompting, bared his teeth into an intimidating snarl. "Where is my father?"

Elvira held up a hand in surrender as her gaze flicked between me and the dog. "Are you carrying around bacon in your pocket or something?"

"Answer the damn question."

"That's what we're trying to figure out, in case you haven't noticed," she snapped.

"You knew he was alive all this time!"

"Yes. And I told you that. I didn't lie."

"But there's clearly a lot more to the story!" I dug my heels into the sand, standing my ground in more ways than one. "I'm not stupid, and I heard you two talking last night. What aren't you telling me?"

Elvira and Calypso exchanged a look but didn't say a word.

"I'm two seconds away from releasing Ark—"

"Kaara wants Cedric," Elvira blurted out, and her composure shattered the moment she opened her mouth. She began quivering, though whether it was from fear, sadness, or more anger, I couldn't be certain. "And he's known that this entire time. All three of us did. It's what she was here to ensure, that he'd arrive in one piece. I warned him not to agree, begged him to reconsider, but did he listen? Of course not. And now he's fucking gone."

My mind raced to piece it all together. "Kaara wants him, and he wants Mother... Gods, he's going to give himself up in exchange for her, isn't he?"

"He's going to try," Calypso said, pursing her lips when we all glared at her. "And before any of you dare accuse me of further deception, I told Cedric Teach from the very beginning he ought not to trust me, *and* that Scarlett Maynard would be the death of him. I'm guilty of many things, but lying isn't one of them."

"Then where is he now?" Yanking my dagger from my belt, I took a threatening step toward the nymph, and Arktos growled again. "The least you could do is take us to him."

"I'd be more than happy to if I knew," she hissed, both at me and the dog. "He's not where he's supposed to be. Scydra lost him."

"Who the fuck is Scydra? And how in hells do you know that?"

"Listen, I know you all want to strangle me, and you're more than welcome to do just that. But you'll never find Cedric if I'm dead, and you"—she gestured to Peter—"will have traveled all this way and killed your fairy for absolutely nothing. Cedric is alive, but if he's going to stay that way, we need to find him sooner rather than later."

I hated that she made sense. "Fine. But if we don't find him by sundown, Arktos gets to use you as a chew toy."

To cover the most ground, we agreed it would be best to split off individually, so we did just that, save for Tink remaining with Peter and Arktos remaining with me. Peter and Elvira searched different sections of the forest while Calypso and I headed in opposite directions along the coast. Though I tried multiple times to get Arktos to track Cedric, the dog either couldn't or wouldn't, so by midafternoon I gave up asking it of him. We walked tirelessly, only stopping a few times for quick water breaks, and though we stumbled upon a handful of wrecked rowboats and other washed-up debris, none of it contained Cedric or any of his belongings.

I hadn't been allowing myself to imagine the unthinkable up until now, but as the night crept ever closer, so did doubt. My father going missing had never been part of whatever Kaara or Calypso had in store for him. They claimed he wasn't dead, but how could they know for certain if they didn't even know where he was?

What if he died thinking I hated him?

I swallowed as Cedric's wounded face flashed in my mind's eye. Though I may have hated him once, and certainly still hated many of his actions, my resentment had undoubtedly grown into something softer. It wasn't affection, and I didn't quite *like* him, but he was the only father I'd ever get… and though I wasn't ready to admit as much aloud, I could have easily been saddled with one far worse. *Worse* wouldn't have risked drowning and dodged bloodthirsty monsters to pluck me from the sea. *Worse* wouldn't have called a truce with the one responsible for cutting off his hand, much less gone on to defend him. *Worse* would be a far shittier captain and command a lot less respect, if he was even a captain at all.

And *Worse* wouldn't have thought twice about leaving the woman who had abandoned him to die.

My thoughts shifted to Scarlett as I glanced out at the sea. Unless Adais had lied to me and Hook, my mother was alive, and I was likely to meet her soon. Gooseflesh erupted along my arms at the thought, which both surprised and unsettled me. Even six months ago I'd have leaped at the opportunity to come face to face with the woman who birthed me. My feelings toward her had always been complex, but far more fond than bitter, especially once I learned she hadn't given me up willingly. So why was I suddenly... nervous?

Though my first instinct was to shove the uncomfortable realization aside, I clenched my hands into fists and shook my head. *No. Face your feelings.* Running from them had only caused the most volatile of my emotions to come spilling from me at the most inopportune moments, evidenced by my outburst yesterday, and I didn't need anything else to regret. So I halted, closed my eyes, and allowed the anxiety to wash over me like the tide, all the while asking myself a single question.

What are you so afraid of?

Rejection. Disappointment. Being too much, or perhaps not enough, like him. The truth stung even worse than I had prepared myself for, and I wrapped my arms around my middle as a dull ache throbbed deep in my chest. Old wounds ripped open, and though I was still alone, save for Arktos, I felt more vulnerable and exposed than I would if I were standing naked in a room full of people. Hells, I'd prefer that right about now if only it would make the pain go away.

But it wouldn't, not for a long time, because my sense of inadequacy was rooted deep. The seed may have been planted the moment my mother abandoned me, but I was the one who had fed and watered it. I was the one who had watched dozens of other children get adopted and convinced myself there was something wrong with me for never being among them. I was the one who believed the whispers, believed that 'Wayward Wendy' wasn't worthy of friends or meant to belong. I was the one so hellbent on finding a ship, so determined to run from the past and never look back that instead, I became the fool who ran straight into a den full of monsters... into Neverland.

That's what I feared—that Scarlett would look at me and see nothing more than a scared little girl simply playacting the pirate she and Cedric would have raised me to be. That she would resent me, hate me even, for what she'd gone through in the name of keeping me safe. That I wouldn't be anything like she'd imagined, unwilling or unable to be the daughter she had fought so hard to protect.

That she would no longer want me.

I don't know how long I stood there and cried, but reality came trickling back when a wet tongue began caressing my cheek. I didn't recall kneeling, but I must have sat at some point. The tide lapped against my lower half, offering a bit of respite to the heat of the midday sun, and Arktos was glued to my side. He whined when I made a halfhearted attempt to push him away, insisting upon licking away the rest of my tears, so tangling my fingers in his long white hair, I let him. Little by little, my heart rate began to slow, and my breathing evened out along with it. Even when I had no more tears left to cry, Arktos remained where he was, resting his massive head in my lap as he patiently waited for my panic to subside.

"You really can understand me, can't you?" I asked him after a while, studying the whole of his body for any sign of affirmation. His tail wagged slightly, but I didn't know whether it was because of the question or because he was simply happy to hear my voice.

I laughed. "I've never had a dog, though I've always liked them. But you're not mine, you know that? If Herbert asks for you, you have to go back. And no more biting anyone if they try."

Arktos snarled, but I didn't relent. "I mean it, you silly—"

He stood up, cutting me off, and only then did I realize he wasn't snarling at me. His attention was fixated upon two silhouettes approaching from the opposite end of the beach: Cedric and Calypso.

My heart skipped a beat. After stammering at Arktos to go fetch Peter and Elvira, I stumbled to my feet and broke into a reckless sprint. But the closer I got, the more confused I became; Cedric was leaning heavily on Calypso, and his head was bowed. Was he hurt? I reached them quickly and halted just short of them, not entirely certain what to make of the scene before me. My father looked like absolute hell. His soaking-wet clothes were in tatters, his hair wild and unruly, and scrapes and bruises covered nearly every bit of visible skin. He wasn't wearing his hook and instead clutched the prosthetic to his chest, but none of that worried me nearly as much as the way he was acting. At first, I'd assumed he needed Calypso's shoulder to lean on for extra support, but that wasn't it at all. She was dragging him, and he was fighting her every step of the way.

"No," he pleaded, eyes wide and frightened, and he made a desperate attempt to turn back toward the direction from which they'd come. "No, no, *no*. She's here, I saw her, we have to go back!"

"You saw her. I understand," Calypso repeated patiently. "But right now, we have to meet everyone else. They've been worried about you." The nymph raised her gaze to mine. "Especially Wendy."

Cedric echoed my name as if it struck a chord of recognition in him.

"Your daughter—"

"I know who she is." He looked at me then, and the depth of his stare sent prickles up my spine. "Scarlett told me your full name is Gwendolyn. Well, she didn't tell me, because she's lost her voice, you see, but she wrote in the sand, and I wondered where she had even…"

Cedric continued talking, but I stopped listening at *Gwendolyn*. I hadn't heard or spoken that name to anyone in well over a decade, so if my father suddenly knew it…

"She's alive?"

I hadn't spoken any louder than a whisper, but both Calypso and Cedric stopped talking to look at me. He still seemed confused, so I repeated myself, adding, "You saw her?"

He nodded stiffly. "It was her… but not exactly her. She was a mermaid. Her tail was red. Kind of like her face toward the end, because I think I pissed her off…"

"A mermaid?" I spoke over Cedric and glanced at Calypso given that he wasn't making any sense. "Was Scarlett... always a mermaid?"

"No. She was very much human the day she struck her bargain with Kaara."

"Then what the fuck is he talking about?" Conflicting urges clashed within me. On one hand, Cedric somehow knew my full name, but on the other, it was no secret he'd been seeing things for the past several weeks. He was obviously dehydrated, exhausted, and starving, and those factors combined with his already fragile mental state were making me severely doubt the validity of his claims. "I think he's been hallucinating again."

I had tried to speak out of the corner of my mouth, but unfortunately, Cedric heard me. "I wasn't hallucinating. Not this," he snapped. "She was real, and it was her. I don't know how or what happened, but I know Scarlett when I see her in the flesh."

"Personally, I believe him," Calypso said, shrugging. "Stranger things have happened."

"Stranger than my mother turning into a damn mermaid?"

"Who's a mermaid?"

I whirled around at Elvira's voice, calmer and more collected than I expected from her given the circumstances. She and Peter trudged up the beach, following an excitedly yipping Arktos. Peter was coated in a thin sheen of sweat, breathless, and exhausted, but nodded when I glanced at him, so I turned my attention to Elvira.

She came to a halt in front of her brother, and at first I couldn't tell if she meant to embrace or punch him. But then she threw her arms around his neck, and even though Elvira's back was to me, I easily envisioned the look on her face as her ruthless façade crumbled. Her voice cracked as she pulled Cedric closer and whispered for his ears alone, but I still made out something along the lines of 'never do that to me again' before she released him.

Calypso eyed Elvira with disdain. "Scarlett is evidently now a mermaid, according to Cedric," she said, answering the earlier question while still keeping a firm hold on him. "Which makes sense considering I found him attempting to drown himself."

"You were doing what?" Elvira's raw emotion vanished in an instant. "What the fuck, Ced. There are far easier ways to—"

"I just want to get back to her. Please. That's all I want." Cedric turned to Calypso, falling to his knees as he took her hand and pleaded. "Take me back to Scarlett. Please."

Peter brushed against my side, whistling low under his breath. "I'd be lying if I said I hadn't ever fantasized about bringing that man to his knees, but I didn't imagine it would look quite so..."

"Pathetic?" I finished, reluctantly agreeing with his assessment. It wasn't the display of emotion as much as it was the sheer desperation, the eagerness with which Cedric would throw himself back into the sea if only Calypso would let him. All traces of self-preservation were long gone, leaving behind nothing but recklessness and stupidity.

We watched as Elvira hissed something unintelligible before yanking her brother to his feet. "Right now? You can't be serious. You almost died and had us all worried sick. We should at least take the rest of the night to rest and regain our strength."

"I wish I could tell you that Kaara gave a shit about the needs and emotions of humans, but she doesn't." Calypso still hadn't loosened her vice-like grip on my father's upper arm. If anything, she tightened it as she continued in that same icy tone. "We either go to her now, or she'll send someone, or more likely some*thing* after us."

Peter took a step forward. "I can't believe I'm saying this, but I agree with Hook. Let's get this shit over with."

All heads swiveled to me then, leaving me fumbling with my words. "W-What are y-you all looking at m-me for? Isn't it a-already three t-to one?"

Calypso snorted. "How generous of you. I wasn't aware I got a vote."

"You don't," Elvira snapped.

I bit my lip, weighing our limited options. We could set up camp here for the night, but not only did we bring extremely limited supplies, we'd have to sleep in shifts. That was the best-case scenario. Worst would be if we found ourselves battling Kaara's supposed someone or some*thing* threat. We could also drag ourselves back to *The Jolly Serpent* and spend the night there, but if we did that, I didn't trust Elvira not to take advantage of Cedric's weakened state, mutiny, and sail us all straight back to Afterport. I couldn't do that to Peter; not after we'd come so far and he was so close to getting what he'd always wanted.

That left braving Kaara, here and now. A lump formed in my throat at the thought, but I tried to hope for the best—perhaps the goddess would show us mercy, especially once she had us firmly in her grasp. Adais's words echoed faintly in my mind: *Kaara wants*

Heartpiercer, my trident. Surely she wouldn't allow us to attempt retrieving it if we were exhausted.

Right?

Swallowing, I put on my bravest face before turning to Calypso. "Lead the way."

XIX. THE GODDESS

Featured Song: Ocean's Lullaby

Cedric

I couldn't fully breathe again until Calypso guided us underwater. Everyone else was transfixed as the nymph worked her sea magic, first parting the waves, then encasing us in a massive sphere of oxygen, but I barely paid any attention to our destination or how we were getting there. As long as she led us to Scarlett, we could walk straight into the jaws of some horrifying monster for all I cared.

Within minutes, we were completely immersed. Though the sphere prevented us from getting wet—wetter in my case—it didn't keep out the biting cold, and I began shivering violently. My shirt was ruined, and none of my companions had a jacket that would actually fit my broad shoulders, so other than the shaky inhales I drew through chattering teeth, I was forced to suffer in silence.

I had plenty to keep me distracted as we descended into darkness. I could still taste Scarlett on my lips, feel her arms around me, and picture her mismatched eyes as she stared into mine. I replayed the entirety of our encounter in painstaking, excruciating detail, determined to sear it into memory in case... In case...

No. I shook my head, unwilling to allow my thoughts to stray down such a harrowing path. I'd see her again. I'd hold her again. I'd kiss her again, even if I had to duel Kaara herself for the privilege, and as long as Scarlett still wanted me by her side, I'd never again let her go. She may well be all I had, especially after I'd so thoroughly fucked things up with Wendy, and if there was one thing this voyage had taught me, I wasn't meant to be alone. But even the momentary twinge of doubt had been enough to let fear constrict my chest, not at all helped by the fact that we were descending farther into blackness with every step, and a single thought gripped me in a chokehold.

As much as I loved and needed Scarlett... could she ever again be enough?

She had been once, but that was before we'd had our daughter. Before I'd known her, traveled with her, and loved her. Confessing as much may have caught Wendy off guard and come at a painfully awkward time, but I'd spoken true. I did love my daughter, enough to want to bridge the gap between us no matter the personal cost. And as she herself had put it, it wasn't as if Scarlett and I would be able to ride off into the sunset and live out our happily ever after as if none of this ever happened. As if *she* never happened. She was part of us now, part of the family I never knew I desperately needed.

I didn't care if it took the rest of our lives. If by some miracle the three of us made it out of here alive, I would see to it that we were reconciled. Scarlett would never forgive me if I didn't at least make an attempt, and I would never forgive myself if, after everything, Wendy walked away hating me.

She may have never answered my question, but she didn't have to. Other than to ask about Scarlett, Wendy hadn't said a damn word to me directly since Calypso had plucked me from the sea, and I didn't for one second believe that was an accident. Even now, Wendy trailed behind me, either to pretend I didn't exist or to burn a hole in my back with her glare.

"...hear me? Ced. Holy shit, did that squid turn you into a damn zombie?"

I nearly flung my hook at Elvira's skull for breaking my train of thought. "What do you want?"

She pursed her lips into a thin line. "Excuse me for caring that you almost died."

"I'm not dead, in case you haven't noticed."

"No, but you sure as fuck aren't right in the head."

"What's that supposed to mean?" I'd have halted in place if I wasn't so determined to reach Scarlett as quickly as possible. "I'm focused, that's all."

Elvira didn't relent despite the warning in my tone. Dropping hers, she gripped my shoulder so she could lean in and hiss for my ears alone. "On walking to your own execution?"

"On the woman I love." I shoved her away, and she nearly crashed into the side of the sphere. I had no idea what would happen if we broke it, or if we could break it, but right now I didn't give a fuck. "And if you get in my way, I swear to Adais I'll—"

"Oh, don't worry about threatening me, Ced," Elvira cut across me, gracefully recovering her footing. It was difficult to tell in the little remaining light, but I could have sworn her eyes were glistening. Her voice, however, betrayed nothing. "I know better than to try and stop you now. I'm simply wondering if I should turn back, because I have no desire to watch you do this. I suspect Wendy doesn't either, though I'll let her speak for herself."

"No one is turning back." Though she hadn't turned around, Calypso's booming shout was so loud and forceful it rattled the edges of her sphere, sending ripples all along its outline. "It's far too late for that. Prepare yourselves, for we'll face Kaara shortly."

The nymph snapped her fingers, summoning an orb of bright light and forcing me to throw up an arm to shield my face. Once my eyes had adjusted, I had to do a double take, because Calypso had either shapeshifted or donned a new outfit while I wasn't paying attention. A glittering golden dress hugged her features, and the way it was cut exposed most of her back. Her hair had been secured into elaborate, decorative braids, forming what almost looked to be a crown. She picked up her pace without warning, leaving the rest of us struggling to keep up with her hurried steps.

Behind me, Elvira huffed. "Surely the goddess isn't going any…"

Her voice trailed off as the orb of light began rising, ascending above and beyond the reach of Calypso's protective sphere. From there it expanded, at last illuminating the previously pitch-black area surrounding us, and my mouth fell open in a silent gasp.

We stood in what looked to be a courtyard. Elaborate marble arches and columns were erected to our left and right, while just ahead, a short set of stairs led into a larger, grander area. At least half a dozen nymphs scurried to and fro, utilizing their webbed feet and hands to move about as they worked to tidy up the already immaculate space. They were dressed exactly like Calypso, wearing blue dresses instead of gold, and even had their braids done up the same. Not one of them spared even a curious glance as we passed. Craning my neck, I looked upwards, unsurprised to find that the space had no roof. Several schools of various fishes hovered above, kept at bay by another of Kaara's nymphs.

Though I'd never been in one, and certainly not one that was underwater, I had no doubt we were entering a palace, especially as we began ascending the stairs. Calypso's sphere molded to the space below our feet, allowing us to more easily keep up with her still-brisk pace. Hopeful we were nearing Scarlett, I kept as close to the nymph as possible, barely noticing that Elvira had appeared at my side until she yanked my hook from my hands.

I attempted to snatch it back but missed. "What are you doing?"

"You need to put this on," she said, her tone as urgent as it was serious.

"What could I possibly need it for?"

"I don't know, and that's my entire point. Just let me help you, all right? It will put some of my fears at ease."

I held out my arm and didn't protest as she fastened the prosthetic to it. There was no need to tell her to hurry. Elvira's practiced fingers worked quickly and efficiently, and though we fell slightly behind, we were easily able to catch back up. We walked in silence after that, trailing behind Wendy, Pan, and the dog, but just as I was about to ask Elvira what 'fears' she meant, Wendy halted so suddenly I nearly slammed into her back.

"Do you hear that?" she whispered, remaining immobile as Calypso kept moving both herself and the sphere.

"Hear what?" Elvira asked, looking as confused as I was. Ever since being encased in it, I hadn't heard a single sound that may have occurred outside the sphere.

"That voice." Wendy turned her head, revealing that her face was white as a sheet. "It's Mother's."

Any excitement that had fluttered in my chest evaporated upon recalling that, according to Scarlett, her voice had been stolen by Kaara. Unless that was a lie, and I didn't believe it was, the goddess was already toying with us. "Are you sure?"

"Positive."

We waited and listened, but not only did none of us hear anything, the back end of the sphere was quickly approaching. "Come on," I finally said, gently urging Wendy forward. "We need to keep—"

Then a song came drifting through the stillness, a lullaby I knew more than well, and my blood turned to ice at its achingly familiar tune. Wendy was right: it *was* Scarlett's voice, clear and pure as it sang the mournful melody.

> "*The winds, the waves are howling,*
> *The sailors watch by night,*
> *Then come the morn they're drowning,*
> *As storm, she takes her flight.*
>
> *The pirates spurned,*
> *The witches burned,*
> *The colors now they fly!*
> *All men must die,*
> *The crimson sky bleeds out,*
> *And moon soars high.*
>
> *The winds, the waves are howling,*
> *The sailors watch by night,*
> *Then come the morn they're drowning,*
> *As storm she takes her flight.*"

Elvira gripped my upper arm. "That's…"

A lullaby Blackbeard had learned from my sister's mother. "I know." I had sung it for Scarlett once when I'd thought she wasn't listening, but she most certainly had been, and she liked it so much that she wouldn't relent until I taught it to her. "But it isn't Scarlett."

Both my sister and daughter gave me incredulous looks, and Elvira said, "Even I know what her singing sounds like."

"Just trust me, and keep moving." Herding them both despite their protests, we started forward as the back of the sphere began rubbing uncomfortably against my still-sore shoulders. Though it may be see-through and malleable, it was far more solid than it looked.

We reached the top of the stairs, entered an area far less open than the last, and it immediately became obvious why the courtyard had been so simple in its design. If I didn't know better, I may have believed we'd happened upon the ruins of a shipwreck. More likely, several shipwrecks. In addition to the various sections of hull that appeared as though they had literally been chewed on and spit out by some horrifying monster, every inch of available space contained something, from long-ruined cannons, to broken and crumbling statues, to half-rotted crates spilling their half-rotted contents. There existed paths, but they were so narrow that navigating through the chaos was going to take careful and precise maneuvering. I had no idea how we were going to manage it while remaining within the boundaries of Calypso's sphere.

There wasn't time to worry about it, not when Wendy stiffened and froze in front of me. I tried to shove her forward, but she planted her feet and wouldn't move. "Come on, we need to keep—"

"I can't." Her whisper was pleading, desperate. "It's too small."

"What are you talking about? You'll fit."

"That's not what she means." Pan appeared at Wendy's side, taking her hand. "She's claustrophobic."

I vaguely recalled Elvira telling me how badly Wendy had panicked upon being locked inside a small closet the night before we raided Blackbeard's tomb. "She still has to go in there."

Wendy shook her head, pulling against Pan's grasp as she made an attempt to turn back. "No! Please, don't make me."

"I could carry you." The words left my lips before I thought twice about them. "Will that help?"

She considered me, swallowing, but didn't answer until Pan swooped in, handing her a strip of fabric he'd torn from the bottom of his shirt. "Cover your eyes," he said. "It should make it more bearable."

Wendy took the makeshift blindfold, albeit hesitantly, before raising her gaze to mine. "If you drop me—"

"I'm not going to drop you."

She looked unconvinced but didn't argue. After securing the blindfold behind her head, Wendy allowed me to scoop her into my arms. She was light enough but so tense and stiff it felt as if I was carrying one of the statues. "You can relax, you know."

"With your hook poking into my shoulder? No thanks."

"Then at least wrap your arms around my neck."

Heat crept to her cheeks, contrasting against the white of the blindfold. "Gods, you really want to make this as embarrassing as possible, don't you?"

"Just do it, Wendy, unless you want to fall."

With a deep breath, she obeyed, pulling herself flush against my chest just as Calypso's voice came booming once again. "Everyone gather closer together. I need to make this shield quite a bit smaller."

We formed as straight of a line as we could manage, with Pan behind Calypso, followed by me and Wendy, the dog, and Elvira at the rear. No sooner were we in position did the sphere begin to shrink, stopping a mere inch or two above my head given that I was the tallest. It was no wider in width than it needed to be to accommodate Wendy's legs, and even then I pulled her tighter against me, ignoring her whimper of protest.

Navigating through the wreckage was far more difficult than I anticipated, and not solely because I carried my teenage daughter in my arms. The farther we got into it, the narrower the paths became, so much so that the debris on either side rubbed against my profile as I passed, and more than a few times, I was forced to walk sideways. I'd never had any specific fears related to being in small spaces, but the overwhelming feeling of entrapment was beginning to make even me sweat. Wendy was quick to pick up on my nervousness and responded by tensing up, making manipulating her body even harder.

"You need to trust me," I hissed after we nearly got stuck ducking beneath a pair of fallen support beams. "I'll get you through this."

She bit her lip but nodded. Although she didn't fully relax, it became marginally easier to guide her through what was beginning to feel like a gauntlet. Getting from one end to the other took a full ten minutes, and when we were finally through, the first deep breath I took felt like I had just emerged from underwater. Ironic.

Sensing that it was over, Wendy all but leaped from my arms, ripping off her blindfold and racing back to Pan's side. Calypso waited until everyone was out before restoring her protective sphere to its normal size and shape, and I was in the middle of stretching my arms when Scarlett's voice came drifting over us once again, sounding far closer than it had before.

"*The winds, the waves are howling,*
The sailors watch by night,
Then come the morn they're drowning,
As storm, she takes her flight."

Elvira made a face as she came to stand beside me. "Gods, that's fucking creepy."

"If you think that's creepy, just wait." Calypso spoke without turning yet again, solidifying that, at least in this place, she either had eyes in the back of her head, super hearing, or both. "But come. She isn't far off now."

As promised, we only walked for another minute or so, Scarlett's voice the ever-present backdrop, before the setting changed again. The hall opened up into another elaborate circular space, but I didn't bother to take a good look at our surroundings. It was more of the same, though there were two key differences: in addition to the powerful aura that seeped into my lungs and constricted my chest, at the far end of the room sat Kaara herself.

The goddess lay draped over an extravagant throne. Dressed in a simple black gown with a slit up one side, it contrasted starkly with her ghostly white complexion, yet enhanced the beauty of the ornate silver locket hanging around her throat. Her hair and clothing seemed to be acting as their own sentient entities, each swirling and dancing in a current that didn't exist. Coal-black eyes narrowed as we approached, though once she ceased singing in Scarlett's voice, she didn't otherwise move to greet or stop us. I should have been worried about the depth of Kaara's stare, and even more worried about that smirk playing on her unnaturally pale lips.

But the moment I noticed Scarlett, I could focus on nothing else.

She hovered to the right of the throne, the expression on her face unreadable as she stared directly ahead, not looking at anything in particular. Her dark hair was loose as it billowed and swayed in the unseen waves, and her one blue eye glowed faintly. But as my gaze trailed lower, the easier it became to read her. Just as it had on the beach, her red mermaid tail twitched slightly, especially when Wendy came to stand beside me.

My daughter's whisper was shaky and hoarse. "You... You were right. About the voice, and about *her*."

Of course I was, but now wasn't the time to rub it in. We had far bigger problems, namely the way the goddess had lit up upon seeing me and Wendy side by side. She spread her arms, grinning from ear to ear, and spoke in the smoothest voice I'd ever heard. "We meet at long last, Cedric Teach and friends."

If I hated the way Calypso said my name, I had a visceral reaction to the way it sounded on Kaara's lips. Chills erupted along my arms, shooting down the length of my spine, and I had a sudden urge to claw my skin off. Swallowing it, I forced a smile and bowed my head. "We are honored."

Kaara cackled the way a child might upon ripping the head off one of her dolls. "You may speak plainly, Cedric Teach, for you have nothing to fear. I did not allow you to come all this way simply to kill you. At least not yet."

Her idle threat did nothing more than stoke my barely contained rage, because if she thought death scared me, this so-called goddess didn't know me very well. Ignoring Elvira's tug on my arm, I strode forward, only coming to a halt when Calypso's conjured sphere held firm, even when I banged my fist against it. Part of me wanted it to shatter, because drowning would be more than worth it if I did so in Scarlett's arms. "All right, then, let's be plain. You know the reason I'm here. It sure as fuck isn't for you."

Kaara sat up straighter on her throne, narrowing her dark gaze. "That's more like it. And by all means, if you want her, come and claim her."

I dared a glance at Scarlett, whose lips were drawn into such a thin line it was difficult to tell where one ended and the other began. She gave an almost imperceptible shake of her head, but I hadn't come this far to give up that easily. Turning to Calypso, I brandished my hook. "Let me through."

Kaara laughed again before clicking her tongue. "How can someone as bloodthirsty as yourself lack such basic self-preservation? I have to say, I expected more from the man who not only unleashed Jamie Teach's curse on the whole of Neverland, but who survived it."

The goddess stood then, once again drinking me in as though she intended to devour me. "*That* was unsurprising. Your soul is as black as the crow you're named after."

If Kaara didn't release Scarlett this fucking second, I was prepared to show her how right she was. I opened my mouth to tell her as much, but Calypso's whispered warning was enough to shut me up. She didn't move anything but her mouth, continuing to stare straight ahead as she spoke. "Careful. My mistress does not take kindly to threats."

"She's right," Kaara said, though her smile had vanished. "And if we're extending courtesies, I suppose it's only fair to inform you that my magic might make you feel a bit chaotic. You'll feel compelled to do and say things you may not under normal circumstances."

I felt more level-headed than I had in weeks. Scarlett was within my grasp, my sister and daughter were safe, and I had the perfect bargaining chip to ensure they all remained that way.

Me.

Someone said my name, but I ignored it, standing my ground as Kaara approached the sphere. She touched the tip of her index finger to the barrier. It parted like water, and the next thing I knew, I was face to face with a goddess.

Her hair and dress continued their odd dance even out of water, unnerving me more than I wanted to admit, but I managed to keep my composure. Expecting her to linger on or at least speak to me, it surprised me when Kaara did neither, turning instead to my companions and gasping as if noticing them for the first time—

352

which wasn't at all true, given that she'd just addressed Calypso. "You brought spares. How touching. It's not often those who visit my realm bring guests." She clapped her hands, but her lips curled in disgust upon noticing Pan. "Peter Pan—the Golden Child—and his fairy. You're either incredibly brave or incredibly stupid for daring to show your faces here. Elvira Teach, the Serpent, no shock there. Your obsession with Cedric might be endearing if it wasn't so toxic. Wendy Maynard of course, Neverland's Chosen, and her... dog?" Kaara seemed surprised by Arktos's presence but moved on when he snarled at her. "And *you*."

Kaara fixated on Calypso, whose eyes were wide with an emotion I couldn't quite place. "Hello, Mistress," the nymph said, sinking into a respectful bow, but Kaara had already turned away, this time to address Scarlett.

"Well, what do you think? Was she worth everything you sacrificed?"

It took me a moment to realize Kaara was talking about Wendy, but Scarlett understood immediately. She darted to the edge of the sphere, but it didn't part for her. Placing her palm flat against it, Scarlett glanced longingly at me and Wendy in turn. Though Wendy took a startled step back, I mirrored Scarlett's movement, placing my hand over hers all while silently cursing the barrier between us. I wanted to touch her, to hold her, to tell her I was going to get out of here, but with a goddess listening, neither of us dared to communicate with anything other than our eyes.

Kaara cackled, though evidently not at us. "The girl who broke Neverland's curse is frightened of a little *mermaid?*"

"W-what did you d-do to her?" came Wendy's stammer. "Why do you have her voice?"

"She gave it to me," Kaara answered smoothly. "You weren't the only one who needed to be spared of the curse, so in addition to serving me 'as long as her daughter should live,' her voice it was. I keep it right here for safekeeping."

In my peripheral vision, I watched as Kaara held up the locket around her neck.

Wendy's tone dropped to a whisper. "But… But I've heard her—"

"Your whole life? Indeed you have, child, but it was never Scarlett. It was me."

Scarlett banged her fist against the sphere so forcefully that even Kaara flinched. The look of absolute loathing the two exchanged unsettled me to my core, as did a cryptic quip from Kaara in what sounded a lot like Sirenstongue.

Switching back to English, the goddess addressed me next. "As you can plainly see, your Scarlett is as fiery as ever, Cedric Teach."

"If she's too much for you, I'll be more than glad to take her off your hands." I loathed myself for speaking of Scarlett as though she were an object to be bought and sold, but if it got the goddess's attention, so be it.

Kaara's lips twisted into a wicked grin. She sauntered toward me, coming to a halt a hair's breadth from my chest, and trailed a finger along my jaw as she spoke. "Oh, I know you would. The real question is whether Scarlett still wants *you*."

It took effort not to rip myself from Kaara's grasp. "What are you talking about?"

"Haven't you heard? She's to be a married woman. Arranged it herself."

My heart skipped a beat as Prince Herbert's ridiculous declarations echoed in my mind. *I'm engaged, you see, but not to any woman. In fact, she's not human at all.* I had assumed he meant a nymph, but had he meant Scarlett?

"Still want to make a deal, Cedric Teach?" Kaara grinned from ear to ear. "Or are you only interested in bargaining for Scarlett's freedom on the condition that she spends it with you?"

Of course I wasn't, but my throat had gone dry regardless. Though I was more than aware that Scarlett didn't belong to me, and never had, it was no secret that I'd done nothing but fantasize about picking up right where we left off if we were ever lucky enough to reunite. And to claim that marriage to another, especially a prince, wasn't going to complicate things was the understatement of the fucking century. None of that addressed my main question, though; did Scarlett truly want this? Or was this Diego Ruiz all over again, and was the engagement just another ruse for some elaborate plot I wasn't yet aware of?

"If he doesn't want to bargain, I do."

Pan spoke while I was still lost in thought. All heads snapped to him as he stepped forward, raising his chin to look the goddess in the eye. Tink stood perched on his shoulder, more lucid than I'd seen her in days, and in unison, they sank into what were clearly rehearsed bows.

"I have sought you out for centuries—" he began, but Kaara cut him off with an animalistic snarl.

"I don't make deals with *Golden Children*."

I didn't have the slightest idea what Kaara meant by that, but both Wendy and Pan flinched at the venom in the goddess's tone.

"However," she continued, turning back to me, "retrieve the trident Heartpiercer from the Sea of Eternal Woe, and in return, I shall give any of you willing to aid in the quest whatever your hearts desire. Name it, and it's yours."

Pan blurted out something along the lines of 'aging' and 'immortality,' but my desire was entirely different. I whispered it as I glanced at Scarlett's tortured expression, hers still fixated on where our palms touched through Calypso's barrier, then decided that I wasn't willing to see her like that for a single moment longer.

"I'll get the damn trident," I declared, paying no mind to Elvira's stammered protests. "Swear that Scarlett goes free, and I'll do whatever you ask."

"Anything?" Kaara's voice dropped to an unsettling purr, and several strands of her hair stroked my cheeks of their own accord. "What I wouldn't give for you to actually mean that."

"I do. Free Scarlett and her voice, and you can have me."

Elvira wasn't alone in protesting my sacrifice. Scarlett resumed banging on the sphere, and had she possessed the ability to speak, I had no doubt she'd be screaming at the top of her lungs. For once, I was glad that she didn't, because neither of us could afford to see logic or reason right now. Not if she ever wanted to be free.

"If he's going after the damn trident, I'm going with him." Only when Elvira snaked both of her arms around my middle in a vice grip did her words truly sink in, but as I shook my head, someone else appeared on my other side.

"Me too," Pan said.

"And me as well." Wendy stepped forward, trailed closely by Arktos. "Well, 'us,' I suppose."

"No. Absolutely not." I found my voice then, and though I didn't need anyone coming with me, I addressed Wendy in particular. "Let me do this. Alone."

"Touching as your concern for Wendy may be, it's she who has the least to fear." Kaara began pacing around us in a circle, her hair and dress lightly caressing those she passed. "Any of you may enter the Sea, but only one of selfless heart and untainted soul may return to our world unscathed. Wendy may be far from perfect or even innocent, but I'd wager that stabbing herself to save all of Neverland counts as pretty damn selfless to me." Halting in front of Elvira, Kaara's tone switched back to that sultry murmur. "And keep in mind that not even a mother's love and sacrifice were selfless enough. *I* didn't render Scarlett a mermaid. The Sea did."

I stole another glance at Scarlett. Was that why she had refused to tell me what happened to her? Was that the reason behind the set of mismatched eyes she definitely hadn't possessed the last time I saw her? And if what the Sea had done to her was a curse, how the fuck were we going to undo that particular one, if the whole point of the Sea's existence was that it contained ancient magic not even the gods could unravel?

I was still spiraling when Elvira tensed beside me. "So if the rest of us choose to go regardless—"

"Perform a selfless act, remain forever, or emerge marred in some way. Like her." Kaara waved her hand toward Scarlett dismissively. "Your choice."

Wendy, Pan, and Elvira nodded their agreement, but suddenly I wasn't so sure about mine. Not because I feared for my life or even my soul, but because I feared for Wendy's future. If Kaara herself hadn't cursed Scarlett, would Kaara 'releasing' her even mean or do anything? Was Kaara capable of turning her human again? That left me and my fate. If I entered the Sea and became trapped or perished...

Would Wendy become an orphan all over again?

It wasn't out of the realm of possibility, no matter what scenario I played through my mind. Nothing I did from this moment on was certain, but I could at least marginally control one thing: Wendy's perception of me. And I may be many things, but I certainly wasn't a fucking coward.

"All right," I heard myself say. "But before we go, please, let me see her. Just once."

Kaara laughed before materializing in front of me. "Scarlett, you mean? She's right there. Look at her all you want."

"I mean face to face, in here. So I can..." I couldn't bring myself to finish the sentence aloud: *So I can say goodbye.*

"How romantic." Rolling her eyes, Kaara waved her hand in a

quick flourish. "Go on, then."

It happened so fast it took us all by surprise. Scarlett still had one hand on the sphere, but what had once been a solid barrier gave way the moment Kaara's fingers moved, sending Scarlett careening forward. When everyone else staggered back as a torrent of water entered the space along with her helpless body, I darted forward, unwilling to allow Scarlett to strike the unforgiving ground. I caught her awkwardly around the middle and took the brunt of our fall, becoming drenched all over again. The water was fucking freezing, but I didn't care, especially not when she threw her arms around my neck and buried her face in the crook of my shoulder.

She was shaking, though from what, I couldn't be certain. I very nearly asked until I remembered that she couldn't answer, at least not verbally. A mixture of rage and protectiveness ignited within me, and as conversation continued around us, some of it containing raised voices, I whispered for Scarlett's ears alone. "I'm not letting you go. Do you hear me? I lost you once. Never, ever again." I would let her go, though, and we both knew it. If this was what the Sea had done to her once, there was no way she could risk entering it a second time, meaning in another short while, we would be separated once again.

But when my gaze flickered to her tail, there were *legs*. Human legs, fully covered with a pair of loose breeches, but bare feet and toes poked out precisely where they should. *What the fuck?* Gooseflesh erupted all along my arms, and it had nothing to do with the cold.

Scarlett Maynard was human once more.

She lifted her head to meet my incredulous expression, and my words were just as dumbfounded. "What... How...?"

"Did she not tell you during your little beach rendezvous?" Kaara looked anything but pleased at its mention. "Though the Sea may have so modified her, my power is enough to change her form at my leisure, whether it be from human to mermaid or vice versa. And before you ask, no, it's not something she's able to do herself."

I turned back to Scarlett. "Is this true?"

She nodded, pointing to each of her eyes in turn, and suddenly they made a lot more sense, as did her reasons for remaining tethered to Kaara in more ways than one.

The revelations shocked me, but there wasn't time to dwell on them. Wendy and I had a trident to retrieve, and it was becoming increasingly obvious Scarlett had a plan of her own, and I had no intention of standing in the way. This wasn't the first time she would have used a fake engagement to set some elaborate ruse into motion—I didn't believe for one second that she had spent the past sixteen years sitting on her ass, and if I knew anyone who could fool a goddess, it was Scarlett. She was intelligent, more than capable, and, as Wendy had once said, clearly didn't need me to save her, but that didn't mean I wasn't going to aid however I could. Taking Scarlett's hands in both of mine, I pulled her close, touching my forehead to hers. "We're going to get through this. Hold on, all right? I'll keep Wendy safe until we both return."

Scarlett gave me an irritated look as if to say, *You'd better*. Then she rose, wobbling for a handful of steps before coming to a halt in front of Wendy. Producing something small from her pocket, Scarlett placed it in Wendy's palm, covering it with her free hand before I could make out what it was.

Kaara snorted. "Protect that little shell with your life, Wendy, because Scarlett certainly does."

A shell? I tried to search Scarlett's face for any sort of hint, but she wouldn't meet my gaze, and Wendy looked as puzzled as I felt. "What does it do?" she asked, holding it as though she was worried it might burst into flames.

The goddess shrugged. "What all shells do. Nothing. It's Scarlett's supposed 'lucky charm,' so evidently she thinks you need some."

Yet another clue that wasn't adding up. I had never known Scarlett to be superstitious, and she had certainly never relied on luck to get her through anything. Nagging questions posed themselves once again as I watched Pan approach Scarlett. *What are you hiding, and what are you trying to tell us?*

Buzzing wings broke my focus. Pan had lifted Tink from his shoulder and now held the protesting fairy out to a wide-eyed Scarlett. "She's far too weak for the Sea, and you were a friend to the fairies once. Will you keep her safe until I return?"

Scarlett took Tink in her hands. Her eyes flicked from the fairy to Pan, and even to Wendy, but after a brief hesitation, she nodded. A satisfied Pan rejoined the others, and it looked as though everyone was gearing up to go. Calypso, Scarlett, and Kaara all stood back as the goddess surveyed us for a final time, trailing a finger across her cheek as she scrutinized us individually.

To Elvira, she said, "You look well-prepared, but something tells me you'll need more knives." With a snap of Kaara's fingers, half a dozen more appeared, all strapped in various places on her person. Pan was gifted a new jacket given that his had been ripped while searching the jungle. Arktos received an instantaneous groom, clipping some of his excess fur and making it much easier to see the leather pack now strapped to his back. Hopefully it contained food and water, because I was fucking starving.

Wendy was next, and though Kaara stared at her for an unnervingly long time, the only thing my daughter received was a compass whose arrow kept spinning and turning erratically. When asked what it pointed to or whether it even worked, Kaara's only answer was a cryptic, "You'll know."

I was last. Half a dozen tendrils of Kaara's sentient hair slithered along various parts of my body, including beneath the rips in my still-tattered shirt, but I forced myself to remain completely still as the goddess took me in. She giggled, the sound once again reminding me of an overexcited schoolgirl, and said, "You're such a mess that you're going to need the full package."

I barely noticed Kaara tilt her head, but a moment later I was clad in an entirely different outfit, complete with weapons. Everything from my boots to the pistols at each of my hips were shiny and new, and my shirt and jacket no longer had any holes. Shrugging my shoulders and flexing my arms, I was pleased to find that my range of motion remained sound, and that the clothes were a comfortable, yet snug fit.

"Like it?" Kaara asked, clearly enjoying the view.

I liked them so much that I felt more myself than I had in days, but not wanting to stroke Kaara's massive ego, I simply nodded. "Thank you."

"Good!" She rubbed her hands together as she took us in a final time, clearly admiring her handiwork. "I wish you luck, Cedric Teach and friends."

She spoke as if we were supposed to take it from here, and I frowned. "Aren't you going to lead us to the Sea?"

Kaara's irises dilated until her eyes became pools of soul-emptying blackness, and when she spoke, it was in Scarlett's voice. "Only you would stand at the gates of Hell and still ask to be shown the way."

It was the only warning we got before the ground caved out from under us. Instinct had me scrambling for a ledge, but all it earned me was something sharp slicing into my palm. With Scarlett's name on my lips, I fell, catching a fleeting glimpse of her tear-stained face before tumbling into nothingness.

XX. THE SEA
Wendy

Bones broke my fall, and it was far from painless. The agonizing impact tore a strangled cry from my lips, and I wasn't the only one shocked by the sensation. Screams echoed to my left and right as my companions landed around me. Even Arktos yelped when he struck the mound of decaying skeletal fragments, some of which were so sharp they sliced into my flesh. Others poked at my back and rear, reminding me far too much of the blades that had once prodded there, and I scrambled upright at the first opportunity, resisting the urge to vomit at the overpowering stench of death that invaded my nostrils.

It was dark, but not so dark that I couldn't see. Blinking in the eerie light that lacked an obvious source, I made out several silhouettes, groaning but alive.

Elvira muttered a string of curses as she struggled and failed to stand. "Where are we?"

"Hell." Cedric dusted off his arms, lips curled in disgust as he picked bone fragments from his brand-new jacket. "Or did you not hear the goddess?"

"I was too distracted by the way she was fondling you."

"And you're blaming me for that? All I did was stand there!"

"Holy shit, shut up, both of you," I snapped, making my own feeble effort to stand and cursing again when I couldn't get my footing. "Is everyone all right? Peter, where—?"

"I'm here," came his voice from behind. Bones snapped and crunched as he half-shuffled, half-crawled in my direction, and only when he took my outstretched hand did I notice the cut on his cheek. A thin trail of golden blood seeped from the wound, but it appeared to be superficial.

"You're bleeding," I said, pointing.

Peter nodded toward the slices on my arms. "So are you."

"Get used to it." Cedric seemed to be the only one making any headway toward where the mountain of bones at last came to an end, down a steep incline. "Come on. The sooner we get out of this graveyard, the sooner we can find that damn trident and get out of here."

"Get the hell out of Hell?" Elvira was the only one who laughed at her terrible joke.

Rolling my eyes, Peter and I followed Cedric's lead, still hand in hand. He acted as my anchor any time I slipped and vice versa, but the sweat coating Peter's palm soon made gripping it nearly impossible. The slimy sensation only got worse the farther we trekked, and by the time we stood at the edge of the incline, I became thoroughly convinced it wasn't sweat at all. Unable to stand the sticky sensation any longer, I released his hand to cling to his shoulder instead, and that's when I noticed it.

"Peter, what the fuck is *that*?"

He did a double take upon glimpsing the black smeared all over his palm and flicked his wrist in a panicked attempt to remove it. When that didn't work, he wiped it on several bones, but that, too, failed. "I don't know, but it won't come off."

"Does it hurt?"

He shook his head.

"Let me see." Once he placed the back of his hand within both of mine, I leaned in to examine what looked rather like a welt. Black, angry, and oozing, it explained the mucus-like liquid I'd felt, but that was where logic ended. Though it could have been a trick of the dim light, the longer I stared, the more convinced I became that its outline was rippling and changing before my eyes. "It won't come off because it's part of your skin. It's moving."

Peter ripped his hand away, holding the afflicted limb by the wrist as he visibly quivered. "I don't know when or how I got this. Do you have one?"

I showed him my completely normal palms, and he cursed just as Cedric's irritated shout rattled the smaller bones around us. "What's taking so long?"

He, Elvira, and Arktos had made it safely to the bottom of the bone mountain, and judging from the way Arktos kept dancing around and whining, even he appeared agitated. "Peter has some kind of mark on his hand," I called back.

Elvira scoffed. "And does he need his hands to walk all of a sudden? Hurry up, we need to keep moving."

"Wait. I think I have one too." Cedric spoke over his sister as he examined his palm. "Do you?"

"Of course no—shit, why is it moving?" A look of pure horror crossed Elvira's face, confirming that she, too, possessed a mark. "Do we all have one, then?"

"Wendy doesn't," Peter called back before I could.

Elvira's shocked expression was replaced with a glower in an instant. "Kaara did this."

"If that's true, then why did she mark me and not Wendy?" Cedric countered.

"Can you at least wait for us before deciding what the hell those are for?" Still clinging to one another, Peter and I were doing our best to make it down the bone mountain without falling on our asses. "We're com—*ahh!*"

My shout morphed into a scream as bones shifted beneath me, causing me to lose my footing completely, and then we were tumbling. Jagged fragments grazed my clothing and skin alike, lacerating both as my helpless body slid down a twenty-foot incline, and seeing the ground fast approaching, I squeezed my eyes shut and braced for impact.

But it never came, at least not as hard as I'd been expecting. There was a wall of fur, a muttered curse, and then arms encircled me, followed by a string of questions my brain wasn't yet prepared to process, let alone answer. I wasn't badly hurt, but I had obtained a number of fresh scratches, probably twice as many bruises, and my head throbbed as if I'd struck it. Had I?

Only when the cool metal of a hook grazed my arm did I snap out of the pain-induced trance. Shoving Cedric away, I growled, "I'm fine," before attempting to stand too fast. Far too fast. Dizziness overtook me, my knees buckled, and those arms were back, this time ignoring my feeble protests.

"Adais's sake, Wendy, sit down and stay down. And *shoo*, dammit," Cedric snapped, though it didn't sound like that last bit was directed at me. "She's all right. See?"

Something wet nosed my cheek before giving it a few licks, and it took me a moment to recall that I had a dog. *Shit. Perhaps I did hit my head.* But not wanting to admit as much aloud, especially with Cedric within earshot, I wrapped my arms around Arktos's neck and said instead, "Correct. So you can stop hovering."

"I'm not going anywhere until you can stand. Unassisted," he added when I made an attempt to do just that, using Arktos as a crutch.

Though my protests were out of habit, my logic made a lot more sense than Cedric's did. "We can't stay out in the open like this, and I don't want to be the one to slow us down."

"She's right." Elvira watched from a distance while Peter stood behind Cedric, but both appeared antsy and more than ready to get moving. "If you want her to rest, at the very least we need to find shelter."

"Then find it." Cedric spoke without taking his eyes from me. "We'll stay here, and I'll guard her."

"*Ced.*"

He whipped around then, and the vehemence in his tone was enough for me to picture the look on my father's face. "You heard me. We may not be on *The Jolly Serpent* anymore, but I'm still the fucking captain, and I'm telling you to go find shelter. Both of you."

Peter scoffed. "Since when have I taken orders from you?"

"Since right now, unless you want me to—"

"Just go, Peter," I cut across Cedric, shutting them both up as they stared at me with even more concern. They were probably wondering why I was suddenly agreeing with my father, but truth be told, rest sounded heavenly, and given that he'd pulled the captain card, I could already tell this was an argument I wasn't going to win. Releasing my hold around Arktos's neck, I motioned for the dog to go to Peter's side instead of mine. "But take Arktos."

The dog only whined once before obeying but happily trotted back over when Peter closed the distance between us. Frowning, I opened my mouth to ask what he was doing just as he held out his hand. "This fell out of your pocket."

I'd nearly forgotten about the compass Kaara had given me until I plucked it from his palm. Its arrow still spun and turned erratically, without any sense or pattern, and even though part of me was tempted to toss the more-than-likely useless thing into the pile of bones behind me, I nodded. "Thanks."

"We should stick together, boy." Elvira motioned with her head for Peter to join her. "Something tells me it isn't safe for any of us to go off alone."

"I have a name, you know."

"Ah, right. Golden Child, was it? Has a nice ring to it, and I like it far better than Pan."

Peter bristled. "Do you call anyone by their name?"

"You won't have a name if you don't get your ass moving, because you'll be dead."

"Fine," Peter said over his shoulder, but then addressed me, gaze darting between me and Cedric. "Are you sure you're good?"

"Positive."

Though Peter didn't seem convinced, he didn't say so aloud. A reluctant Arktos trailed after him as Peter turned to follow Elvira. Before long, their silhouettes had completely vanished in the eerie haze, and it was then that I became acutely aware of just how creepy this place was. It felt empty and full at the same time, because other than the bones, there was quite literally nothing. No warmth, hardly any light, and no sound other than whispers I could make out, both screams and pleas alike. The longer the silence lingered, the louder the voices became, and ducking my head, I prepared to cover my ears.

Cedric must have heard them too, because he cleared his throat awkwardly. In an instant, the whispers stopped, though they'd likely start up again if it got too quiet. "How are you feeling?"

"Like I fell down a mountain of bones."

He sighed. "Wendy—"

"What?" I snapped. "I may have agreed to be alone with you, but that doesn't mean I have to like it."

"Right. Because you hate me. My mistake." Pushing off one knee, Cedric stood and began to pace like a caged animal, and the sight agitated me in more ways than one. I hadn't intended to pick a fight, especially after what he'd just gone through, but his retort was enough to push me over the edge right along with him.

"Don't you dare put words in my mouth. You asked, but I didn't say it."

"You didn't need to. Your hesitation was more than enough." He didn't slow his hurried steps. "Either you hate me, or you hate yourself because you don't, and I'm not sure which is worse."

I suppressed a wince, and my words came out far more pleading than I intended them to. "Why does it matter either way?"

"Because this isn't how it's supposed to be between a parent and their child!"

"How is it 'supposed to be,' then?" I didn't recall standing, but I somehow managed to keep my balance on aching, wobbly legs. "You'll have to enlighten me, because it's not like I would know."

"I don't either!" Cedric ran his hand through his hair, shouting now. "In case you've forgotten, my father didn't exactly set an ideal example, but that's my entire point. He never gave a fuck, yet the harder I try with you, the more it feels the way it did between me and him. We're powder kegs waiting to explode, and either of us could be holding the matches."

"Then stop trying!"

He froze. "What?"

"If you 'trying' was what got us here, then stop." I closed my eyes, recalling what I'd told myself on the beach mere hours ago: *face your feelings*. Right now, my feelings wore Cedric's face, so I raised my gaze to his and uttered perhaps the truest words I'd ever spoken to him. "You're right. Whatever is between us is twisted and complicated, and it's going to be for a long time. Maybe even forever. But I don't hate you." I clenched and unclenched my palms as it suddenly became much easier to breathe. "It became abundantly clear when I thought I lost you. I couldn't stand the thought of that awful fight having been our last interaction, or"—I hesitated before mumbling the last bit—"never seeing you again."

Cedric's face had gone from wounded to something else, though he looked just as likely to cry as he had before. He said my name in a voice choked with emotion, but I shook my head to silence him.

"Don't misunderstand me. I still don't like you. But if that's ever going to change, I need time and space, okay? This can't be forced, not by either of us, and you certainly can't go around telling me that you *love* me. While I still feel this way, that's the equivalent of hugging a feral cat. You're going to get scratched, and I'll have you know I'm not above biting, either."

He laughed then. "You sound like Elvira now."

"Bad news for you if that's true."

"No, a challenge. One that will keep me sharp, which is a good thing considering I'm not getting any younger." Cedric's eyes narrowed as he considered me. "I'm willing to agree to a truce, but are you? It's hardly fair that you keep backing me into a corner so you have yet another thing to hold against me when I inevitably lash out. I may not be claustrophobic, but I still don't like being trapped. Powder keg and matches, remember?"

That truly was a perfect metaphor for what we were. "Fine. I'll hide my matches if you hide yours."

Cedric held out his hand as the corner of his mouth played at a grin. "Shake on it, Wendy Maynard. I may be a pirate, but I honor my word."

I swallowed my *I'll believe it when I see it* retort and accepted the handshake, grimacing at the familiar slimy sensation of his black mark rubbing against my palm. But before I'd even pulled away, the compass in my other hand began quivering, and it startled me so much I nearly dropped it.

Cedric frowned when he noticed. "What's going on?"

"No idea. Seems broken, though."

He shook his head. "I highly doubt Kaara would have made such a show of giving you something useless. Let me see." I handed him the compass, and he inspected it with both hand and hook, quickly making a discovery. "Have you seen this? There's an inscription on the side here."

"What does it say?"

"'*I show not your heart's desire, but what you need most dire.*'"

I groaned. "Didn't we leave all the riddles behind in Neverland? How the hell is that supposed to show us anything when it's spinning like that?" The needle seemed torn in opposite directions and switched erratically between the two, sometimes adding a handful of spins for good measure.

Cedric brightened all of a sudden, handing the compass back. "I don't know, but Scarlett might. Didn't she give you something else?"

"Yes, but it's even more usel—"

"Nothing, and I mean nothing," he cut across me, deadly serious, "Scarlett Maynard does is ever unintentional or without thought. Show it to me."

It took a moment to pocket the compass and instead locate the small shell, but when I did, my fingers closed around a third object, something unexpected. *Paper?* I pulled it out along with the shell, holding one in each hand. "She must have written a note as well."

He released a breath of wonder as I began unfolding it. "Of course she did."

My eyes scanned over the nonsensical words twice before I spoke them aloud. "'*Marks vanish when you're safe to emerge. Speak to the shell for further guidance.*'"

Cedric immediately began muttering the message under his breath, his gaze faraway as he attempted to unravel Scarlett's meaning. "The marks. Does she mean the ones that all of us have but you?"

"And maybe Arktos," I offered weakly. "No one thought to check his paws."

"They vanish when we're safe to emerge, and to do that, Kaara said we need to do something selfless. Or be selfless, in your case, which is probably why you're the only one who doesn't have one."

"That's why they're moving. Must be magic."

He nodded. "Makes sense. They're a warning and will disappear when we're able to leave the Sea unscathed. All right, that's one clue dealt with, and the other is hardly cryptic. Do as Scarlett says."

My mouth fell open. "What? You want me to talk to a damn shell?"

"If you won't, I will." He made a reckless grab for it, but I snatched my hand away.

"No. If Scarlett wanted you to be the one to do it, she would have given it to you." But when I held the shell closer to my face, I completely blanked, especially with Cedric staring at me like that. "What the hell should I say?"

"She said to ask for guidance, so that would be a good place to start."

It felt beyond ridiculous to be talking to a shell, but it wasn't as if we had any other options. Sighing, I asked, "May we have some guidance... please?"

I only added the 'please' after Cedric mouthed something that looked like 'manners,' but common courtesy appeared to have gotten us nowhere. Nothing happened, not even after I asked a second time, and turning back to my father, I threw up my hands.

"Never does anything 'without thought,' huh?" I mocked in his overconfident tone, but before I'd finished speaking, the shell vibrated in my palm as a deep but familiar voice sounded from it.

"Hello again, Wendy Maynard. Is Cedric Teach with you?"

Adais. Gooseflesh erupted along my arms, and my mind spun with this new revelation, but despite the sudden dryness in my mouth, I managed to utter a response. "Yes."

"Good. Have you secured my trident yet?"

I may have appreciated the fact that he'd gotten straight to the point if there weren't a million questions running through my mind—*where did Scarlett get this? How had she kept it secret from Kaara? And how long had she been talking to the Sea God, plotting and scheming up gods-knew-what,* literally?—but unable to voice any of them, my lips somehow formed another curt reply. "No. We only just arrived."

Adais made a disapproving noise. *"You must hurry. Well-laid plans have been set in motion, but we have no hope of succeeding until I have Heartpiercer in hand."*

Cedric snatched my wrist so suddenly I yelped. He brought the shell mere inches from his lips as he spoke, his words tense and rushed. "What plans? What's going on? Is Scarlett involved? Is she all right?"

"Your task is retrieving Heartpiercer. Until you do, nothing else matters."

377

My father clenched his jaw, tightening his grip on my arm at the same time. "Does that mean that if we don't, she'll die?"

"Don't ask questions you already know the answers to, Crow."

Cedric cursed as I yanked myself from his grasp. "But how do we find the trident, and what do we do once we have it? How do we get out of here?"

*"Heartpiercer is not difficult to find, Wendy Maynard, and that compass will aid you if only you let it. Once you have secured my trident, all you need to do is grip its shaft—you, and anyone accompanying you— and say, '*What belongs to the sea will always return.' *Heartpiercer will do the rest, but remember, only those who are touching the shaft will be brought to the surface. Hurry, because far more than your mother's life is at stake if you fail."*

How were we meant to succeed when even the Sea God was being so vague? Were there traps we needed to watch out for? Monsters? What awaited us that wasn't this stupid mound of bones? There were so many more questions I wanted to ask that I didn't know where to begin, but before I could select one, Cedric ripped the shell from my palm and rattled off pleas of his own.

"Tell Scarlett that we're safe, all right? Tell her that I love her, that we're coming, that Wendy is—*fuck.*" Cedric let it tumble to the ground with a flick of his wrist, not looking the least bit apologetic when I shot him an incredulous glare. "What? It shocked me."

"You could have broken it, and then we'd be even more fucked than we already are." Bending over, I picked up the shell, inspecting it for cracks before dusting it off. It appeared to be in one piece, thank whatever gods would listen, but it was clear Adais was no longer one of them. "Looks like we're on our own."

"We shouldn't be. We need to find Elvira and Pan. Are you all right to walk?"

I nodded both in answer and agreement. They should have been back by now, and the fact that they weren't concerned me. Was there truly no shelter in this place? Had something happened? Were they even alive? *Get a grip*, I reminded myself, and before my thoughts could spiral any further, I fell into step beside Cedric. Reaching back into my pocket, I deposited the shell before trading it for Kaara's compass, turning it over in my hands as my father retraced our companions' steps. A strange mist shrouded much of what lay ahead, but at least I could still make out the things in my immediate vicinity.

"'*I show not your heart's desire,*'" I repeated, reading the first part of the inscription aloud. "Seems straightforward. It won't point to what someone wants, but rather '*what you need most dire.*' But how 'dire' are we talking? Does my life need to be in danger before it will point to anything?"

Cedric shrugged before muttering that he didn't know, and if that didn't make it obvious that his mind was anywhere but here, his furrowed brow did.

"You're worried about Scarlett."

"Of course I am."

"You shouldn't be. She's outsmarted a goddess, schemed with a god, and has a role far larger than any of us expected. Possibly the largest."

"Is that supposed to reassure me? That only worries me more, but not because I think she isn't capable." Cedric placed a hand on one of the pistols at his hip. "It's that whether intentional or not, she's entangled herself in an impossibly complex web, one she might not be able to extract herself from, and I didn't come this far to not… to not…"

"Be with her?" I finished quietly. "You heard what Kaara said, though. Scarlett's engaged."

"Oh, trust me, I fucking heard," Cedric snapped. "But the union is a ruse. I may not know how or why just yet, but I do know that Scarlett doesn't want anything to do with that moron prince, if that's who she's marrying. Not truly."

Gods, he was far more in denial than I thought. Ordinarily I'd just let it go, but this seemed to be a scenario in which it would be far better to rip the bandage off in a single pull rather than do it slowly, and Cedric seemed to be in enough pain as it was. "Are you sure?"

"Positive." He took a deep breath before exhaling just as slowly, yanking whatever story he was about to tell along with it. "Years ago, before you were born and before Neverland, Scarlett and I were capt—wait. Is that your dog?"

I assumed Cedric was stalling or had made an extremely poor attempt to change the subject until those telltale hairs rose on the back of my neck—the ones that told me a beast was near—and a moment later, a fluffy white shape came bounding toward me. Arktos showered my face in licks after I knelt to meet him, but when I ran my hand over the fur on his flank, it was warm and sticky, and my palm came away coated in crimson. "Is that blood?"

"Better that dog's than your boyfriend's."

I heard Elvira before I saw her, but her slender silhouette soon reappeared from the mist. Though her hair had been ruffled and she held a bloodied knife in each palm, she appeared unhurt. Peter was a different story. Trailing closely behind Elvira, he gripped his right shoulder with his opposite hand, features contorted in pain. I had been attempting to locate the source of Arktos's wound, but the second I noticed Peter, I sprinted to his side instead, poking and prodding at his injury even when he groaned.

"Don't tell me you dislocated this again," I started, but Elvira shook her head.

"Not dislocated and nothing's broken, though both are a shock to me. That fall was nasty."

"What fall?" Cedric glanced between the trio. "What happened?"

Elvira snorted. "Goldy over here tried to play the hero when it's that dog who *actually* saved the day."

"I wasn't trying to be a hero, I was trying to be selfless!" Peter protested before puffing out his chest proudly. "I think it worked, too!"

"If that were true, you wouldn't still have this." I held up the palm containing the black mark. "They disappear once you've proven yourself."

"Anyway," Elvira continued in that nonchalant tone, "this strange cat-like creature leaped at me. Pan thought it would be a good idea to get between us to fulfill his noble little quest, but it was Wendy's dog who ended up ripping the thing limb from limb. We were up on a ledge, though, and there wasn't enough room for all that commotion, so Pan fell."

Understanding dawned on me as Arktos licked his chops. "That blood isn't Arktos's?"

Elvira shook her head as Cedric asked, "Why were you on a ledge?"

"You mean you haven't seen them?"

"Seen who?" Cedric snapped, frustrated now, but Elvira beckoned with her finger.

"This way."

She led us through the haze, her strides confident and sure even when the mist got so thick that I could barely see my own hands. Not wanting to lose my companions, I laced my fingers with Peter's and hovered close to his side, gripping his palm even tighter when those whispers started up again. They were far louder this time, closer, and more numerous. Even Arktos's hackles rose as we neared our destination, but as I was about to voice my fears aloud, the mist parted, and Elvira gestured in front of us.

"This," she said grimly, "is everyone who's ever died."

Crammed into the space ahead were millions upon millions of ghostly silhouettes, and I couldn't immediately tell if they were solid. Most wandered in dozens of never-ending lines, dragging their feet as if weighted with chains, but others simply stood in place, lips parted and eyes glazed over as if even their spirits had long since given up. My mouth dropped open as I drank it all in. There was nothing gruesome or even particularly sad about it—everyone died at some point—but my eyes began to glisten regardless. They weren't people anymore, but they had been once, and each one of these souls had a life, a purpose, families, friends—

"...stretches as far as we tried to walk in either direction, and they lash out when we get too close. Yes, they can touch us, because one of them tried to bite me. There's no way through," Peter was saying when I finally managed to tear my gaze from the horde of wandering souls, and then it dawned on me.

"There may be one way."

Everyone turned to stare at me as I produced the compass, which for once, wasn't quivering. The needle pointed straight toward the souls, its message more than clear.

"Well," I said to Cedric, "it looks as though our need is 'most dire.'"

Before any of them could stop me, I took a deep breath, approached the souls, and held the compass straight ahead. What was it Adais had said? *That compass will aid you if only you let it.*

"I'm letting you," I whispered, ignoring the fact that at least a dozen of the souls had turned to stare at me. "Take us to Heartpiercer. We need it to save my mother. To save *Peter*." At first, nothing happened.

Then little by little, they parted.

I could hardly believe my eyes as the souls shuffled back, offering us a clear path through what had previously been a tangled mass of bodies. Once in place, they turned their heads to look at me, and I couldn't decide whether that was unnerving or reassuring, so I turned around, smiling weakly at my companions.

"See? Someone just had to ask nicely."

Cedric ran a hand through his hair, his face pale enough to rival the souls'. "Is there anything that doesn't listen to you?"

You, I wanted to blurt out, but I managed to keep my mouth shut until I turned back around. "Come on."

Getting through the souls was the easy part and, strangely, didn't trigger my claustrophobia. Maybe it was the extra room they seemed to know to leave me, or maybe it was their presence alone. Either way, I appreciated the gesture as they allowed us to pass. The whispers turned reassuring, and the fact that I was now the leader kept my thoughts from spiraling. I was able to simply walk. And walk.

We trekked for what was probably several miles. The slow shuffling of boots scraping dirt combined with Arktos nosing my hand every now and again kept me energized, but my confidence was rapidly dwindling. What if I was wrong and led them all this way for nothing? What if all these 'things' I felt were just lies I told myself? What if we'd already failed and Scarlett was already dead, what if—

"What if all you needed was a reason to believe in yourself?"

Chills erupted down my spine as the faintest whisper drifted from my pocket. It was Adais, and he was right, and my companions deserved to share in my sudden boost of confidence. "I can't explain how I know," I said, raising my voice so it would carry to everyone behind me, "but we're close."

They had to think I was mad, because we didn't appear close to anything right now. There was nothing but barren, rocky wasteland as far as the haze stretched around us, and we'd long since left the whispers from the horde of wandering souls behind. Between the compass, the prickles trailing across my flesh, and Adais himself in agreement, the only thing I could do was trust them, and a few minutes later, light caught my eye as the mists parted. "There!"

Heartpiercer hovered in midair no more than fifty yards out. Though it was difficult to tell at our current distance, the golden three-pronged weapon appeared to be longer than I was tall. Humming and faintly glowing, it radiated power even in this bleak place, as if to say it would bend to the wishes of anyone who would aid in its mission of reuniting with its master. The trident was quite near the edge of what looked to be a steep cliff, and the path to reach it was littered with rocky outcroppings, but so long as whoever retrieved it watched their step, the sudden drop-off shouldn't be a problem.

Peter's voice cut through my train of thought. "I'll get it," he declared, and would have taken off sprinting if Cedric hadn't snatched his arm.

"No," he hissed, gaze darting around wildly. "I don't like this."

"Unless you want to lose your other hand, I suggest you get

it off me."

Cedric paid Peter's threat no mind, still fixated on the trident. "It's far too easy. Wendy, can you sense anything? Any monsters?"

I shook my head. "Nothing." Arktos was the only creature I picked up in the near vicinity, but like Cedric, that didn't give me anywhere near the amount of confidence it should have.

Elvira snorted. "Definitely too easy, which is why I'm going first. I still need to perform a 'selfless act,' remember?" Before any of us could stop her, she darted forward. Ignoring Cedric's cries of protest, she stepped lightly, utilizing the outcroppings both as shortcuts and shelter, remaining on high alert for any sudden threats as she made her way toward Heartpiercer.

Cedric tensed as we watched helplessly, and I gripped his arm. One wrong step and Elvira could set off a booby trap. One wrong breath and she could die. If something were to happen to her now, we were too far, too hindered by all those outcroppings to assist.

Just as thoughts began to spiral, Elvira came to a halt just short of the trident. Cedric and I released a collective sigh of relief as she spread her arms, a victorious grin forming on her lips. "Well, brother, I guess it *is* that ea—"

Something slammed against her chest with nearly enough force to throw her over the edge of the cliff. As Elvira scrambled to regain her footing, face contorted as she clutched her middle, one of the strangest and most hair-raising noises I'd ever heard rose up from the silence.

An insect more monstrous than anything my worst

nightmares could have conjured up appeared from behind one of the largest outcroppings. A formidable pair of pincers came into view first, followed by a spiny carapace, eight legs, and lastly a tail that hung curved over its back. Attached at the end was some kind of blackened barb, but there wasn't time to worry about its purpose. With another cry consisting of a series of hissing clicks, the monster made a wild grab for Elvira with one of its massive pincers.

I reacted without thinking, closing my eyes as I recalled what I'd done with the dragon only a few short days ago. Opening them again, I stepped forward, balling my hands into fists as I screamed at the top of my lungs. "Leave her alone!"

Nothing happened, though it was quite possible neither of them heard me. Having recovered from her near-fall, Elvira was back to being light and quick on her feet, leaping from ledge to ledge as she attempted to put as much distance between her and the creature as possible. Whipping out a pair of knives, she hurled one and then the other between jumps, but despite both being well-aimed, the daggers bounced uselessly off the insect's protective carapace.

She spared a glance in our direction as the monster slammed its barb into the space she'd occupied a split second previously. It attempted to land another blow in quick succession, one she barely dodged, and the carelessness of it caused her to trip and stumble. Elvira crumpled against a rocky ledge, limbs quivering as she tried and failed to prop herself up on her arms. My heart nearly stopped. Was she hurt? Could she get up? Though her wispy blonde hair covered most of her face, it didn't conceal the genuine fear in her eyes as she fixated on the presence beside me.

Cedric barrelled past me, but not without barking orders. "Stay here, no matter what happens! And for fuck's sake, get back. *OI!*"

Cedric had still been standing in close proximity to me when he addressed the monster, and I flinched at the volume of his shout. Stripping off his jacket, he strode forward before waving it over his head like a flag. "You want blood? Have a taste of mine."

The monster turned then, but not without ramming its tail into several rocky ledges in the process. Debris rained down on Elvira's battered body, but with the beast's sights set on him, Cedric couldn't get to her, especially now that he was the one dodging that intimidating barbed tail. He made a grab for his pistol before shoving it back in its holster, and even as I wanted to scream at him to shoot the damn thing, it dawned on me that he was likely afraid he'd shoot one of us instead, especially in this chaotic mayhem.

Terrified determination surged through me as I pointed a shaking finger in Elvira's direction, nodding to Arktos. "Go dig her out, boy," I ordered, and he raced to obey, but as I moved to follow, a hand gripped my shoulder.

"What are you doing?" Peter hissed. "We need to go get that trident, especially while that thing is distracted!"

I couldn't have given less of a shit about Heartpiercer in that moment. "They're going to die if we don't help!"

"Then *help*! Can't you talk to it, like you did the dragon?"

"It won't listen." My breathing quickened as I watched Arktos frantically dig Elvira from the rubble while Cedric continued to make himself an enticing target, dodging pincers and that terrifying tail alike. Though he managed well enough for now, it was only a matter of time before he ended up like his sister or worse. "And I'm not entirely sure I can. It's beasts I've spoken to, not insects."

"Then we need to get what we came for and get the fuck out of here," Peter said, and then he was gone, using my shoulder as a boost to prop himself up on one of the outcroppings before tearing off.

"*Peter!*" I screeched, but my cry was swallowed among the chaos. Arktos had started barking and wouldn't stop. A few of Elvira's pained groans reached my ears, and Cedric remained locked in his game of cat and mouse with the monster. The longer it went without killing anyone, the more frenzied and frustrated it became, and the creature acted far more battering ram than beast at this point. Between the boulders it hurled and the outcroppings it reduced to rubble, it didn't seem to care whether it was those or its own appendages which succeeded in ending my father. By some miracle, Cedric remained on his feet, though I was more than aware that could change at any moment.

But he had held his own for this long, and I was much closer to Peter than I was to Cedric, so there was only one option which truly made sense. My body made the decision though my heart protested, pulling and yanking itself to the top of an outcropping before scanning for Peter. He was halfway to the trident, and if I hurried, I could catch up.

Forcing myself not to pay attention to anything other than what was right in front of me was one of the hardest things I'd ever done, especially when Cedric began screaming my name. *The trident, the trident, the trident,* I chanted in my head, utilizing the syllable pattern to help me keep a hurried pace as I leaped from outcropping to outcropping, though it became much harder the closer I got to my prize. They were spaced much farther apart here, and finally, I reached a dead end. There was no way I'd be able to jump to the nearest one without a running start, and there simply wasn't room for that on the ledge upon which I currently stood.

It was up to Peter, then, and judging by the fact that he was nearly within arm's reach, he'd succeed. "Hurry," I urged him, finally daring a glance over my shoulder and immediately wishing I hadn't. Though Arktos had managed to extract Elvira from the debris, she looked far too weak to aid Cedric, who sorely needed a reprieve. He breathed so heavily that each inhale was audible even from where I stood, and his face was so red that the outline of every strained blood vessel was clearly visible. His legs quivered, so much so that he wobbled when dodging the monster's barbed tail, and it was clear he didn't have many—if any—dodges left in him.

Peter's agonized cry had me whipping back around. He stood next to Heartpiercer, but flicked his wrist, grimacing, and yelled, "It burned me when I tried to take it!"

"Use your jacket!" I called back, though even as I said it, I knew there was no way the trident could be fooled that easily. Sure enough, the moment the fabric grazed Heartpiercer's handle, the jacket burst into flames.

Peter yelped before tossing the flaming garment aside, shooting me a glare before it even struck the ground. "Any more brilliant ideas?"

"Just one," I muttered for my ears alone, because I had tensed up to do something quite the opposite. Balancing my heel on the very back of the ledge, I bent my knees, steadied my breaths, and tried not to think about the fact that I wasn't particularly athletic as I took what wasn't nearly enough of a running start.

Then I jumped.

Peter's mouth opened in a silent *O*, or perhaps he was screaming, and I simply couldn't hear him. I was airborne for what felt like an eternity, hovering precariously between victory and a concussion before gravity took hold of me far too soon. I wasn't going to make it, not even if I stretched out my arms. I was going to fall in that dark narrow space between the ledges where no one could reach me, and not only had I failed, I'd condemned everyone I had ever cared about, including Scarlett, to certain death.

Just when my mind had been about to follow my body into the depths of despair, fingers encircled my wrist. I fell forward instead of down, and though the subsequent slam into the outcropping's edge was enough to knock the wind from me, I'd never been more grateful to feel anything in my life. Peering up, I glimpsed Peter's contorted face as he held my arm in both of his hands, including the burned one. "I've got you. I've got you," he said over and over, as if words would be enough to keep him from dropping me. "But I could use a little help."

I utilized both the outcropping's jagged edge and my free hand to scale up the cliff, and a minute later, Peter and I collapsed in a tangled heap of limbs on the ledge's face. "What the fuck," he said without lifting his head. "You could have broken your leg!"

"But I didn't." Heartpiercer pulsed from where I lay draped over Peter's chest, but I couldn't bring myself to move until I had at least caught my breath. "Besides, wasn't it you who told me to help?"

"You're no help to anyone dead," he shot back as I extracted myself from him. "Or with a burned hand. Wendy, you don't mean to touch that, do you?"

"Someone has to."

He remained silent as I approached the trident, and if our circumstances were any different, here was where I may have hesitated. I may have halted, taken time to assess whether or not the heat radiating from the weapon was meant to be welcoming or a warning, or even attempted to fashion some other way to get Heartpiercer down without using my bare hands. But there was time for none of that, and it was now or never. So I curled my fingers around the trident's shaft, squeezed my eyes shut, and tensed for all hell to break loose.

It did, but not in the way I'd expected.

I'd all but forgotten about the monster, but the moment Heartpiercer fell into my hands, its guardian released a cry so piercing that it brought me to my knees. Through watering eyes, I made out several vague silhouettes: Peter throwing himself at the creature's hardened carapace, Cedric sprinting at full speed toward me, leaping from ledge to ledge in single strides, and that horrific barbed tail pointed straight at my chest.

A scream, a shove, and then I was falling, both hearing and feeling an excruciating *snap* a moment before the world went dark.

XXI. THE TRUTH

Featured Song: Far Across the Seas

Cedric

Burning. My right arm was on fire from shoulder to wrist, and no one would extinguish it. Not when I screamed so fiercely it felt as though it would rip me in half, not when I thrashed against the hands that held me in an attempt to do it myself, and especially not when I tried to form words through the foam and drool pouring from my mouth.

Cut it off, I tried to plead. *Cut the entire thing off*. Even without anything to numb the pain, there was no way that amputating what was left of my arm could hurt any worse than this torturous agony. Each time my muscles spasmed of their own accord, fresh jolts of pain shot from the wound on my shoulder in every direction, some even creeping up my neck, and if I could have reached inside to forcibly rip the venom from my veins, I would have without hesitation.

The coolness at my back was the only thing that brought me any shred of solace. I vaguely recalled my shirt being sliced from me prior to my hook being removed, so I lay bare, exposed, and completely at the mercy of the same evil bastards who refused to douse the fire eating me alive. Couldn't they tell *that* was what I needed, not to be held down and immobilized, forced to drown in my own spit and vomit? That I'd never been in this much pain, that I would do anything to get it to stop, even run a blade through my chest, even curse Scarlett's name—

"...for Scarlett," some faint, faraway voice said. Had I said her name aloud? "If you won't stay awake for me, do it for Scarlett."

The flames reignited then, causing my back to arch and another involuntary scream to tear from my throat, but with my pirate queen's face in my mind's eye, I got through it without attempting to tear my arm off. The pain wasn't anywhere near bearable, but knowing she was watching helped me pretend that it was. I couldn't let her see me like this, no matter how much it hurt, and I certainly couldn't let her listen to me beg.

"I'm going to extract the barb now. It's going to get worse before it gets better, Ced."

I almost laughed at such a cruel joke. *How could it possibly get any worse?*

Then, a knife. That was a *knife* digging into my flesh, and I couldn't move, couldn't fight it. It was my older brother holding me down and laughing as he carved me up like an animal, licking my blood from his blade between cuts, threatening that my tongue would be next if I screamed. It was Compton stringing me up by my wrists before opening up every slice Jamie had ever made and adding more of his own. It was every time a dagger had been shoved in my face simply to get me to scream or flinch, and Blackbeard or one of his crew had made a mockery of my trauma. It was that unmistakable feel of cool metal against my sensitive, wounded, unprotected flesh, and I was as powerless to stop it now as I had been every other time a blade had left a permanent mark on my skin.

I wailed. I cried. I kicked and thrashed, bit and squirmed, but all it did was both exhaust me and allow the venom to work faster. I couldn't move or hear, and I certainly couldn't think. My world had been dark for some time, but the blackness beckoning me now was the deeper, more sinister kind, an abyss from which I might never emerge. An entity. And upon discovering my weakness, it became ravenous.

Opening its maw, it met no resistance when it swallowed me whole.

Of all things, I woke to music.

The voice was soft and raspy, but its melody was pure and clear, repeating the same verse in an endless, haunting loop. From the way it swirled and echoed, it became obvious we were in an enclosed space. A cave, perhaps? I allowed the song to be my guide as I eased back into the world of the living, and I soon recognized its mournful lyrics as well as the voice giving them life.

"The tide is ever rising through the night,
Silver waters bathed in restless light.
Far across the seas,
Together you and I will be."

Elvira realized I was awake halfway through this particular repetition but finished it before tightening her hold around my uninjured shoulder, avoiding the bandages wrapped around my other half as she pulled us closer together. My head rested in her lap, but she wouldn't meet my gaze when I blinked up at her bruised and swollen face. Tremors wracked her body, and that combined with a few shaky inhales informed me she was crying, but only when she leaned forward and wispy blonde hair draped across my cheeks and upper chest did I become aware that she wasn't simply crying. She was *sobbing*.

My pain and my voice returned around the same moment, so it cracked when I tried to utter her childhood nickname, the one reserved solely for situations like these. "Elle, don't cry. I'm here."

"Are you?" she whispered between sobs, her nails digging into my scalp as she tangled her fingers in my hair. She began rocking back and forth, cradling me as if I were a child. "Are you really? I'm not dreaming?"

"You're not if I'm not."

Elvira didn't quit crying or rocking. "I thought… I thought…"

"I'm alive." *Somehow.* "You wouldn't be able to get rid of me that easily."

That made her laugh, at least, but her terror returned in an instant, causing her to trip over her words. "I thought I'd killed you. There wasn't enough juice left in that damn barb to make a proper antivenom, and cutting it out of you made you panic far more than I anticipated. You were screaming Jamie's name, begging him to stop, but I had no choice but to use a blade, not if you were going to live. I had no choice, Ced." A choked wail escaped her lips. "Please, forgive me. I'm so sorry."

I gripped her wrist with my good hand then, squeezing just hard enough to get her attention. "Me salvaste la vida," I said slowly, taking a moment to recall my Spanish. "There's nothing to forgive, and never was."

"Are you sure about that?" Though she had stopped rocking the moment she felt my touch, Elvira's tears still flowed freely. "I've been such an ass to you these past weeks, and I was wrong. About everything."

"What do you mean?" Ordinarily I'd have considered it a great victory to yank any semblance of an apology out of my sister, but I was still struggling to recall what had happened prior to me passing out, let alone the past month.

"I mean that Scarlett is alive. I didn't believe it until I laid eyes on her, but she was precisely as you said. You didn't lead us all this way for nothing. And you certainly weren't willing to give up Wendy in the process, proven by this."

Elvira took my hand before holding out my palm for me to see, and I was deeply confused until she went on to explain, "Your black mark. It's gone, and has been since the moment you sacrificed yourself, taking that monster's sting in your daughter's place. It was selfless, and you really did save her life. With her being so much smaller, I suspect the venom would have killed her."

My daughter. I'd have bolted upright if I possessed the strength. "Where is she? Is she all right?"

"I don't know if you'd consider a broken leg 'all right,' but she's alive. Just sleeping."

Elvira gestured to where Wendy lay huddled against the side of the cave, closely flanked by both Heartpiercer and Arktos. The trident's dim light pulsed rhythmically, and the dog lifted his head when he noticed me staring. Unless I was hallucinating, I swore he nodded, as if to say *Don't worry, I've got her.*

My sister either hadn't noticed or didn't care, because she kept talking. "You, ah, pushed her a bit too hard when you shoved her out of the way, and she fell down one of those ledges. After we fished her out, Pan helped me set the break, and we splinted it as best we could. She'll recover, but she won't be walking for quite a while."

"Shit." I made a feeble effort to stand or at least sit up, but neither my body nor Elvira would let me.

"Wendy's more fine than you are, Ced. The worst of the symptoms may be over, but venom is still in your system. You need to rest, and you definitely need more sleep."

"No, we need to get that trident to Adais and get the fuck out of here." Shoving Elvira aside, I managed to pull myself into a sitting position, but not without sending white-hot spikes of searing pain shooting from my wound into my chest. Through gritted teeth, I forced, "Where's Pan?"

"*Adais*?" Elvira made a noise of disbelief. "Aren't we giving the trident to Kaara?"

I'd forgotten that Wendy and I were the only ones who knew that, but there wasn't time to fill my sister in. "Where is Pan?" I repeated.

"Off somewhere trying to make his mark go away. Mine's smaller, but I still have it. And in case you haven't forgotten, neither of us can go anywhere until those disappear, so unless you intend to leave us here—"

"I don't, dammit!" I had raised my voice to a shout, but when Wendy stirred, I lowered it to a whisper. "It's imperative that you both do whatever you need to as quickly as possible. The moment you're both free and not a minute after, we're getting out of here. *All* of us," I added when Elvira shot me a pointed look.

"Fine. I suppose I should go make sure Pan is alive, at least. He's been gone for hours." She stood, then hesitated. "Are you sure you'll be all right?"

I nodded. "Go."

Elvira got to the mouth of the cave before darting back to my side, kneeling, then pressing her lips to my forehead. "I'm not going far. If anything happens, anything at all, just yell, and I'll be right here."

"I'm not dying, Elle. Not today."

"Good. Because if you scare me like that again, I'll kill you myself."

"Looking forward to it."

When I blinked, she was gone. Despite Wendy's presence, my

sister's sudden absence left me feeling more vulnerable than I had anticipated, and I wrapped my uninjured arm around my still-bare chest, shuddering. It took only seconds for those whispers to come drifting from the cave's entrance, filling what would have otherwise been silence, but I was grateful for the noise. At least it gave me something to listen to other than my own anxiety and guilt-ridden thoughts, thoughts that had wandered back to a certain person in particular. Or mermaid—whichever form she currently occupied.

"You're doing it again."

I must have slipped deeper than I thought, because Wendy's voice caused me to start. Turning, I found her propped against the cavern wall, still flanked by her dog. Her right leg lay tucked beneath her and the other had been splinted with some driftwood, albeit awkwardly given our lack of proper supplies. Wendy clutched Heartpiercer in one hand while idly scratching Arktos's ears with the other and watched me with an expression that very much suggested she held metaphorical matches right now.

Just as well, because I badly needed an excuse not to close the distance between us and throw my arms around her. Even the sight of her awake and alive was almost too much, so it was no shock that my voice cracked when I said, "Sorry. Old habit."

"'Habit,'" she echoed, still studying me closely. "Is that what you're calling what you did for me, too?"

The question startled me so much that I didn't have an immediate answer, nor could I tell where Wendy was going with this, so I kept my mouth shut and let her continue.

"Is that how you got all those scars? Saving people? I... I didn't realize you had so many."

Her mask slipped, and emotion shone in her gaze, but I forced myself not to acknowledge it, at least not yet. Repositioning myself so she could get a better look, I gestured to the marks on my chest and shoulders. "Each of these has a story, but they're not nearly that exciting or noble, I'm afraid. A good number of them were left by two men, both of whom hated me very much."

"Was Jamie one of them?"

I winced. "How do you know that?"

"You were screaming his name."

"Ah. Right." Elvira had mentioned as much. "He used my body as his own personal form of celebration the night Blackbeard was kil—wait. Why are we talking about this?"

Wendy didn't answer other than to mumble an apology, so I took my own guess.

"We don't have to talk about what happened if you don't want to, but I'd like the night my brother tortured me off the table as well."

"It's not that," she blurted out, looking increasingly guilty. "I'm just confused. You nearly died."

"You *would* have died."

"And? It's not like I didn't know what I was risking."

"Hold on, now I'm confused." The longer we talked, the harder it was to keep in mind our truce, but I did my best to keep my tone from slipping into antagonism. "Are you upset with me for saving your life?"

"Yes. No. I don't know." Wendy chewed on her lip. "You just have so much more to live for, so much more that depends on you, needs you."

"Are you talking about Scarlett again? If you think for one second that she wouldn't skin me alive if I ever let anything happen to you, you don't know her very well. But that's not why I did it."

Wendy didn't make me say the dreaded 'I love you' again, but her flinch told me she was thinking it, so I changed the subject.

"And that's not true in the slightest, and hardly a fair comparison. We each have different things to live for, different people who need us, but that doesn't make either of our lives more valuable than the other's. What about Pan and Tink? What about Scarlett? She'd be beyond disappointed if, after all of this, she didn't get to meet you properly."

I nearly added *what about me*, but decided against it, especially when I noticed the silent tears running down Wendy's face. She didn't say a word, even when I left room for her to speak, and continued stroking Arktos almost hypnotically.

I wasn't sure if I should keep going or let silence overtake us. We stared at each other for a long while, but when those whispers came creeping back, words tumbled from my lips. They probably weren't what she wanted to hear, but I uttered them anyway. "I know what it is to be scared of the dark. I also know what it is to be allured and seduced by it, to let it convince you that you're undeserving of even the tiniest shred of light. But, Wendy, the only reason you can't see it yourself is because you're the fucking *beacon*. You shine so bright for everyone else that you're living in your own shadow.

"But I see it. Pan sees it. Elvira sees it. Hell, even Scarlett sees it, and she barely knows you. We've all benefited from it in one form or another. It's high time you do too. Allow yourself to be as worthy as I know you are. Allow yourself to be loved."

As I spoke, I inched closer, both because of my physical limitations and because I didn't want to push her, but I wanted to be there to catch her if she fell. And into my waiting arms, she did.

Some faraway corner of my mind registered pain, but it was easy to shove aside while my daughter sought me out for comfort. Wendy buried her face in the crook of my neck, tucked her arms flush against my chest, and sobbed, her anguished wails finally drowning out those damn whispers.

I continued murmuring words I hoped were reassuring as I draped my right arm around her shoulders. My free hand rested atop her head, eventually beginning to stroke her hair, and I rocked her just as Elvira had rocked me, only vaguely aware of the fact that Wendy wasn't the only one crying. For the first time since losing Scarlett all those years ago, that gaping hole in my chest had been filled, and now that I no longer felt like I was drowning, I was left gasping for breath in an entirely different way.

It was difficult to tell who pulled away from whom, but we managed to extract ourselves from one another once we'd both regained control of our breathing. Wendy resumed her position against the cave wall, tucking a strand of hair behind her ear as she raised her gaze to mine. Her cheeks were flushed from crying, but she looked far more at ease than she had before. "When the hell did you become so wise?"

I shrugged my uninjured shoulder. "I didn't. You're just getting easier for me to read."

"Oh?" She brightened at the challenge. "What else have you observed?"

"I'm not sure you want me to answer that."

"I wouldn't have asked if I didn't!"

I didn't believe her but obliged anyway. "All right. You didn't protest or correct Elvira when she called Pan your boyfriend. You two have been sharing a bunk for weeks—"

Wendy grimaced and cut across me. "It's not like that, I swear. We're very close, but nothing more."

"I don't give a shit, I'm just curious." A lie, but only because it was Pan of all people. For Wendy, though, I'd force myself to accept it if he truly made her happy.

"I like Peter a lot, but we're just friends. We couldn't and won't be more, because..." She hesitated, then blurted out, "I like girls."

I blinked. "Oh."

Heat flamed her cheeks. "Yes. It's been a while since I've had a crush, but H-Herbert's advisor was q-quite pretty."

"The mean one? Amira?"

She nodded, and I laughed.

"Well, to be honest, I like the idea of that far better than you and Pan. But be with whoever you want. As long as they make you happy, I'm happy."

Wendy immediately bristled. "I wasn't aware I had to ask your permission to do anything, much less when it comes to *that*."

"Back to snipping at me, which means you're feeling better. Good, because we need to get the hell out of here." It took less effort than I anticipated to pull myself to my feet. Perhaps the venom had finally run its course.

"But Peter and Elvira—"

"Have been gone for at least an hour, which means they either can't do what they're supposed to but are too stubborn to ask for help, or they're in trouble. Either way, I'm going after them." Having located one of Elvira's spare daggers, I tucked the sheathed blade into my waistband. I decided against donning my hook given the weakened condition of that arm and shoulder.

Wendy's mouth fell open. "You're leaving me here? Alone?"

"No. You have your dog, don't you?" It was difficult to keep my tone even, because while I didn't like the idea any more than she did, it wasn't as if she was capable of walking at the moment. I nodded toward Heartpiercer. "Do you remember what to say to get out of here?"

She looked insulted that I asked. "*What belongs to the sea wi—*"

"Don't say it now!" I snapped. "Keep that trident close, and if anything happens, don't hesitate."

Wendy shook her head and blurted out another string of protests, but I had already turned to leave. Though I hated to abandon her, each step I took helped to clear the mind fog the venom had left behind, and the surer I became that I'd made the right decision. Something felt off, and we'd stayed sedentary for too long. What's more, Elvira wouldn't have been gone this long without explanation, Pan hadn't been seen for far longer, and my suspicions were confirmed the moment I set foot outside the cave.

It was hauntingly silent.

Gooseflesh erupted along my arms, and it had nothing to do with the fact that I wasn't wearing a shirt. Those rhythmic whispers had been present since the moment we'd tumbled into that pile of bones, so for them to have gone quiet couldn't mean anything good. Instinct had me yanking out the dagger, but a deeper and more primal one warned that one measly blade wielded by a man at half strength wasn't going to do shit. Still, it wasn't as if I had any choice, so I crept forward, scanning my surroundings.

We hadn't gone far from where we'd battled the monster. Though partially veiled in a cloud of mist, I could make out the outline of the creature's lifeless corpse draped over piles of rubble. The carapace had been pierced from above, nearly cracking it in two, and the curved tail lacked the barb that had poisoned and nearly killed me.

My arm tingled at the unpleasant memory, and I turned away, taking note of two distinctive paths to my left and right. Both led back to the monster and then beyond, though the barrens we'd crossed to reach this place were obscured by that mysterious fog. Was that where Elvira and Pan had wandered off to? Had they retraced our steps and backtracked that far? Or were there other paths I simply hadn't seen? Elvira had mentioned she intended to stay close. Surely she wouldn't—

A scream from the mist. Not a warning, but a cry of pure fear that seeped into my skin and bones alike. I remained in place when I should have darted back to Wendy's side, but a combination of curiosity and stupidity won out, keeping my feet firmly rooted to the ground. Was it my sister? Pan? Or was it yet another monster, this one designed to lure me to my death, or worse, away from Wendy?

I didn't have to wait long. A silhouette came staggering from the path to my left, and upon emerging from the fog, I recognized Pan's terrified face. Judging from how out of breath he was, he'd been running for quite some time and struggled to regain his footing. "The souls!" he half-gasped, half-yelled, eyes wide and pleading. "They turned on us!"

Of course they had, and my sister was nowhere to be seen. "Get to Wendy," I ordered Pan before sprinting toward the path to the right. A low roar grew louder with every step, but only when I was a dozen feet from the mist did I register them as voices. Angry and buzzing, their combined volume soon became overwhelming, but I pressed on, because I meant what I'd said to Elvira. I wasn't leaving without her.

She burst from the fog a moment later, looking even more bedraggled than Pan. Her clothes were ripped and torn, her hair plastered to her cheeks with sweat, and she didn't slow her limping stride when she spotted me. "Those fucking ghosts," she managed between gasps. "They've gone mad, chased me, tried to grab me—"

"Come on." I snatched her wrist in a vice grip, abandoning the useless dagger as I dragged her back toward the cave. "Pan has Wendy. We're getting out of here."

"But the mark, it's still there!"

"Would you rather be cursed or alive?"

"Are you saying you'd give me the choice?"

"Come on," I repeated, because the honest answer was no; I

wasn't any more ready to lose Elvira than she was to lose me, and she knew it. "Heartpiercer can take us to the surface."

We remained linked as we made our way back to the cave. Though we moved significantly slower than I would have liked thanks to Elvira's limp, we were otherwise unhindered, and Wendy, Pan, and Arktos were waiting for us by the time we arrived. They looked ready, but far from relieved or welcoming. Wendy was only standing thanks to Pan and Heartpiercer's help, both of whom she utilized as crutches, grimacing as Arktos emitted a series of agitated barks, but it wasn't until Pan lifted a shaky finger that I whirled around. "Behind you!"

Souls began pouring from both paths, effectively blocking any form of escape. Some looked ravenous while others looked downright murderous, with a handful wielding ghostly weapons. They formed a mob so tightly packed that they were tripping over and trampling one another, but for every soul that got crushed, three more were there to take its place. Within a minute, we'd be overwhelmed, and whether they intended to beat, swarm, or tear us limb from limb, I could think of few worse ways to die. Without slowing my pace, I roared over Arktos's frantic barking, "Everyone grab that trident NOW!"

I shoved Elvira ahead of me, ensuring she got within reach of Heartpiercer before I did. The moment she touched her palm to it, I followed suit, and even Arktos jumped up to place one of his paws on the shaft. That left Pan, but of all things, he hesitated.

"What the fuck are you doing?" I snarled. "Grab it!"

"It burned him last time," Wendy protested.

"A burn is better than death. Take it, Pan!" I'd have forced him if I had another hand, but I wasn't willing to let go of the trident for his sake. The souls would be upon us within seconds and their screams were deafening, but my heart was pounding so loud it drowned them out. "*Now!*"

Swallowing, he reached, but the moment his fingertips brushed the metal, he yelped and yanked his arm back. The scent of singed skin flooded my nostrils, and I may have felt sorry for him if ghoulish and clammy hands hadn't brushed my back a moment later, informing me we were out of time. In a split second, I made my decision, placing the safety of my sister and daughter over that of Peter Pan's.

Forgive me, Wendy.

Tightening my grip on Heartpiercer, I whispered, "What belongs to the sea will always return."

XXII. THE BATTLE

Wendy

It was like drowning and dying of thirst all at once.

One moment we were sedentary, the next, my body was yanked and pulled in a million different directions, all while I couldn't breathe. It wasn't excruciating, but it certainly wasn't comfortable, and I had no way of making it stop. We were moving so fast that I didn't dare let go of Heartpiercer's shaft, nor open my eyes to witness time and space bending around us. And given the viscous liquid pooling around my mouth and nose, I didn't scream. I had to bear both the itchiness in my throat and the pain in my lungs as they demanded air, but just when I became genuinely fearful for my life, I surfaced.

Gasping, I inhaled saltwater and oxygen alike as I fought to keep from slipping back under the frigid water. Agony shot up my broken leg as it was jostled in the choppy current, and I barely stifled a cry as the waves only grew stronger. They pummeled me mercilessly, crashing over my head multiple times before I was finally offered a reprieve. Tears streamed down my face from all the seawater I'd inhaled, making it doubly hard to fixate on the glowing object just a few strokes away, but once I recognized it, I paddled my arms and functional leg until I reached it.

Why or how Heartpiercer hadn't sunk remained a mystery as I closed my hand around its handle, but I had never been more grateful to touch anything in my life. Though it wasn't anchored to anything, the trident remained immobile even as another round of waves assaulted us, forcing my head underwater another half dozen times before I was able to more clearly make out my surroundings.

To describe it as chaotic would be an understatement, and every one of my senses became overwhelmed. Ships and monsters littered the waters in every direction, smoke and lightning flooded the skies, and to top it all off, it was pouring rain. The *booms* of cannon fire combined with the roaring of the beasts were almost enough to drown out the thunder, but every few seconds, those telltale *cracks* rattled me to my core. Breathing through my nose soon became impossible thanks to the acrid stench of gunpowder lingering in the air, and I coughed and sputtered as I clung to Heartpiercer, fighting to ignore the searing pain in my broken leg. What I'd thought were smaller waves were actually part of the torrential downpour, which dumped literal sheets of water over my head every single time I thought it couldn't possibly get worse.

"*Wendy!*"

I thought I'd imagined the voice until a bobbing head came into view. Elvira swam in my direction, her strokes as impressive as her speed. Once she reached me, she gripped my upper shoulder as if she thought I needed the support, though her attention remained fixated on the complete and utter mayhem unfolding around us. "We need to get out of here."

No shit, I wanted to say, but what came out were a series of panicked questions. "Where are Peter and Cedric? What's going on? Whose ships are those? Where are—"

"I don't have a clue, but there's your dog."

The surrounding cacophony had masked Arktos's barking until he was nearly upon us. He paddled through the water at a pace that rivaled Elvira's, then draped his front paws over Heartpiercer's shaft to anchor himself and showered my face in licks. But as happy as I was to see him safe and alive, I wouldn't be in any mood to celebrate until I knew Peter and Cedric were as well.

As if she'd read my thoughts, Elvira shook her head. "We don't have time to wait for them. We're sitting ducks if we stay here."

"You'd leave your brother?"

"I'd get both of us to safety so we can *help* him," she spat, clenching her jaw. "Unless you'd rather get blown to smithereens by stray cannon fire!"

I didn't have a compelling argument, and the selfish part of me desperately wanted to be out of this water. Though it was fucking freezing, my injured leg felt as though it was on fire, and I wouldn't get an ounce of relief until I immobilized it again. Squinting, I did a quick scan of all the surrounding ships, recognition dawning on me when I took note of their colors. "Is that Prince Herbert's emblem?"

Every vessel in our immediate vicinity displayed the same golden flag *The Glistening Pearl* had so proudly waved, quite possibly the only beautiful thing about that ship. But unlike Herbert's oddly shaped and wastefully adorned one, these members of his fleet were capable warships, their guns giving the various creatures they fired upon a run for their money.

Elvira fixated on a different vessel entirely and brightened as she lifted a quivering finger. "I don't know about those ships, but I've never been happier to see *my* ship—or her."

Following where she pointed, my mouth dropped open, but not because *The Jolly Serpent* had just opened fire on a gigantic fish with teeth.

Because *my mother* stood at the prow.

Even from this distance, I could make out the whiteness of Scarlett's knuckles as she gripped the rail. Fully in her human form, she was dressed simply in a white shirt, leather corset, and breeches, though the weapons strapped to her were anything but. Among a collection of knives to rival Elvira's,

Scarlett possessed a pair of pistols as well as a longer cutlass sheathed at her hip. Lifting one of her boots to the railing's lower rungs, she leaned forward, scanning the ocean for gods knew what, but judging from the way her face lit up, she found it a moment later. Gesturing wildly, she made a series of over-exaggerated movements, clearly in an attempt to communicate with whatever she had spotted.

The hairs on the back of my neck stood at attention around the same time Elvira scoffed. "Gods, not that slimy thing again."

I turned to look where she and Scarlett were staring and screamed. Hurtling toward us was some kind of fish-horse, and given how our last run in with a monster had gone, I didn't trust myself to make it go away if it proved to be unfriendly. But it slowed to an eventual halt before reaching us, whinnying a greeting, and I recognized the beast at the same time Cedric leaned over its neck.

"So we get to drown while you get the royal treatment? Typical."

"How in any way is that *typical*? Phorcys found me somehow, but it's not like I asked him to help me. I'm not Wendy with her magic powers." He shot his sister an incredulous glare before turning to me. "Speaking of, are you all right?"

"Where's Peter?"

Something flashed in Cedric's face, but it was gone a moment later. "Haven't seen him, and we can't wait around. Take my hand."

Eager to escape the frigid and choppy waters, I slipped my palm into his more freely than I ever had before. Elvira and

Arktos kept hold of Heartpiercer while Cedric pulled me onto Phorcys's back, which was far more awkward of a process than it needed to be given his lack of two hands and my mangled leg. The pain was unbearable any time I moved, and despite biting my tongue, a handful of anguished cries tore from my throat. Cedric mumbled encouragement, but I didn't register a word of it until I sat straddling the beast's back, and even then, I couldn't keep my balance without gripping my father's shoulders for support.

"—not well at all. Need to get her out of here," I heard Elvira say when I wasn't feeling quite as dizzy, but Cedric shook his head.

"How the fuck is she going to scale the ship in her state? There isn't time to lower a longboat, and Scarlett can't spare the men."

"Scarlett?" I echoed. "Is she captaining, then?"

Cedric turned his head, speaking over his shoulder to me. "She's doing a lot of things, but all *you* need to do is stay alive. Phorcys and Arktos will keep you safe."

"What?" Elvira hissed. "You intend to leave her down here?"

"It's a hell of a lot safer than bringing her aboard the ship most likely to be targeted and sunk!" My father shouted now, but whether it was because of agitation or because he needed to be heard over the cacophony, I couldn't be certain. "Besides, if anyone wanted Wendy, they wouldn't think to look in the water, and even if they did, Phorcys can outswim anything that isn't another hippocampus."

"Is anyone going to ask my opinion?" I snapped.

"You don't get one, not about this." Cedric placed his hand on my uninjured knee. "I'm sorry, Wendy, but this is for the best."

I glanced helplessly at Elvira. "You're letting him leave me?"

Cedric answered before she could. "We're not leaving you. We're getting that trident to Adais, and he's going to do whatever it takes to free Scarlett. Even if it means killing Kaara."

"Wait, what?" Elvira tightened her grip on Heartpiercer. "You struck a deal."

"And then I struck another deal. Your point?"

"We technically didn't swear a damn thing to Adais," I muttered, but this only agitated Elvira further.

"Wendy is in on this too?"

"Look," Cedric pressed his sister, glancing at *The Jolly Serpent* and then back again. "I know it's a lot to take in. But I never hid anything from you, I swear. I've picked up scattered clues over the past several days, and Wendy happened to be with me through much of it. Only just now did I piece it all together, when Scarlett showed me that."

Elvira and I glanced where Cedric pointed into the storm clouds on the horizon. I didn't immediately see anything out of the ordinary, but when lightning flashed, it illuminated two distinctive silhouettes, both fighting tooth and claw, and one looking very much like…

"Kaara," Elvira breathed, finishing my train of thought. "And that's—"

"Adais, yes. He and Scarlett have been working together for I don't know how long. His goal is to get Heartpiercer back, hers is to regain her freedom, and they both orchestrated all of this."

"Scarlett looks pretty damn free to me," Elvira muttered, but Cedric kept going.

"She's doing what she can, but still lacks her voice. She pointed to her throat and then to the gods, and I don't know quite what that means, but hopefully Adais can help her somehow. In the meantime, we need to help *him*." He nodded to Heartpiercer. "Herbert's fleet is only going to buy us so much time."

A realization struck me. "You were right. The engagement was a ruse. All Scarlett wanted were his ships, and he was stupid enough to believe her."

Cedric nodded, and I didn't miss the proudness in his voice. "Starting to believe me when I tell you your mother is something special, are you?"

I didn't answer that, because as far as I was seeing it, they were all something special—everyone but me. They all had a job, a role in this elaborate plot, yet they expected me to sit on my ass and watch while they saved the day. Even considering my broken leg, it seemed beyond absurd. I had influence over monsters, for fuck's sake, and it wasn't as if there weren't plenty in my immediate vicinity that I could attempt to communicate with. But when I opened my mouth to say as much, Cedric peeled himself from my grasp before slipping into the ocean to join his sister. Arktos abandoned Heartpiercer to swim in my direction, and to my surprise, Phorcys didn't protest when the dog used his tail to pull himself out of the water. He climbed up behind me before doing a massive shake, completely useless in the continuous rain, but I was too focused on Cedric and Elvira to scold him.

"Where are you going?" I asked again, loathing the way my voice cracked. "I need to be with you. I can help! I can talk to the monsters, or at least try—"

"Like you did with the last one?" Cedric shrugged the still-bandaged wound on his shoulder, keeping a firm grip on Heartpiercer as Elvira swam toward *The Jolly Serpent*. "It's not worth the risk, and we don't need any help. We're holding our own just fine."

"For now," I snapped, but Cedric ignored me.

"Please, just stay here and stay out of the way. Phorcys, keep her safe."

He may as well have uttered the only words I was used to hearing as often as my own name while still at the orphanage—*sit down and shut up*—and rage boiled my blood, because fuck that. Where was the Cedric who had, merely an hour ago, held me while I sobbed and made up all this sappy shit about a beacon? Who had whispered over and over again that I was worthy, that I was loved? I didn't know precisely what to call this, but it sure as fuck didn't feel like love.

It felt like rejection.

I kept my mouth shut when Elvira began scaling the ladder that had been rolled down for her, and I didn't say a word when Cedric followed suit. Combining their strengths, brother and sister managed to lug the trident up the side of the ship and, when they finally succeeded, were greeted by Scarlett. After pressing his lips to her cheek in a quick kiss, Cedric spoke words I couldn't hear, and both he and Scarlett stole glances in my direction once he finished. My mother gave me what was probably meant to be a reassuring nod before turning back to her captain duties. Cedric bellowed orders, and just like that, *The Jolly Serpent's* sailing pattern changed, altering course to sail straight for where Adais and Kaara were attempting to kill each other.

And just like that, I was discarded and abandoned, left behind by *both* my parents... again.

I may have burst into tears if I wasn't so damn angry. My arms quivered as I snaked them around Phorcys's neck, and though I badly wanted to scream, I gritted my teeth instead, because it wasn't in any way worth the effort. No one would notice or care, because as had been proven time and time again, without Peter and Tink, I had no one. And where the fuck were they? I didn't even know where to begin to search for Peter, and last I'd seen Tink, she was with Scarlett—but the moment my mother's name popped into my head, I sat up. I'd bet anything that Tink was aboard *The Jolly Serpent*, and if anyone could help me find Peter, it was her.

Digging my uninjured heel into Phorcys's side, I nodded toward the ship. "Get me close. There's someone I need to find."

The hippocampus seemed reluctant but obeyed, tossing his head before gliding forward. Though the waves continued to churn around us, Phorcys was unaffected, remaining steadfast even when faced with waters that would have overtaken me if I had been on my own. The smooth ride made keeping my broken leg still and marginally comfortable a hell of a lot easier. We reached *The Jolly Serpent* without incident, and though a handful of crewmen shot me incredulous looks, I cupped my hands and shouted Tink's name.

"Are you there? We need to find Peter!"

A head popped over the side of the rail, but not the one I wanted to see. "What the fuck are you doing?" Elvira snapped. "Didn't Ced tell you to get out of here?"

"Get Tink and I will. She's my best chance at finding Peter."

"That boy is going to be the death of you."

"Just do it, Elvira!"

She disappeared, but I didn't know whether it was to tell on me or obey, until she returned with something cupped in her hands. Though I couldn't see Tink from my current position, the faintest whisper of bells was enough to make my heart flutter.

"Do I just... let her go? She doesn't seem strong enough to fl—*wait*!"

Elvira made a wild grab for Tink's tiny form but missed, and the fairy hurtled toward the dark waters below. Halfway down, she spread her wings, and though she didn't flap them, they were enough to turn her freefall into a glide. I released the breath I'd been holding, held out my hands, and sagged my shoulders when Tink finally landed within my grasp.

"Thanks for the heart attack," I said, but she wasn't listening, curls bouncing as she glanced around wildly.

"Where's Peter?"

"Not here, which is why I came to find you. I was hoping you'd know where he is, or at least how to find him."

Tink shook her head slowly. "I would if he hadn't shut me out right before you entered the Sea. I haven't felt him or our bond since."

Ripples of concern shot down my spine. What could have kept Peter from reactivating his bond with Tink the moment he returned to the world of the living? Was he injured? Captured? Or was he…

No. I refused to believe it unless I saw irrefutable proof, and until then, Tink and I would do anything and everything within our power to get him back. "Okay," I forced, reassuring myself as much as Tink. "Okay. That's okay. We just need to be methodical about this, then. We got separated upon our return and emerged in different places, so he's probably just somewhere we haven't…"

My voice trailed off as Tink visibly began to quiver. Fixated on something behind us, she opened her mouth to utter something, but it was Elvira's shriek that damn near pierced my eardrums. "Wendy, *look out!*"

I hadn't ordered him to move, but Phorcys shot forward with such zeal that Tink and Arktos nearly tumbled into the sea. Throwing an arm around the hippocampus's neck just in time, I held on for dear life while he transported us a fair distance from *The Jolly Serpent*, and only when Phorcys slowed did I see why.

The fish with teeth was back, and it was pissed. Though wounded from the last round of cannon fire that had been unleashed upon it, it fueled the creature's rage far more than it had been weakened, and as I watched, the fish sunk its massive teeth into the hull near the prow. Screams resounded, the masts shuddered, and the entire ship began to groan as the fish whipped its tail back and forth without letting go, seemingly determined to either rip a hole in my family's flagship or drag it to the bottom of the ocean. It was difficult to tell at my current distance, but I swore I made out Cedric covering Scarlett's body with his own as water and debris alike flooded the deck, the force of it sending several bodies tumbling into the unforgiving ocean.

Red clouded my vision, and I balled my hands into fists, because if *The Jolly Serpent* was ever destined to sink, it sure as fuck wasn't going to be today.

An explosive combination of instinct and rage fueled my summons. Not wanting to miss the fish getting what it deserved, I didn't bother closing my eyes as my thoughts drifted far below the depths of the stormy sea to the dragon I inexplicably knew lurked below, watching and waiting for my orders alone.

You are needed.

At first, silence, but then, the slightest rumble before the dragon posed a question it had asked me once before. *Are you certain, Wendy Maynard?*

Yes.

There was no confirmation or agreement, and as quickly as the dragon had entered my psyche, it disappeared, leaving only silence behind. I could do nothing but watch as the fish continued its merciless assault, wrecking the vessel that had survived Neverland, its curse, and a goddess's realm all in a matter of minutes. Its desperation rose with its determination, and it began thrashing even harder before an eventual agonizing *crack*.

But it wasn't *The Jolly Serpent*—it was the dragon, quick and cruel, as it burst from the waves before slamming its much larger body against the fish's wounded side. Either it had been struck with enough force or its wounds amplified the pain, but either way, the fish unhinged its jaw, and *The Jolly Serpent* was free once more. The dragon and the fish turned on one another then, as ravenous as they were vicious, but the dragon at least had enough sense to guide the fight away from the ship.

Now that the chaos had died down somewhat, I made out Cedric's voice bellowing various orders. "Smee, batten down the hatches. Elvira, secure the remaining guns, but make sure they're loaded. Hudson, I need you to—Scarlett?"

My head snapped up at that, but given that my mother was still standing, I didn't immediately know what Cedric was referring to. She stared at him, wide-eyed, brought a hand to her throat, then opened her mouth and moved her lips. I could only make out shouting given the distance, but judging from the whooping and cheering that rose up, followed by Cedric wrapping Scarlett in a fierce hug, my mother had just spoken for the first time in sixteen years.

Before I could wonder why or how, my gaze darted to movement in my peripheral vision, and my breath hitched. At least a dozen humanoid creatures were scaling up *The Jolly Serpent's* sides. Their skin shone an unnatural green, appeared as slimy as Phorcys's scales, and though they possessed two arms and two legs, they moved more like insects than humans. As if sensing they'd been spotted, one of the creatures whipped around, bared its pointed teeth, and snarled, and only then did I find my own voice.

"Those things—*look out!*"

My warning became swallowed among the mayhem, because several had already boarded. Still reeling from the fish's attack, even our best fighters were caught off guard, and the strange creatures met little to no resistance as they began slaughtering without mercy. What should have been war cries were shrieks of agony, and as crimson began splattering across the deck, for the first time, I was grateful I wasn't anywhere near that ship, because I was likely to have vomited.

But I couldn't sit here and watch it happen. Heart beating out of my chest, I urged Phorcys forward, all the while praying I wasn't too late to do *something*. My options were severely limited thanks to my leg, but I could warn or be a lookout, summon the dragon again, or stab any of the fuckers stupid enough to get close to me, and surely that had to count for something.

In the minute it took me to arrive, though, it was over. As if a switch had been flipped, the creatures dove back over the side of the ship and disappeared into the waves, having seemingly gotten what they came for. None of the ones that I noticed had anything within their grasp, but clearly something had been taken, because Cedric was losing his goddamn mind.

"—*kill* her for this. She can't do this to me!"

Though I couldn't see her from where I sat, Elvira's voice had no trouble reaching my ears. "None of us saw them take her, Ced. Maybe she just fell. We can send out a search party."

"No," he snapped. "*We're* the search party. All of us."

It hit me then that there was a voice I had yet to hear, and given the rest of the context clues, my blood turned to ice. "Where's Scarlett?" I called to whoever would answer.

There was an awkward pause before Elvira leaned over the rail to address me. "We don't know. She's just… gone."

"We're getting her back." Cedric appeared at his sister's side, not looking the least bit shocked to see me still here. "That means it's up to you now, Wendy. You need to get the trident to Adais."

I blanched, and my voice squeaked, because of all the things I'd been expecting him to say, that wasn't one of them. "Me?" I'd asked for a job, pleaded for one, even, but this wasn't a job—this was being a whole ass heroine. And hadn't I already done that once, in Neverland, and only by sheer, dumb luck? How could I possibly be expected to do it a second time?

Oblivious to my self-doubt, Cedric nodded. "I'm going after Scarlett, and this ship is in no condition to sail for the gods. But you and Phorcys can make it. I know you can."

My father's confident '*I know you can*' echoed in my head long after he'd uttered it, and tears sprang to my eyes. He did believe in me, and I was a fool to have ever thought otherwise. "All right."

I waited as Heartpiercer was loaded into a longboat before being lowered down from *The Jolly Serpent*. From there, I placed the trident horizontally in front of me, keeping a firm grip on it with both hands as Phorcys began to glide toward the storm.

Stealing a final glance at Cedric, I nodded before whispering, "Thank you." Then to Phorcys, I said, "Get us there as fast as you can."

I held on for dear life as I finally experienced the true extent of a hippocampus's speed. The world around us became a blur as Phorcys zipped and dodged, avoiding obstacles with ease despite his breakneck pace, and within a few short moments, we had reached the massive wall of clouds.

Patting the hippocampus's neck, I allowed him a moment to catch his breath before gently urging him forward. "You've done brilliantly. Just a little farther—*fuck!*"

I nearly lost my grip on Heartpiercer when Phorcys reared up, kicking his front legs the way a horse would when spooked. Arktos yelped as he slipped part way off the hippocampus's back, and even Tink swore as she, too, almost tumbled into the ocean.

There was good reason for Phorcys's panic, though. A wall of violet flames had burst up from the sea, stretching in both directions and completely blocking the way forward. Even after backing up, the heat seared my exposed skin, the smoke made my eyes water, and drawing a breath that didn't send me into a coughing fit became nearly impossible.

Trapped. It was the only word for what I was, because Phorcys couldn't get me any closer, and I couldn't swim beneath the flames with a broken leg. I'd come this far only to fall short at the last moment, to prove myself a disappointment—

"Wendy!" I only heard Tink say my name when she shouted at the top of her lungs, which still wasn't very loud. When I turned to her, I did a double take, because cupped in the fairy's hands was no more than a pinch of a substance I thought I'd never see again.

"Is that... dust?"

"The remainder of what I have. You may not be able to walk or swim, but with this, you can fly. It's the only way you'll be able to get Heartpiercer where it needs to be."

My heart skipped a beat. I hadn't flown since Neverland, and I'd missed it dearly, but my excitement only lasted for a moment. "If I take your dust, what happens to you?"

"Don't worry about me. Everyone else is more important."

"You don't mean—"

"I'm not going to die if you take it, Wendy, at least not any faster than I already am. Please, just do it. If not for me, for Peter."

I nodded even as a lump formed in my throat. "For Peter."

After depositing the dust into my waiting palm, Tink sat back and watched as I sprinkled it over the crown of my head. Closing my eyes and ensuring I had a decent grip on the trident, I waited expectantly.

But nothing happened.

"It's not working," I told Tink, my voice choked and panicked. "Why isn't it working?" I'd used her dust countless times in Neverland, and never once had it failed me. Why now of all times, when I needed it most?

The fairy's voice was barely audible. "Dust alone may not be enough when I'm this weak. If you want to fly, you need to think happy thoughts."

Surely I'd misheard her. "Happy thoughts?"

"Yes, and I suggest you hurry."

As much as I wanted to oblige her, how was there anything remotely happy about the chaos ensuing around us? Dozens of sailors had died, a number of ships had sunk, monsters had perished for the sole reason that their gods had ordered them to fight, and Kaara and Adais remained hellbent on murdering one another.

Then there were my personal relationships. Peter remained missing, Cedric and Scarlett had been all too eager to leave me behind, and my sole companions now were a half-dead fairy, a dog, and a hippocampus. Ending this ancient fight between gods rested squarely on my shoulders, and not only was the weight of that responsibility beyond crushing, I couldn't do it without conjuring at least an ounce of happiness in this bleak and dying place. I'd fail, just as I'd failed at being captain, at earning my father's love, at being the kind of friend who couldn't locate one of their own, and this time, the price was losing everyone and everything I'd ever held dear.

Though my heart continued beating out of my chest, something shifted when I closed my eyes, because beneath my insecurities, there was an incredible amount of love. I cared so much because I loved these people, and I loved them because, as infuriating as they could sometimes be, every one of them brought me joy in their own unique way. Peter never failed to make me laugh and knew precisely how to comfort me any time I needed a shoulder to cry on. Cedric had made me smile more times than I could count in the past few days, had been willing to give his life for mine, and though I remained furious with him, deep down, I knew his only goal was to keep me alive and safe.

And finally, Scarlett. She and I hadn't exchanged any more than bewildered glances, but I couldn't deny that I felt a connection to her, stronger than anything I'd ever felt with Cedric. There was a warmth to her, a gentleness he simply didn't possess, and perhaps it had been artificially forged by my attachment to the music box she had given me, but above all, my mother made me feel safe. I could almost envision a life with her—and Cedric, if she could wrangle him—one where we sailed the seas by day, with both of them acting as my mentors, and drank and laughed ourselves silly by night. We'd tell ghost stories and legends alike, and they could tell me about their previous daring ventures. We could solidify a proper bond and forge new memories to replace the old.

We could be… *happy.*

No sooner had I thought it than I began to rise. Heartpiercer nearly slipped from my grasp, but I hoisted it over my shoulder at the final second before shooting forward.

The flight was beyond uncomfortable, and not solely because my broken leg dangled uselessly beneath me. Rain pelted me harder the higher I ascended, with each icy drop feeling more like the stab of a blade, and my teeth began chattering so violently I feared I might bite off my tongue. But through the lightning and the storm, I pressed on, even when I had risen so high I could no longer make out the waves or flames below. I was close, and Heartpiercer knew it too.

I had expected the trident to grow heavier in my hands, but if anything, it felt as light as the air caressing me. It began vibrating, humming softly at first, but its song soon expanded into a triumphant symphony. Its master was close, it needed him, and after centuries, they would be reunited at last.

But I still couldn't make out either of the gods, and this concerned me most of all. Judging from the sheer mass of their silhouettes, they should be gigantic, and I assumed I would have spotted at least one of them by now. Nothing but an expanse of storm clouds and lightning lay ahead of me, and I could see no visible end.

Was this how I would meet mine?

Out of options, I did the only remaining thing I could think of and whispered into the blackness. "Adais? What do I do now?"

Heartpiercer pulsed in my hands, but nothing else happened.

"Please," I pleaded. "Show me the way."

Another pulse, stronger this time, and the trident tugging itself against my grasp. Surprised, I loosened my grip, but not enough to drop the weapon. Thunder boomed to my left, though it could have just as easily been a deep chuckle, followed by a flash of lightning so close it had every hair on my arms standing at attention from the static.

"*What 'way'? Wendy, all you have to do is* let go."

Let… go? Was it really that simple? Could I unclench my hands and let Heartpiercer find its way, trust that it knew its true master? Could this all be over, finished at last, and could the happy thoughts which had ascended me into the sky become my reality at last?

No. Nothing is ever that easy. Doubt shadowed me then, twisting my gut into knots. What if this was just another trick orchestrated by Kaara, another of her ruses? Or what if, when I released the trident, it tumbled into the waters below, never to be seen again? What if it sank even deeper, worming its way back into the Sea of Eternal Woe, and our efforts to retrieve it had been for nothing? Cedric's sacrifice, my broken leg, Scarlett's curse, Elvira's near-death experience, and Peter's burned hands… for *nothing*.

My palms quivered, and Heartpiercer nearly slipped from my hands due to that alone. I was being torn in two, and every time my mind began leaning one way or another, an argument cropped up for the opposite. How could such a decision have been placed on my young shoulders? How was this in any way fair? How could I be expected to survive this without the weight of that decision crushing me, or at the very least leaving me scarred?

Then a scarred face popped into my mind's eye, and the four words he uttered were more than enough to solidify my choice.

I know you can.

I let go.

The action was both effortless yet monumental, terrifying yet exhilarating. I watched as Heartpiercer plummeted, at first at the mercy of gravity, but just as Tink had spread her wings, so did the trident. It shot forward, piercing the clouds in a deafening crack of thunder, and when I threw my hands over my ears, the vibrations rattled me to my core.

Then, silence.

The storm ceased, the rain slowed to a halt, and sensing that Tink's dust was beginning to wear off, I began my descent. As I floated back to Earth, trembling and breathless, three words cut through the harrowing stillness, as final as they were clear.

"*It is done.*"

An hour later, a small crowd had gathered on the beach. The remaining ships had anchored in the cove, and the only ones who had come ashore were those who wished to be present for Kaara's humiliation. Two distinct groups had formed: one made up of Prince Herbert and a handful of his subjects, and the other made up of me, Tink, Arktos, Elvira, Cedric, and Mr. Smee. Given that the dust had worn off, I sat leaning against Arktos while an unconscious Tink had been tucked into the front of my shirt. Despite both of us asking anyone who would listen, there was still no sign of Peter, but he wasn't the only one missing. Scarlett hadn't been seen since her mysterious disappearance, a fact which Cedric had let none of us forget, but he'd silenced when Elvira reminded him that he was likely to see her soon if only he kept his mouth shut.

In front of us, a human-sized Adais held Heartpiercer to Kaara's pale throat. She alternated between looking mortified and murderous, but any time the goddess so much as flinched, Adais anticipated it, shoving the trident into her neck hard enough to draw beads of blackened blood from the superficial wounds. Though they healed almost instantly, streaks of charcoal marking where the blood trailed down her flesh remained, elevating her already terrifying appearance to an entirely new level. Just as they had while underwater, Kaara's hair and dress moved of their own accord, but unlike before, they kept their metaphorical hands to themselves.

It had been silent for so long that it startled me when Adais finally spoke. "Kaara of the Moon, you stand accused of conspiring to murder a god."

"I wasn't the only one," she spat, but hissed when Heartpiercer illuminated, its glow a warning.

"Don't be dramatic. My actions were never motivated by anything other than self-preservation, a fact to which Scarlett Maynard can attest."

"She's not here." Cedric stepped forward then, addressing the Sea God. "She hasn't been seen for over an hour."

"She's not the only one," I added. "Peter Pan is still missing as well."

Kaara took one look at me, threw back her head, and laughed. "Missing? You can't be serious."

Unease prickled down my spine at her tone. "I'm dead serious."

"You're not the only one, because Peter Pan may as well be. Just ask your father. He's the one who left him behind."

I suddenly couldn't breathe, both because of Kaara's declaration and because my body was recalling our journey from the Sea of Eternal Woe. But prior to that, prior to our departure, Peter had tried to grip Heartpiercer's shaft, and it had burned him. Cedric had forced him to take it, I assumed, but what if he hadn't? What if he whispered those words knowing full well that Peter wouldn't be coming with us?

What if he left one of my only friends to *die*?

Kaara said something else, but I didn't hear it over the blood roaring in my ears. My broken leg momentarily forgotten, I threw myself forward in an attempt to crawl across the sand toward Captain Hook. I had no idea what obscenities were pouring from my lips, but hoped that somewhere among them, I was taking back every kind and loving word I'd ever said to him. *He* was the one who deserved to have his hands burned, *he* was the one who should have been left behind, *he* was the one who should have died.

I barely dragged myself half a foot before Elvira's arms encircled me, rendering me immobile as I screamed and cried. Hook's face was as pale as a ghost, but he held my gaze as I forced him to look at what he'd done, at what he'd made me.

"I was right," I seethed. "You get to have your Scarlett, while I get fucking nothing."

Adais sighed. "None of this is helping anyone, Wendy. Peter Pan is lost. He's as good as dead."

"He wouldn't be if your trident hadn't burned him!"

"That's enough," he snapped in a tone that made me flinch. "Though I may be unable to help the dead, I *can* help the living, which includes Scarlett Maynard."

"No one's seen her," Hook repeated, turning away from me in an instant. "She just… vanished."

Kaara scoffed. "And that worries you, Cedric Teach? It's not as if your pirate queen can't take care of herself. I'm told this is all her doing, after all." She pursed her lips into a thin line. "It's quite impressive, really, and I'm not sure if I ought to be thanking or punishing her."

"You'll do nothing but *release her*—" Hook started but silenced when Adais held up a hand.

"The Crow is right. I seem to remember a bargain was struck, and a goddess must never break her word. Right, Kaara?"

"Our bargain was off the moment I was betrayed," the goddess snarled. "My price for releasing Scarlett was Heartpiercer, which I don't have, and now will never get, so she remains *mine*. She already has her voice thanks to him smashing my locket." Kaara nodded toward Adais. "Is that not enough?"

Hook roared something along the lines of 'no the fuck it isn't,' but wanting an excuse not to dwell on Peter's fate, I stopped listening. A memory surfaced, recent and clear, of the moment Kaara had first mentioned the locket. I paid incredibly close attention, especially after the goddess revealed she was the one who had been speaking to me in Scarlett's voice my entire life. Word for word, Kaara had said, *In addition to serving me 'as long as her daughter should live,' her voice it was.*

Except I *hadn't* lived. In Neverland, I had died, which meant...

"The deal is off."

Everyone fell silent and all heads swiveled in my direction. Though they had stared when I yelled at Hook, this felt like a different kind of attention entirely, more intimate and vulnerable. Still, I gathered my courage, cleared my throat, and repeated, "Your deal with my mother. It's off and has been for quite some time."

Kaara opened her mouth but shut it when Adais jabbed the trident at her neck. "Explain yourself, Wendy Maynard."

"I may be living and breathing at this very moment, but several months ago, back in Neverland, I died. Delivered the blow myself, actually." Lifting my shirt from my abdomen, I revealed my scar for all to see. "I'm only alive thanks to a Nightstalker giving its life in exchange for mine, and if it hadn't, I would have remained dead."

For a while, there was silence. I held Kaara's intense glare, swallowing as her pupils darkened and energy swirled in her palms, but just when I thought she was going to smite me, a disturbance in the tide behind us had me turning around.

"Cedric?"

Clad in nothing but a white, almost see-through gown, a woman had appeared on the beach. Between the sputtering coughs that wracked her quivering form, she barely had time to lift her head before Hook rushed to her side, raising her chin as he checked her frantically for any sign of injury.

"Scarlett," he whispered again and again in a tone that made me want to gag. "Are you all right?"

She nodded, pressing her forehead to his. "I'm here. I'm here."

Was she? I couldn't explain it, but something didn't feel right. Kaara gave in much too easily. Without any proof, though, I could do nothing but sit and watch as Hook leaned in for what was presumably a kiss... and then it struck me like a bolt of lightning.

Not only was Scarlett human—which didn't make any sense given that her curse dictated that she transform into a mermaid upon touching the water—she hadn't acknowledged me.

The latter was a tiny, almost insignificant, detail, but every single time she'd been present in the same space as me, my mother had always thrown at least one longing glance in my direction, and that was before she'd been able to speak. Now that she could, for her not to greet me in her own voice wasn't simply unusual, it only had one logical conclusion. It *wasn't* her, a fact solidified by her lack of a mermaid tail.

I reacted out of pure, adrenaline-fueled instinct. The moment before Hook touched his lips to what he thought were Scarlett's, I yanked a knife from Elvira's thigh, hurtling the blade straight for the impostor's back. It found its mark, burying itself firmly near her left shoulder blade.

Two screams erupted at the same time: one from the imposter, and one from Kaara. As the woman in his arms began to morph and change, Hook shoved her away, horrified, and I only caught a fleeting glimpse of Calypso's distinctive curls before blinding pain erupted in my broken leg. An involuntary cry tore from my throat, followed by another as the pain grew to agony, and when darkness clouded my vision, I didn't bother to fight it.

So long as the blackness came with numbness, I'd choose it every time.

XXIII. THE AFTERMATH

Cedric

It didn't matter how many times I pricked myself with my hook or gnawed at the inside of my lip. It didn't matter how many times I rubbed my eyes or blinked profusely, nor how many times I ducked from the room for a quick word with Elvira. The scene I returned to remained unchanged, meaning I wasn't hallucinating, dreaming, or otherwise allowing my addled mind to let its fantasies run wild, and that everything in front of me was the reality I'd dreamt of for so long.

Scarlett—the *real* one, not that bitch Calypso—sat perched on a stool, hovering over Wendy's unconscious form. She had reappeared from the forest shortly after Kaara fled with an injured Calypso cradled in her arms and revealed that the goddess had indeed whisked her away from the battle. The intention had been for me to let my guard down long enough for Calypso to stab me, which I was still kicking myself for not anticipating, but at least Wendy had been paying attention. Yet again, I owed her my life. I liked to think I'd repaid the favor after preventing Kaara from ripping Wendy's broken leg clean off her body, but I'd just as happily keep repaying it time and time again.

Though there would have been more space in the bed in my quarters, Scarlett and I decided to place our daughter in Peter's hammock, where she was accustomed to sleeping. A slumbering Tink lay curled against her chest, and Arktos had insisted upon remaining by Wendy's side. He seemed less-than-thrilled about all the poking and prodding that had been necessary to get her healed and arranged, but other than a few half-hearted growls, the dog hadn't given us any trouble and now lay quietly at Scarlett's feet.

Both Scarlett and Wendy were battered and undoubtedly shaken. Scarlett sported various scrapes and bruises, and Wendy hadn't woken since Adais had mended her broken leg, but given they would both no doubt recover, it was a price I'd happily pay a thousand times over. Sharing a space with them was such a simple thing, and though I was more than aware I didn't deserve it, I was grateful for every damn second. The two people I loved most in this world were not only sitting in the same room with me, they were so close I could reach out and touch them. Prompted by the thought, I leaned forward to rest my hand on Scarlett's shoulder, offering a gentle squeeze. "She's not going anywhere, you know."

Scarlett entwined her fingers with mine but didn't otherwise respond or take her eyes off our daughter. It came as no surprise. Eighteen hours had passed since Kaara's defeat, and ever since she'd been formally released from the goddess's service, Scarlett hadn't left Wendy's side to so much as piss. Barely having a voice, given her long-neglected vocal cords, hadn't stopped Scarlett from reading, whispering, and even singing to Wendy, both with and without the help of the enchanted music box, but most of the time, she simply stared. There was no way Scarlett hadn't memorized Wendy's features several times over by now, but as I watched, her free hand traced the freckles dotting Wendy's cheeks for what had to be the tenth time.

If it were up to me, I would have let Scarlett sit there for as long as she wanted, but her body had other ideas. I didn't miss the tremors she attempted to conceal, nor the way she had to fight to keep her eyes open. Squeezing slightly harder, I asked, "When was the last time you ate?" Only silence answered me, and I sighed. "When was the last time you slept?"

"I'm not sleeping until she wakes." Scarlett's damaged voice cracked as she spoke. "I want to be here when she does."

"You would probably also prefer to speak in coherent sentences for the first real conversation you have with your daughter, and that's if you can speak at all. Stay awake for much longer and you won't be able to do either." Though I chose my words carefully, my tone didn't leave room for argument. "I'll have Elvira watch over her while you're gone and, of course, Wendy has Arktos. We'll be right down the hall. We aren't going anywhere, and neither is she."

Scarlett didn't respond right away, and when she did, it wasn't any of the ones I had anticipated. "I thought the fairies were dead."

My gaze flicked to Tink's corpse-like form. Her light had gone out, her wings were still, and the faintest rise and fall of her chest was all that told me she was still alive. "I did, too, until Pan brought this one out of hiding. He kept her well-concealed while Jamie hunted her kind."

"Smart boy, and he seemed capable too. He and Wendy are friends?"

"Were," I corrected, dropping my voice to a whisper as a sudden wave of guilt threatened to drown me. "Who knows if she'll ever see him again." *All thanks to me.*

"Don't," Scarlett said, threading her fingers tighter within mine. "You had no choice."

"I did, but according to Wendy, I made the wrong one." I'd told Scarlett the full story regarding what happened in the Sea, and while it felt good to get it off my chest, reliving the memory was doing nothing for my frazzled nerves.

As if sensing my discomfort, Scarlett changed the subject. "This fairy isn't likely to last the night."

My chest tightened yet again at the thought of what Tink's loss might do to Wendy, especially so soon after losing Pan, but there was nothing that could be done for either of them now, so I simply nodded my agreement.

"And if Wendy wakes to a dead fairy on her chest, I doubt it's the mother who abandoned her she will turn to for comfort."

Another true statement, but this time, I didn't have the heart to say so aloud. Scarlett's love for Wendy may be obvious and palpable, but they were strangers given how little they knew about one another. Establishing any semblance of a relationship was going to take time and effort on both their parts, and it certainly wasn't going to happen in the exhausting aftermath of us battling gods and monsters alike. "Come," I urged softly, pulling at Scarlett's hand. "Both of you need to sleep. You have the rest of your lives to forge a bond."

"But I missed her first *sixteen years*." Her voice was faraway and haunted, and she didn't move. "We both did. That's time not even Adais himself could give us back."

"I'll never get back the sixteen years you spent here."

Scarlett visibly tensed. "That's—"

"Living in the past will do nothing but detract from your future." I had so far avoided touching her with my hook but, not wanting to release her hand, I brushed the prosthetic lightly against her cheek to turn her face toward mine. Only then did I notice that her eyes were red and swollen, indicating that Scarlett had been silently crying for some time. Resisting the urge to take her in my arms was difficult, but I swallowed the lump in my throat and continued. "I'm living proof of that, and trust me, dwelling on previous mistakes and 'what-ifs' isn't going to change a damn thing about your current reality. And why would you want to? Look at her. She's beautiful."

That summoned a tearful laugh. "She is, isn't she?"

"And alive, warm, and safe, all thanks to you."

"I had a little help." Scarlett brushed her lips against the back of my hand, sending my knees damn near buckling. "But all right. You win, given that I'm out of arguments. Since when are you the rational one?"

"He's not." We both turned toward Elvira's voice, who leaned against the doorframe with her arms crossed. "If Ced is making any sense at all, I'd question whether he hit his head. Wouldn't be the first time. He's as dramatic and irrational as ever, I'm afraid, so truly not much has changed."

The corner of Scarlett's mouth twisted into a half smirk. "Hello, Elvira. I've missed you." Though they had interacted briefly during the battle and its aftermath, this was the first one-on-one conversation the two had a chance to share, and certainly the first formal greeting, especially now that Scarlett had her voice back.

Elvira merely shrugged. Her body language was nonchalant enough, but the way her tone wavered told me she wasn't nearly as unaffected as her façade suggested. "Me, or the knives I used to throw at you?"

"The whole package." Scarlett laughed before pushing herself off the stool, approaching Elvira with her arms spread wide. "Come here, you psychotic bitch."

Old habits had me holding my breath as Scarlett pulled my sister into a tight embrace. Bewildered and unsure what to do with her hands at first, Elvira simply stood there, but around the same time I exhaled, she snaked her arms around Scarlett's shoulders. They held each other for far longer than I expected, their bodies gently swaying even though we had run the ship aground. Elvira even closed her eyes after a while, especially once Scarlett tightened her grip.

"How are you feeling, by the way?" Scarlett asked once she pulled away, though she kept a hand on Elvira's shoulder. "Your mark—"

"I'm fine, as far as I can tell. Haven't turned into a mermaid or even had the urge." Elvira glanced at the black lingering on her palm and shrugged. "Perhaps I got lucky."

Scarlett narrowed her gaze and very much looked like she wanted to argue, but she dropped it to change the subject. "Can we leave Wendy in your charge? Cedric keeps insisting that I go rest."

"I can't imagine why. I've seen you look far worse."

Old habits died hard with Elvira, too, it seemed, but that didn't mean I had to tolerate her love for insulting Scarlett at every opportunity. "Will you keep an eye on her or not?"

"Fuck's sake, Ced, of course I will." Elvira rolled her eyes. "Unlike Fish Princess over here, *I've* gotten plenty of beauty sleep."

Not even a coma would grant you enough beauty to rival Scarlett, I almost fired back, but swallowed the retort when she gave me a pointed look.

Turning back to Elvira, Scarlett said, "Thank you. But work on some cleverer nicknames, will you? While Fish Princess has a nice ring to it, surely you can do better."

Elvira cackled. "Challenge accepted, *princess*." She was still laughing when Scarlett and I exited the room and could be heard chuckling to herself even when we reached the end of the hall.

"Did you have to encourage her?" I muttered, keeping close to Scarlett as she led the way. "You know that's only going to make it worse."

"I think it's rather endearing. Don't you?"

449

"No, because she doesn't mean it to be anything other than irritating, just like he—"

Scarlett moved so fast I was taken off guard. Spinning on her heel, she threw out an arm on either side of me before leaning forward, pinning me against the wall with her body. Though her tone was serious, I knew her well enough to recognize a twinkle of amusement in her mismatched eyes. "More often than not, *you're* nothing but irritating, yet I tolerate you just fine."

I may have laughed if my heart wasn't beating out of my chest at our sudden intimate proximity. Since the moment she had emerged from that forest, human, unscathed, and whole, I wanted nothing more than to kiss her. To place my hand on her cheek, tangle my fingers in her hair, and pull her body flush against mine, precisely the way we stood right now. *Surely Scarlett needs time to recover*, I'd told myself. We had all the time in the world to ease back into things, to ease back into being partners. Yet she had initiated the closeness, not me. Was she as ready as I was? Did she want this, want me, as badly as I wanted her? All I had to do was reach, and—

"Let me enjoy this, Cedric. I missed it. All of it, even the shitty and irritating parts. Your sister included."

Scarlett was gone as quickly as she'd pinned me, leaving me damn near panting as she continued down the hall. The distance at least gave me a chance to catch my breath, though by the time I slipped into my quarters and closed the door behind us, my heartbeat hadn't slowed. If anything, it only quickened when I lifted my gaze and took in the sight before me.

It was difficult to say whether Scarlett walked around my cabin as though she was seeing it for the first time, or if she knew precisely where everything belonged and was simply reminding herself of its place. She trailed her fingers over every surface, from my desk to my chests, and finally the bed, lingering there the longest. When she noticed what sat in the far corner, her mouth dropped open in a silent gasp. "Is that…?"

"It's nothing," I said without thinking as heat crept to my cheeks. "Well, it's *not* nothing, but it's certainly nothing I need anymore."

Scarlett was silent as she strode toward her shrine and tilted her head as she took it all in. It was all there, from her portrait, to her old chemise that had stopped smelling like her at least a decade ago, to her old hand mirror, and even one of her daggers. The handful of candles surrounding the assortment of items had been illuminated, though by whom, I didn't know.

"You made this for me?" Scarlett's whispers were growing faint and ragged as she continued to abuse her damaged vocal cords. "How long has it been up?"

"Since about a week after you disappeared. Prior to that I was, ah, inconsolable." That was putting it lightly, but she didn't need to know that.

Scarlett didn't take her gaze from the shrine. "You waited for me."

"Yes," I answered, though she hadn't phrased it as a question.

"I waited for you too. All that shit with Herbert, the entire engagement, it was a sham—"

"I know. I think you kneeing him in the balls was a pretty good indication of that." As reckless as it had been for Scarlett to physically assault a prince, it certainly got the rejection across, because he and his remaining fleet had already begun their voyage back to wherever it was they'd come from. "But even if you hadn't, I couldn't have blamed you. Sixteen years is a long time."

"For you, as well. You're telling me you were never tempted?"

Heat flamed my cheeks as I recalled all my interactions with Calypso, but thankfully, Scarlett wasn't looking. "Temptation is another thing entirely, but I never acted on it, not truly. Any time I got close, all I could see was your face, and all I could hear was your voice. Your laugh. I've already told you that my mind never forgot you, Scarlett, but my body didn't, either. How could I expect to be kissed the way you kiss me, touched the way you touch me? How could anyone else ever compare?"

She looked up then, and the candlelight revealed more wetness glistening at the corners of her eyes. Wrapping her arms around herself, Scarlett looked smaller and more vulnerable than I'd ever seen her, and the sight nearly brought tears to my own eyes. "Easily. There are countless other women able to offer you far more than I can. I abandoned our daughter to fend for herself, abandoned and lied to you, and I can't even set foot in the goddamn sea without cursing myself to live as a mermaid for the rest of my days, and we're pirates, for fuck's sake. You really came all this way just for me? For *that*?"

While she spoke, I closed the distance between us, speaking only when her erratic breathing had slowed slightly. "Scarlett," I whispered again and again, her name both a prayer and a plea on my lips. "'Just' for you? You say that as if you're nothing. How can you be nothing when you're my everything?"

We stood chest to chest. Her fingers played with the edges of my jacket and our lips hovered dangerously close, but I refused to kiss her until she not only heard but believed me. "I don't want another woman. I want any version of you I could possibly be worthy of. The clever stowaway, my vengeful enemy, my pirate queen, even a mermaid. Be all of them or just one, I don't care, because I love you as you are, as you were, and as you've always been. I want nothing more than…"

My voice trailed off as Scarlett knelt before me. Heart hammering, I found myself unable to do anything but watch as her deft fingers worked to undo my belt and unfasten my breeches. She worked slowly, giving me ample opportunities to protest or stop her, but transfixed, I did neither. *Fuck.* She was beyond beautiful on her knees, a position she'd reminded me time and time again was reserved solely for me, and the sight of it alone made it difficult for me to keep still as she worked. Only once she'd freed my hardening cock did it occur to me to speak, though forming a coherent sentence was a battle all its own. "Are you su—*ohhh.*"

She took me in her mouth before I could finish, her lips and tongue already working in tandem to create enough friction to drive me wild. My hips bucked before I could stop them, thrusting my length to the back of her throat, but Scarlett seemed to have been hoping for it judging from the shuddering moan the movement elicited.

After bracing one of her hands on my thigh, she extracted herself before raising her gaze to mine. I still wasn't used to the way her one blue eye seemed to glow, but especially now, its eeriness only enhanced her beauty. "I'm listening. You want nothing more than what?"

I could barely remember my own damn name, but one thought at least rang clear. "Your voice—"

Scarlett shook her head, cutting me off. "For sixteen years, my voice, mouth, and even throat," she whispered, touching her fingers to each in turn, "haven't been mine. But today, I reclaimed them, and tonight, they belong to you." Still holding my gaze, she gripped the base of my shaft, and it was a struggle to stifle the moan I wanted badly to utter. "You may not know what you want, but I do. I want you to keep saying those lovely things while you fuck my mouth, and yes, I can take it. Don't be gentle, and don't hold back."

I swallowed, but not out of apprehension or fear. Of course I wanted this, but I didn't want to hurt her, physically or otherwise, and we were meant to be resting, for fuck's sake, so I asked again. "Are you sure?"

"Sure of what?" She gave me a quick stroke, smiling when it elicited a shudder. "That I love you and have since you risked your own neck to keep me safe aboard *The Night Rose*?" Another stroke, rougher this time. "That I want it quick and hard? That I want you, want this?" Scarlett laughed, the sound clear and pure. "I didn't wait for you all these years to go *slow*, and I've wanted you since the moment I first held a knife to your throat. But aren't you supposed to be the one doing the talking?"

I groaned as my cock twitched in response to both her words and her touch. Tugging sharply on her hair, I brought her lips to my groin, but the encouragement was hardly necessary. Scarlett swallowed me down more than gladly, taking me nearly all the way to the back of her throat in her first go. I cursed as more shudders rippled down my spine and forced myself to break eye contact if only not to come on the spot. "Tap my thigh three times if you need me to stop," I managed through haggard breaths, and remained completely still until she gave a slight nod.

Only then did I begin fucking her exactly as she'd requested—fast, rough, and hard—but it was damn near impossible to speak, let alone intelligibly. She felt far too good, looked too damn beautiful on her knees for me to concentrate on whatever curses came spilling from my lips. I was, however, hyper aware of her hand resting on my thigh. Scarlett squeezed and even dug her nails into my sensitive flesh on more than one occasion, but she never tapped, not once. Her endurance only fueled my own.

In a rare moment of clarity, I spoke between frantic thrusts, simultaneously chasing and denying my own orgasm. "You take me so well. *Gods*, you're gorgeous, you know that?"

Scarlett raised her gaze then, locking her eyes with mine as I fucked her throat for the last handful of times. The tears streaming down her cheeks marked both victory and a ceasefire and had my heart fluttering all over again. Loosening my hold on her hair, I allowed her a chance to catch her breath, but she didn't remain on the floor for long. She rose to claim me in a kiss, her hands roaming everywhere as she began stripping off any piece of my clothing she could reach.

"I want you inside me," she breathed against my cheek, and had I not been reeling over tasting myself on her lips and tongue, I may have obliged her right then and there. But a stronger urge rose within me, one I refused to ignore no matter how much Scarlett begged, though begging might certainly enhance things.

"Soon," was all I said before leaning down and scooping her in my arms. Ignoring her squeal of surprise, I laid her on the bed, wasting no time tugging off her breeches and undergarments first, then pulling my shirt over my head and tossing it aside. The hook slightly complicated things. I somehow made it work without ripping or damaging anything, not that either of us would have cared if I did.

Scarlett lifted her head, propping herself up on her elbows as I knelt at the edge of the bed and got into position between her legs. Bracing my good hand on her inner thigh to spread her open, I used my free arm to pull the other toward me, trailing gentle kisses from her knee to her groin. She was visibly wet, and likely already ready to take me; that didn't mean I wasn't going to return the favor she had so graciously shown me regardless. But when I glanced up to tell her as much, her gaze wasn't where I thought it would be.

It was on my hook.

A nauseating mixture of bile and something else rose in my throat, and I became unable to swallow it down. The hook and my missing hand were both things we hadn't yet discussed and things I had actively worked to conceal, but in these moments of passion, I'd forgotten to hide them from her view. It didn't matter that Scarlett had already seen me without the prosthetic. Removing it during a moment as intimate as this and revealing my amputated limb to the woman who had only known me with two functioning hands seemed unfathomable. Lowering it, I tried to pull away, but Scarlett's fingers ensnared me at the wrist, gripping the iron sleeve that held the hook in place.

"What's wrong?" The concern in her eyes made this no easier. "Cedric, talk to me."

Unable to string together my thoughts in a coherent fashion, words came out in fragments. "The hook, I can cover, you don't need—"

Scarlett said my name again but didn't loosen her hold on my arm. "Are you ashamed of this? Did you think I was staring at it because it disgusts me?" She scoffed. Lowering her whisper even further, she spoke so softly I almost didn't hear her. "I was staring because I was envisioning all the ways that hook might *enhance* things for us."

Heat flamed her cheeks, and realizing I wasn't alone caused all my shame to vanish in an instant. "Really?"

"Yes." She unraveled my arm from her thigh and guided the hook between her legs. "Tease me with it."

Unsure if I was more impressed or aroused, my lips parted in wonder. "It will be cold."

"I know." She shuddered. "I'm ready."

She sat back, surrendering completely as I spread her legs as wide as they would go. As gently as I could muster, I brought the hook's tip to her sensitive, glistening flesh, marveling at the way it met no resistance as it glided through her folds.

Scarlett's reaction was immediate. She arched her back, took the sheets in her fists, and moaned my name, summoning yet another wave of arousal straight to my cock. It took effort to keep doing what I was doing, but I was determined not to fuck her until neither of us could stand to be apart a moment longer. I tormented her mercilessly, alternating between nudging at her entrance and circling her sensitive bud, working her into a frenzy, but never over the edge.

"Please," she half-whispered, half-sobbed. "I need…"

Her plea became a moan as I replaced the hook with my tongue. I went slow, both relishing the taste of her and refusing to speed up, even when Scarlett tangled her fingers in my hair and attempted to steer me where she wanted. Her thighs quivered on either side of my skull, proving just how close she really was.

She cursed my name then, and I laughed against her warmth. Pulling away, I frowned. "That wasn't very nice."

"Neither is whatever the fuck you're doing, you ass." Her cheeks were flushed and her hair a tangled mess. "If you don't finish me off right this second, I'll do it myself."

"There's no need for that." I slipped a pair of fingers inside her as I spoke, slowly moving them in and out while my thumb circled her bud. "But I do have one condition."

Scarlett whimpered, bucking her hips in an attempt to get more friction. "Anything."

"I know your voice is shot, my pirate queen, but just once,

will you scream my name?"

"The gods themselves will hear us—*fuck!*"

I'd kept her so close to the edge that she came apart almost the moment I began touching her the way she liked. True to her word, Scarlett shrieked my name so loudly that I almost needed to cover my ears. Limp and quivering, she collapsed back onto the sheets when the orgasm eventually released her, though that wicked look in her eyes told me she was far from finished.

"Your turn, Captain Hook."

My villainous persona had no business sounding as good as it did on her lips. Leaning forward, I climbed onto the bed, covering her body with mine before capturing her mouth in another kiss. Scarlett responded with passionate enthusiasm, placing her hands on either side of my face as she wrapped her legs around my hips, pressing my erection to her entrance. The combination of that, her breasts against my bare chest, and her tongue entangling with mine was more than enough to keep me distracted until the moment she made her move. Pushing against my chest, she forced me upright before straddling me, making her intentions clear.

I was more than happy to let her ride me, but a sensible thought broke through the haze of lust. "Wait," I said when she reached between our legs. "Are you protected?" We very much didn't need another child until we at least sorted out our first.

Scarlett nodded before I finished speaking. "I took a preventative while at Kaara's court, and it's still effective. I wasn't going to let her take any more children from me."

I tried to nod my approval, but all that came out was a groan when fingers wrapped around the base of my shaft. Scarlett held my gaze as she guided me into her, taking me to the hilt far quicker than I expected and leaving me the one breathless. I bit out a curse when she began grinding her hips against me, not fast, but not slow, either. "Keep doing that and I'm not going to last."

She raised an eyebrow. "You'd better, because I plan on at least one more."

The next time I moaned, it was against Scarlett's lips. She rode me with every ounce of ardor I'd waited sixteen years for, wrapping her arms around my neck and clinging to me as though she was fire, and I was her oxygen. We kissed, fondled, and worshiped various parts of one another's bodies, though I focused mainly on the area I'd so cruelly neglected earlier, tucking my hand between her legs and manipulating her with my thumb. It wasn't long before she began approaching her second climax, and unable to restrain myself when she tightened around me, I shifted my weight and began pumping into her.

The feel of her was far too much. Her heat, her breasts bouncing against my chest, her lips sucking on my neck as I drove into her again and again. "I'm close," I warned through gritted teeth, and Scarlett came undone a moment later. Throwing her head back, she released another shuddering cry, raking her nails across my chest as I continued bucking my hips. I followed her over the edge soon after, slumping forward to take her in my arms as my orgasm rippled through me.

It was difficult to say how long we remained a sweaty and trembling entanglement of limbs, but some hours later, we were cleaned up and settled beneath the sheets, at last prepared to rest as we had originally intended. Scarlett lay draped across my bare chest, her fingers lazily tracing my various scars. Though her body was relaxed, she had been silent for a long while, which told me her mind was anything but. "We have a long road ahead of us," she finally murmured, saving me from asking her what was wrong.

"Aye. But it doesn't seem half as long now that you're here." I pressed a kiss to her forehead.

"I wasn't lying when I said it wasn't your fault," Scarlett said slowly, clearly choosing her words carefully. "But do you think Wendy will ever forgive you for leaving her friend behind?"

I opened my mouth to respond just as the door barged open. Scarlett reacted fastest, yanking at the sheets in a hurried attempt to cover her naked form, but it took me a few seconds longer to recognize Smee's cowering silhouette.

"Fuck's sake," I snapped, bolting upright. "Someone had better be fucking dead."

"N-not that we know of, C-Cap'n," he stammered. "B-But—"

"Is it Wendy?" Scarlett used what little of her voice she had left to ask a question I hadn't immediately considered, and it turned my blood to ice.

Smee wrung his hands and nodded. "She's…"

"She's *what*, Smee?" I leaped out of bed and was already throwing on my clothes. "And where is Elvira?"

"That's just it, C-Cap'n. Wendy, the fairy, the dog, and Elvira. They're gone. All gone."

XXIV. THE RETURN

Wendy

Waking to an empty room and what I'd assumed to be a dead fairy on my chest certainly counted as one of my gloomier mornings, if it even *was* morning. After calming my erratic heart and allowing the last of my nightmares to abandon my racing thoughts, I took a closer look at Tink's condition. I wasn't at all used to the fairy lacking her glow, and her breathing had become so shallow it was nearly imperceptible. Her wings were frayed and shriveling, and her body limp and cold when I took it in my hands.

Tink was going to die. I'd known it since she'd given me the last of her dust, since she'd lost Peter and, seemingly, her will to live. Recalling what Peter had said all those weeks ago, returning to Neverland was her only hope, but even if I could get her there right this instant, I wasn't certain it would be enough. Tink was so far gone, so battered and broken that there may well be nothing that could save her now.

That didn't mean I wasn't going to try.

After bundling her small body tightly against my chest, I dressed in the darkest clothing I could find. I wasn't certain of the time but planned on keeping to the shadows regardless, and I needed to be inconspicuous. Well, as inconspicuous as someone with a huge fluffy dog could be, because I'd discovered Arktos under the bed, and knew better than to try and order him to stay behind.

It only took a few short minutes to gather my belongings. With a dagger in one hand and the satchel containing my music box in the other, I left the room Peter and I had shared for a final time, unwilling to spare it a final parting glance. If I did, I might break down, and that was the last thing any of us needed right now.

"Come," I whispered to Arktos, but I needn't have bothered. The dog was at my heels the moment I crossed the threshold, and though I didn't have the slightest idea where I might be leading him, I was grateful I wasn't alone.

The oddest thing about traversing the hall wasn't that my leg didn't hurt, but the lack of movement beneath me. I vaguely recalled Adais healing my break, as well as the ship being run aground rather than remaining anchored in the cove. Just how long did they plan on staying here? Then again, no one else had any reason to hurry, and there was reasonable justification for the opposite. *The Jolly Serpent* and its crew had been through much in the past few weeks, and had Peter and Tink been safe and whole, I would have been all too happy to join in their well-deserved rest before they began the long and complicated task of resupplying.

But Peter was as good as dead, Tink was set to follow, and no one gave a shit except for me, evidenced by the fact that the noise drifting from the crew's quarters was a celebration. Smee and his band played a lively tune, a drunken chorus accompanied it, and it was likely to go on for days.

An overwhelming sense of grief and dread gnawed at my chest. I couldn't stay here. I didn't belong and never had. Hook and Scarlett and perhaps even Elvira would be upset, but they would find a way to go on just as they always had—without me. I didn't yet know where I'd go, but anywhere was better than here, and the beach was as good a place as any to begin plotting my next move.

Other than a pair of tipsy cabin boys who didn't bat an eye in our direction, Arktos and I didn't meet an ounce of resistance until we crept onto the main deck, and even then our escape remained far simpler than it should have been. It was nighttime, and the darkness aided our efforts to remain unseen. I gripped my dagger tightly as I rounded each corner, on the lookout for Elvira in particular, but the most difficult task proved evading the trio of men keeping watch. I had to command Arktos to stay behind me and remain hyper aware of our surroundings, but other than a close call in which I almost knocked over an empty rum barrel, at last, we reached the rail.

I stole a glance over the side. It was about a ten-foot drop onto a soft bed of sand. Too high for me to risk jumping, especially so soon after breaking my leg, but Arktos had no other choice. "You first, boy."

He cocked his head and whined softly but didn't need telling twice. The briefest of hesitations, and then he leaped, rolling once before coming to a skidding halt. Not bad for a giant fluffy dog.

He waited while I maneuvered myself and the satchel over the side of the ship. After sheathing the dagger, I carefully shimmied myself and Tink down the ropes and onto the beach.

I exhaled deeply before whispering, "We made it," both to Arktos and to Tink's unconscious body, trying my hardest not to dwell on the fact that though the fairy was still breathing, she remained stiff and cold.

Or that Peter was dead.

Or that I'd failed both of them.

No. Shaking my head, I snatched my satchel from the sand and began marching up the shore, leaving *The Jolly Serpent* behind for what part of me hoped would be forever. Just three weeks ago I'd have given anything to have the ship back under my command, but now it was nothing more than a vessel containing memories I'd much rather forget.

I wanted to forget it all. Peter, Neverland, my father, and even my damned mother, though the fact that I'd brought my music box along suggested otherwise. *Shut up. It means nothing, and you despise her as much as you do the rest.* Gritting my teeth, I picked up my pace, my hurried stride now bordering on a run. I still had no idea where I was going, but literally anywhere was better than here.

Arktos trotted beside me, oblivious to my conflicting emotions. Every so often, he'd take a detour to sprint through the tide, and it helped to know that at least one of us was enjoying ourselves. It really was a beautiful night. A gentle breeze caressed my skin, the tide lapped rhythmically, and the briny scent was a comforting one. The moon glowed brightly, illuminating the beach and ocean alike, but upon remembering who conjured it, a stab of grief shattered my façade as Adais's voice echoed in my memory.

"Peter Pan is lost. He's as good as dead."

I don't remember whether I fell or collapsed intentionally, but somehow, I was on the ground on all fours. The dam holding back my carefully restrained emotions broke, releasing a flood of violent, ugly sobs, and I began hyperventilating as they poured from me in waves. I was barely aware of Arktos's tongue lapping at my cheeks, barely aware of the rocks that had sliced open my knees, barely aware of anything other than my failure. It was as if I'd traded one family member for another. And the worst part?

I didn't yet know if it was a fair one.

It was a long while before I caught my breath, but I eventually managed to pull myself into a sitting position. Wrapping my arms around my knees, I buried my face against them, silently willing the tears to cease falling, or at least for this to stop hurting so much.

It didn't.

"Why do you cry, Wendy Maynard?"

My breath caught in my throat, and having sensed a presence standing over me a moment before he spoke, I didn't dare glance up.

Arktos snarled fiercely, but knowing our visitor wasn't likely to leave even if I asked him to, I waved a hand to silence him. Clenching my palms into fists, I cleared my throat before responding. "Adais, our deepest apologies for disturbing you."

"There was no disturbance, therefore no apology is necessary. Look upon me, child."

I didn't dare disobey. The corner of the Sea God's mouth twitched as I scanned his hardened features—his beard, his loosely tied half-ponytail, his skin glowing faintly in the moonlight—but I didn't linger on his face for long. Adais was dressed precisely the same way he had been for battle. Four loaded pistols adorned his front, a sword was sheathed at each hip, and in his right hand he clutched Heartpiercer. The sight of so many weapons unnerved me enough that I couldn't keep my curiosity to myself. "Are you expecting another attack?"

"Always," he said without hesitation. "Kaara never sleeps, so neither can I."

I nodded toward the trident and smiled weakly. "Well, hopefully that helps."

"It will, Wendy Maynard, more than you know." Adais looked to Arktos, who whined and laid down. "Which is why I'd like you to answer my question, so I may know how to help you. It's the least I can do after what you did for me."

The better question would have been why *wasn't* I crying, but I didn't dare say that aloud. "We won a great victory yesterday," I began cautiously, "but it wasn't a victory for me. Not completely."

Adais's brow furrowed. "Are you referring to your friend, the Golden Child that Kaara mentioned? The one who remains trapped in the Sea of Eternal Woe?"

I nodded.

"Then you must also know there is nothing I can do for him. The Sea's power extends to me as well, and no god will be able to rescue your friend from its clutches."

"But Peter never stood a chance," I blurted out. "Heartpiercer burned him any time he tried to touch it. Why?"

Adais frowned. "Of course it did. He is a Golden Child."

"Other than the fact that his blood is gold, I don't know what that means. He never told me."

"Ah. That was either very smart or very foolish of him." He paused, tightening his grip on the trident before continuing. "Golden Children are so named both for their blood and the fact that they rarely live to see adulthood, though not for the same reason Peter wishes to freeze his aging. It's because while they are born mortal, Golden Children have the capacity to become gods should they fully mature into adults."

I still wasn't connecting the dots. "But why is it they so rarely live that long?"

"Because *actual* gods see them as competition and will do anything within our power to keep them from becoming one of us. But trust me, that power is severely limited, because we are unable to kill Golden Children by our own hand."

My blood turned to ice at the realization. "Which was why Kaara baited him into entering the Sea. She knew he'd be trapped there."

"It's also why Heartpiercer rejected him. It doesn't like competition."

"Peter isn't *competition*," I snarled before I could stop myself. "He's a human being."

Adais shrugged. "For now."

"And you still won't help him? Not even to reward the fact that he aided us?"

"Even if I wanted to—and I don't—as I already told you, Wendy, I can't. I cannot pluck him from the Sea and onto your doorstep any more than Kaara can, so my suggestion would be to grieve and move on."

Of course he couldn't do anything meaningful. Peter was gone forever. *Dead.* Tears blurred my vision, and it was a fight to keep them from spilling down my cheeks. Afraid my voice might crack if I spoke, I didn't for a long while, and Adais had to pose his question a second time.

"Is there anything else I may do for you? Think long and hard. Believe it or not, there are few instances in which my power is limited, and I am more than happy to utilize it for the one who returned my trident to me."

I idly thought about asking him how and why I could communicate with certain creatures, but just when I opened my mouth to do just that, Tink stirred against my chest for the first time since leaving the ship. I touched my fingers to where she rested, working hard to untangle my cluttered thoughts. "This fairy is dying. Can you heal her?"

"Show her to me."

I removed Tink from her wrappings and held her out for Adais to see. He knelt in the surf to examine her, his dark eyes darting back and forth as he drank in her decrepit appearance. It was a while before he spoke, and when he did, his tone was curt and detached.

"She is bonded to the Golden Child."

"Yes." My voice trembled, and I was crying again. "Is there no way to save her?"

"Her life force is equally tethered to both Neverland and that boy. Without at least one of them, and soon, you will lose her in a matter of days. Perhaps hours, by the looks of her."

And if Adais couldn't save Peter, that meant… "She must return to Neverland, then?"

"At once."

A chill that had nothing to do with the night air crept up my spine. *Neverland.* The forest I'd fought so hard to escape, the place where I'd died. For all I knew, those blackened trees were still crawling with Nightstalkers, the beasts who whispered in my mind, who had haunted my nightmares for weeks on end, who had chosen me for their own nefarious purposes. And they were far from the only monsters I'd be likely to face, because sirens, mermaids, nerisas, fairies, and gods knew what else were likely to still call Neverland home. But if I wanted Tink to live, returning there was our only chance.

The only way forward was to go back.

"All right." I forced the words before I could change my mind, working to tuck Tink back into her wrappings before placing a hand on Arktos's back. "Take us there. All three of us."

Adais raised an eyebrow. "You're certain?"

I wasn't, but affirmed it anyway. "Yes."

The Sea God rose to his full height. The water surrounding his feet began to ripple and swell, and when he spoke again, his already low-pitched voice was so much deeper that it had the hairs at the back of my neck standing on end. "A wave will wash over your heads, and when it recedes, you will be standing upon Neverland's shores."

My heart began beating out of my chest. This was my final chance to turn back. I could still stop this to be with my mother and father, our family whole and reunited at last. I could turn my back on the sea and its magic, never speak of the gods again, forget Neverland, forget Peter, and live my life for me and only me.

But there would be no wiping Tink's blood from my hands, no absolving myself of the role I'd played in Peter's death, as unintentional as it was. I'd carry the guilt and shame with me forever unless I did everything within my power to make it right... or died trying.

Shoving my thoughts aside, I nodded. "We're ready," I said, and at his silent command, the tide began to recede. The god took a few steps back as the waters swelled behind him, gathering into a mini tsunami.

His lips twisted into a grin. "Now would be the time to hold your breath."

I gripped a handful of Arktos's scruff, trying not to quiver as I whispered, "Stay close to me, boy."

What happened in the next few seconds was a blur. With a twitch of Adais's fingers, the wave came crashing down. I kept my eyes open until the moment of impact, bracing myself to be swept off my feet, and that's when I saw her. Blonde hair flashed in my peripheral vision, a familiar grip ensnared my wrist, and before I could shake her off, the tsunami swallowed the four of us whole.

EPILOGUE – THE SHADOW

Peter

I'm betting you thought I was dead. That my soul had joined the wandering, that I spent nearly half a century seeking immortality only to be thwarted at the very last moment. That Peter Pan was no more.

Sorry to disappoint. Other than a burned hand and fingers, I'm very much alive. The souls left me alone the moment my companions were gone and haven't bothered me since.

I can hardly blame you. They all think I'm dead, because not a single one of them came back for me, or even tried. I know because I waited. Walked all the way back to that grotesque pile of bones, plopped my ass down, and waited for what felt like days. They had a mission to complete, but surely they wouldn't forget about me. Surely they wouldn't *leave* me.

It's my mistake, really, and I should have known better. Everyone always leaves, even if they make it seem like they won't. Even if they share your bed for weeks, even if they hold you when you cry, even if they guide you through the worst of your anxieties and self-loathing.

Even if you love them.

Tinker Bell, are you listening? You were right. I love Wendy Maynard, though I had good reason for not acknowledging it sooner. It's a very unique kind of love. It's not romantic, not exactly, but what I feel for her is definitely deeper than a friendship. It's why her betrayal cuts deeper than any knife that's ever stabbed me.

It's why I did what I did.

I expect she'll hate me once she finds out, and that's fine. I probably deserve it, even if Hook deserves what's coming to him more. But Wendy will see sense eventually. She'll see that I'm doing her a favor and realize she's better off without the man who made her life—and mine—a living hell, even if he does happen to be her father, because aiding in her creation was the only decent thing Captain Hook ever did. I don't for one second regret tearing off my shadow and ordering it to kill him.

I do, however, regret that I won't be there to watch.

AUTHOR'S NOTE

You made it! Welcome back from the Sea of Eternal Woe. I'd apologize for putting you through such an arduous journey if I hadn't also felt every one of those highs and lows daily (and nightly) for the past, what, eight months? I poured so much of myself into this book, and while the final product was more than worth it, I have a lot of feelings now that I'm sitting and reflecting back on what it took to get here. I wish the story behind writing this book was as joyful and triumphant as *A Land of Never After's* was, but it wasn't; writing *A Sea of Eternal Woe* was pure, unbridled chaos, and while I'd do it all again in a heartbeat (and I'm sure I will when I go to write *A Forest of Blackened Trees*), I think it's important to be one hundred percent honest with both you and myself, possibly for the first time in my life now that I have the answer I've sought for so long.

(I'm going to discuss mental health in moderate detail in the section below, so if you're not in a space to read that, skip to the final section.)

I went through an extremely tough time after finishing my master's degree in mid 2019. I remain in a transitory phase in my life, certain things weren't moving along like I hoped they would, and then the pandemic hit. By January 2021, I got a new job that had me working completely from home, and I'd never been more excited for such a mundane job (I work in 401k's). I thought I'd get on a nice routine, have plenty of time to write, be able to take better care of myself and my pets, and just all around have a better quality of life. And in a lot of ways, I did (and I wrote *A Land of Never After* before things started to take a serious nosedive), but in a lot *more* ways, it highlighted that something was very, very not right with me. My anxiety was through the roof, I became terrified to leave the house, chores were piling up despite me spending more time at home than ever before, and the only way I could be any semblance of productive or meet a deadline was if I worked myself into a panic-induced frenzy. I'd get it done, but wouldn't feel any sense of accomplishment afterwards. If anything, I'd feel completely exhausted and borderline worse. It was beyond humiliating, and it took me longer than I want to admit to get help because I tried and tried to 'just push through,' but of course that didn't work. The more I tried, the harder I failed, and it made no sense to me. How was it that I'd been running myself ragged for years, jumping from accomplishment to even bigger accomplishment, working insane hours (including a full time job while pursuing my master's degree, yes, I am serious) and hardly ever being home, to not being able to bring myself to wash the massive pile of dishes that were stinking up my kitchen or even take a damn shower?

Sound familiar, my fellow ADHDers?

It sure didn't to me, because until I was diagnosed in March of this year, I knew next to nothing about ADHD. The picture I had in my head was of the stereotypical hyperactive adolescent boy always fidgeting in his chair and completely unable to pay attention in school. He had bad grades, didn't get along well with adults given his behavior, and he certainly didn't achieve things on the level that I achieved when I was his age. That wasn't me.

Except it was, because not only does ADHD present differently in every single person who has it, it often looks wildly different than the example above for those of us who were assigned female at birth. Like so many of my fellow AFAB folks, I flew under the radar for the first twenty-seven years of my life because I was quiet, compliant, and accomplished. I got through grade school, a bachelor's, and a master's with decent grades, could hold down a job, and finish projects when given a deadline. Never mind that doing all of these things ran me into the ground, forced me to mask the majority of the time, and caused me to develop destructive habits and coping mechanisms that to this day I'm struggling to identify, let alone unlearn (and probably will for the rest of my life).

While all of that is of course terrible, I think the worst part, for me, is the complete lack of a sense of accomplishment, and it sneaks up on me every time. As I neared the end of writing this book, I used the thought of getting to write the Author's Note as motivation to see me through those final chapters. *It will feel amazing to finally be done!* I reassured myself with glee. *You'll be basking in the glory of having finally finished your best book to date, and you'll get to reflect back on what you've achieved.* I pictured writing this note as a reward, a celebration, and couldn't imagine feeling anything other than relieved while I did so.

That's not what happened, because of course my dopamine-deprived brain said, 'You wrote an entire book? So do lots of people. You're nothing special.' When I should have been assembling this book for my ARC readers, I've instead spent the past week procrastinating, catching up on shows and movies I haven't been able to watch until now, and eating copious amounts of ice cream, all while wondering why this tightness in my chest won't go away (I knew why, deep down, I just didn't want to admit it). Part of it is no doubt a habit given that I've spent the past several months in a constant state of panic and anxiety as this deadline hung over my head, but the rest is a delightful cocktail of so many things: doubt, guilt, grief, and really awful impostor syndrome to name a few. The main thing, though, hurts worse than Elvira punching me in the gut (because we know Cedric would never): ADHD often makes your accomplishments feel like accidents.

Am I calling *A Sea of Eternal Woe* an accident? No, of course not. Logical brain knows full well I worked damn hard for this, and that I deserve to feel proud and accomplished. ADHD brain is loud, however, and given that I managed to mute it while I marathoned finishing the book, it's been screaming this week.

Good thing I finally invested in noise-canceling headphones.

(Mental health stuff over!)

I said at the beginning of this note that the story behind writing this book wasn't a triumphant one, and in many ways, it wasn't. I missed multiple deadlines, my poor editor had to edit in chunks, I didn't take care of my health or my house for days and sometimes weeks at a time, I neglected relationships with a few of my friends, pulled all-nighters and wrecked my sleep schedule in general, and these are just to name a few of the uglier things.

But *I made it*. And it's all thanks to you.

No, seriously. If I didn't have so many people clamoring for this book, commenting on my social media posts, sending me kind messages, and taking pictures of their books in the wild, *my* books, I'd not only have burned out a long time ago, I'd have probably given up. It's what happened with my music career: I loved it, but love wasn't enough. I needed to know that my performances meant something, that I was making a difference in this world, a meaningful impact, and I simply wasn't getting that. Not the way I do with writing and telling these stories. These beautiful, raw, dark, LGBT+ positive and diverse stories that so many of you love so much and that you beg me to keep writing.

I don't know about you, but that sounds pretty triumphant to me.

If you made it this far, thank you so much for not only reading my book, but for caring about me as a human being! It would mean the absolute world to me if you could take a quick moment to leave a review. Even a rating helps, but if you're willing to write a line or two, that's even better! To show my appreciation, here's a sneak peek at the third book in the Curses of Never series, *A Forest of Blackened Trees*, where we return to Neverland… but as before, Neverland is not as any of us remember.

A Forest of Blackened Trees
Prologue – The Enemy

Tiger Lily

I always felt Shimmer's presence strongest near the southern shore. It wasn't where he was buried—we laid him to rest in the village graveyard among the other fairies—but it was where he'd died.

Mother said I needed to stop going there. Doing so only fueled the storm cloud that hung over my head since the day I lost him, and only widened the emptiness eating a hole through my chest. I promised her I wouldn't, but there would have been no fooling her even if she couldn't literally *see* the cloud. Aura-readers like her always knew such things, which was why Bright Eyes had started coming to me directly every time Father needed more medicine. Daydream moss favored the humid conditions near the shores, giving me the perfect excuse to visit, and I began anticipating what my sister's fingers were about to sign even before they formed the shapes. With her help, sneaking out of the village had become easy. Too easy, which probably meant that even the dogs had given up trying to keep me contained.

Good. Better for all of us this way. I would be far more willing to accept that their way of dealing with the fairies' loss was by pretending they never existed if only they could accept that this was mine.

Having at last reached my destination, I fought to steady my ragged breaths and fluttering heart before setting my sights on a small and otherwise unassuming hawthorn tree. There had never been any need to mark it; not with what happened here so irrevocably seared into my memory. It was near a cliffside that sloped into the nearby beach, perched proudly and sporting fresh white blooms. Kneeling at the tree's base, I touched my fingertips to the precise spot where Shimmer had laid when his light went out, flinching when a painful jolt shot up my arm and down my spine. I had known it was coming, but didn't bother to brace myself for it, because it wasn't just any pain. It was *his* pain, and as his bonded, it was my duty to feel it in death just as it had been in life.

My voice cracked when I regained control of my trembling lips enough to speak. "Hey, Shim. How have you been?"

Nothing but the roar of distant waves answered me. I expected nothing less, but kept talking anyway.

"Me first? All right, but it's just been more of the same old shit. Mother worries too much, mostly about me. Bright Eyes is her usual giggly self, but I can't help but wonder for how long. Father's pain has only gotten worse. He's taking twice as much daydream moss as he was at the beginning of his illness, and it makes him sleep a lot. It's also not enough. He tries to hide his grimaces and thinks we don't notice, and maybe Bright Eyes doesn't, but Mother and I certainly do." I paused to switch positions and turned so my back rested against the hawthorn's trunk. I was careful both not to disturb Shimmer's death site or loosen my grip on my bow, and kept my gaze fixated on the surrounding forest. Neverland's curse may have broken weeks ago, but the monsters certainly hadn't gone anywhere. "I'm worried about him, and he's not the only one who's sick. A third of the village is symptomatic now. A *third*."

We called it the black haze. Though it had afflicted my people since before I was born, we still didn't know what caused it or how it spread, because it had predated even the curse. The disease brought on terrible headaches which only progressed with time, and though the black haze wasn't deadly in itself, the severity of the symptoms had caused nearly a dozen of our villagers to take their own lives. I've been told the pain gets so intense it feels as if an arrow is splitting the forehead. Daydream moss is the only remedy which brings any semblance of relief, but there comes a point where it isn't enough.

Father had reached that point.

I'd held my tears back for as long as I could, but the stress of the past few weeks combined with my grief were more than enough to yank them from me. A gentle warmth settled over my shoulders as I silently sobbed—Shimmer's spirit, no doubt—and it made me want to scream my frustrations one by one into the still-decaying forest.

Our chief was in pain and I couldn't help him. Our forest was dying and I was powerless to stop it. Our fairies were dead, and nothing could bring them back.

If I had my way, I would shriek all that and more at the top of my lungs before cursing the spirits and our elders, and possibly even the white man's precious gods. I would wail until my throat was raw, if only so I had an excuse not to talk to Mother when she inevitably interrogated me over where I'd been, or better yet, pain that wasn't this constant, aching grief.

But I couldn't yell or scream any more than I could afford to snap a twig beneath my feet. The Nightstalkers had always been sensitive to noise, but their hearing seemed to have been amplified ever since the curse had been broken, something I had unfortunately learned firsthand. What should have been a quick and simple trip checking the hunting traps around the perimeter of the village had turned into a near-death experience after Leaping Deer had laughed a little too loudly at one of my jokes.

We didn't joke anymore.

But I didn't blame him or even the Nightstalkers that had nearly mauled us; I blamed *her*.

Wendy fucking Maynard.

I hadn't thought it possible to hate anyone more than I hated Cedric and Jamie Teach until she came strutting along, sporting that ridiculous mop of blonde hair and acting as if the whole of Neverland bowed to her. I'd heard the whispers of *Neverland's Chosen* and we may not have to kill to survive anymore, but so what? And what in hells had she saved us from? The forest was still fucking dying, my people were still diseased, and the monsters were as horrifying and murderous as ever, so as far as I was concerned, Wendy Maynard had done nothing of actual value, and she certainly hadn't *saved* us. I may have counted the time she'd plunged a knife into her own gut, but of course she hadn't possessed the decency to stay dead.

She'd had the decency to leave, though, and we hadn't seen her or any other pirate in weeks. With any luck, they and their ship had at last been swallowed by the depths, and after nearly two decades of living in secrecy, my people were finally free to reclaim the land that was rightfully ours. If it weren't for the monsters, we would have already moved back to our ancestral grounds, but especially given how many of us were sick and weak, Father hadn't thought it wise.

I agreed with him, but that didn't mean I had to like it.

"You'd know what to do, Shim," I whispered into the salty breeze, though I barely heard my own voice over the agitated ocean behind me; perhaps it, too, wanted to scream. "You always know what to do." If nothing else, my fairy would have been able to make me smile… but the thought was far from comforting given that I'd never see him again.

I remained at the hawthorn tree until an hour before dusk, which gave me just enough time to gather daydream moss for Father and return to the village before nightfall. My limbs were stiff and my ass had been numb for the better part of the day, so standing was a chore, but I managed to do it without allowing a whimper to escape my lips. It wasn't the most painful part of leaving, though; that was reserved for my final goodbyes. Swallowing, I addressed Shimmer once more. "I don't know when, but I promise I'll be back. Soon."

At first, there was nothing, but following the crash of a particularly large wave, I heard it.

Fairy bells.

My heart skipped a beat, because I knew immediately I hadn't imagined it. Losing Shimmer had been hard enough, but the silence that had permeated the forest ever since the fairies had all died had been almost harder. There had been no music, no whispered words in Fairiestongue, and certainly no bells. It had been so long I'd nearly forgotten what they sounded like, but upon hearing these, recognition struck me like a war drum.

The bells weren't alone, though—they were accompanied by a dog frantically barking as well as voices. Shouts. Human voices, human shouts, spoken in that clumsy English tongue, and by the time I'd darted into a nearby bush for cover, my brain had adjusted to make sense of the language I hadn't heard in weeks.

"...followed me? What the fuck!"

"What the fuck, yourself! Neverland, Wendy, really?"

"You think that after losing Peter I'd be willing to lose her, too?"

My blood turned to ice.

Wendy?

Surely I'd misheard. Surely my eyes were playing tricks on me, and that wasn't Wendy Maynard and the Serpent standing drenched on Neverland's beach.

Surely that wasn't a *fairy* cupped in Wendy's hands.

The possible illusion continued without waiting for me to catch up, and Wendy held out the fairy for the Serpent to see. It was difficult to tell given my current distance, but she almost looked like Tinker Bell, Peter Pan's bonded fairy. "See? It was worth it. She's alive."

The Serpent scoffed. "She looks the damn same to me."

"But her bells! I haven't heard those in weeks."

"I'd have been perfectly happy never to hear them again!"

Their shouts were nearly drowned out by the massive white dog sprinting up and down the coast and barking like mad. Its fur was plastered to its frame in a way that would have been comedic if my mind wasn't racing with questions: How the fuck had they gotten here, and when? Had I truly been so preoccupied with visiting Shimmer that I'd missed it? If that fairy truly *was* Tinker Bell, the last known fairy in existence, where in hells was Peter Pan? And most importantly, by making all this noise, did the four of them have a death wish?

The Nightstalkers would be on them within minutes, if not far less. They'd rip the dog to shreds first—for whatever reason, the beasts seemed hellbent on eradicating dogs—before turning on Wendy, the Serpent, and poor Tink. And if I stayed here, I'd be next.

It briefly crossed my mind to help them, or at the very least warn them. But one look at Wendy Maynard, at her flushed cheeks and soaking-wet frame, and I decided against it. With a smirk playing on my lips, I slipped back into the blackened trees, a single glorious thought fueling my silent strides.

Let her die as she should have all those weeks ago.

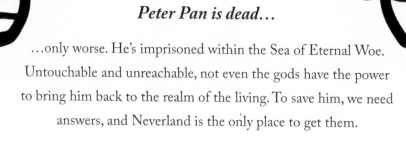

Peter Pan is dead…

…only worse. He's imprisoned within the Sea of Eternal Woe. Untouchable and unreachable, not even the gods have the power to bring him back to the realm of the living. To save him, we need answers, and Neverland is the only place to get them.

But we're not alone.

Everything remains as dead as it was the day I first laid eyes on it, and the handful of survivors are desperate and starving. Only this time, they aren't monsters. They're *people*. And they hold me responsible for their suffering.

Any attempt at peace turns to all-out war, and once again, I'm at its center. Long-buried secrets rise from the grave, and the more we learn, the less I understand. What is clear is that to save Neverland, we need Peter. And if he doesn't die in that Sea?

I'll happily kill him myself.

A Forest of Blackened Trees arrives on July 25th, 2023.

PREORDER NOW!
https://books2read.com/afobt

ABOUT THE AUTHOR

Raelynn Davennor is an author of fantasy and science fiction, a musician and composer, and a creature of the night.

Nestled among her fictional worlds full of darkness, dragons, and sassy heroines, you'll often find a musical number or two. An accomplished performer, she's made appearances with artists such as The Who, Weird Al, and Hugh Jackman on many of the largest stages in the United States.

Raelynn is usually lost in her head, dressing up in costume, or humming a tune she can't wait to scribble down. When not obsessing over her latest idea, she enjoys pampering her menagerie of pets and pretending she isn't an adult. Her home base is https:// rldavennor.com where you'll find more information, her newsletter, and links to social media.

Made in United States
North Haven, CT
21 October 2022

25741753R00300